WHERE YOUR TREASURE IS

WHERE YOUR TREASURE IS

HOLMAN DAY

WILDSIDE PRESS

Originally published in 1917.
Published by Wildside Press LLC.
wildsidpress.com

I

BEING THE STRUGGLE OF AN AMATEUR AUTHOR TO GET A FAIR START

Speaking of money—and it's a mighty popular topic—the investment of the first twenty-five cents I ever earned, all at a crack, ought to have directed my feet, my thoughts, and my future along the straight and narrow way. Ten minutes after I had galloped gleefully home with that quarter-dollar from Judge Kingsley's hay-field, my good mother led me down to Old Maid Branscombe's little bookstore and obliged me to buy a catechism.

I earned that money by hauling a drag-rake for a whole day around behind a hay-cart, barefoot and kicking against the vicious stubbles of the shaven field. I honestly felt that I did not deserve the extra penance of the catechism. However, that first day's work gave me my earliest respect for money—earned money. And I also remember that Judge Kingsley, when he paid me, sniffed and said I hadn't done enough to earn twenty-five cents.

I hated to walk up to him and ask for my pay, because Celene Kingsley was within hearing; she had come down to the field to fetch him home in her pony-chaise. That's right! You've guessed it! I'll waste no words. It was only another of the old familiar cases. Barefooted, folks poor, keeping my face toward her, as a sunflower fronts the sun (though the sunflower has other reasons than hiding patches), I was in the shamed, secret, hopeless, heartaching agonies of a fifteen-year-old passion. Of course, I don't mean that I had loved her for all that time—I'm giving my age and hers.

Yes, I hated to walk up. And the judge gave me the quarter only because he did not have any smaller change.

And really, for the times, it was considerable of a coin for a single juvenile job.

The services of youngsters in those days in Levant were paid for on a narrower scale—ten cents for lawns and a nickel for shoveling snow, and so on. And tin-peddlers were mighty stingy in their dickerings for old rubbers and junk. To get rags one had to steal 'em—our folks made rugs and guarded old remnants carefully.

So much for my first financial adventure of real moment—for the biggest coin I had ever clutched; and right now I lay down my pen for a moment and spread out two human paws which have juggled three million dollars' worth of gold ingots as carelessly as one scruffles jack-straws. That was maverick treasure. But there's a big difference between earned money and maverick money. If you don't know what maverick means I'll save you the trouble of looking the word up in the dictionary. Once on a time, in Texas, old Sam Maverick wouldn't brand his cattle. Therefore, a maverick was a cow or steer unbranded. And to-day it means any kind of property at large which a bold man or a dishonest man may grab if he can beat other thieves to it.

I had an early taste of maverick money, and the taste was so sweet that I never have lost my hankering for more.

In the fall of that "year of the catechism" the line gale blew down the chimney which had stood after the old Pratt house was burned. I was there before the dust settled, for all the boys knew that there were wrought-iron clamps high up in the bricks. But I left the clamps to the next corners and picked up a dented tin box, rusty and dusty and soot-blackened; I shook it; it rattled and I ran away into the woods. When I had knocked the box open and looked in and spied coins I had the heart-thrilling conviction that money worries were over for me in this life. My first thought was that I would marry Celene Kingsley and settle down and live happy ever after. If there had been in the box what I thought at first there was, I could wipe my pen and close my story.

I dove both hands into the box and brought them up brimming—coins scattering and clattering back over my trembling fingers. They were big coins—and I had read much about the days of the bold pirates.

"Pieces of eight!" I whispered.

But they were not. When I had winked the mist out of my eyes I found that they were old-fashioned coppers—bung-downs they used to be called. Mixed in with them were a few copper tokens, a Pine Tree shilling, a sprinkling of Speed The Plow cents, and the only coin of any account at all was a Mexican dollar with a hole in it.

It wasn't in my nature to bury that treasure. I knew it was pretty worthless junk, but I had a hankering to carry it about with me, to feel its drag in my pockets, to reach in and chink it when no one could hear. I walked around weighted with it as afterward I have been weighted with the leaden chunks of my diver's dress. As early as that in my life I found that money was a burden as well as a vexation. I didn't dare to frisk and frolic with the boys at school; I was not exploiting my new wealth; I had grounds for caution because there were plenty of Pratts left in Levant. At home I moved about so

6

quietly that my folks thought, I reckon, that I was entering an early decline. My mother used to look at my tongue quite often and made me drink hardhack tea.

But there is one impulse in the male animal which is not easily controlled by prudence; it's that cursed itch to make a show in front of the female of the species—in front of the special one, the selected one, the beloved one. Some sort of a jimcrack-peddler came into the school-yard one noon, and Celene Kingsley, daughter of a plutocrat, tendered a big, shiny silver dollar and the man could not change it for her. I walked up, trembling with both pride and panic, and said, trying my best to act the part of a matter-of-fact bank on two legs, "Let me handle it for you!" It was the first time I had ever spoken to her, and my voice was only a weak squawk.

When she turned to me and opened her big, blue eyes, I was nigh to running away.

The boys and girls came crowding around, and I couldn't blame them for showing interest; the sight of a Levant Sidney with money on him was a new one in town.

I had separated from the coppers the aristocrats of my hoard, the Pine Tree shilling and the Mexican dollar, by wrapping them in a wisp of paper. I brought them out first.

"I don't know exactly what they are worth in real money," I told her. "But you can have 'em at half price."

She had been considerably surprised before, but now she was plain dumfounded. That system of changing a dollar was brand new.

Then I dredged a trousers pocket and produced a handful of the bung-down coppers. I began to count them, down on a corner of the school-house steps.

"Somebody get a wheelbarrow," advised one of the boys. "That's the only way she'll ever tug-a-lug her change home."

"Really, you needn't bother," she said, stammering a little. "No, don't trouble yourself. I have changed my mind about buying any-thing."

They all laughed.

"That isn't money," said the jimcrack man. "I'd never take that stuff for my goods."

A girl ran up and grabbed into the coppers I had been heaping on the stone. She was a Pratt.

"Ross Sidney, you stole that money," she squealed. "It was in my granny's notion-box. We couldn't find it after she died. You stole it!"

"I didn't steal it—I found it," I told her. But all the courage had gone out of me.

"You ain't the first thief to lie about your stealings."

"But I did find it—I found it after the chimney blew down."

"You knew it was ours. You didn't bring it to us—that's stealing."

"It might have been put there before—"

"It was my granny's money. Don't you suppose I know? She saved old coppers." She spread down her handkerchief and began to pile the coins upon it.

There did not seem to be any room for argument. In my shame I fell to wondering how I had ever convinced myself that this money was treasure-trove. I dug down and gave her the rest of it. Instead of proudly showing myself a person of means before Celene Kingsley I was barely escaping the suspicion of being a thief.

"If it belongs to the Pratts you're welcome to it," I said. "I don't want anything which belongs to somebody else."

"You'd better remember as much the next time you find money," snapped the Pratt girl. "Your conscience will be easier when you die."

They say that dying men live over their lives in a flash—that's so! When I was dying in black darkness, five fathoms deep under the waters of the Pacific, with a bar of gold in either hand, I remembered what that Pratt girl said to me that day in the glory of the autumn sunshine, my face as red as a frost-touched leaf; it was the day of my bitterest humiliation; I slunk off without daring to look at Celene Kingsley.

I think I know what my main mistake was in my first attempts at writing this tale; I tried to tell the story as if it had happened to somebody else and the thing was stiffer than a mud-caked tug-line and squealed like a rusty windlass. Of course, I hate to be saying "I" here, there, and everywhere—but there'll come a place in my tale—you'll think of it if ever you get as far as that—where there'd be nothing to the story unless you could see with my eyes and feel with my hands. So, bear with me and I'll reel off the yarn as best I know how, making no apologies after this confession.

Oh, about that first maverick money I ran afoul of!

I never saw that money again, of course.

But I did happen to meet Ben Pratt right in front of Judge Kingsley's house. I'll not say how big Ben Pratt was, because you'll think this is only a bragging story. He called me a thief and I decided it was about time to show Levant that the name was not a popular one with me.

I licked him.

Judge Kingsley rushed out with a horsewhip and lashed us apart just as I was finishing Ben up.

"Young Sidney, you're a cheeky, tough, brazen character," said the judge. I did not answer him.

It is my nature to take a big lot from all women, considerable from some men, and devilish little from most men. I had nothing at all to say to Celene Kingsley's father, even though I was rubbing half a dozen swelling welts where his whip had connected with the back of my neck.

"You come of a tough family," stated the judge.

Right then my uncle Deck arrived at the party; he had been watching the thing from the tavern porch.

"What's that you say about our family?" he asked the judge.

"I don't care to stand here and quarrel with you, Decker Sidney."

"When you horsewhip my dead brother's boy in the main street you'll come pretty nigh to having a quarrel with me, seeing that his own father can't protect him."

"I merely came out here and stopped a fight which was disgracing our village."

"It's a nice thing for one of the 'forty thieves' to talk about disgracing a village," said my uncle.

As young as I was I knew what was meant when folks called Judge Kingsley one of the forty thieves. He belonged to the syndicate that had grabbed the State's principal railroad away from the original shareholders; there was political shenanigan and a good deal of foreclosure trickery. I never understood the details, but the fact remained that the syndicate got the railroad.

"A cheap slur from a cheap man," said the judge, walking away.

I can't say that I resented that remark very deeply, though I suppose family loyalty should have prompted me to do so. I never in my life came close to my uncle Deck when he did not have the smell of liquor on his breath. On each side of his nose there was a patch of perfectly lurid crimson. He was a horse-trader and he made considerable money.

"That slur of *yours* is a high-priced one," my uncle shouted. "I have my eye on you, you old hypocrite. There'll come a day when that slur will cost you more than you can afford to pay. That's how high-priced it is, Judge Kingsley."

I didn't know what my uncle meant then.

It was a wicked time for me when I did find out, a long while afterward.

II

ENDING WITH A MEETING
ON PURGATORY HILL

My mother was a good woman—a thrifty, kindly, helpful woman, a good neighbor, in spite of her poverty.

My short temper, my cheeky disposition, my generally ready impulse to grab in on short notice, all belong to the Sidney side, I guess. All we know of the family has come down by word of mouth, and I suspect that the first rovers who came over in the old days when New England was really new were pretty tough characters who had plenty of original nerve to start with and then developed more as occasion required. Well, some of that sort had to come on ahead and smooth things with the ax and crowbar—yes, and with the musket, so that the country could get a good running start.

My mother was a good neighbor, I repeat. Up in the attic, hanging in dried bunches from the beams, were spearmint, thoroughwort, hardhack, mullein, pennyroyal, and other pasture herbs which she sent me forth to gather. Her thoroughwort syrup was guaranteed to cure any case of whooping-cough—and she gave freely to all who came to her.

My father was a helpful sort of a man in his own way. He used to volunteer as boss of all the barn-raising bees in our section—but his enemies, made up of a considerable army of the men whom he had licked in his life, said, behind his back, that the only reason he had for helping at a barn-raising was to show off by running the ridge-pole first of all the crew, and then to start the regular free fight. He fell off a ridge-pole one day and my mother was widowed.

I take it that her chief ambition in life was to tame the Sidney disposition in me—that earnest desire explaining my involuntary investment in the catechism. My mother's axioms and teachings would have made excellent addenda and foot-notes for any catechism. Always did she counsel me to count ten before speaking angry word or performing angry act; I don't remember that I ever did as she told me, though the Lord Himself knows how much I have suffered in my life on account of that lack of self-restraint. Two days after I bought the catechism my good mother thought it was having its effect on my nature. She saw a boy heave a rock at me in our dooryard and I stood perfectly motionless and speechless.

10

"That's right, my own son! Count your ten!" she called to me.

But just at that moment a bumblebee was crawling around over my bare foot and I was in no mind to disturb him. Therefore, my enemy was enabled to collect a full supply of rock ammunition and to defy and rout me when at last I was free from the restraint of the bumblebee. It would have been the same if I had waited to count ten. Somehow, as the world is constituted, I have never taken much stock in this watchful-waiting game while your enemy is hustling to pile up his ammunition and you know he is doing so. I may be wrong. Maybe this story of mine will show that I'm wrong. But I hear you say, let's get on to the story!

I mean to do so at once; but if I have paused to pull the curtain aside from my family and my character a bit you may be able to understand some parts of the story a mite better, because, in spite of that catechism, in spite of mother-influence, and perhaps mother-goodness deep down in me, I have butted into adventures which you will not find set down in the volumes of any well-conducted Sunday-school library.

I didn't have my mother long, after my fifteenth birthday.

I was her sole heir; five minutes before she closed her eyes she gave me all her little fortune—to wit, the sweetest smile good mother ever left to bless memory of her, a pat on my hand, a few whispered words in my ear.

And then Uncle Deck took me in hand to make a man of me, so he said.

He wasn't all bad—don't understand me as saying that. He would pass a sleepless night if he failed to cheat a man in a horse trade, but he would sell his shirt before he would allow any old folks in our town to go onto the poor-farm. He would sneak around with wood and groceries after dark, that big, red face of his like a harvest moon, and when they would start to thank him he would curse the miserable old creatures so horribly that my blood used to run cold. He prided himself on language which, so he said, "would break up a Sunday-school picnic if a little bird sat overhead and twittered it out of a tree." He saved his choicest profanity for his comments on Judge Zebulon Kingsley. His hatred went far back. I don't know what started it. Perhaps it began in the natural antipathy such a man as Uncle Deck would entertain for a cold, proud, punctilious, professedly religious man like the judge. Uncle Deck would have it that the judge was a hypocrite, a thief at heart, and my uncle's constant boast was that some day he would show the judge up; but all that vaporing seemed to be silly spite, without foundation. Judge Kingsley was

11

our rich man; he had been judge of probate, and after retiring from that office he was trusted with funds as a sort of private banker; folks whose estates he had handled as judge just naturally insisted on his keeping control; and he had been town treasurer of Levant for years.

I hated to hear my uncle rave on about such a man; it was as irritating as the barking of a cur.

I have said that my uncle was a horse-trader. Rather, he was a general country dickerer, if you know the kind. He dealt in everything from a sheet of fly-paper to a clap of thunder. He had car-loads of horses sent to him from the West and peddled those to farmers, taking cash or bills of sale or produce or second-hand furniture or anything else which he could turn in a trade. He set me to peddling and collecting, and it was a mean job. At first I used to believe everything which debtors or sellers would tell me, and the result was that Uncle Deck bawled me out most dreadfully; and thus being abused by both parties, I got so at last that I believed nobody.

Therefore I was in a fair way to be made just the sort of man Uncle Deck desired me to be.

And continually, after I was sufficiently hardened, he impressed on me that I mustn't be bothering him all the time, asking this and that about running the business. I must act for myself and then report to him when he called for an accounting. You shall see how his trying to make a man of me in this fashion turned me into ways which neither he nor I could have forecast. Don't tell me that the activities of this life are very much a matter of individual election, after all. To be sure, a man might elect to live a hermit and might get away with the job in good shape; but if a person throws himself into the ruck of the living, into the running of humanity, he'll be apt to find himself leaping from crag to crag because he has been shooed or jarred.

I ran up against one Juvenal Bird, newly come to town from the rural fastnesses of Vienna plantation—plantation meaning an unorganized township. I had never heard of Mr. Bird, and when he came within range of my vision I rather wondered because I had not; he seemed to be a person of some importance. To be sure, his frock suit was rusty and his plug-hat was fuzzy, but the garb was distinctive.

Mr. Bird was in search of furniture and I showed him our second-hand stock; he ordered liberally and largely—especially largely. He took the biggest stove, the largest bedsteads, the most expansive tables, and bureaus of breadth. That plug-hat impressed me. When he told me to send the goods out to his house on the Tumbledick Road, and to call for the pay at my convenience, I did not presume to ask for an advance instalment, after our usual custom.

I promptly found out that this was one affair of business with which I should have bothered my busy uncle, who knew all the cheats of the section.

Mr. Bird was one of the most notable cheats. His raiment was garb discarded by an up-country parson, who pitied Mr. Bird after the latter had been evicted from timber-lands as a dangerous squatter, careless of fire. Mr. Bird installed the furniture in a shack which he had hired, then acted as his own carpenter and narrowed all the doors and the windows. I went out after the money and learned that the law provides for the replevin of furniture, but does not allow a house to be mutilated in order to remove the furniture. Mr. Bird grinned at me through a cracked window and thumbed his nose.

When I reported to my uncle he told me to go and get it. I refrain from quoting the words in which he voiced that command.

"But the law says—" I ventured.

Again I suppress details. My uncle Deck's opinion of the law would lack authority.

However, being a Sidney, and resenting Mr. Bird's betrayal of my innocence, and needing a home and a job, I accepted my uncle's opinion of the law for the time being. I collected a gang of my boy intimates. We went in the night and ripped the stuffing out of Mr. Bird's nest.

There's a queer kind of senseless and secret gratification in doing a mob job. The human animal has a lot of primeval instincts which need tickling once in a while. I reckon we boys gratified the wolf streak on that occasion, running in a pack in the night-time.

We enjoyed it so much that we held a meeting a night or so later and organized ourselves as the "Skokums." I can't remember how we happened to light on that name. I was chosen as leader.

That first sortie was a great success—Mr. Bird was not in a position to prosecute. We had had a wonderful night, had defied the law, and had escaped punishment.

Judge Kingsley was the only man in town who proclaimed indignation loudly and openly. He expressed himself before a crowd in the post-office and declared that hoodlums had disgraced the town of Levant. He looked straight at me and said he would give a reward of ten dollars for evidence on which the ringleader could be convicted.

"And I would give one thousand dollars to pay for law to set him free," said my uncle.

"Some day the plug-uglies will be rooted out of this place—and good riddance to 'em," snarled the judge.

"The snout that goes rooting into that business will get twisted off'n the face of the rooter," retorted my uncle. He was never very choice in his language. How those crimson patches on his face did glow and how his eyes sparkled!

So, it will be seen, I was not getting on at all with my love-affair.

It is pretty presumptuous in me to refer to it as a love-affair. That would intimate—calling it that—a bit of reciprocation on the part of Celene Kingsley. But she never showed any visible interest in me, even to looking my way when she met me on the street. I would have liked to attract her attention, for at last I wore shoes and had clothes without patches on them.

The Skokums flourished under cover of the night.

There was Oramandel Bangs. He was rather simple, and always carried his mouth open, and nobody in Levant ever forgot that once a hornet flew in and stung his tongue and it swelled and stuck out of his mouth for days like the end of a bologna sausage.

Oramandel had a sneaking suspicion that witchcraft had never been wholly stamped out by his forefathers in New England.

We decided to convince him that he was right—there's nothing like clinching a man's faith in the good judgment of his ancestors.

We hoisted one of his calves into an apple-tree. He "unwitched" the animal by cutting off its ears and tail before taking it down from the tree.

We tied cords to his ox-chains and hid ourselves and slashed the chains about the dooryard; he ran to the neighbors and reported that the witches had changed his chains into big snakes. We did a lot more things, and then imagination began to do the rest for him. He said the witches wouldn't allow him to do his farm-work, even though he had sumac-wood splinters in all his tools and stuck shears around his churn to make the butter come. Before we realized what mischief a lively imagination can do to a man, they were obliged to carry the old chap away to the asylum for the insane.

And again Judge Kingsley held forth in the post-office.

I guess he did a lot of talking at home, too.

At any rate, Celene Kingsley was mighty well posted, so I discovered.

I met her on Purgatory Hill one day—and never did that name seem to apply so well! I had been out on my uncle's business, and among other plunder in the beach-wagon were two shotes in a crate, and they certainly were taking on about leaving home and mother.

She was alone in her pony-chaise and the shaggy little brute she drove was frightened—and I didn't blame him. I pulled as far into the gutter as I could and waited; I poked the butt of my whip into the

14

crate and prodded those shotes, but that only made them screech the louder.

So she came leading her pony past me. I didn't expect that she would stop and speak to me, but she did. I nearly fell off my seat. And she called me "Mr. Sidney." It was the first time anybody had ever given me a handle to my name. I had pulled my hat off when I saw her coming; when she spoke to me I put it back on again and then took it off so that I could show her that I knew a little something about manners. However, I wasn't at all sure just what I was doing; my head was in a whirl, and I was damning those pigs in my heart.

"I thank you, Mr. Sidney," she said. "Pedro acts like a fool sometimes."

Two hours afterward, I guess it was, I thought of just the right reply to that remark; as it was, I didn't say anything to her. I couldn't.

She started on and then stopped and looked at me.

Perhaps she guessed something—I don't know. Girls can act as if they never notice anything and still they have an eye out all the time; and what they don't see they know by instinct. At any rate, there was a lot of kindness in her face, and perhaps there was pity in her thoughts.

"I'm afraid I am very bold, Mr. Sidney. I hope you'll forgive me for speaking to you."

She hesitated. Right there was another beautiful chance for me to say the good thing which came to me that night after I was in bed. All I could do at the time was duck my head.

"I'd hate to have any of the boys who went to school with me get into trouble on account of their thoughtlessness. I'm sure it's only thoughtlessness and skylarking. But older folks, you know, don't understand and cannot sympathize with young folks. Now you won't tell anybody that I told you something, will you?"

Just think of it! A secret between Celene Kingsley and myself!

I gulped and shook my head.

"Won't you tell the boys—you'll know just how to pass the word—that folks are talking of having a detective to watch the village nights?" She probably saw that I was incapable of uttering a sound and she went on, hurrying her words. "Mr. Sidney, of course you understand that I am not picking you out as the ringleader. That's not why I am asking you to pass the word. But I know you are popular among the boys. They all speak so well of you! And I was so sorry when I heard that your dear mother had passed on. I wanted to write a bit of a note, but they are very strict at the boarding-school—we are not allowed to write to young gentlemen."

Think of two shotes, squalling their heads off, furnishing accompaniment to that! But I'll say this of the shotes, they had spirit enough to use their voices—I was dumb.

"It would be terrible to have anybody arrested here in Levant for boyish pranks—it's all thoughtlessness, I'm sure. You and I ought to be able to straighten everything out."

I stood up.

"Enough said!" I shouted.

She flinched. Then I realized just how I must have sounded, for she said, "I didn't mean to make you angry!"

I couldn't blame her for mistaking my looks; I was so mad at myself that I wanted to lash my back with my own whip.

"No, no, no! It isn't the way you seem to think it is! I want to say that after this—after what you have said to me—if there's any more cutting-up in this village I'll strip the pelt off the chap who does the job." I beat my hand on my breast. "It's the proudest day of my life when I can take orders from you."

"But I haven't given orders, Mr. Sidney."

"You have. They're orders to me. The littlest thing you can wish for is orders to me. If you said for me to cut my hand off I'd do it. Oh, you don't know! I have—I don't know how to say it—but for years—oh, I'm crazy—" And I was. It was lunacy provoked by the passion of love trying to outvoice those devilish shotes.

By the funny look she gave me she was taking me at my word. She hurried to step into her little chaise.

"All I mean is this," I quavered. "I'll make 'em quit. You look to me. I'll be responsible. Don't you worry."

"I'm sure everything will be all right after this," she told me. "I'll depend on you, and I thank you."

She went on her way, and the burden I had assumed seemed lighter than feathers and more precious than golden ingots.

She had given me her confidence—she had asked me for a service!

She had thought of me and my trouble when she was away at school!

A few minutes before I had not dreamed that she was conscious that such a person as Ross Sidney walked the earth.

Now, at all events, my poor self was in a little corner of her thoughts. She was looking to me for help in something which she had made her own concern.

I rode down Purgatory Hill, hugging my joy and cursing those shotes.

III

ON ACCOUNT OF A GIRL

I trust you have noted, by this time, that my yarn is not a mere chronicle of disconnected incidents. Linked circumstances seemed to be tying me up. One happening had pushed me on to another and I had allowed myself to be pushed. It might be urged, of course, that I had no business in inciting a mob to play hob with Mr. Bird—but I had my own interests to consider, and I had been listening to my uncle's teachings on the subject of looking out for number one.

"You know what happened to your father when he went to running his legs off on somebody else's business," he told me. "If it hadn't been for me helping him in his other scrapes, your mother would have been playing hungryman's ratty-too on the bottom of the flour-barrel oftener than she did. I hope you've got an ambition to be somebody and to have something."

I did have, but you may be sure I did not tell my uncle that my principal hankering to get money was so that I might lay it at the feet of Zebulon Kingsley's daughter.

Now, by the expressed wish of that daughter, I started out to control happenings and to set myself in new ways.

I passed the word to the Skokums, keeping my promise to Celene.

I was obliged to be indefinite, for I was guarding that little secret between her and myself as my most precious treasure.

As I remember it, I put it to the gang this way: "We ought to behave ourselves and protect the good name of the town." They laughed at me and asked me if I had joined Judge Kingsley's Sunday-school class.

I knew they didn't suspect the truth, nevertheless that dig nearly put me out of countenance on account of the secret I was cherishing. I blushed and stammered and I lost my grip then and there as a leader—and it was the same old story—it was on account of a girl. A girl does rattle the gear of man-business!

One of the fellows remarked that I was getting almighty pious after I had used them to clean up my own dirty job. He said the most of them had matters of their own which needed attention, and wanted to know if I proposed to sneak out on them after all the help they had given me.

I told them that I had thought the thing over carefully and had decided that what we had done to Mr. Bird was not right or lawful and we'd better make no more mistakes.

"Then perhaps you want us to correct that mistake and make up a bee and carry the furniture back to the old cuss," suggested one of the Sortwell boys.

When I failed to welcome that notion they turned on me in good earnest, and in my own heart I had to admit, looking on the surface of the thing, that they had good reason for thinking that I was both selfish and ungrateful.

In the Sixth Reader, at school, I had found the story of Frankenstein's monster. I saw that in organizing the Skokums I had built a lively little monster of my own.

"I have a special and a private reason for asking you to quit and be good, boys," I told them.

"A member who keeps his private and special reasons to himself and doesn't trust the rest of us isn't much of a help in time of trouble," said Ben Pratt. "I have never taken a whole lot of stock in you, Ross Sidney, and now I take less than ever before."

From remarks which were dropped I gathered that the rest of them held similar sentiments.

"They're going to have a detective in here," I told them.

"Who said so?"

But that was Celene Kingsley's secret.

I had hoped that the threat might scare them. It had just the opposite effort; the boys of Levant had never seen a detective, but they had read every five-cent thriller on the subject. To be the object of a real detective's attention seemed like glorious adventure—and they were sure that they were, when on their own prowling-grounds, match for any sleuth who ever dodged behind trees.

But I had stood up before her and had beaten fist upon my breast and had assured her that she could trust all to me. What sort of a knight was I to wear lady's favor and then fail to do and dare in her behalf?

"I had hoped that you knew me better and that I stood higher with you fellows," I said. "I'll admit that you did a big job for me, and I am grateful. But you all had your fun out of it, for you have said so, over and over. You'll have to admit something, yourselves; you'll have to own up that we are ashamed of what we did to poor old Bangs. If you keep on you'll do other things to be ashamed of. I'm advising you to stop."

"We don't want your advice," said Ben.

"Then you'll get something from me which you'll like a blamed sight less than advice."

Plainly they were hungry for information.

"What'll that be?" asked one of the Sortwell boys.

"Try on any more of your doodle-busting in this town and you'll find out," I said. Then I left them and went home.

Some bright chap has made a simile about having as much privacy as a goldfish. At any rate, by leading an open life, one may be in a position to prove an alibi.

I took to spending my evenings in the bar-room of the Levant Tavern.

That was by no means such a roystering sort of a life as it sounds to be. They used to sell liquor in the tavern in the old stage-coaching days, when the place was a post station; the little catty-cornered bar is there in the big room, its worn wood shiny from the dragging of rough fists and from many scrubbings; behind is the cupboard, with wavy glass set in diamond-shaped panes. But the cupboard was bare in my boyhood days and the shelves were dusty. Dodovah Vose, the landlord, was a tee-totaler and believed in impressing that principle on others.

"I have seen what liquor will do and undo," he said when he used to get on to the subject. "In my young days, when the West Injy trade flourished and rum held its place without blushing, I have set in meeting and seen the parson soop a sip of rum-and-water between the firstly and secondly, and so on. It may have improved him and the sermon—I'm not arguing. But do you think that liquor would ever have improved my brother Jodrey and made him the best deep-sea diver on the Atlantic coast, as he is to-day? No, gents! Where a man needs the strength of his arms, the full power of his ten fingers, the quickness of his brain, and the help of his lungs and a good heart—then he'd better let liquor alone. That's what my brother says and he has been deeper underwater than any other man—and you can look around you and see some of the queer and wonderful things he has brought up for the peerusal of mankind."

The old foreroom was really a storehouse of curious pickings and gleanings which had been sent up-country, from time to time, by the diver brother. It had been one of my earliest haunts, for I had always hit it off nicely with Dodovah Vose. I did not lark about the room or molest the curios, as other boys in the village sometimes did.

On the contrary, I always surveyed them with respect and interest; the awe I felt when I first laid eyes on them never left me, entirely. I have not been able to determine, exactly, whether my boyhood study of those objects inspired the hankering I developed, the burning desire to go down into the depths of the sea some day, or whether the queer things merely catered to my natural instinct in the matter. At any rate, I touched them reverently and I asked many questions of Landlord Vose and he told me hair-raising stories which, he said, his brother had told him. I remember that when I was so young I was still wearing a plaid kilt, I got down on all-fours and stuck my leg in the air at his request; he called it "playing circus," and gave me a penny. He said I was a smart boy and allowed that a smart boy might grow up and be made a diver by Jodrey Vose. So there was an idea put into my head at an early age. And Dodovah Vose used to call me "Lobster Sidney"—a truly deep-water nickname! He had a rather droll idea of a joke—it was to prompt youngsters to go and make fools of themselves. My folks gave me the middle name of Webster. In order to plague the new schoolma'am, Dodovah Vose told me to insist on the first day of school that my name was Ross Webster Lobster Sidney—and I did, even though the boys in the school laughed themselves sick. Mr. Vose praised me because I had obeyed orders, and gave me a conch-shell on which, by the aid of three finger-stops, one could play more or less of a tune. He had already given to me a shell which whispered in my ear the everlasting murmuring of the great ocean I had never seen.

It was a big fountain-shell from somewhere in the West Indies, and it fairly boomed, deep in its spirals, when I held it to my ear; I sensed all the vastness and the mystery and the solemnity of the ocean depths. The more I listened the better acquainted I seemed to be with a wonderful stranger far away at the other end of a wire.

It really seemed like a call to bigger things, and my job with my uncle was getting less and less to my taste. If there's any such thing as the angels looking down on earth over the parapets of heaven in their hours off duty, some of the things my uncle would do in horse trades, in order to get back at other cheaters, must have grieved the judicious in the upper spheres.

I didn't realize it at the time, but I can look back now and see how my lashings to the life in Levant were in the way of severance, one by one.

I found no comfort in the lull of Skokum activities; I reckoned that the boys were reorganizing and getting ready for a really big slam. I felt as a timid girl must feel in a thunder-shower when the thing is right overhead and there's an extra wait between claps.

I continued to visit the tavern evenings and I came into closer intimacy with Dodovah Vose. He brought out old letters written by his brother and read them to me. In one Jodrey Vose described his venture on the sunken British frigate *Triton* somewhere off the coast of Nova Scotia. She was bringing pay to the Hessian troops in the American colonies, so old reports had it. Jodrey Vose was more of a diver than a writer and his letter had no frills. He informed his brother, who had invested modestly in the gamble at Jodrey's suggestion, that the thing was a failure, though the frigate had been located by dragging and Jodrey himself had gone down and explored her where she had lain for more than a century.

Diver Vose stated bluntly that he believed, from what he saw down there, that the *Triton* had been scuttled or blown up by certain of her officers, who secured her treasure, escaped to the main in small boats and reported her loss in a storm; tradition has it that there was always considerable doubt about that storm. Also, tradition has it that those officers settled in America and lived happily ever after. Diver Vose tried to help pay expenses by raising the cannon. But though they seemed sound enough under the sea, they crumbled into lumpy masses after they were exposed to the air.

"But I never begrudged the money I put in," Dodovah Vose told me. "I got my curiosity scratched where it had been itching for a good many years, ever since Jodrey and I first began to talk about the *Triton*. And I helped my brother get something off his mind. He wouldn't have died easy if he hadn't made sure about that treasure. I stand ready to invest in another scheme of his if he ever gets ready to tackle it. That's to go down and dig in the bottom of the river Tiber, providing he can fix it with the town officers of Rome. As near as we can find out from history, Jodrey and I, when the Romans wasn't throwing their treasures into the river to keep 'em away from one another in their civil wars, the barbarians were up to the same game, because they didn't enjoy art. And, of course, there's always the treasure of the *Golden Gate*! That's in modern times."

But it was not in times sufficiently modern so that I knew anything about it, as my blank stare showed.

"She caught fire on her way from San Francisco to the Isthmus and was run ashore with three or four million dollars' worth of gold ingots in her. That's fact! But Jodrey says there's been so much blasted lying done since by owners, underwriters, divers, claimers, and others, that nobody knows for sure just what has become of the treasure. That's another of his hankerings—to find out!"

More and more did I fed the spirit of adventure stirring in me!

I could not understand why the whereabouts of that great treasure should remain in doubt, and so I expressed myself to Mr. Vose.

"There's some sort of a mystery about it—and so far's my brother is concerned he can't drop regular contracts to go chasing dreams—only once in so often. That *Triton* case made a hearty meal for his curiosity—he hasn't been hungry for high-spiced stuff since." He looked at me with shrewd kindness. "Maybe he'll let you go on that job after he has made a diver out of you."

I felt a flush in my cheeks.

"I suppose you have been poking a little fun at me all along when you have hinted at my being a diver, sir. Do you really believe your brother would give me a thought?"

"He might, if you went to him backed up with a letter from me."

"I have a mind to ask you for that letter."

"And you'll not get it, my boy! I don't propose to have your uncle Deck come yowling and clawing at me like an old tom-cat because I have coaxed his handy-Andy away from him."

"I don't like the kind of work he puts me to, Mr. Vose. I have grown up to be a man, almost, and I understand better than I did at first."

"You understand, for instance, that when you took that cow away from Andrew P. Corson last week you left his baby without milk!" He stroked his nose and peered at me from under eyelids that were cocked like little tents.

"There was a bill of sale! He made me go and get the cow."

"But do you know what your uncle did, after that?"

"No, sir!"

"He went to Andrew P. Corson and said you acted without orders. He lent Corson the money to buy another cow."

I stammered out something about not understanding that.

"But I do," said Landlord Vose. "Your uncle Deck wants to get into politics in this town—he wants to get into politics far enough so that he can do something to Judge Kingsley. He reckons you don't need any popularity. He is starting you out with considerable of a handicap if you mean to live and prosper in your own town. However, I won't do anything to encourage you to leave! I've got to keep on living in the town—alongside your uncle Deck!"

A flash of family loyalty prompted me to assert that my uncle was good to the poor.

"That he is," said Dodovah Vose. "He is a queer man, your uncle is. But I don't want to make a pauper of myself in order to curry favor with him."

It came to me that I'd better have a talk with my uncle, and I started out, crossing the village square on my way home.

All at once something landed heavily and violently on my shoulders, and the attack was so sudden that I was borne to the ground with such a crack of my forehead on the hard earth that I became unconscious, but not until I had felt claws of some sort tearing at my cheeks.

When I came to my senses I was back in the tavern foreroom and Dodovah Vose was swabbing my face with a sponge wet in warm water. In a corner of the room Constable Nute and two helpers were hog-tying old Bennie Holt, the village fool.

"I ain't a dove of peace no longer—I ain't a rooster no longer," he was squalling. "I'm a bald-headed eagle! They told me I'm an eagle. I allus knowed I was some kind of a fowl. They lied to me when they said I was a dove of peace. I'm an eagle. See what I've done! I've mallywhacked him. He made fun of me when I was a dove. Others made fun of me—but now they'd better look out. I'm an eagle."

Whatever the old idiot had been or thought he had been, he was then plainly a raving maniac. In his struggles he was shedding turkey feathers with which he had thatched his coat. As far back as I could remember old Bennie Holt, he used to stand in the square with feathers of various sorts stuck around his hat, harmlessly indulging his vagary. But never before had he raised his hand against any human being.

"I reckon that this time you fired a boomerang, young Sidney," stated the constable, reproachfully. "Old Bangs didn't fly back and hit you, but this one has. The village will be glad to hear it."

"You'd better be careful what you report about me," I told him. "I had nothing whatever to do with old Bennie. Mr. Vose will answer for me."

"We know where to plaster the blame when anything happens in this place," insisted Nute. "Now you've sent another one to the bughouse!"

It did not seem to be of much use to talk to that raving old man, but I tried it. I asked him who had been talking to him.

"My guardeen angels," he screamed. "They all come to me and told me. They was in white and they told me."

I myself had furnished the pillow-case cowls to the Skokums out of the second-hand stock in my uncle's storehouse!

"There must be some mistake this time, Nute," said Landlord Vose. "Young Sidney has been spending his evenings here in the tavern for quite some time."

"Trying to put up a bluff, that's all. The one who torches on a fool can't complain if the fool kicks back. Here's more expense to the town, boarding an insane man at the State hospital. It didn't cost us anything as long as he e't broken crackers out of the grocery-stores and slept in the livery-stable. I reckon Town-Treasurer Kingsley will say that this ends up his patience."

"Don't you dare to tell Judge Kingsley that I had anything to do with getting old Bennie in this state," I cried. My face smarted dreadfully, for Dodovah Vose was putting on some kind of stuff to kill the poison of the fool's finger-nails, so he explained.

"I don't need to tell him; he'll know it for himself."

"I'll find out who did do it! I know well enough!"

"Of course you know."

It was maddening—this determination on the parts of Levant to put me in the wrong in all matters of local disturbance. Here was I, victim of the resentment of the Skokums because I was trying to obey my promise to Celene Kingsley, now in imminent danger of further repute as the ringleader of the latest atrocity—even though I was the sole sufferer after the devil had been stirred up in the old loafer.

"You fired him, and the boomerang swung around back and hit you—that's all," insisted the constable. "His mouth has been full of something you have done to him. If it wasn't you he wouldn't be talking about you."

While Dodovah Vose was finishing with my lacerated face I pondered on what he had said about my uncle's indifference in regard to my popularity in town.

Then I stood up in the tavern foreroom and cursed family and foes and town with such lurid invective—my vocabulary and force being so far beyond the ordinary capabilities of youth—that even the crazy man was shocked into silence. I was ashamed of myself even as I ranted. But then, as in after-times, my temper swept me out of myself. I was blind and dizzy and there was a roar in my ears like the rush of water. I swung the fires of anger about myself as a juggler whirls his flaming torches. I was sorry as soon as it was over—I have always been sorry when my frenzy has passed.

When I bowed my head and walked out of the tavern I heard the constable clucking away like an offended old hen.

"It's all a matter for the judge to consider—language and all," he declared.

"But I insist that he is a good boy in his heart," said Dodovah Vose.

"Can't be—coming out of that family—and with the general reputation he has got since he has worked for his uncle the last four years," insisted the constable. Fine dwelling-place for me—Levant, eh?

My uncle was in bed and asleep when I got to the house—and perhaps it was just as well, because I was quickly forgetting my shame and was ready for a further squabble; a disposition on my part which has never been especially helpful during my life.

I made careful and disgusted study of my striped face in the looking-glass before I went to bed. In spite of my innocence, there I was, the labeled participator in an affray. In this world, as you have probably noticed, the man who carries around a blacked eye or a bunged lip never succeeds in dissipating the suspicion that he has been in some sort of a disgraceful mix-up, in which he was more or less to blame. You may remember how you yourself have felt in the case of your friends, even when a sliding rug or a closet door has been saddled with the blame. A man with a marked-up physog is never at his best as a defendant. I dreaded the next day, for it seemed pretty certain that I would have to face Judge Kingsley. But the feeling that his daughter might be brought to doubt the sincerity of my promises, when she heard the story and beheld my face, kept me awake more effectually than did the pain of that ferocious clapper-clawing.

IV

THE TRAINING OF
THE QUEEN OF "SHEBY"

I was awake so long in the night I overslept next morning, of course. Breakfast had been cleared away by the time I got dressed and was down-stairs.

I had made up my mind to have a run-in with my uncle, but I was starting with a disadvantage. Coming late to breakfast in that busy household amounted almost to a crime, and the look of disgust my aunt Lucretia set on my face made my courage drop tail. She was never amiable, and she considered me an intruder in the family, as well I knew.

"I have left your doughnuts and coffee in the but'ry—and your uncle wants you in the stable." She turned her back and went on with what she was doing at the stove.

I ate the doughnuts on my way to the stable, trying to whip up my rancor. I expected to be received with a hoot and a howl, and depended on those spurs to start my own temper on the gallop.

Uncle Deck was just pushing a bottle back into the oats in the bin. He slammed down the cover and wiped his mouth and grinned at me. He was in the best of good humor. I was chewing on food his money had bought, and, I repeat, he was as pleasant as a basket of chips. In the face of that I couldn't screw a mean word out of myself.

"She sure was some operator with her claws," he remarked. But he wouldn't listen to my indignant explanation; he plainly had his own business on his mind that morning, and it was business which seemed to be affording much satisfaction. He gave me a push toward the harness-room, the sanctum where he performed most of his deviltry in horse matters.

In that harness-room was hitched the worst-looking old pelter of a plug I had ever laid eyes on.

Uncle Deck put his hands on his hips and swapped looks between myself and the horse. He was master of a certain kind of cheap, horse-jockey patter which he employed at fairs when he wanted to call a crowd around. He struck a pose and "orated."

"Having a knowledge of hoss pedigree, relatives, previous condition of servitude, religious preferences, and other matters pertaining to, and so forth, even going back to the fact that the hoss Bucephalorus, that was owned by the late Aleck the Great, cocked his left hind leg when he stood in the stall, had a nicked right ear, and a wind-gall puff behind each fore shoulder, I want to say that I reckon that never before was there gathered, collected, and assembled on four legs every kind of a pimple, bump, wheeze, scratch, spavin, horn ail, hock bunch, trick, and bobblewhoop, that's laid down by old Medicombobulus, in his book entitled 'Things a Hoss Can Get Along Without.' I call this ancient Gothic ruin 'Carpenter Boy,' sired by Pod Auger, dammed by Hemlock Maid—and, in fact, damned by everybody who has ever owned him. Speed is developed in him by feeding the celebrated spiral oats, produced by crossing shoe-pegs with bedsprings, which in process of being digested uncoil and carry the animile in leaps like the mountain-goat."

After that outburst I definitely, in my own mind, set forward to some future date the matter of an understanding with my uncle.

"How did it ever happen that anybody could unload this on you?" I asked him.

"Because I went out hunting for it, sonny. It was the worst I could do on short notice. If it had looked worse and had had more ailments and outs I would have paid more for it. Now ask no more questions, but lend a hand to what I tell you to do."

I have no time to go into the details of what my uncle Deck did to that equine framework, but if I could describe it all I'd be furnishing considerable of a handbook for the uses of tricky horse-swappers. I had helped in many similar jobs in that back room of his stable, but I had never seen him put so much art and soul into the work before; he seemed to have special reasons for his painstaking toil. He chuckled whenever he secured a particularly good result; at times he gritted his teeth and swore under his breath regarding some party whom he did not name. But I gathered that this transformation of a horse was intended as satisfaction of one of his bitterest grudges.

He had everything to do with in that horse beauty-parlor of his. There were ointments and colorings, false hair for mane and tail, skin-patches and disguises for puffs and swellings. But still the horse remained gaunt; the rafters of his ribs suggested that he needed to be shingled in. To my general wonderment as to what my uncle was about, anyway, was now added more lively curiosity; how was this living skeleton to be disguised as to skinniness? I found out before long. My uncle put on the poor brute a bridle with a wicked twist-bit and told me to hold him, no matter how much he kicked about.

Then Uncle Deck brought out a bit of board into which shoe-pegs had been set thickly. He began to clap the pegged board against the horse's skin. I had my work cut out for me after that, I can tell you. The pain must have been excruciating, for the bradding-pegs raised blisters. In a little while the ribs were hidden by this new and deceptive plumpness. The horse took on the appearance of an animal which had been well cared for in the food line. And he certainly displayed the spirit of Phœbus's nigh wheel-horse. His nostrils snorted furiously and his eyes flamed. It seemed incredible that this animal with flowing mane and tail, with round barrel and smooth limbs, was the decrepit old creature I had seen on my arrival in the room.

Lastly, my uncle Deck oiled the horse from stem to stern, smoothing the hair into place, and then stood and admired his handiwork.

"Now let's see what the needle will do for style and knee action," he said. He gave the horse a jab with the hypodermic—I had seen him do that at horse-trots just before the race was started. He hitched a long rope into the bridle and led the animal out into the yard. In a few moments the horse was prancing and curveting and whickering like a blueblood of youth and spirit.

"But he won't last this way!" I said.

My uncle turned withering side-glance on me. "Do you think you're telling me something I didn't know? Of course he won't last. I don't want him to last. If he would pop like a blown-up paper bag when I got ready to have it happen I'd like it all the better. But, as it is, it'll be bad enough. Don't you know a good name for him out of some of those books you have read, son?"

But while I was hesitating my uncle clipped in with his usual impatience.

"I have thought of it already! 'Judge,' that's his name. When she hears Trufant call him 'Judge' the coincidence will catch her interest, likely enough. She will prick up her ears!"

Right then I pricked up my own ears. I understood mighty sudden. I had seen the writing tacked on the notice-board in the post-office the day before. Judge Kingsley had let it be known that he was in the market for a driving-horse, suitable for use by ladies. I had read it with mingled emotions, realizing that Celene Kingsley had grown to girlhood out of childhood; no longer a pony-cart for her!

"But he'll never buy a horse from you?" I blurted, staring at my uncle.

"Who won't?"

"Judge Kingsley."

"Probably he wouldn't if he thought it came from *me*. But I'm baiting a hook that he'll swallow or I'm no guesser."

My eyes were full of questions and he saw fit to humor me.

"Seeing it's all in the family, son, I'll tell you. I've got to let out a few holes in my surcingle or I'll bust. 'Squealing John' Runnels, of Carmel, will drive this hoss into Judge Kingsley's dooryard to-night, around dusk, representing that he is a poor woman who needs money in a hurry so that she can get her husband out of trouble. 'Squealing John' has got a woman's voice, and he will wear some of his wife's clothes."

"I don't see how you can get a man to do that," I objected.

My uncle raised his hand above his head and slowly clinched his fingers.

"A man will do 'most anything when you've got a foreclosure clutch on his weazen. I'm making the whole thing plenty crazy so that the laugh will be bigger when the truth comes out. He'll buy this hoss—there's no doubt of it. Old John will give him only twenty minutes to decide. Short notice on account of the hypo juice I'll shoot in up around the turn of the street! Must have a quick decision because I reckon the hoss will stagger up against a fence and die mighty soon after old John gets out of sight. Clek-clek! Gid-dap!" He yanked on the rope and the horse frolicked. "Whoa, Judge! Plenty of knee action! Sound in wind, limb, and peepers! Safe for the ladies!" He pulled in on the rope, grabbed the bridle, and led the horse to a stall. "If we get over two hundred I'll slip you ten dollars for your part of the job," he called to me. "It's time for you to understand that there's good money in a sharp dicker."

I did not have the courage to tell him what I thought. I tried to frame some sort of a reproach when he went to the oat-bin and pulled out his bottle. But he grinned over his shoulder at me! If he had had any short and sharp words for me that day I would have burst out, I'm sure of it.

But he was wonderfully kind to me that last day I ever spent in his home, under his thumb.

"You'd better stay close around the house till your face looks less like the battle-flag of freedom, son," he advised me. "Cats will be cats, and girls will show claws!" He went away about his business and I hung around the stable, taking a look every now and then at the preposterous horse.

I was made party to a most horrible deceit on Celene Kingsley. To be sure, the fraud most nearly concerned her father and his money. But the horse was destined for her. I could not get that idea out of my thoughts. Probably, after the trade had been made, my uncle would brag that I had helped him. How would she view me? It must seem to her that some of my promises had already been broken, for I was certain that the matter of old Bennie was being canvassed that day in the village. There was such a thing as family loyalty, I admitted, as I pondered on the situation. But to allow my tough uncle to tramp through the little sanctuary where I enshrined my love, to pull me into a vulgar scheme which must ruin forever all my hopes, poor and futile though they were, these were sacrifices I did not feel called on to undergo. I had my own pride to consider. I no longer dreamed of ever possessing Celene Kingsley. What was in me was a romantic hope that she would think on me once in a while when I was far, far away—remembering that I was her slave in what she asked and that I had asked nothing of her.

However, to have her memories of me mixed in with thoughts of the horse-trading cheat which I had connived at was reflection unendurable.

I went to the wood-shed and secured an ax. It occurred to me that when a horse had so many bumps on him, one more and a deadly bump on his forehead would not attract much attention; furthermore, my uncle seemed to think that the animal's course was nearly run.

I faced the brute. His ears were hanging in despondency. His eyes were dropping tears; those blisters must have been stinging like the martyr's skin under the shirt of fire. When I looked on that woe all my resolution left me. I dropped the ax. There were tears in my own eyes. I felt as if he were my brother in common sorrow. So I went to the cellar and fetched apples and carrots and fed them into his gratefully slobbering mouth until he sighed and spraddled his legs and went to sleep.

Constable Nute came for me during the day.

"There ain't any subpeny to this, young Sidney," he informed me. "If you feel too guilty to face Judge Kingsley, who is making an informal investigation, you needn't come."

"I am not guilty. I'm not afraid to face the judge." And I went along. There was no one else in his office. He had been calling in persons and examining them one by one. I was alone with him after Nute left.

I gave in my version of what had happened the night before and declared that I had had nothing whatever to do with putting notions into the noddle of the village fool.

"But as to this society of young vandals which has been disgracing the village? Certain members of the gang have confessed to me that you are the organizer and the ringleader."

"And I confess that I *was* leader at first," I owned up to him, just as manfully as I could. Then I told him about Mr. Bird. "When I realized that I was making a mistake I stopped being leader. I have had nothing to do with the society since."

He had a way of shooting speech out through his pinched nostrils with a sort of a jew's-harp twang. He leaned back in his chair and gave me a good looking-over.

"Becoming an angel overnight by the natural piety of the Sidney disposition, eh? Young man, you are lying to me! Now tell me the real reason why you quit your devilishness."

I had no mind to tell him, and I was silent.

"You had another reason, didn't you? A better reason?"

I confessed that I had. But I wouldn't tell him what it was, even when he raised his voice to me and pounded on the table with his fist. If he had been the right kind of a man I would have told him, for a proper man would have been proud of his daughter under those circumstances. But I knew that Judge Kingsley would consider that she had disgraced herself by talking to me.

"You can't tell the truth—you won't tell the truth—for the truth isn't in you," he stormed. "You are convicted by the tongues of the boys who have owned up."

"I knew there were sneaks in the crowd—that's another reason I had for getting out, Judge Kingsley."

"If anything else happens in this village we shall know where to place the blame."

"It isn't fair, Judge Kingsley!" I remonstrated. "I'm not getting a square deal in this thing. I know that old Nute has been talking to you the way he talked to me last night. They are all bound to put the blame on to me."

"I know for myself."

"No, sir! You don't know for yourself. You say I can't tell the truth! I'll show you that I can, even when it's to my own hurt—yes, sir, to my awful hurt! You have advertised for a horse, haven't you?"

"Yes."

"My uncle is going to send around a man dressed in woman's clothes—this very evening—so as to fool you in the dusk with the worst fraud ever propped on four legs."

That confession didn't help me a bit and I ought to have had sense enough to know it before I opened my mouth. I had made the judge more thoroughly angry than ever; I had offended his pride as a shrewd business man.

"What cock-and-bull yarn is this? Do you think I can be fooled by cheap horse-jockey tricks? You young fool, what do you mean by insulting me?"

"You just wait till you see the horse," I retorted. "I helped fix him and I didn't know him, myself, after the job was done. But I don't want to see you gulled, Judge Kingsley. I am following new ways from now on. You know my uncle and how I am beholden to him! When I open up to you about him it ought to show you that I want to be honest, no matter how much the truth is going to harm me."

"There's no decency in this town—not even honor among thieves," snarled the judge. He pointed to the door. "That's all for now, young Sidney! Remember for yourself—and tell others—that the grand jury sits in this county within a fortnight! Upon actions from now on depends what the county prosecutor will be inclined to do."

Judge Kingsley's office was a sort of ell affair built out from the side of his mansion. When I left it I ducked around to the rear of the house and made off down through the orchard, having no relish to show my clawed face to the public. I had my day to myself and I did not hurry; I had many things to ponder on.

All at once I heard the sound of somebody running on the turf behind me. I turned and faced Celene. I curved my forearm across my countenance, ashamed of my appearance, her own flushed cheeks were so radiantly beautiful!

"I know how it happened. I'm sure it wasn't your fault," she said, graciously,

"They ste'boyed him on to me!" I told her. "I have tried to make 'em stop their tricks, just as I promised you. So they did this to put me in wrong. Your father is hard on me! I tried to make him understand that I—well, I wanted—"

"I overheard—I couldn't help overhearing." Then her cheeks grew rosier. "I'll own up. I listened at the door. I wanted to know. And that's why I came after you. You have kept our little secret and I know you have done your best in other ways. So that's why I'm here. I want to thank you. And—I— Well, I think that's all!"

It seemed to finish it as far as I was concerned, too; I couldn't pump a word up out of myself. So we stood there and looked up into the trees.

"Father has been talking to them to-day," she said, after a time. "Perhaps they are warned now and won't be up to any more mischief. And they ought to be sorry for what they have done to you. I think you can have a lot of influence over them after this."

"I don't know about that. I'm going away from here."

That statement astonished her just as much as it astonished me.

32

I had not thought of announcing my departure ten seconds before; it had not been in my mind that I was going away. But all of a sudden the memory of what I had told the judge about the horse popped into my thoughts. Considering what would be my uncle's state of mind after the exposure, I reckon the going-away idea followed as naturally as the right answer in a sum of addition.

"I had supposed that your outlook—your position with your uncle—was very promising," she said. "The town needs smart men."

The fact that she had spent one thought upon my condition interested me more than the implied compliment.

"If I stay with him I'll only be a country cheat and horse-dickerer. I want to be something else," I told her. "This very day my uncle is trying to put up a job on your father. I have told the judge about it."

"I heard you. It was another reason why I wanted to speak to you—to encourage you in being honest. There's no need of father bringing you into the matter at all. It would only make trouble between your uncle and you. I'll speak to father."

"You'd better not, for then you'd be making trouble for yourself. I'd rather take all the blame of it."

We stood and looked at each other for a long time.

"I'm not a coward," she said.

"But it will come out about me blabbing—some way it will come out. There's no need of you being in the scrape. I'm going away, and I may as well go flying while I'm about it!"

"I hope—" she said, and that was as far as she got. I know how I was feeling inside and perhaps my feelings showed too plainly on that striped face of mine. She looked scared and turned and hurried away. I didn't know whether she hoped I'd stay in Levant or hoped I'd do well wherever I might roam. I watched her out of sight and she did not turn to look at me. I couldn't exactly figure that out—whether she didn't want to give me a last glance or didn't dare to.

I fingered in my vest pocket while she was running away; when she disappeared I pulled out a packet and opened it. There were three rings in it. One was a coral ring; I bought it when I was fifteen and paid thirty cents for it. I never had the courage to give it to her when we were at school. There was a silver ring which I bought a year later when my circumstances were a little better—better than my courage. Lastly, there was a gold ring which I had secured in a dicker soon after our meeting on Purgatory Hill. I am not going to discourse on the fool impulse which prompted me to buy those rings and stick them in my vest pocket. Nor will I say anything concerning another impulse which made me wrap the rings up and drop them into a cleft in the trunk of an apple-tree. If I did not dare to give them to her, at least I could leave them on her premises. Then I went by back ways to my uncle's house.

Before I was out of sight of Judge Kingsley's mansion I looked behind me several times. I didn't know but I might see a flutter of a handkerchief from some window, for a vague and queer kind of hope was still in me. I saw no flutter, but I did see a strange man who was strolling along my trail. I was too busy with other thoughts to wonder who he might be.

I found my uncle admiring the transmogrified horse.

"I have been whetting the old hellion's appetite," he said, and I knew by the expression on his face that he was referring to Judge Kingsley. "I have had half a dozen fellows from the back districts drive one old skate after another into his dooryard, and inside of an hour he'll have a chance to inspect a few more skeletons and bone-piles. By nightfall he'll be hungry for a peek at something which doesn't look as if it would have to be pushed on casters by iron reins. Oh, he's hungry! He'll swallow this one."

More than ever was I coming to understand into what complicated and precious gears I had flung my trig—and what the consequences to me were likely to be.

"Now come out into the harness-room," commanded my uncle. "I want you to have a look at the Queen of Sheby."

I had never seen "Squealing John" Runnels, but that this was he I had no doubt. He sat on an upturned grain-bucket with his skirts pulled up about him, wore a woman's broad hat of dingy black felt, and a veil partly draped his face; he was smoking a corn-cob pipe.

"I'll be cussed if I see any good sense in being titrivated out like this the whole afternoon," he complained, in tones as strident as a scolding woman's. "It's getting on to my nerves."

"You've got to get used to 'em, you old fool," barked my uncle. "I don't propose to have you forgetting yourself. It would be just like you, right in the middle of that dicker-talk, to pull up your dress and reach into your pants pocket for a plug of tobacco. Now get up and let me see you practise walking; and forget that you're wearing pants."

Runnels went grunting and limping around the room, whining like a teased quill-pig. His feet were pinched into women's shoes. My uncle seemed to see much humor in this exhibition, but I couldn't find any. It looked to me only like a grotesque sham, and pitiful, too, for I knew it was not going to succeed. "Squealing John" appeared to be of the same opinion. He kept complaining that he would not be able to fool a sharp man like the judge, and asked, anxiously, what the law penalty was when a man dressed up like a woman.

"I'm a good mind to let ye foreclose and be shet of the thing," he said, facing my uncle and cracking together his bony little fists. "All that will come of this trick is that I'll be took up and sent to jail. I'm a good mind to go to the judge and tell him how I'm persecuted and hectored and see if he won't take up that bill o' sale."

"I'll kill you if you do—I'll kill anybody else who blows on me and my plans. Now, Queen of Sheby, remember that this is my champion performance. I ain't in any frame of mind to be trifled with."

He went to the oat-bin and brought in his bottle.

"You need to be teaed up a little so that you'll have some courage, you old angleworm."

After the two of them had swallowed stiff drinks my uncle turned on me.

"I have half a mind to dress you up instead of Runnels, son. Your face is smooth and you've got nerve enough to act the thing out right."

"I'll not turn any such trick," I said. I was angry in a moment. So was he.

"You will if I tell you to."

"I won't; and I'll say further that I don't think much of this business, anyway."

"Nor I—and that's two against one," declared Runnels, the tip of his thin nose beginning to glow as if new courage had hung out a banner.

Liquor had also given my uncle's temper an edge of its own; he cuffed Runnels until that lamenting "lady's" hat fell off. I jumped up and ran away into the fields, for I knew that Uncle Deck was merely warming up on "Squealing John"; as chief mutineer, I was ticketed for the real bout. I lurked about in the pine grove till after sunset. Then I stole back into the village with all the stealth of a criminal.

V

SHOOING AWAY A SCAPEGOAT

I reckon it's best for innocence to go boldly in this world. At any rate, I would have come off better that night if I had not lurked and prowled. However, I was only obeying very wise dictates of prudence; my uncle had been sufficiently savage in the harness-room when rebellion was merely in process of hatching. To meet him after Judge Kingsley had exploded the bomb—and I was sure that I would be revealed in the matter—would be like getting in the path of a Bengal tiger with snap-crackers blistering his tail.

I wasn't at all certain what I would do after I found out that I had been exposed to my uncle's fury; first of all, so I felt, it was essential to learn what had developed in the horse trade.

So I stole in the gloom around behind the buildings of the village and retraced my trail up through the judge's orchard. While I was still some distance from the mansion I heard considerable of a hullabaloo above which rose the shrill voice of "Squealing John" Runnels, who was issuing warnings about "laying a whip on that hoss." Then there was a racketing and a splintering and down past me came an outfit which I recognized. The horse was certainly the brute my uncle had doctored into false shapeliness; the mane was dangling in shreds where the apple-tree limbs had raked. Runnels, his woman's hat hanging on his back, was kneeling on the bottom of the wagon, both hands full of false hair which he had reaped from the horse's tail in effort to check the animal; he had lost the reins and they were dragging uselessly on the ground.

Not far from me the wagon was flailed against a tree and Mr. Runnels was violently dislodged; but I judged that he was not injured because, after rolling over and over on the turf, he rose and ran away with his skirts gathered around his waist.

It was evident that my uncle's plot had failed ingloriously.

I could understand the flash of fresh spirit in that moribund horse; Runnels had shrieked warnings regarding a whip; a lash laid across those tingling water-blisters must have made that poor old pelter develop a hankering to outfly Pegasus. He disappeared with fragments of the thills clattering on his heels.

Then there were immediate and further developments in that orchard. I thought for a startled moment that it was enchanted ground. White figures began to pop up here and there and came flocking to me. I found myself surrounded by the Skokums, wearing the pillow-case masks I had furnished.

They seemed to think I had some information regarding the runaway or was concerned in it, but I had no news to give out. One of them brought the old felt hat with its broken feather.

"I didn't know there was any woman in these parts, who could cuss like that one did when she went down through the orchard," said one of the Sortwell boys. "I reckon that detective is finding mysteries piling in on him pretty thick."

"What detective?" I asked.

"The one that Judge Kingsley has been hiding in his home. That detective was hid in a closet in the office to-day when the judge was asking questions of us."

"How do you know he was there?"

"Cigar smoke was coming out of the cracks in the closet door. So somebody was hid. And since then he has been outdoors and we piped him off. He followed you home. Didn't you see him?"

I did remember the strange man who had been loafing along behind me, but I kept my own counsel. I had a more important matter on my mind.

"I want to know which of you fellows told Judge Kingsley to-day that I am ringleader of this gang?"

No one answered me. They went on making fun of the detective, and I'll admit that it seemed to me that he was putting up a poor job in his line. My reading had given me a rather exalted idea of detectives, but a man who smoked behind a closet door while eavesdropping, and through whose identity those country boys saw straightway, was certainly a clumsy operator. Therefore, I lost interest in him and persisted in my own business with them.

"I'm going to overlook your dirty work in setting old Bennie on to me," I said. "You may have done it only for a joke, and there's no telling what a fool will do when you start him off. But there's no joke in blowing on me to Judge Kingsley—and you say there was a detective listening behind a door. Now own up!"

Nobody volunteered.

"I told him myself that I was in it at first. But when I said I was out of it he made it plain that some of you are still putting the blame on me. Whoever has said anything of that kind to him is a sneak."

No word from any of them.

"And the fellow who won't speak up to me now, so that we can settle this thing, is a coward."

There was no such thing as picking out a guilty face in that crowd; they were hooded with those pillow-slips. I wasn't sure which was which; I couldn't locate even Ben Pratt in the gang, and he was the special chap I had in mind as informer.

"I can say this," stated one of the boys, "that I didn't mention your name to the judge, Ross. So there's no chance for a fight between you and me. But when you come to twitting about the throwing-down business, let me remind you that you did the first job in that line; you threw us all down. And that was after we had turned a trick that saved you and your uncle good money."

"But what the rest of you wanted to do was go around in the night and raise the devil in this town, simply for the sake of mischief. I wouldn't do that, and I told you so."

"But how about a case where we'd be protecting ourselves against somebody who was doing us dirt?"

"Nothing like that has been put up to me."

"It's going to be in about three seconds. You organized this society; now do something for it. We're going to coat that detective with molasses and feathers and ride him out of the village on a rail. We call on you to boss the job."

"I won't do it."

"Then join in with us and help."

"No!"

"This isn't mischief—it's tackling an enemy. You haven't got any good excuse for throwing us down."

"I've got an excuse that suits *me*. I have made up my mind to travel straight in this town, after this. I'm going to do it. I have my own good reasons for doing it."

"Lost your courage, hey?"

"It takes more courage to stand up here and say what I'm saying than to lead this mob."

"So *you* say, but that doesn't convince *us*. Go home, then, and get out from underfoot."

It came to me all of a sudden and with sickening force that it required more courage to go home and face my uncle than to undertake any other project which my mind could grasp just then.

I stood stock-still and they began to suspect my motives in sticking around.

"You won't head the party, you won't go along as a member, you won't get out of the way," growled a voice, and I recognized Ben Pratt. "What do you intend to do—make a holler?"

I could be just as stiff in temper as any of that Levant bunch.

"A good deal depends on what you devils intend to do," I said.

"You may as well know at the start-off! We intend to have that detective out of Judge Kingsley's house! If he doesn't come out when we call him we shall go in and get him."

"That's a prison crime—entering a house like that," I warned them. "Also, think what a report that is to go out from Levant! A guest of our leading citizen dragged from a private residence by a mob! There's a sacredness about a home—"

"What book did you get that out of?" asked some one, and they laughed.

I suppose it did sound mighty top-lofty and unlike anything else that ever came from me. But I was thinking with all my might of Celene Kingsley and what an awful thing it would be to have those young hyenas invade that house in the night-time. You can say what you want to about hoodlumism in the city—it's bad! But you've got to go back into the country for unadulterated hellishness, when a mob really gets started. Furthermore, nobody is especially afraid of a village constable. I could foresee dirty doings that night in Levant. I had seen one mob in Levant when I was a youngster; they tarred and feathered a fanatical evangelist, and he died of fright.

I tried to think up something in the way of argument and I stammered about local pride and so forth, but my talk didn't ring true, and I felt it and they knew it. Personally, I didn't care a hoot about that clumsy fool of a detective, and I was not remarkably fond of sneering Judge Kingsley. If I could have stepped up to those boys and explained my love and my hopes and my fears for Celene Kingsley I might have made some impression on them. But that was not to be thought of.

While I talked I saw them crawling toward me, spreading out, two by two. It was plain enough—they intended to start their foray by making me a captive so that I could not interfere.

Therefore, I made hasty resolution and turned and ran with all my speed toward Judge Kingsley's house. I wasn't at all sure just what I intended to do, but my impulse was to forewarn the household so that Celene might not be frightened. The Skokums came on my heels on the dead jump. But I had a good lead of them when I came around the corner of the house.

Then a man tripped me, pounced on me, and sat on me; I was a submissive captive, for the breath was knocked out of me when I fell. The instant the Skokums appeared my captor began to shoot off two automatic revolvers. I was lying on my back and saw by the flashes that he was shooting into the air. The boys had been chasing me rather than intending to rush the house at that time, and they broke and fled in all directions, scampering in a way which suggested that they were not prepared for artillery defense and that the hostilities were over for that night.

After a time there was silence, and the man who was sitting on me rose and yanked me to my feet.

He was a stocky man with a big, black mustache, and he looked savage.

There was a sound of drawing bolts and Judge Kingsley appeared at his office door.

"You have the right one, have you, officer?"

"Sure thing! He was leading the rush—ahead of 'em all. This is the chap you told me to follow in the afternoon."

The judge came down the steps and stared into my face.

"It's the right one—the ringleader," he said.

I knew that she was listening above. She must be listening! And other folks were flocking outside in the street; that fusillade had been a signal as effective as a general fire alarm.

"Look here," I cried, full of panic, seeing the position I was in, suddenly become the scapegoat of the whole affair. "I have done nothing wrong. I rushed up here to warn you—"

"You rushed up, all right," declared the detective. "Do you think you hicks could hold a mass-meeting down in that orchard and fool me as to what you were planning to do? I was ready for you. What's orders, Judge?"

"Take him to the lock-up!"

God of the innocent! I'll never forget how that sounded. It was as if somebody had hit me on the heart with a hammer. There is some sort of dignity about a real prison! But that little, red, wooden coop in our village where an occasional drunk was cast in or some lousy hobo harbored—it had always seemed to me and to others such a shameful place—to leave such a badge of utter discredit on the person who had been lodged there!

"I'll never go in there! I'll die first," I wailed.

I was telling the bitter truth as I felt it.

I was eager to die in my tracks rather than to have such a foul blot on my name.

The next instant I had sudden revulsion of feeling in regard to that lock-up. In bitter fear, in almost frenzy of apprehension, in default of better retreat, I was quite ready to flee to that loathsome coop.

For I heard my uncle raving in the street!

I never remembered his words; my feelings were too much

stirred just then. But the hideous screech of rage in his tones I'll never forget. I knew he had found out my betrayal of him.

"He is going to kill me," I told the detective. "It's about the horse!"

"Yes, I reckon he will peel you if he gets his hands on you," stated the man, who seemed to know what I was referring to. My uncle was threshing his way through the crowd toward me, making slow progress in the jam. The detective took advantage of that delay and rushed me off, with Constable Nute swinging his key and leading the way. Before I was fairly in my right senses I was in the lock-up alone and my two defenders were on guard outside the door.

My uncle frothed about the place for an hour, circling the little building again and again, plucking at bars and clapboards as a monkey might pick at a gigantic nut which resisted his attempts to get at the juicy meat for which he was hungry.

Never had I thought that I would be thankful to be in jail till then!

Furthermore, my hopes were sustaining me. I was young and trustful, and I was sure that innocence would be victorious. I could not understand how anybody would believe that I was guilty when morning came and I could explain it all. And I resolved to make some of the Skokums speak up in my behalf on threat of exposing the whole gang.

At last my uncle went away, staggering and hiccoughing curses—for he had brought his bottle with him and had been consulting it quite often.

I fell to wondering whether my innocence would stand me in good stead, providing it vindicated me and secured my release from the lock-up? The lock-up was surely proving a sanctuary—and my uncle's threats had been horrible ones.

Then the crowd which had been hanging around the place with a sort of hope, I suppose, that my uncle would be able to get at me, went away, for the hour was late. Mr. Detective went, too. So did Constable Nute, who was the village night-watch and had his rounds to make. They considered the cage a secure one, I suppose, for there were big bolts on the door and iron bars on the windows.

I sat on a stool and mourned my lot as a prisoner, when I was not dreading my release to be a victim of my incensed uncle. A good many times I had watched Bart Flanders bring a trapped rat up from his cellar and set it free in the village square for the entertainment of his terrier. I was in a position to sympathize with trapped rats.

In the silence of the night something clicked on the glass of a window and a voice outside hailed me cautiously. My first thought was that the Skokums had come to rescue me, and I was not especial-ly pleased, for I felt that they would be impelled more by the spirit of vandalism than by any love for me. I did not answer.

Then the window-frame grunted and squeaked and I saw that somebody was prying with a chisel. I rose from the stool and saw the face of Dodovah Vose.

"I take it that it's another job they have put up on you, young Sid-ney."

"Yes, it is, Mr. Vose," I cried, and I began to whimper. I couldn't help it. He spoke as if he understood, as if he were a friend. "I was trying to stop their devilishness, and they—"

"You needn't bother about going into details—not with me, young Sidney. I have been watching you lately. You have been a good boy. I know you haven't been rampaging round town nights. No matter about telling me anything. There's no time to listen. Nute may be drifting back here any minute."

He was working with his chisel while he was talking.

He pried a couple of bars out of the rotten wood. He pushed the window up.

"Light out o' there!" he commanded.

"But I hate to run away, and—"

"The way things stand now in the village you'll be made the goat," he insisted. "And if you get clear of the gang part there's your uncle to reckon with. He has been stamping around the tavern and telling about you. I don't blame him much. What in sanup did you betray own folks few?"

I couldn't tell him.

"After what you did to him you can't expect me and others to say nay if he takes it out of your hide. Trigging own folks in a regular hoss dicker comes nearer to being a crime than anything the judge can lay against you. So you've got to simplify matters by getting out of town. You mustn't stay here and get hurt, son. Climb, I tell ye!"

So I climbed.

He led me down into a lane and pushed me into a top buggy whose curtained sides hid me well. He crawled in after me and drove off at a good clip.

"I have written that letter to my brother," he said, after a time. "Here it is." He put it into my hands. "How much money have you got about you?"

I was never at any loss in those days as to my exact financial standing.

"Three dollars and sixty-four cents, sir."

"Here is ten more. You must remember to pay it back. It will take you to the city and give you a little extra to come and go on. I have backed that letter to my brother with full address and directions how to get to the Trident Wrecking Company. Mind your eye, keep your money deep in your pocket, and go straight."

I realized that we were on the way to the railroad station at Levant Lower Corners.

"I'll do what I can to stand up for you in the current talk that will be made, young Sidney," said Landlord Vose. "I won't say where you have gone, and you can bet that I won't give it out how I helped you to go there. But I can tell folks how you have been sitting evenings with me instead of cutting up snigdom. I'll help your name what I can."

"I have been trying to get my tongue loose so as to thank—"

"Don't go to spoiling a good thing at the last minute," he snapped. "Come back and thank me when we both are sure that this jail-robbing was the best thing that could be done under the circumstances. I had only short notice and I took a chance that it was the right thing to do."

So, after a time, we came to the railroad station, and he left me. I sneaked in the shadows till the night train came along.

After this fashion I left Levant. Looking ahead or looking behind, I did not feel especially joyous.

VI

HAVING TO DO WITH JODREY VOSE'S MAKING OF A DIVER

I sat up in the smoking-car all night, straight as a cob, making myself as small as I could on one of the side seats nearest the door. I was not used to riding on a railroad train. At every stop, when men came in and looked at me in passing, my heart jumped. Things had been happening pretty fast in my case. In the upheaval of my feelings, I was not exactly sure just what special crime I had committed. I merely knew that I felt like a combination of coward, renegade, and malefactor.

The idea which stuck most painfully in my crop was the certain knowledge of what everybody in Levant would be saying—"He had to skip the town!"

That's a mighty mean tag to be tied to a chap when it's tied on by a country community; it never comes off. Even if he makes good in fine shape some old blatherskite is always ready to shift his chaw and drool, "Maybe he's all right *now*—but ye have to remember that he had to skip the town!"

I had run away!

However, Ase Jepson let drop a remark once which sounded pretty good to me: "I'd never run from a bear-fight, because if you lick the bear there's the pelt, the steak, the oil, and the reppytation. But who in blazes ever got any sensible satisfaction out of sticking to the job and licking a nestful of hornets?"

I got a little satisfaction out of thinking that I had run away from hornets, even if they would be sure to call me coward behind my back.

But what I knew of the world outside my home town could have been put in the eye of a mosquito without making the insect blink. I felt as helpless as a wooden shingle latching a furnace door in tophet. I had never seen Jodrey Vose. Either I had dreamed it or had heard that he was considered a pretty hard ticket in his early days. As a diver, a man who passed much of his time under water in the mysteries of the sea, he seemed to me like something unreal. I studied the superscription on the letter and felt as if I were carrying a line of introduction to a bullfrog.

And so I went bumping on toward somewhere, my thoughts

44

heavy and my possessions mighty light; I hadn't even a clean hand-kerchief.

If I had not so many bigger matters to hurry on to in this tale, I'd like to describe how I was all of two days locating the Trident Wrecking Company and Jodrey Vose, after I arrived in the city. The folks in Levant always seemed to think I was a cheeky youngster, and I guess I was, to a certain extent. I had plenty of temper and when I wanted a thing I always had to go and get it—it wasn't hand-ed to me. But in that big city I was more meeching than a scared pup in a boiler-factory.

I had no idea how large a real city was, anyway. Furthermore, all of a sudden, I found myself becoming very crafty, according to my own reckoning. I had decided that I was a fugitive from justice and that every policeman was on the watch for me. Therefore I avoid-ed policemen, turning corners whenever I saw brass buttons. As I looked on everybody else in the hurrying multitude as a sharper, on the hunt for country picking, that left me without anybody to ques-tion. I had my nose in the air and must have sniffed the water-front after a time. At any rate, I found myself down there, dodging drays, tramping dirty alleys and as completely lost as a bug in a brush-pile.

I lived on chestnuts because I found men selling them on the street. I drank water from horse-fountains. After I walked all day and most of the night, and napped for a while, standing up against a building in a dark corner, I began to feel more or less like a horse; I had eaten so much dry fodder and had gulped so much water! There were many adventures, of course, but I have already stated why I may not deal with them.

Staggering from weariness, I fairly bumped, at last, into a door which was labeled: "Trident Wrecking Company, Anson C. Doughty, General Manager." This was no accident. I reckon I had tramped all the water-front and had read all the signs except that one.

I went into the outer office, holding my letter by one corner.

Nobody paid any attention to me for half an hour. There were men writing in big books behind a counter, and finally I pushed the letter over to one of them who had stopped to light a cigar. He pushed it back.

"Not here," he said. "Doesn't come here."

"But where will I find him?"

"Don't know. He's a diver. They don't do their diving here in the office."

There was not a place in that office where I could sit and I was so tired I was sick. The man turned his back on me and I did not dare to ask him any more questions. I backed away from the counter and stood in the middle of the floor, swaying and blinking. I reckon I must have looked like a down-and-out bum. At any rate, when a big man came showing a caller out of a door labeled "General Manager, Private," he bumped against me when I did not get out of the road and almost knocked me down.

I suppose it was due to my state of mind and body—but till that moment I had never felt what ugly, vicious hatred—desire to kill—meant. The feeling came up in me so suddenly that I was frightened.

The big man went right on with his friend and took no notice of me. He had hairy hands which he flourished as he talked, and the coat of his brown suit had long tails which ended in a sort of scallop at his knees, behind; it came to me in the flush of my boiling hatred that he looked like a fat cockroach. And that bump dealt to me when I was so miserable, that suggestion of the cockroach which always popped up at me as long as I knew him, later made for another decisive turning-point in my life. Again I am calling attention to the fact that matters which I did not reckon on as to amounting to much at the moment have been my mile-stones. As I look back I recognize the mile-stones, though I could not distinguish them at the time. For instance, if you keep on with me far enough, I shall tell you how an affair which counted, perhaps, as the biggest crisis in my life was dominated by a plain, ordinary monkey with an artificial tail.

I followed after that big man with a raging desire to kick him under the sleek tails of that coat—to pound my fists into his fat back. I might have given quite an account of myself, at that, for I was full grown at twenty and as hard as hickory.

"As I say," I heard before he slammed the door behind him, "you better come along with me down to Trull wharf and talk to Vose himself. He can tell you—"

I gathered my wits and chased along behind. The two of them paid as little attention to me as they would to a prowling cat. But if they were on the way to talk to "Vose himself," that surely was my opportunity.

It was some distance and by way of devious alleys, but we came at last to where a lighter was tied beside a wharf.

There was a derrick and the scow was loaded with blocks of granite. A man was slowly and ceaselessly turning the wheel of a queer-looking machine, another was carefully handling hose which passed over the side of the lighter and down into the water, and still another was tending ropes. It did not occur to me at first what this activity indicated.

But when the big man called out, "Is Vose about due to come up?" I understood at once and was mightily interested.

I looked down into the dock and saw water like liquid muck, filled with floating refuse, and a good deal of the glamour of a diver's life departed from my imagination. Somehow I had thought that Jodrey Vose spent his days in blue depths of pure ocean water, looking around at strange fishes and exploring mysterious caves. That he was obliged to go down into any such mess as that and work on blocks of stones with his two hands was a depressing discovery.

After a time there was a bubbling of the turbid water close beside the lighter, and for the first time in my life I saw a diver's helmet emerge; the goggling eye-plates, the grotesque excrescences, the sprouting antennæ of the hose lines, the venomous hissing of the air from the vents—it all seemed uncanny, and made me shiver.

Men reached down to help him up the ladder, and when he was on deck in full view, scuffing his huge, weighted shoes, a balloon-like creature, as shapeless as the doughnut men my mother used to cut for me when she was in good humor on frying-day, I was sure I had never seen so curious a sight.

After he sat down they twisted off the helmet, and the fat man, whom I reckoned must be Manager Anson C. Doughty, escorted the other man aboard the lighter and the three started a conversation which I could not hear.

I knew the diver for Jodrey Vose because I had seen his picture at the tavern.

The business, whatever it was, did not take much time and the manager and the other man went away. Helpers began to shuck the diver from his suit; it was nearing sundown and work for the day was over, it seemed. When he was free from the bulk of the stuff and was starting for the cabin of the lighter I went to him and gave him the letter.

"From Dod, hey?" Then he told me to follow him.

I looked at him while he read the letter by the light of a bracket lamp. He was a wiry man with a twist of grizzled chin-beard. I was much comforted when he looked up from the letter and grinned.

"Ben Sidney's boy! Well, your father was the only critter on two legs in Levant, in the old days, who could stand in a barrel, like I could, and jump out without touching the sides. You look as if you have some of his spryness and grit!"

"I hope so, sir. I have always worked at what has come to my hands to do."

"Dod says business is a mite slow in Levant and that you want a job."

"Yes, sir."

Now there was gratitude in me as well as comfort; it was evident that Dodovah Vose had not written that I was a runaway.

The diver laid down the letter and went fumbling for his street clothes in a closet.

"At any rate, you can come up to my boarding-place with me for the night and we'll talk it all over," he said, in a very kind way. "If you had only made yourself known a few minutes ago I could have introduced you to Manager Anson C. Doughty. But to-morrow will do as well."

I did not dare to offer comment. I wondered what there was about Anson C. Doughty to keep my hatred of him so stirred.

"He takes my recommendations as to my helpers," said Vose. "There is one thing a diver has to be sure about—that's picking his helpers. We'll talk it over, I say. If I find there's considerable of Ben Sidney in you, I reckon we can make a go of it. Have you a hankering to learn the business, itself?"

I blossomed under the warmth of this kindness. I was full of words by that time. I hadn't opened my mouth to talk for two days. I told him about my evenings in that tavern, my poring over his curios, my ambitions, my dreams and hopes after hearing the stories his brother had to tell me.

When he had finished dressing he clapped me on the shoulder.

"Oh, I calculate you're going to do," he told me. "Don't get your expectations too high. I have given up all the deep work—too old. Five or six years steady at deep work finishes a man. I have nursed myself along. Wharf work—fifteen to thirty feet—that's my limit these days. But I like your spirit, son. Can't find boys in the city like that! I should say that you've got the real hankering. Cigarettes, ever?"

"No, sir! No tobacco."

"No cider jamborees? No express packages from the city?"

"No, Mr. Vose."

"Good! I reckon I'll keep the old town of Levant on the map in the diving line. I know the game, my boy. And I know how to teach it to the right kind of a pupil."

"I'm sure you do, Mr. Vose."

"So we'll talk it all over this evening—and while we're about it, if you don't call me Captain Vose down this way they'll think you don't know me very well."

I blushed, then I followed him out and away.

Before I tumbled into bed that night we had settled upon the future so far as our words to each other went; the bargain only needed the ratification of Anson C. Doughty—and that was secured next morning. I had expected that sleep would soothe my nerves and remove my ugly grouch in the case of that gentleman. However, there must have been something instinctive in my dislike for him; he looked me up and down and caught my scowl.

"You seem to have picked out a pretty surly up-country steer, Vose! However, put him to work if you like that kind!"

So to work I went.

I cleaned diving-suits and thus became familiar with the parts and the mechanism. I soaked out mud-caked ropes, I tended lines and learned signals, and was always busy with a hundred other odd jobs as a satellite of Diver Vose. He used me well enough, though he was never as warm toward me as he was at our first meeting.

After some weeks I lost my fear that I would be followed and taken back to Levant. I was not sure whether I felt more relief than rancor. To be considered as not worth chasing, to know they were saying "Good riddance!" behind my back, gave me thoughts which hurt a certain kind of pride.

I was afraid of the city and I went nowhere except to my work and to my boarding-place. So there was an epoch in my life which was bare of adventure until Diver Vose sent me down for the first time.

He had given me a fine course of sprouts previously, of course.

But in spite of all that the first sensations nigh paralyzed me. I reached bottom and wallowed around without the least thought or remembrance regarding what I had been told to do. A freight-train seemed to be roaring around inside my helmet and I was gasping like a dying skate-fish.

Then in scuffing around in a sort of panic, taking no care of what I was about, I hooked my shoe onto something and began to yank and thresh around in a perfect frenzy. The result was that I pulled the shoe off and my lightened foot was snapped above my head in a finer spread-eagle than any acrobatic dancer ever pulled off. To drag that foot down was beyond my powers, and I tripped and went onto my back. Being up-ended is a diver's chief peril, because the air bellies up into the legs of the dress and leaves scant supply in the helmet.

In that crisis there was one idea which stuck to me: I must get that lost shoe!

And I did get it. I groped and rolled and struggled and pulled until I did get it. A half-dozen times in my efforts I felt them trying to haul me up. I suppose I must have given signals telling them to quit that. I fought them as best I could, anyway, until I had recovered the shoe; then I yanked for a lift and went up.

Captain Vose was standing in front of me with the helmet in his hands when I had recovered my wits enough to notice anybody.

"Been dancing a jig?" he inquired, caustically.

I shook my head, for I was not able to utter words.

"Which did you lose first down there, your nerve or that shoe?"

When I hesitated, he snapped, "Give me the truth, now, or we sha'n't get along after this!"

"My nerve!" I told him.

"So I knew—for I lashed on that shoe with my own hands. Very well! What good are you as a diver without your wits or your nerve?"

"No good, sir."

"You can buy an eighteen-pound shoe at any equipment loft. But how about buying nerve?"

"I reckon it can't be bought, sir," I confessed.

"Still, you were almighty *particular*," he sneered, "to bring back that shoe with you even if you didn't bring your nerve. Left your nerve on the bottom, eh?"

He was mighty nasty in his tone and his manner, and the men standing around were grinning. Perhaps even all that would not have put grit back into me, for I was dizzy and scared and was owning up to myself that I was better fitted for dry ground than a wet sea-bottom. But just then Anson C. Doughty bellowed from the wharf:

"Say, look here, Vose, let that coward go back up-country to his steers! We have no time to fool away on greenhorns."

"If I did leave my nerve on the bottom I'm going back after it, and I'm going right now!" I told the diver. I was holding the shoe and I dropped it on deck and shoved my foot into it. Captain Vose kneeled and began to lash it.

"What are you doing, there?" demanded the manager.

"Making a diver," stated my teacher, calmly.

"I'm paying you fifty dollars a day to do what I tell you to do, Vose."

"That's right, sir!" The captain kept right on with the lashings. "There's a contract between you and this young man which tells me to teach him how to be a diver, if he shows the capacity."

"He hasn't shown it."

"He is going to in about five minutes, sir."

He picked up the helmet and bent over me.

50

"I had a reason for twitting you about that shoe," he said, in my ear. "You showed what was in you by bringing it back. If you hadn't brought it back I would have stripped this suit off you and sent you hipering! You've got it in you! You're all right! Now go down, son, and set that chain where I told you to set it. The first scare is the vaccination for this kind of work. You're in a way to be immune from now on!"

The last sound I heard was the snarl of Anson C. Doughty. That sound helped me to go to my job that day. I went down and did what was required of me, and, as I worked below there and became convinced that there was nothing to harm me if I kept my head, I found my nerve, I reckon, for good and all, in the diving business.

And now that this story seems to be settled into a rut of adventure in my chosen line of work, hold breath with me and prepare for a couple of most "jeeroosly jounces," as old Wagner Bangs used to term his occasional falls from his state of natural grace.

First, I leap as nimbly as I can over three years and a half of hard work, the story of which would hold as little interest as the biography of a mud-clam. I slipped and slid and dug in slime, I shagged granite blocks and dragged chains, I pried into wrecks and had my whack at fumbling in the watery shadows for the drowned—pitiful bundles floating as if they were attempting posthumous gymnastics, head down and fingers trying to touch toes.

I did "deep work" on ticklish jobs.

So I came into the fifty-dollar-a-day class of workers, to the grim content of my mentor.

I have just remarked that the snarl of Anson C. Doughty sent me in earnest to my first job. Also, just as suddenly, that snarl pried me loose from my job.

I wish I did not have to confess what I have to say now. I come to jounce number two!

I have spoken a ways back of mile-stones in my life and suggested that Anson C. Doughty was connected with one.

I wish I could give a real, compelling, manly reason why I tossed my hopes and my prospects so wildly into the air all of a sudden. I have spoken of my ready temper—but that's no reason.

In fifteen seconds I shifted the life I was living as completely as a derailing-switch shoots a runaway engine off the main line.

The borers of that mysterious hatred for Anson C. Doughty must have been burrowing in me all the time, even as those little teredinoid bivalves we call ship-worms gnaw into submerged piles with the edges of their shells. I was full of burrows and went to pieces all of a sudden.

For I came up one day out of thirty fathoms—and that's man's work—and Doughty was giving me green help out of his general meanness—and my head was far from steady; in addition he gave me his snarl for the last time, instead of snarling at his infernal dubs who were risking my life.

I stepped on his foot with a shoe that was loaded with twenty pounds of lead—and that's some anchor!—I walloped him into insensibility with the end of a rubber hose. Then I resigned informally, while he lay on the deck of the lighter, grunting back to life again.

Nobody stopped me when I said I was going and announced that it would be dangerous to get in my way.

They stood back while I shifted my clothes—and I got away with my diving equipment, even! It was the newest thing out for those days and the going styles of gear, and I had paid good money for it.

I say again, I wish I had a more cogent reason to give for throwing up my work. But I'm giving the truth of the matter. I left just that way. I knew that Anson C. Doughty would have me put in jail if he could catch me. I knew that I couldn't do any more diving, for divers are marked men and are easily located. It was up to me to go and hide; so I went and hid.

VII

THE PSYCHOLOGY OF A PLUG-HAT

I had been about a bit during three years and a half. I own up frankly that I had found out that I had more or less of a cheap streak in me. I'm not disguising it wholly by the name of curiosity; though, of course, a country fellow has a keen hankering to look in on some of the sights of the big city.

When we boys up in Levant used to hand around among ourselves by stealth some of the flashy papers, I didn't believe there were such things as I read in print and saw in pictures. After some of my sporty associates of the Trident workers began to take me around with them evenings I kept perfectly still about my earlier disbeliefs, and my cheap streak began to talk up to me. Somebody came distributing free admission cards to concerts, managed by religious and fraternal bodies—but I preferred to pay money at the door of a burlesque theater. I liked to go scouting in dance-halls, and I haunted low resorts to hear what I could hear and see what I could see.

We went boldly, for we were husky youths. As for myself, I had licked the boys of Levant at every opportunity—and my Sidney temper afforded me opportunities aplenty. I was never afraid when I went about alone, either. I had a rather quiet way of minding my own business and impressing it on the other fellow that he'd better mind his.

So, it may be guessed, most of my wanderings had been done in the lower quarters of the city.

That's where I went to hide. And I had knowledge enough of the locality to hide myself effectually and keep hidden.

I did get in touch with one of the fellows who had been around a great deal with me and whom I trusted—for he had no special use for Anson C. Doughty.

Anson C. Doughty was out of doors once more, after spending a week of retirement in the company of a few busy little leeches, and, as to eyes and nose, he was not looking so very badly on the outside, but was evidently having a great amount of trouble with a volcano raging within, so my informant told me. Mr. Doughty was proclaiming that he proposed to catch me so that he could make an example for the sake of discipline in his crews in the future; but according to the program he had promulgated, he proposed to cut me up with a meat-chopper before turning me over to the law. So I decided to keep under cover for an indefinite period.

Then I sent word to Captain Jodrey Vose and had him call on me in my castle, because I did not want him to think that he had wasted all his efforts when he had made me a diver.

However, the captain did seem to think so. He frankly said so.

"You'll never get another job diving on the Atlantic coast," he told me. "In the first place, you won't dare to show up as a diver where Anson C. Doughty can grab you. In the next place, Anson C. Doughty has posted you with all the wrecking companies as being as dangerous as an Asiatic tiger with lighted kerosene on his tail. Now tell me what made you do it."

I told him.

He looked at me with his eyes squizzled up and a frown on his forehead.

"I'm getting along in years and I'm probably losing my mind to some extent," he said, "but I'll be cussed if I believe I've got entire softening of the brain. It must be that I'm deaf and can't understand—because I don't get the least idea of why you did it to him. Tell it over."

I told him again.

"Yes, I must have softening of the brain," he grunted. "It's all a riddle-come-ree to me!"

"It is the same to me—and that's why I can't explain," I told him, frankly. "I hung onto myself all that time, wanting to do it, and then I let go and did it!"

"About as you went to cutting up in Levant before you skipped out," he snapped.

Up to that time, not by word or look had he let me know that he had any knowledge of why I had left my home town.

"Dod explained it to me in the letter he sent with you. But he had excuses to give."

I had to admire Captain Vose's ability to keep his thoughts to himself, as I remembered the placid countenance he showed to me when he had read that letter.

"Now I reckon that Dod was prejudiced in your favor and that you had been a young devil the folks wanted to boost out of town. Dod's judgment was never very good in the case of any critters who were willing to cater to him. I don't suppose you dare to go back up there?"

"I don't want to go." But all of a sudden a queer wave of homesickness seemed to come swelling up in me and to choke me like water chokes the throat of a dredge-pump. "I'm done with that town for good and all," I told him. "I got along all right while I was do-ing dirt as fast as the rest of 'em, but when I tried to be decent they didn't give me a show!" I snapped my finger. "I wouldn't give *that* for anybody in Levant!"

I knew I was lying and I think Jodrey Vose knew it, for he was a keen old chap. He scowled at me and grunted.

"Got any money left after all the rake-helling you've been doing for a year past?"

So he knew all about that, too!

"I'm fixed all right!" But I looked up at the ceiling of my room when I said it, and I knew I was not fooling him. I ought to have had a bank account, considering what I had been pulling down. I had all my capital in my pocket—a roll about as big as my thumb. I had con-siderable of a string of memories, such as they were, regarding mon-ey I had spent; I had a brand-new diving-dress, and, above all, queer as this may sound, I had a specially new outfit which was my chief pride: a frock-coat and pearl-gray trousers, waistcoat modestly fan-cy—my real tastes in that direction having been gently suppressed by an honest tailor—and a plug-hat whose shininess fairly put my eyes out. And up to that time I had had no opportunity to wear that suit except in front of the mirror in my hiding-place!

I had tested the tilt of that hat at a dozen different angles; I had nearly broken my neck in efforts to see just how the coat-tails flared in the back. With a chart as help, a card stuck in the side of the mir-ror, I had practised tying a scarf in Ascot style until my staring eyes watered and my fingers ached. Then I had walked back and forth, trying to get the hang of a cane.

Again I suggest that this may sound queer. But it was only an-other manifestation of that cheap streak in me, so I reckon. I was not modeling my appearance on the looks of any real gentleman I had ever seen; I had not bought that garb in order to appear at church or to climb into better society. But from the time I was ten years old I had nursed one special, hungry, despairing ambition. At the county fair I saw "Diamond Dick" Shrady marshaling his painted beauties in front of his tent, and, according to my notion, his rig-out was ap-parel which shaded even the robes of royalty. I could not conceive higher height of happiness than to own and wear for "every day" a suit like that.

Consider the lily—as I considered "Diamond Dick"! Then con-sider me as I stood in front of that tent!

I had on brogan shoes which I had fresh-tallowed for the day. My stockings were home-knit and bulged out in folds over the tops of my shoes. But I was not so keenly self-conscious of my footwear as of the rest of my outfit, because Levant boys wore brogans quite commonly. My trousers were my special sore point, for even in Levant they had been ridiculed. In the first place, the cloth was a glazy, stiff stuff; in the second place, my good mother did not understand how to cut out a boy's pants. There was just as much fullness in the front as in the back. I kept denting in that fullness with my fists when I was unobserved. I found that by stooping quite a bit when I walked or stood I was able to keep the fullness caved in and less noticeable. It was a wonder I did not become permanently hump-backed while I was wearing out those pants. The legs of them were like twin stovepipes, and almost as unyielding. They crackled at the knees when I sat down. Add to these items of attire a hickory shirt, for which I had made a false bosom out of a shingle painted white, a paper collar, and a butterfly bow made of a gingham rag, a hard hat which was a paternal hand-me-down; they called them "dips." It was a good name. The hat was exactly the shape of the bowl of a table-spoon.

As I leaned back and gaped up at that gorgeous stranger on the platform, straightening myself and letting my forward fullness swell as it would, there was born in me that unconquerable hankering—wild desire to be dressed like that—sometime! To say to myself—sometime—"Now I am dressed right! Everything about me is just as it should be!"

To base my ideas on the outfit "Diamond Dick" wore was probably evidence of the cheap streak in me, I say, but when you consider me as I stood there, and then consider the lily, is there not some excuse?

I confess with some shame that during my hiding in the city, while I was tucked away in that boarding-house room, my chief regret was not that I was out of a job, was not that I had battered the face of my employer, but was because I could not go out and swell around the streets and the amusement places wearing that suit and looking that picture of myself which had been the ideal that lulled me to sleep every night during my boyhood.

I was having some of those dreams while I sat there and gazed up at the ceiling. At last a big dream had come true. I owned that suit and I knew I looked mighty well in it. I had put in a good many hours in front of the looking-glass making sure of that fact. But now that I owned it I was getting none of the thrills and but little of the satisfaction I had looked forward to. Realized ambitions in my case—and probably it's true in most cases—have always seemed to have a lot

56

of discomforting tag-ends tied to them. I was practically a prisoner in a dingy room, I could not go out and sport around in my new regalia, and Jodrey Vose, who had undertaken to make a man of me, was sitting across the table, scowling at me with a great deal of disfavor.

"Have you taken up drinking along with the rest, young Sidney?"

"No, sir; and I never shall. I'm sure of that, sir."

"What are you going to do next?"

"I don't know."

"You'd better go back to Levant."

"I'll never do that."

"Dod writes that your uncle has been enlarging his business and is making a lot of money and is going to run for town office. He must need a chap like you and has probably forgotten any little trouble he might have had with you."

But I shook my head.

"You don't expect me to do anything more for you, do you?"

Again I shook my head. That homesick feeling was swelling up once more.

"I hear that they are fitting out another Cocos Island expedition to hunt for the Peru treasure-ship. You might be able to sign on there. But it's a fake job. There's no sunken ship. However, you'll get wages."

"I believe I'll try the Pacific coast, sir."

He did his forefinger back and forth slowly under his nose.

"It might do, son. I have thought of the same jump, myself. I have waited now till I'm too old. What started me thinking about it some years ago was the *Golden Gate* proposition. What troubled me about making up my mind was that some said the treasure had been got out of her and others said there was some guesswork. Nobody seemed to be willing to produce any proof that the treasure was still there. Looking back, I can see now why all interested parties would naturally rather have it thought that the treasure wasn't there. But when a fellow like me has his living to make he doesn't want to take too many chances. And the one job I did go on sickened me of treasure-hunting on somebody's guesswork."

He was silent for a time.

"I am sorry you are in your scrape, young Sidney. You're done for as a diver in these parts for a time. Try the Pacific. I don't say it's a bad idea." He grinned at me. "If you recover the *Golden Gate* treasure drop me a postal card."

Then he went away, making no more ado about the matter of our parting. I was not surprised by that manner of leave-taking. I am a

Yankee myself, and I had found myself wishing that when he went he would walk off without jawing me or coddling me.

I counted my money and sent out for some railroad folders and trailed my finger across the map—and stayed right on in the city, week after week. I don't know exactly what I had lost—ambition or pluck or what it was! But that was a spell in my life when I was a plumb, square loafer, and rather enjoyed myself—reading cheap novels and playing solitaire in the daytime, then getting in with some of the rest of the boarders and playing poker evenings. In Levant we used to play for beans in barn-chambers. I had a country boy's shrewdness in that game, and the city fellows did not get much of my money away from me; nor did I get any particular amount of theirs.

However, the pastime did bring me into touch with some sporting characters and with some queer characters, too. There were men who were hiding the same as I was. The fact that I was under cover gave me open sesame to their confidence. They talked a great deal, whiling away dull hours in the day. Several were in the house where I was stopping, and after a time I dared to go visiting around a bit evenings and went along to other houses in the locality.

It was all new to me, this "flash" side of life, and I listened to their stories with eyes and mouth open. I conceived an idea of writing out these stories into a book, and after I got back into my room nights I would jot down all I had heard, names and all. I had all the nicknames of operators down pat—those names rather fascinated me. There were names which were based on personal peculiarities or blemishes or system of operating. I found out that a great many of the parties were linked, either by relationship or by gang ties, and that the wise boys among the crooks or the police officers could tell in many cases just what crowd had operated, providing the identity of one man could be revealed. I reckon I calculated in those times that I was going to make an exposé, for I made many notes about the different coteries and their associates.

I will say at this point that I have no intention of writing such a book, and I have gone into a bit of detail about the matter in order that certain following activities of mine may be understood. Otherwise, I might, later on, be thought to be advertising myself as one of those know-it-all and do-it-all heroes of fiction instead of a plain and ordinary chap who has been swayed by circumstance and governed by accident in large measure.

But I did get a lot of fresh and lively information out of those chaps with whom I was thrown in.

After a time they were not at all bashful about asking me if I wouldn't like a lay in some of their operations.

They frankly said that they had the best luck in country communities. Understand that they proposed nothing except brace games! No safe-breakers in that lot! They said I had an honest way about me that would take well in the country districts.

My money was getting so low I listened with increasing interest. I cannot say that I was tempted, exactly. But I was beginning to wonder how I was ever going to make a go of it if I didn't get some money. My Pacific trip was all off by that time! My capital had shrunk below the price of a ticket.

They told me that a regular village skinflint with lots of money was, in most cases, a prime victim if the right bait was offered; with the right bait he bit more easily than the more liberal kind of an individual, because the skinflint was more crazy to make money fast and was already used to getting high rates of interest for all money he let out. They were making constant search for old chaps in country communities, well-to-do men who would be tempted to grab at a rich chance or could be induced to serve as decoys to pull in the neighbors, provided a sufficient rake-off were offered.

There, too, was another thing which surprised me—that so often really prominent men could be secured as decoys. The knaves I was training with gave me a lot of stories of the kind; in most cases, so they said, the men seemed to talk themselves into believing that they were offering the neighbors an opportunity to make money.

If I had not been idle and very curious, and all the time wondering how I could make a little money for myself, a lot of this would have gone into one ear and out of the other. But I was in the mood to take it all in, and so, in that foolish belief that I could write a story, I set down many names and many instances until I had well filled a sheaf of papers which I sewed together into a sort of note-book.

There were various side-lines of the craft of cheaters where I was allowed to be an observer. I watched one of the chaps make up his face for a trip and learned about false beards attached by spirit gum. There was a cute little mustache in his kit and I asked him to affix it to my upper lip. He allowed me to keep it on when I asked permission.

I felt so much confidence in that alteration of my features that I went directly to my room, put on that raiment of my yearning ambition, took in hand my cane, and went forth into the open.

One who has remained long within-doors gets used to the confinement after a time and the desire to go out is dulled; there are persons who have voluntarily remained in bed in perfect health for years; but, once the plunge outside is made, the desire for further liberty grows by what it grasps in the blessedness of outdoors. I determined to be free from then on and to test the quality of that freedom. It was astonishing what confidence I felt in myself when I walked abroad in that rig, casting side-glances at myself in store windows as I walked. It is amazing what the right sort of clothes will do for a man's grip and grit.

I went down to the docks and walked about, deliberately seeking to put myself in the path of Anson C. Doughty. He did come face to face with me after a time, looked at me with considerable interest, for plug-hats were none too common in that locality, and passed on with bland indifference. My transition was too much for him; I was the butterfly that had emerged from the pupa of a diving-dress. After that I bestowed no further thought on dangers to be apprehended from Anson C. Doughty.

I was more concerned with speculation on where my next meal was coming from, for I was flat broke. I suppose that fact had something to do with driving me out on the street; it was not wholly proud eagerness to show myself in that suit of clothes.

All of a sudden I received direct proof that a plug-hat is occasionally something to conjure by.

Perhaps it is on the principle that advertising pays; a man with slick, silk headgear is supposed to be at least something which can be classed under the title of "professor." At any rate, I was hailed by that title by a man who stood in a broad doorway. I stopped and he had something interesting to say to me.

VIII

"TAKING IT OUT" ON A
SUIT OF CLOTHES

That doorway was solidly banked with banners frescoed in gaudy colors and roughly painted; they advertised a show within. A few glances I had time to give while I walked toward the man who had hailed me, revealed that there were on tap such features as "Petrified Mormon Giant," "Siamese Susie," "Mammoth Peruvian Cockatoo," and others. Over the door was heralded in big letters: "Dawlin's Mammoth Wonder Show."

I guessed that the man in the doorway might be Dawlin. He wore a corduroy suit, with gaiters, and a broad-brimmed cowboy hat was canted on one side of his head. By the way in which he was looking me over I could see that I was suiting him.

"Hitched up with a show?" he asked.

I told him that I was not, and I said it with considerable curtness. To be sure, the personality and garb of Showman Shrady had formed my early ideal, and I ought to have felt gratified, I suppose, when this man took me for a showman. But I was pricked a little by the thought that my appearance seemed to grade me on that plane.

"Want to hitch on?"

"What makes you think I'm in the show business?"

"I had you sized that way on account of the scenery."

I gathered that he meant my clothes.

"I don't see any circus signs on this suit of mine," I told him.

"Oh, say, I didn't mean to offend—but it's usually only sports and professionals who tog that way down in this part of the town. If you're a gent you seem to be off your beat."

There was nothing offensive about the man—he seemed a good-humored chap who was a little cheeky.

"Well, what if I had been a showman—what about it?"

"I was going to offer you a lay—here at the door."

"Selling tickets?"

"Good gad, no, man! I want you for the spiel—for the oratory—tongue-work—hooking the hicks! You're rigged out just right. You must know that the better the front we put on at the door, the better the business inside! But excuse me if I got the tags shifted!"

I swung my cane with one hand and with the other hand in my

pocket sifted coins through my fingers. There were not many coins. I needed more in a hurry. It had been impressed on me that in spite of all my pride in my attire I did not look like a "gent"; it was certain that I did not feel like one. Disappointment was curdling pride in me; my clothes had gone back on me. I entertained a sort of a grudge against them. All of a sudden I made up my mind to get back at those garments which had cost me so much money and now repaid me in contentment so niggardly.

"It would be all new business for me. Can I do it, do you suppose?" I asked the man.

"Looks are half the battle. You've got capital in your clothes to start with. You don't look like a souse! The last two I have had on the door pawned their rigs for rum. I've got the patter stuff all written out. All you've got to do is study it and reel it off like you used to recite pieces in school."

"What's the pay?"

Seeing surrender in my face, he winked and crooked his finger in invitation to me to follow him inside. He led me into a narrow little office. He offered a drink and a cigar, and I refused both.

"Gee! Some principles, hey? Now, if you're a church member I reckon you won't stand for the lay!"

"I'm devilish far from being a church member," I told him.

"I don't like to open up too much till I know a little something about you. Can you tell me?"

I told him enough to make him pretty much at ease.

"Do you know any of the right kind in this locality—the sporting bunch?"

I gave a roster of acquaintances that made his eyes glisten.

"Oh, then, you're all right!" he cried, slapping my knee. "In *my* business a fellow has to try the ice before he slides out too far. I'm coming right across to you." He waved his hand to indicate his establishment. "This show is only a hinkumginny, you know!"

"I thought so," I said, calmly. I hadn't the least idea what he meant, but I knew that one needed to act wise with wise gentlemen.

"We run the gazara game and phrenology."

I nodded and winked an eye as if I had been quite sure of that fact right along.

He scratched a few figures on a wisp of paper and pushed it to me across the desk-slide on which he had set out the whisky-glasses.

"That's the split," he said, grinning. Still it was all Greek to me.

"I know places doing half our business and paying twice as much—and every once in a while having to settle a squeal, at that!

But I've got a cousin at headquarters—see? Nothing to it! Now you can understand what a sweet little pudding you're pulling alongside of."

I was wishing I could understand better, though I was developing a dim notion that he was talking about money paid for protection from the law. He pulled back the paper and tore it up.

"Only fifty a week," he said; "it's nothing. I'm thinking of throwing in another twenty-five without their asking. It beats laying up treasures in heaven!"

I agreed.

"Now as to a lay for you! Of course, first of all, I have to grab off my fifty of the net—it's my show and my pull! Then there's the 'Prof'—Professor Jewelle. He has his twenty-five per cent. I'll tell you straight, now, I have been getting by with those dickerdoodles I've had out on the stand for fifteen per cent., and 'prof' and I have divided the other ten. But they were crumby! Their suits were wrinkled worse than an elephant's dewlap, and the nap of their plug-hats was fruzzled up like the fur in the mane of the Australian witherlick. No pull to that class! The jaspers jogged right past without being a mite impressed. If you grab in with us your looks and your style make you worth a lay of twenty-five per cent. Now what say?"

"I'll grab," I told him, and never did a man hire with less idea of just what kind of a business he was entering or what pay he was going to get for his labor.

"You say your name is Ross Sidney," said the boss, remembering what I had told him. "Mine is Jeff Dawlin, Ross, and there's no mistering among partners." He gave me a few dirty sheets of paper. "There's your spiel all written out. You can add your own talk as you work into the spirit of the thing. The idea is get them to stop, look, listen—and then coax till they come in. If they come out squealing, you go on and bawl them—bawl them down! There's some good work to be done in that line—and you're husky and can scare 'em, providing Big Mike hasn't already scared 'em enough. There isn't a thing in the show but what's a fake—of course you understand that. Most of 'em are too ashamed to squeal."

He was leading me into the inner mysteries of the place while he talked. He made no reference to the objects which were ranged around the sides of the big room, plainly despising them as curiosities which could not possibly interest anybody. But they interested me mightily and I lagged behind to give each one a glance in passing.

"Siamese Susie" was made up of a couple of big wax dolls confined in a single dress. "The Peruvian Cockatoo" manifestly had been, when he was alive, the humble master of some up-country barn-yard; now he was tricked out with all sorts of dyed false feathers, including an enormous topknot. The "Mormon Giant" was a papier-maché figure, and there was a hideous thing labeled "Mermaid" constructed of the same material as the giant. There were a few other nondescript exhibits in dingy glass cases or mounted on stands draped in dirty hangings. I had never seen a collection of more shameless frauds. I began to understand that I had not been let in on the main proposition for money-making.

On one side of the room there were curtains lettered: "Professor Jewelle, the World's Greatest Seer." The professor came out when Dawlin called for him. He wore a wig and false white whiskers, and had watery eyes, and a breath like a whiff from a distillery chimney. A big brute of a man was loafing in one corner of the room, and I reckoned that this person must be Big Mike; I had seen many such of the bouncer sort when I had made my rounds, hunting for experiences.

Mr. Dawlin introduced me, and I seemed to make a good impression.

When he slyly slid out the information that I, too, had been having troubles which had kept me under cover for some weeks, I noted that I stood even higher in their estimation.

As we talked on I began to feel a bit ambitious. I thought I might be able to improve business.

"Look here," I suggested, "why not put a tank in here and let me do some of my diving stunts? It would be a novelty—there really doesn't seem to be much to the show as it stands."

"Say, I haven't pulled a greenhorn into camp, have I?" inquired Mr. Dawlin with a good deal of tartness. "Show? Good gad! who ever said we wanted a show?"

I did not know what to say to that and so I did not answer.

"What do you think I would be doing, or the 'prof' would be doing, while the jethros were crowded around you? We wouldn't be doing a thing in the line of the regular graft. The main idea of this concern is to get 'em in here where there's nothing to take up their minds after they've had one look around the place. Then they begin to feel that they want to get something for their money. So the 'prof' hands 'em the dome dope—feels their bumps—and I feed 'em the gazara stuff. How many times have I got to tell you what this place is?"

"Oh, I'm wise," I said, trying hard to look that way. "But of course I'm anxious to do all I can to help."

"The zeal of youth! The zeal of youth!" prattled the professor. He seemed to me to be pretty much of an old fool. He had that smug, cooing way with him—all put on like the airs of a country undertaker. He came across to me before I could understand what he was about and stuck his thumb onto a spot on the top of my head and pressed with his forefinger a little lower down. "Yes, approbativeness well developed and conscientiousness—this where my finger—"

"Oh, shut up!" snorted Mr. Dawlin. "Don't try to put that stuff over among friends."

"However," the professor went on, continuing to fondle my head, "the development of the brain upward, forward, and backward, from the medulla—"

"Save it for the cud-wallopers, I tell you!"

"If this young man is going to have his say about me in front, I want him to know that the science of phrenology has a good exponent here," said the professor.

I reckon he had seen me looking him over without a great amount of liking and was anxious to put on a bit of a front.

"He'll say that you'll read all heads free of charge, and that's *all* he'll say," stated Mr. Dawlin. "It isn't necessary for him to know the difference between a medulla and a free-lunch pickle—and I don't believe *you* know, yourself. Ross, we want to open the doors again to-morrow. Do you think you can get the gist of that patter into your head overnight?"

I thumbed the dirty sheets and said I'd do my best.

Therefore, I went to my room and applied myself. There was a lot of extravagant guff about the curiosities, flowery flapdoodle of the usual barker sort.

The next morning I was able to make some sort of a try at it from the stand, for I have said before that I always was more or less cheeky. A sort of a fluffy-ruffle damsel with bleached hair was in the ticket-office and there never was a young fellow yet who did not try on a little extra swagger when a girl was hard by. She smiled at me encouragingly when I had arrested the attention of a few passers, some of whom bought tickets and went in. I guess I must have smiled back, for Dawlin, who was standing in the doorway, appraising my first efforts, came and climbed up beside me and growled in my ear.

"You're breaking in fine. Only put a little more punch and sing-song into it! And, by the way, the dame who is shuffling the pasteboards—she's private goods—mine!"

"I don't want her," I said, with considerable heat.

"I don't say you do—but a lot of trouble has sometimes been made in partnerships by women. So that's why I have flipped the buried card at the start-off. Now tune up and let it went! If your voice gets husky I'll send out a handful of bird-seed and a hunk of cuttle-fish."

I reckoned he was trying his cheap humor on me to smooth the insult about the girl. It seemed to me like an insult, and he understood pretty well how I felt.

So I went to my job and minded my own business most exclusively.

Day after day, for several weeks, I stood up on my rostrum and cajoled folks into that joint, and I say frankly and honestly that for a long time I did not have full understanding of just what went on inside. Possibly that statement makes me out a mighty stupid chap.

But I was ashamed to ask any more questions after what Dawlin had yapped out about his suspicions that I was a greenhorn.

I did not have any special conversation with him, anyway. I was still ugly when I thought upon his warning about that painted girl—as if I wanted her! And I was careful that she should have no word to carry to him about me; I never looked in her direction.

Furthermore, I did not want to know very much about what they were up to inside. I was ashamed of my job. It struck me that if I came to know all the fraud of the thing I'd jack the proposition. An ostrich sort of attitude, to be sure, a foolish evasion, but that's just how it was, like other things which came up in my life, things not lending themselves readily to explanation as I look back on them now.

I saw patrons come out, some angry and with red faces, some ashamed, some laughing—but only a few of the last, and they were plainly chaps who took it as a joke when anybody could put something across in their case.

Man after man came out with a broad piece of paper in his hand, crumpled it up, swore, and dashed it down on the sidewalk.

It was a chart purporting to be a reading of bumps, as Professor Jewelle sized up the patron's cranium. Nobody seemed to be very well pleased. A lot of them pitched into me and said that I had promised that the reading was free.

Well, the reading was free.

But once the victim had ventured inside the curtains and after the free reading, the professor handed over the chart and demanded three dollars for it.

Disputes ended promptly, for Big Mike was always present. The vocabulary of that bellowing bull was limited to two words in those séances—"Three dollars!"

Of course I had to find this out before long or stand convicted in these records as liar and half-wit combined.

I also found out about the gazara game, Mr. Dawlin's special project.

There was an oblong box in which were stacked leather envelopes, each envelope bearing a numbered card.

Mr. Dawlin seemed to be a very generous individual; he would allow patrons to win considerable money by picking prize envelopes into which he had slipped crisp bills; he also seemed to be a careless operator. For instance, he would quite openly put a twenty or a fifty dollar bill into the envelope holding the card numbered 0. Then he would shuffle the envelopes and with carelessness utterly blind would leave the corner of that card sticking up a bit, revealing the upper part of the numeral. Feverishly excited patrons would bid high for the privilege of drawing first—sometimes almost as high as the prize itself, for Mr. Dawlin had plainly left a good thing exposed. But, strangely enough, what had seemed like the figure 0 was revealed in the drawing as the figure 9 with an exaggerated upper loop. If the patron made moan and let out the secret of his grief, Mr. Dawlin reproached him for trying to take advantage of an oversight in an honest game. Such was the activity known as "gazara" in our establishment! I don't know who gave the game that designation. I believe that in Maccabees a town of that name is spoken of—and being in Apocrypha seems well placed. It may be that the game started there—at the same time the gold-brick game was hatched in Gomorrah. Both schemes must be very ancient—for they are true, tried, and certain.

Mr. Dawlin had much information to give me regarding games in general. He told me about his brother Ike, a proficient gold-brick artist. He said that if I cared to go into that line he would put me next to his brother. Mr. Dawlin, as had the others of his fraternity, complimented me on my honest looks. When I dared to suggest that the gold-brick scheme must be known to everybody, and all played out, he laughed at my ignorance. He said that getting a whole lot for a little always had been a bait for human greed and always would be; as to getting at the yaps in these days, it was only a matter of fresh style of approach and men like his brother were thinking up new methods of approach all the time.

Men who needed money in a hurry to make up a balance were

almost always ready to gamble heavily and desperately.

He said his brother had a deal on at that very time, but that it was too late for me to get in on that, for the thing was all set and pretty near ready to be pulled off. It was an up-country case, of course.

"Plant by 'Peacock' Pratt," said Dawlin. That was a new name for my roster of rascality, and I stuck it into a mental pigeonhole. "Pratt is a white-vest operator. Paunch scenery!" He saw that I wasn't catching him very well and explained that Pratt affected the manner of a prosperous Westerner who regularly stoned neighbors' chickens out of his garden with gold nuggets.

Speaking of gold, I was not specially dissatisfied with the rake-off I was getting from there precious rascals, though, of course, it was small as compared with my diver's wages. But standing in the sunshine under a plug-hat with nothing to do but gabble nonsense was a softer snap than grubbing under muddy water with a diver's helmet stuck over my head. I was truly in a way to succumb to the blandishments of my cheap streak and settle down into the practice of roguery.

But I had some sense of shame left in me. I kept on that disguising mustache when I was before the public. It was not much of a mask, to be sure, but it comforted me a bit to know that it made me look unlike myself.

And that's why the Sortwell boys from Levant did not recognize me when they halted on the sidewalk one day and listened to my barking.

There they were, the two of them, grown up to manhood; but they were mighty green specimens. They were looking at the banners rather than at me. I wagered with myself that it was the first time they had ever been in the big city; even one trip would have rounded off some of the rough corners they were showing. For instance, they surely would have had experience with such a peep-show as we were running and would not have been tempted.

They walked over to the painted maiden and asked her if she could recommend the show; they grinned and gaped at her amorously. She fawned on them and they bought tickets and went in. I wasn't a bit sorry, nor did I try to stop them. My last experience with the gang in Levant had not implanted in me any hankering to hug and kiss the Sortwell boys.

I watched for them to come out, for I felt pretty sure that they would be properly trimmed and I anticipated secret relish in looking on their faces. I told myself I didn't care. If a good jolt should be handed to them it would help in satisfying my grudge against the town which had sent me flying. Bitterness was in me at that moment. I was glad I was out of the jay place. If I had stayed there I would be looking just like those simpering rubes who had gone in like lambs to be sheared. I'd never want to go back to that town, I decided all over again.

When they came out each one carried one of Professor Jewelle's charts, and they were crying like great calves—actually guffling slobbering sobs. They went away a little distance and stood on the sidewalk, looking at each other and scruffing tears from their eyes with the palms of their hands. Awhile back if somebody had told me I would see a couple of big, larruping chaps from Levant doing that on the street in broad daylight, I'd have predicted a good laugh for myself.

Well, there was nothing like that in my case!

A lump swelled in my throat. I don't know what it was—whether 'twas homesickness, longing for my own people of my own kind, spectacle of boys who had gone barefoot with me, sight of their sorrow, mindfulness of what the cruel city had done to me, reflection that I had helped in a measure to get them into their scrape—I say I don't know just what it was. But my throat gripped and tears flowed up into my eyes. Those poor devils, who were children in spite of their size, were helplessly adrift—I could see that. Something special must have happened to them.

I seem to be stopping to analyze my emotions. At the time I was doing nothing of the sort. I felt a comforting sense that I was not a rascal down in my heart, in spite of what I had done and of the job I was holding down.

I left my rostrum, ran into the little office, and tipped Dawlin's bottle of whisky against my upper lip; the alcohol dissolved the gum and I ripped off the mustache. Then I chased along after the Sortwell boys. They were far up the street, plugging slowly with bowed shoulders.

When I came close upon them I took my time to get my breath and control my emotions. Then I called to them, and they turned around and stared at me with eyes which expressed all the range of feelings between interrogation and stupefaction.

"Well, haven't you anything to say to an old friend?" I asked.

"It ain't you," faltered the older. "It may look like you, but it ain't."

"There ain't anything in this place that's looking like it really is," whimpered the younger. "There was a card with a zero on it and it wasn't a zero—it was a nine—and he took our money."

"Have you lost your money, boys?"

"All of it—every scrimptom of it," bawled the older. "We 'ain't got anything to get home with. We saved up to come down and see the city for a couple of days—and now it's all gone."

"We worked all winter logging—sweating and freezing in Cale Warson's swamp—to earn that money, and that hellhound down there took it and jammed it into his pants pocket. And how'll we get home?"

Oh, I knew what logging in a swamp was! I knew what sort of wages were paid and how hard it is to save! That one sentence fairly lanced my conscience. "He jammed it into his pocket!" To Jeff Dawlin, who reached out and took in his money so easily, those bills were hardly more than so much paper, as he handled them.

But he had not been a boy in a country town where money is not come at so easily, where the little hoards grow so slowly, where there are so many dreams about the big world up in the attics under the patched coverlids—dreams which the little savings may bring to realization!

These were boys from my home town. Thank God, a lot of the cheap in me, the soul-dirt I had rubbed off in my associations, the cynical notions about right and wrong, the inclinations of a swaggering sport—yes, a whole lot of that slime was washed out of me right there and then by my new emotions. I don't say I was made anyways clean—not all of it went. I have done many things since then to be ashamed of. But I was a blamed sight more of a man when I went up and patted those poor boys on their backs, standing between them.

"Don't take on about it any more, fellows," I said. "I guess I'll be able to do something for you." My tone was pretty important and they began to look me over; they had been so fussed up that they had not taken full stock of me till then.

"Golly! You're rich, ain't you?" gasped the older.

"Now about losing this money—where did you lose it?" I asked, swelling a little more because I knew I was in the way to make a big impression.

"Down the street there—where those fraud duflickers are all billed out! It looked like a zero—"

"And they charged three dollars apiece for feeling of our heads!" put in the younger. "There was a big man who cracked his fists—"

"Never mind! I know all about all such places, boys. I won't allow any such things to be put across in this city on any friends of mine!"

I was talking as if I owned the town. They goggled at me as if they believed that I did own it. When I started back toward Dawlin's joint they followed me like hounds at heel.

I flipped a lordly gesture at the girl in the ticket-office and walked in without paying—herding my clients ahead of me. That was visible evidence of my mysterious importance, and they looked up at me as if they were ready to fall down and offer worship. For in America any man who can walk past ticket-sellers and pay by a flip of the hand, displays a power which autocrats may envy.

"You are sure this is the place?" I asked the Sortwell boys.

They breathlessly assured me that it was.

"And there's the man who made us pay him six dollars," declared the older.

Professor Jewelle had stepped out through the slit in his curtains. I walked up to him.

"Did you charge these gentlemen six dollars—take the money from them?" I asked, sternly.

He saw that there was something on and, like a rogue, believed, of course, that I was plotting further graft on these innocents. He played up to me with shrewd promptness.

"If I have done anything wrong I ask pardon," he whined.

"These are particular friends of mine. Hand over their money at once!"

He turned his back on them while he pulled out the money and gave me a wink which indicated that he was on and approved whatever game I was playing. I kept my face straight and stern, for the boys were surveying me with adoration.

I handed them the money and went across to Mr. Dawlin's booth, the hicks at my heels.

Mr. Dawlin was by nature more suspicious of his fellow-man than was Professor Jewelle, and he evidently resented the fact that I had not tipped him off in advance. He regarded me with much sullenness when I commanded him to return the money he had taken from the gentlemen. His sour unwillingness, mingled with his uncertainty, really helped my game along. It looked as if I had the power to force even such a balky mule as Dawlin seemed to be.

"I don't know about this!" he growled.

"I can't help that! You'll have to take my word—till you can get something better," I added, and I put a little significance into my last words.

And Mr. Dawlin, being a rascal who thought he could sniff a plant, decided to grab in on a partner's game. "Why, sure, boss," he cried, heartily, "if that's the way you feel about it! Take any gents

71

that's friends of yours and all you have to do is speak the word!" He pulled out of his trousers pocket a big wad of crumpled bills. "Do you know how much they spent backing their opinion against mine?"

"It was twenty-two dollars—it was just twenty-two dollars," piped one of the boys, and the other one helped out on the chorus.

"The rising young financiers seem to have no doubt," sneered Dawlin.

The older boy looked at the big swatch of bills and rasped his rough hands together.

"Perhaps money don't mean much to you, mister, handling it the way you do! But if you earnt twenty-two dollars by day's work, getting into a popple-swamp before sunup, I guess you'd know it when you counted those dollars out to anybody."

"So that's the way you earned this money? How much more did you earn?" Dawlin screwed a look at me, showing fresh suspicion.

"I'll do the talking," I said. "I'll talk because I know what I'm doing! I say only this: hand over the coin!"

"And I say again, I don't know about that!"

I reckoned I was overplaying my air of importance, so I found a chance to slip him a wink which promised a good deal.

"But you know who I am!" I told him.

"Yes," he admitted.

"Then pay!"

He began to grin, finding this little comedy amusing as well as mysterious.

"Sure thing, boss! And seeing that it's you and your orders, here's five dollars for your friends on top of the twenty-two. Go and buy five dollars' worth of corned beef and eat your heads off! Nothing like going the limit when you come down to the big burg!"

I gave Mr. Dawlin a knowing look when I turned to leave.

"My friends are much obliged for the extra five—but they can use it for something else besides eats. Come on, gentlemen! You will be my guests at dinner."

I could see by Dawlin's face that he took that last as a straight tip from me that I had designs on the countrymen—and that he would understand why I was quitting my job for a time. He gave me a most benignant smile when I left.

Professor Jewelle smirked and bowed when we passed him.

Big Mike, the ogre of the place, stepped politely to one side and twisted his ugly mug into a one-sided grin of apology.

So we went out in state.

There was a new feeling in me. It was a longing to be with those boys from home. Up to then I had been ashamed to meet anybody from Levant. And out of that shame had come a sort of dread to hear any news from my old town. Now I was hungry for news.

To be sure, just at that moment I was in a fool's paradise of spurious importance. It was comforting, however, to be set on a pedestal by those Sortwell boys, and to know that at least two persons from Levant had stopped thinking of me as a runaway scalawag.

Along with my new feelings had come a sort of vague hope.

I walked out of Dawlin's place with a hazy notion that I would never go back. Dawlin was evened up with me as to finances—I had my last week's rake-off in my pocket.

And I may say right here that I never did go back—not to stand up and coax suckers! When I did go back I played Mr. Jeff Dawlin for one!

IX

A GRISLY GAME OF BOWLS

I did not bother with any of the victualing houses in that low-down locality. I led the Sortwell boys up-town and ushered them into a very fancy restaurant. I could see that their opinion of my greatness was growing all of the time. I could not induce them to touch the bill of fare or even look at it. They gaped in such a frightened way when I mentioned fancy dishes, that I helped to set them at ease by ordering steak and potatoes. They ate to the last scrap, cleaning their plates with morsels of bread, even as grateful pups lick their platters. They confessed that they had not dared to go into an eating-house, and I remembered that first day when I had roamed the streets of the city.

I wanted to ask questions about Levant, but I delayed. Dave Sortwell, the older, opened up the subject, but he did not do it very gracefully.

"I reckon they can't slur the Sidneys after this, like they have always done past back," he said. "Here you are, something big down here in the city—and your uncle Deck is first selectman of Levant."

So my uncle had achieved his political ambition! When I heard that news I had inside me a feeling of apprehension which I could scarcely account for.

"Elected last week at the March town meeting," affirmed Ardon, the brother. "We younger fellows that have come of voting age went for him—most all of us, because he says he is going to turn politics in our town upside down and dance a jig on the bottom of 'em."

"He was into the tavern the other night, pretty well teaed up," giggled Dave, "and he said he was going to gallop Judge Kingsley to hell and stand over him with a red-hot gad while he shoveled brimstone. He has got it in for the judge—and a good many folks in Levant ain't sorry. Judge Kingsley has always gouged folks."

"Did they put the judge out of the treasurership—did my uncle bring that about?" Hearing that the feud was on worse than ever made my heart sick. I had been hoping!

"O Lord, no! I guess the judge is forever fixed in that job. Folks can't seem to think of anybody else as treasurer. He's a financier," said Dave, reverently. "He knows all about handling money. Folks trust to him for that."

"But you say my uncle—"

"Your uncle is doing most of the saying. Folks stand round and listen. I don't know what he is trying to do to the judge. Nobody seems to know. Guess he can't do much of anything except talk. You know, yourself, Ross, how he keeps sparked up most of the time. Maybe he don't know just what he says, himself."

I began to skirt the edges of conditions in Levant, asking questions about this one and that, showing as much indifference as I could. But the Sortwell boys showed even more indifference about their home town. It was all too familiar to them. They were displaying increasing interest in me, and were emboldened to ask questions, now that their early awe was wearing off.

I found out—and I was rather surprised—that the folks in Levant had not heard a word about me since I left the town. I had rather expected that Dodovah Vose would drop some hint as to what had become of me—and yet, on reflection, I could see that prudence required him to keep still. He had helped a prisoner to escape, and could not well let anybody suspect that he knew the whereabouts of that prisoner.

"I'll tell you, boys," I said, when they had flanked me with questions from every approach and had finally and fairly pounced on me to find out what I was doing for a living and how I was so important, "I am hitched up with big business interests who don't allow their men to talk. I'd tell you if I could tell anybody. It isn't one special kind of business—it's all kinds—a sort of a syndicate—a combination. You understand!"

They hastened to say that they did—and I was glad of that because I didn't understand, myself.

"But you'll let us say that you're in this big business, won't you? When we get back home we want to tell all of 'em that they'd better not slur you any more."

"I suppose the backbiters have been busy, eh?"

"Oh, not much nowadays except somebody remarks once in a while that you had to skip the town. You know how such things pop up in talk. Your uncle being prominent nowadays, you get mentioned once in a while. But Dodovah Vose has always stood up for you!"

"And a lot of folks didn't believe what that detective said. He wasn't a real detective, anyway. He was only a deputy sheriff from Pownal," added Ardon, and the next minute I felt like hugging the boy. "I was always ashamed of how us fellows put you in bad, Ross, and so I owned up when Celene Kingsley asked me—"

I couldn't help it! I came right up in my chair.

"Celene Kingsley asked you?"

He misunderstood my heat.

"Don't be mad, Ross! I stood up for you, I say! I was sorry for what I did. I was ashamed."

"But you said Celene Kingsley asked you something!"

"Well, I can't remember whether she came right to me and asked me or whether it just happened that the thing came up somewhere or—"

"But you would surely remember if *she* came to you!" I could not conceive of Celene coming to anybody without it marking a milestone in life.

However, the Sortwell boy had plainly decided to be non-committal until he had a better line on my feelings in the affair.

"I don't want you to be mad because I talked it over, Ross. I stood up for you!"

"But did she come *asking*?"

"We-e-ll, I guess she must have asked—or—or something! Anyway, it came up in talk—somehow—"

Confound his haziness!

"And of course I stood up for you. It was only right! I told her how you tried to bust up the Skokums! I said you threatened to bat out the brains of the whole of us if we didn't stop cutting-up. I told her that they hadn't ought to have arrested you that night, for you was trying to stop us from raiding her father's house to grab that detective. You said something about a home being a castle—or—or something. Anyway, Ross, I did the best I knew how—I ain't so much good in talk as you are. Honestly, I did the best I could to put you straight when she asked. Yes, I reckon she did ask."

I was looking at him with such rapturous expression that his face cleared of uncertainty regarding my feelings.

"Sure, she must have asked, for I wouldn't go to blarting that around, making the rest of us out as pirates, unless she had pinned me down. I reckon she did just that! Pinned me down. But I was glad to help you out that much!"

It came to me with a rush of sentiment that all I had done that day for the Sortwell boys had been fully paid for long in advance, and I was sorry because a whole lot of my actions had really been dictated by my selfishness and my desire to show off.

I reached across the table and took his hand.

"Ardon, I'm going to own up that I have had a lot of bitter thoughts about the folks in Levant since I left home. But if I had known that I had only one friend there like you have been in this matter, I would have put all the bad things out of my mind."

"I only told the truth, Ross."

"But that's the hardest job a man undertakes to do in a lot of cases." I was thinking just then how hard *I* would find it to own up about myself, and how I had secured that money from the clutches of the rogues in Dawlin's joint. And there I was, making a lot of capital out of that deceit!

But after what I had just heard I was resolved to go ahead and make more capital out of my pretensions to greatness.

"You're going to let us say that you have made good, aren't you?" asked Dave.

"I'd like to get back into the good opinion of the old town, boys. If you feel like saying something nice about me when you get back to Levant, I'll be grateful."

"Say, if we don't blow your horn!" they cried in concert.

"But not too loud, boys! I don't want to have too big a reputation to live up to when I come back home."

They stood up and clapped me on the back.

"By gorry! you will come, won't you, and show 'em?" pleaded Dave. "Come and show 'em!"

"But there's one thing to be thought of first," I said, with a grin. "Has my uncle Deck stopped threatening to kill me on sight?"

That stirred their memories and fetched a laugh.

"He wouldn't dare to give you as much as one yip if you walked up to him looking like you do now," said Dave.

The thought which he suggested was comforting; so much in this world does depend on outside appearances. The hankering in me to go back was whetted; just to make a show in the face and eyes of Levant, to stop their tongues for good and all! But I was conscious that deep under those cheaper motives was something more compelling. I had felt the thrust of it after Ardon Sortwell had told me of his confession to Celene. She, at least, knew that I had not been a renegade, and she had taken enough interest in me to make sure on that point.

"When are you coming back, Ross?" demanded Dave.

"Don't tell anybody I am coming back, boys. Promise me that."

They did.

"But you may say that you saw me in the city, and that I am doing well, and sent my best regards to all my friends."

"We'll make their cussed old ears sing," declared Ardon. "Don't you worry about us!"

"If I can arrange my business so as to leave it, I may run up later."

I showed them some of the city sights that afternoon and they started for home that night—and I saw to it that they were safely aboard their train.

That I should dream of Levant that night was entirely natural. They were enticing dreams and they made me homesick and I found out that I was not such a bold man, after all, in spite of the shell I had grown; I felt very much like a boy when I woke next morning. I was hungry for my own folks.

In my haste to be gone I forgot all my caution. I went down to the water-front just as if there were no such person as a vengeful Anson C. Doughty.

I had cached, temporarily, my diving equipment. I went to the storage-man and arranged for its care, paying in advance.

Then I was bold enough to go hunting up Jodrey Vose because I wanted to carry some fresh and direct message to his brother in order to secure continued favor in the case of the tavern-keeper; he certainly had been my best friend in Levant. I intended to lodge with him and I dreaded his keen questioning in case I went to him with lies about when I had seen his brother last.

I found the captain on his lighter and we had a good talk during his rest-spell.

"I'm sorry it has turned out for you as it has, young Sidney. But it's a good idea for you to run up to the old town and hang round with Dod for a while and sort of get your feet placed all over again. Maybe something will turn up down this way later!"

"Anson C. Doughty's toes, perhaps."

He wagged his head, soberly.

"I'm glad you came down to take leave, son, but you're running chances. Anson C. Doughty is mighty ugly. He was beaten up in front of his crew—and folks haven't got done talking and he knows they are talking. You'd better be hipering, I reckon."

He sent one of the helpers to his cabin for a parcel and he put it into my hands.

"It'll be handier than sending it by express to Dod," he said. "It's a skull I found in the dock. Tell him to make up a pirate yarn to go with it."

Being thus equipped with full credentials as to my continued comfortable standing with Jodrey Vose, for the purposes of my further intimacy with Dodovah Vose, I started up the wharf in excellent spirits, my thoughts on my home-going.

And half-way to the street I fairly bumped into Anson C. Doughty. It was no coincidence—I ought to have reckoned on that meeting—the manager was regularly up and down the wharf at all hours of the day. But, as I have said, I had lost my caution. I had met him once face to face, and had not been recognized. But I was no longer wearing that mustache.

He swore a blue streak and danced back and forth in front of me, waving his hairy hands to shoo me back. He looked just as much like a cockroach as ever.

"You belong in State prison and you're going there," he snarled.

There were two wharf loafers near by, the only men in sight. He called to them, and they came to us, a couple of husky stevedores.

"You know *me*!" shouted Doughty. "You two men hold this sucker till I can fetch a cop. Hold him! Don't let him get away!"

He ran off toward the street.

I had not a chance to get away from those big chaps on that narrow wharf—and it was plain that they knew Anson C. Doughty and recognized his authority in those quarters.

So here were all my fresh plans, my hankering for home, my new-laid reputation for Levant consumption about to be kicked into the black depths of tophet by the grudge of Anson C. Doughty!

I could see that the stevedores despised my size because I was wearing a plug-hat; they glowered at me with the natural enmity the man in overalls feels for the dandy. It was perfectly damnable—that situation! To be arrested—to be shown up for what I was—the thought screwed my desperation to the breaking-point.

I pulled my wallet and began to flick out bills.

"He's only trying to get back at me on account of a grudge, fellows; he's using you for tongs," I told them. "I was one of the divers and I batted him when he insulted me! I want to get out of town! Here's a piece of money! He won't give you anything."

I had the skull under my arm and my wallet in my hands, and I wasn't paying much attention to the men while I counted out money.

"Who was the gink who told us to hold the guy?" muttered one of the men. "Was it Doughty?"

"Sure! You know him," said his companion.

"But he don't know *us*!"

"He won't remember who you are!" I hastened to put in. "Take some money, and—"

"You bet we'll take some money," barked the two of them in chorus, and the next instant one of them clutched me and the other grabbed wallet, money and all, and they ran away, ducked into an alley between storehouses, and disappeared.

I was free at a high price.

I ran after them, of course, but they were nowhere in sight when

I reached the parallel wharf, and so I started for the street; and Anson C. Doughty saw me, for he was running up and down the sidewalk, wildly hunting for a policeman. When he undertook to head me off I pitched the wrapped skull at him with all my might; it plunked him squarely in the face and dropped him, and then went bounding along the pavement at a lively clip. I was conscious that a lot of people were looking on and that a hullabaloo was started. But in spite of that I stopped to pick up the skull before I fled from the place. I reckon I must have felt considerable of a sense of responsibility where the interests of my friends, the Voses, were concerned!

I got through a short street on the jump, caught a passing car and when I was once aboard I was lost to pursuers—I was merely one of the city's mass, and my garments testified for me.

I dug down into my pockets and found a few crumpled bills and some silver—the loose money I carried outside my wallet. The whole of it amounted to mighty little—only about enough to take me to Levant, as I remembered what the train fare had been.

I did not stop to figure on any further resources; I did not dare to go and seek aid from any of my acquaintances; I did not go back to my room for any of my belongings. Panic was on me. To be caught at that time meant the toppling of my cardboard house of hopes and reputation. I did not know to what extent Anson C. Doughty would throw out his drag-net—but I was pretty sure that he would drop all his other business for a time and attend strictly to what concerned me. He surely was the angriest man I had seen in many a day when he went down under the impact of that package.

To get out of that city just as quickly as I could, before he could set persons on my trail, or put spies at the city's outlets, was the only sensible course open to me.

So in less than half an hour I found myself on the train, home-ward bound, just as much of a fugitive *from* the city as I had been in other days when I headed *toward* it.

I had a little spare change in my pocket and a skull under my arm.

X

THE ART OF
PUTTING ON A FRONT

Having caught a train out of the city at a fairly early hour in the forenoon, I made a daylight ride of it to Levant, and I stepped out upon the platform at Lower Corners just before sundown.

I remember that the red March sun was almost touching the rocky edge of the beech ridge, and, with the bare trunks of the trees striping it, looked like a coal fire with the stove cover off and a griddle on. In fact, as I looked up at the sun and reflected on the general condition of my affairs, I felt as if I were the particular live lobster destined for the griddle in Levant.

But I walked past the platform loafers, leaving my satin-lined overcoat open so that they might get the full effect of my frock suit. No one seemed to recognize me; Levant Corners is all of three miles from Levant village, and there was never much mixing between the communities when I was a boy. I set off at a good pace to walk the three miles to Dodovah Vose's tavern.

Men in several teams which overtook me offered a lift, and one of them addressed me as "Elder." Evidently my clothes were producing an impression! But I declined all offers. I had waved the stage-driver aside, and now if I accepted a free ride I might have brought suspicion on my financial ability. So I told them all politely that I needed exercise and walked on in all my dignity—and, being encumbered by nothing except a skull under my arm, I found my tramp pleasurable.

I went along at such a clip that I topped the long rise from the river where the railroad winds and was able to look down on distant Levant village before the lingering dusk had settled into night. The stripped trees had left all the houses bare and rather bleak; there was no beauty anywhere. The afternoon chill had hardened the road mud into iron ridges. Being back on my native heath was not so consoling and heart-thrilling as I had pictured. That faded, sodden, frozen landscape was depressing. I looked like a millionaire, but I belonged on the town farm. There was one thing to remember, however. My uncle as first selectman was also overseer of the poor, by virtue of his office.

I wondered what he would say to me if I walked up to him and tried to borrow money! On second thought, I knew so well what he would say that I promptly decided that I would keep my mouth shut in regard to my finances.

I hurried on, for there was an inviting twinkle of light in the windows of Vose's tavern. I was carrying a rather gruesome ticket of admission, but a message from Jodrey Vose went along with it and it would make me especially welcome.

For some distance the highway was bordered by woods, and at last I saw a roadside sign which gave me a bit of a thrill, for it bore the magic name of Kingsley.

"FOR SALE. THIS WOOD-LOT. APPLY TO Z. KINGSLEY." That's what the sign said.

Before I was fairly on my way, after stopping to read, I was able to put eyes on Z. Kingsley, himself. He was in a carriage which was coming in my direction and his daughter was driving a horse which was too likely-looking to have been furnished by my uncle.

I did not reflect or consider. I had no clear notion in my mind at that instant. I suppose I was overcome by an irresistible hankering to hear her voice—to speak to her.

At any rate, backed by that longing or by courage or cheek or whatever else it might be called, I stepped out into the middle of the road and put up my hand. I reckon if Judge Kingsley had been driving he would have run over me. His blessed daughter pulled up short.

I took off my hat and he gave me a sharp glance and recognized me. And so did Celene, for she smiled even while she looked a bit startled.

"Drive on!" snapped her father.

"Judge Kingsley, I want to—"

He checked me with much impatience, and I was glad of it, for I was not prepared to tell him just what I did want. I knew I wanted to rush up to her and say a lot of things, but I was conscious that the action would not have made much of a hit with her father.

"I have no time to waste on you, sir. I have to catch a train."

"But the train has gone along," I stalled. "I just came in on it."

"I am going the other way—to the city!" He showed considerable temper.

"We have plenty of time before the down train is due, father," Celene told him. He reached after the reins, but she held them away from him, showing that she had more or less of the Kingsley obstinacy, herself.

"What do you want, sir? Quick!"

It was a rather contemptuous command, but it was showing more consideration for a member of the Sidney family than I had dared to hope for. If he had taken up the whip and lashed at me at first meeting I would not have been surprised. It was evident that my personal appearance was having weight with him. I ventured to believe that the Sortwell boys had been advertising me in town, though they were only a few hours ahead of me.

I rolled my eyes around, trying to think of something sensible. I saw the sign again.

"What is your price on this wood-lot, Judge Kingsley?"

"I can't stop to talk business, sir."

"But I'm simply asking the price. You're advertising it. You must have put a price on it."

"I'll be back in a week or ten days. Come to me then. I'm in a hurry."

I put on a fine air of importance.

"So am I, Judge Kingsley! So are the big interests which I represent. But we are never in too much of a hurry to answer polite questions in business. I say, what is your price?"

"Two thousand dollars," he cracked out.

"How many acres?"

"Forty."

I raised my hat and stepped to one side.

"That's all, sir. I'll investigate and be ready to talk with you when you return. Good evening!"

I could see that he was taken aback a bit by my own shortness in the matter. He sat there holding his mouth open as if he intended to say something more, but I walked on; it came to me that perhaps he was going to say that he wouldn't do any business with a Sidney—and I was avoiding all argument on that point.

Celene gave me another flicker of a smile when she started the horse. They went on at a good clip, and the moment they were out of sight around a bend in the road I turned back, climbed the fence, and sat down beside some bushes. My heart was so warm within me that I was not afraid of a chill.

I was guessing that she would not waste any time in making that trip to the railroad station; you see, I was building high merely on the glances she had been giving me—on the flush which was on her cheek when she drove away. Would she hurry back to overtake me? She did.

When I saw her coming, snapping her whip to make the horse trot at a brisker pace, I climbed back over the pitch-pole fence and leaned against it. It was pretty dark, but she spied me and stopped the horse.

"I have done something rather foolish," I told her, staying where I stood.

"Yes?"

"And I have found out all over again that haste makes waste. I wanted to get a peep at that stand of timber and I went racing around in the dark—and so I have wrenched my ankle."

"Oh, I am so sorry!"

"It's my own fault! It's what the city does to a man! Keeps him on the gallop! Makes him too impatient to wait for morning."

"Can you get to the carriage?"

"But I don't like to trouble you, Miss Kingsley! If you will send a team—"

"No, you shall ride with me! The idea of my leaving you in the woods alone! I'll come and help you."

"No, I'll manage!"

So I limped to the carriage and climbed in. She watched me anxiously and asked after my hurt with solicitude. I was doing a pretty mean thing, I knew, but the opportunity to be alone with Celene Kingsley that first hour of my arrival in town was a favor to be grabbed for and hugged jealously. She walked the horse, and I sat beside her and was so happy in that first intimacy that I was not a bit ashamed of my deceit.

"So you are doing wonderful things in the city!" she said, after a time. I had not spoken, for I was afraid of blurting out something foolish.

"Nothing so very grand," I faltered.

"But Dave and Ardon Sortwell have had something to say about that since they have been home. I am very glad for you, Mr. Sidney."

"I'd rather please you than anybody else." That was a mighty awkward answer and I was just as much embarrassed at she was.

"Good news about Levant boys pleases us all up here."

"Sometimes I have thought they liked the bad news best—the most of 'em. The way they drove me out and then talked behind my back was—"

"I know all the truth of it—and most of the folks do now, I think," she broke in. "You must put it all out of your mind. You must not come back with resentment toward anybody. There's too much of that in the world. There's too much in Levant."

She hesitated a moment and then burst out with a tremble in her voice.

"Oh, Mr. Sidney, I am so thankful because you have come home! I do hope you can have some influence with your uncle. I ask your forgiveness for bringing it up so soon. But my heart is so full of it all! I hurried back, hoping I could overtake you."

So that was why she had hurried!

"I don't know about having influence with my uncle," I said, and I could not keep all of the rasp out of my voice. Her welcome of me simply as an uncle-tamer had pricked me in a mighty tender place. "I don't believe he is going to give me either three cheers or a hug and kiss when he sees me."

"But you are an important man, now, and he must be proud of you and your success. He will look up to you now that you have money and position."

Like a bang on the head the conviction struck me that I had cut out a fine bit of work for myself when I dropped back into my home town.

I had been all too well advertised by my loving friends.

Celene Kingsley had touched squarely on one truth: the only way to handle my uncle was to appear important even if I were not important. Mere bluff would go a little way—but not far. I must have money!

And here I was picked by her as her champion in the family feud!

If I had only stayed in the city! There was money to be come at there. Dollars in Levant were nailed down with spikes.

"We haven't one happy hour in our home," she wailed. "Your uncle is breaking my father's heart, Mr. Sidney. I don't understand what your uncle is doing; mother doesn't understand it! Father has never told his business to us. But he sits in his office and figures and figures. Sometimes he stays there 'most all night. And it's all on account of your uncle! I know that! For my father says your uncle is hounding him to death. You must find out what he is doing. I know you will find out and tell him he must stop."

"I will look into the matter," I said, as bravely as I could. "Of course there's been hard feeling between my uncle and your father for a good many years."

"But my father is sorry now for anything in the past. He says so to us, to mother and me. He sent mother to your uncle to ask him if he would not stop persecuting. Yes, she went to your uncle because father asked her to do so."

That statement nigh took my breath away!

Mrs. Kingsley going as suppliant to my uncle Deck? Judge Zebulon Kingsley requesting her to do it? I shut my eyes and could picture her—frail, pale, aristocratic. The exigency must be desperate when Judge Kingsley would submit his wife to such employment.

"But please keep that a secret," she pleaded.

I saw that I was headed into something which was bigger and more baleful than I had dreamed of. And more than before did I feel my deficiencies as a fraud who could not even turn a trick for his own wants, let alone those greater affairs in Levant.

"This mystery in our home is killing us all," she went on. "There have been strangers in town and they have been much with my father. I do not like their looks. He would not tell us, but I am afraid they have coaxed him away to the city on this trip he is making. Perhaps your uncle has set those men on to harm him."

I had never gauged my uncle Deck as a hirer of assassins, but I had not seen him for some years, and I admitted to myself that there was never any telling where a man's grudge would lead him.

"Mother and I tried to make him stay at home. But he would not stay and he would not tell us why he was going to the city. Oh, how I hate those strangers, for I believe they have coaxed him away."

I looked sideways at her, and a little shiver tingled in me. There was real venom in her tone and I saw that I had not guessed the depths in Miss Celene Kingsley.

"I wish I had a brother," she mourned. "I believe he would feel as I feel now, and would follow up and kill the man who would harm my father."

It was so strange an utterance from a girl and seemed so contrary to what I had supposed her nature to be that I remembered that outburst for a long time.

I juggled the skull on my knee and pondered awhile before I said anything, and she was silent, too, evidently trying to get control of her emotions.

"I want to say this to you, Miss Kingsley. The Sortwell boys gave me some news of the home town and they told me that my uncle was after your father in bitter fashion. That's one reason why I have hurried up here. I don't know just what I can do with my uncle, but I'll truly do my best."

We had come into the edge of the village and had passed the first houses.

"I put my trust in you," she said, gently. "I always knew you had good impulses in you. I remember our talk that day on Purgatory Hill. And I know you kept your promise you gave to me then. You did your best to make the boys good."

"And I'll do my best to make my uncle good."

"I do hope your business will not call you away until you have straightened matters out. Oh, you asked about the price of the wood-lot! Does it mean that you expect to have some business with father?"

I had not given another thought to the wood-lot since I had used it for an excuse in an emergency. I did not see at that moment how I could use a wood-lot for anything else than that excuse.

"If only you could have some business with my father—it would smooth things so much for all of us, perhaps," she pleaded.

"We'll see what can be done," I assured her. "This syndicate—this combination—a very large concern," I floundered on, trying to think up some sort of a plausible lie to account for my interest in a wood-lot, "it's—er—ah!—you see, I can't give out much information locally because we do so many kinds of business—it's all linked up—it's necessary to move carefully, but I think I'll tell you this much, confidentially, just between ourselves!" Again my hankering to have some sort of a secret between Celene Kingsley and myself! "One branch of our business is building all the tall brick chimneys in the eastern part of the country. We use millions of bricks and so we need a great deal of wood for burning the bricks. So that's why, maybe, I can pay your father's price for the wood-lot. Now you understand!" I ended up with a lot of relief, for I had to dive pretty deep for that lie.

"I do see, and I'm glad there's a prospect you'll stay in town. And then, too, there's your ankle to nurse!"

I was glad she mentioned the ankle, for I had forgotten all about it, and would certainly have betrayed myself when I jumped out of the carriage at the tavern. Really, to be a good liar a fellow should take one of those courses in memory-training! As it was, I descended carefully and promised her to apply cloths and liniment that night. She tendered her little hand, and I pressed it, and she left with me the memory of a smile which was like a rose gemmed with dew—for there were tears in her eyes.

I waited in the tavern yard till she was well on her way, and then I marched in without any limp, for I was not minded to keep up that special lie for the benefit of all Levant.

Dodovah Vose walked behind his catty-cornered counter, plucked a rusty pen from its potato scabbard, whirled the register around under my nose, and tendered the pen.

"Rather nippy evenings, though pleasant enough daytimes for this time of year, Squire," he said, by way of welcome to the arriving guest.

87

That tickled me. He didn't recognize me. He was looking at my rig rather than at my face. When I had splashed my name on the page he pulled his spectacles to the end of his nose and inspected the signature. Then he snapped upright and stared at me.

"Godfrey domino Peter!" he bawled. "Then them Sortwell boys ain't such condemned liars as I suspected they were! When Jod wrote me that you had quit diving I reckoned you had gone plunk square to tophet!"

"Oh, there's always a chance for a fellow in the city, if he keeps hustling," I told him. I chinked the little handful of small change in my pocket. "I'm going to stay here with you for a spell, Mr. Vose. Have you a rule that guests without baggage must pay in advance?" I grinned and he took it as a great joke.

"If you can tell me enough about Jod I may adopt you and give you free board the rest of your life," he chuckled.

Then I handed over his present with a word of explanation, and he unwrapped the grisly object and surveyed it with as much satisfaction as if it had been a golden nugget.

"Jod always knows what will hit me to a T. Of course, he says to you, 'Tell Dod to make up a story to go with it'!"

"Exactly what he said, sir."

"Sure! That's what I have done with every curio he has given me."

For the first time I realized that in my boyhood I had accumulated a fine line of fiction from Dodovah Vose.

But I forgave him in my thoughts, for he took me into the big kitchen and fried me the finest chicken I ever ate. And while he fixed up my supper I told him how I had learned diving with his brother. I comforted him, too, by telling him that I had given up the work only temporarily.

But I switched him when he tried to find out what I was up to at that time. The plug-hat part of my program seemed to puzzle him very much. I was not ready with any good explanation. I figured that I might have some kind of a story ready in the morning, after I had slept on the thing. I began to rely considerably on my work as a fabricator; I had shown quite a lot of aptitude and readiness on short notice, I reflected.

I found myself holding an impromptu reception in the tavern office that evening—and they were all there with their little gimlets of questions, boring for information, you can bet! Therefore I broke away early and went to bed. I staved them all off in good shape, for I could be dignified in those clothes I was wearing. What I was afraid of was that Uncle Deck would pop in. He would not have used any gimlet; he would have set upon me with a pod-auger of inquisition, and would have ridden on it so as to bear down hard! And I had not my story ready!

XI

THE FAILURE OF
AN UNCLE-TAMER

Furthermore, in the morning I was just as much at sea.

I had gone to sleep as suddenly as if somebody had hit me a tunk on the head; too much fried chicken and hashed brown potato! I did not wake up till Dodovah Vose marched through the tavern halls, playing the long roll on his gong. The March sun, level with the eastern windows, quivered with glorious light when I opened my eyes on it. I had all sorts of reasons to be downcast, but I was not when I waked and saw that sun.

Scattered coins, my whole capital, lay on the carpet of braided rags, where they had slipped from my trousers pocket the night before when I hung the garment over a chair. I gazed over the billowing edge of the feather tick in which I was nested, and counted, for the sun lighted the floor and glinted on the coins. One dollar and thirty-seven cents!

However, in spite of that spectacle, I hopped out of bed and dressed, whistling snatches of tunes furnished by music-hall memories. I was home again, Celene Kingsley had given me glances which my hopes translated into all sorts of dear promises—she had asked me to help her; the sun was shining, breakfast was ready! I went down-stairs whistling.

"Head up and tail over the dasher, hey?" was the greeting from Landlord Vose.

"It's a great world to live in," I told him. After I had tucked away a slice of home-smoked fried ham only a little smaller than a door-mat, along with eggs and the fixings, I felt even more resolute about fronting what was coming to me.

My spirit of boldness was even a bit hysterical, I guess. I rubbed the nap of my plug-hat smooth with my forearm, pulled on my overcoat, and went out and stood on the tavern porch, inhaling the tingling air of the morning, exhibiting myself to Levant like a gladiator stepping into the arena, announcing by pose and expression: "Here I am. Now come on!"

And the first to answer my challenge was my uncle Deck. I think he had been waiting for me to appear. He walked across the village square, coming from the town office, and I hailed him from afar with a flourish of the hand and a "Good morning!"

Ten feet away he stopped and looked me over. "Why didn't you come home last night, where you belong, instead of putting up at the tavern and letting me hear about it by word of mouth?"

"Well, Uncle Deck," I drawled, "you remember—"

"Look here," he yapped, "as I stand here I don't know whether to cuff your young chops or shake your hand. A good deal depends on you. If you go to digging up past foolishness I'll cuff you. As it is"—he stepped forward, hand outstretched—"as it is, son, I'm glad to see you back, and I hear that you have made something of yourself. I'm glad of that, too! Now get your volucus, or whatever your baggage is, and come to the house."

"I'll tell you, Uncle Deck," I explained, dropping his hand after a hearty shake; "I'm here on business this trip, not to go visiting."

"What difference does that make about coming to my house, where you belong?" he demanded.

He had me there—backed into a corner! He had his pod-auger out, ready to use on me, just as I had apprehended—and so help me! I was not ready with a story.

"What is your business?"

Dignified reserve and a plug-hat would not serve to trig my uncle Deck!

It was necessary for me to declare then and there what my business in Levant was. I had been clutching wildly into a lot of nebulous thoughts ever since waking, trying to get hold of something solid.

And I found out then, as I had experienced before, and discovered on many occasions later, that there was in me something which enabled me to leap an emergency barrier when the goad was sharp enough and the danger near.

"I've got to have dealings with a lot of men and I'd be a nuisance around your premises, Uncle Deck."

"What dealings? No secret, is it?"

"Certainly not! I'm buying for a big syndicate. Buying standing timber." I said that because I had already committed myself with Celene Kingsley and it came to me that I'd better have one story and stick to it.

"All right! Buy some of mine."

"But as I remember it, it's mostly black growth—pine and spruce."

"Yes, and cedar, fir, and hemlock! What in thunder does anybody want of any other kind of timber?"

"I can't use it. I'm buying for a special purpose."

I felt like a man trying to get across a brook without wetting his feet. Every time I leaped I was mighty glad and rather surprised to find another stepping-stone to land on.

"Then you must be looking for hardwood?"

"That's it."

"What are you going to do with it?"

"Burn bricks for our factory chimneys."

He did not look more than half convinced.

"I can't go into details even with you, Uncle Deck," I told him. "I'm ordered to buy close, and when names of big concerns are given out the sellers always raise prices."

"There's only one big stand of hardwood in this town," he said, "and I'll see you in damnation before I'll let you buy that!"

"Why?"

The red patches beside his nose began to flame. "Don't come back at *me* with your 'whys'! I'll tell you why you can't buy! It's because you'll be handing over money to that"—(I never heard coarser oaths; my uncle fairly choked on them)—"to Zebulon Kingsley."

"I know the lot belongs to Judge Kingsley. I saw the sign on the fence and I happened to meet the judge right there and had some talk with him."

"Do you mean to tell me that you have been dickering with that—"

I broke in on his list of names. "My concern has ordered me to buy hardwood and I'm buying. I have no quarrel with Judge Kingsley."

"By the Great Jedux, you *have*! Don't you dare to tell me you have forgotten! You *have* got a quarrel with him. D—n you, look out that you don't start one with *me*!"

"I have come in here to mind my own business—"

"Condemn your ha'slet!" he cried. "No wonder you didn't dare to come to my house last night! No wonder you're fighting shy of me to-day!"

In spite of his anger, I felt a sudden sense of relief. I did not need to waste effort and time on minor falsehoods, trying to explain why I did not come to his house; I could devote all my attention to my main lie.

"I'm not fighting shy of you, Uncle Deck. I'm a business man, and—"

He turned sideways to me and switched his arm furiously, as if he held a goad and was trying to start a balky steer.

"You come along over to my office," he commanded with a grate in his tones. "This isn't a matter to blart about on a street corner."

I followed him. He locked the door behind us.

"You know that I have been elected first selectman of this town?"

"Yes, Uncle Deck. I'm glad the citizens—"

"Yah, for the citizens! First and last, it has cost me five thousand dollars to get this office. And it's for their own good I worked to get it—and they thought it was only to satisfy my grudge. That's all the credit a man gets from the fools who vote. But I'm in this office now—I'm headed straight for my mark—and the man who gets in my way will be bored like a cheese target! Do you hear that?"

"Yes, sir."

"They know enough in this town to keep out of my way! I have trained 'em. You don't dare to come back here, do you—my own nephew—and get in my way?"

"I'm only attending to my business."

"Meaning by that you're thinking of buying a wood-lot from Zebulon Kingsley?"

Secretly I was sort of laughing at myself. Here I was, inviting a lot of trouble by insisting on doing something which was a positive impossibility, so it seemed then as I jingled my coins in my pocket.

"I have my business the same as you have yours, sir. I didn't know—"

"You did know!" he shouted. "And if you are such a renegade as to forget what has been done to your family by that skunk, you know *now*—for I'm telling you! You can't do business with Zebulon Kingsley. I say it!" He pounded his fist on his breast.

I kept still. I was trying to work out in my mind some sensible idea as to what I really did intend to do in the matter of that wood-lot.

My uncle leaned toward me over the table in the town office, propping himself on one fist and pounding softly and slowly with the other. His lips were rolled back and he growled his words deep down in his throat, almost in a whisper.

"I know what he is, now. I've got the stuff on him. I've had to work slow. I've had to convince two devilish steers on the board of selectmen without telling 'em what I'm after. But I've got 'em. And he is headed for hell and I'm after him. And he knows it now and that's the best of it! Because I'm taking my time while he is thinking it over! Oh, my gad! if only your father could have lived till now to see how the devilish old gouger and robber is getting his! And he is paying for your mother's tears and sweat with drops of his blood. And he is paying me, too. I stay up nights to see that lamp in his office window. And you say, do you, that you have come here to hand over money to Zebulon Kingsley? To the man who filed your father's heart in two with a mortgage?"

"It's only in the way of ordinary trade," I ventured. I was wondering why I was continuing to provoke my uncle. But I knew I needed to start considerable of a smoke to screen my real condition from him.

"There is to be no trade between you," raged my uncle. "No money from you shall touch that scoundrel's hands!" Just at that moment I was more sure of that than he was.

My uncle gave me a little opportunity to do some thinking, for he went to the office safe and pulled out a bottle and drank.

I wondered what kind of a hold he had on Judge Kingsley. My curiosity was aflame. It was not believable that he could ruin the judge financially, for the Kingsleys had possessed wealth for many generations. Celene Kingsley, as the petted daughter of our village aristocrat, was too far above me for any hopes to bear fruit, even though they budded. But what would the Kingsleys be after my uncle had worked out his revenge, of whose success he seemed to be so sure?

"I know there has been trouble between the families, Uncle Deck," I said. "I know we were not used right in money matters. But what is it you're going to do to Judge Kingsley? What is your grip on him?"

He wiped his mouth with the palm of his hand and set back the bottle. "None of your d——d business!"

"I don't like to go into anything blindfolded. I have business to consider, and I'll have to make explanations."

"You'll get off better by making 'em to the men who have hired you than by explaining to me, if you don't do what I tell you to do."

"But I'm no kid any longer. I'm running my own affairs, sir. If you can't let me in on the plans of this thing—"

He advanced on me, waggling his fist. "You're a devil of a fellow to come and pump me for secrets, you are! What do you want to do—run to him again like you did in the case of that hoss trade? Do you think I have forgotten that?"

"No, and I know you never will, sir."

"And so I say now, ask no questions and do as I tell you."

I edged toward the door, for I was pretty well mixed up in my own thoughts and did not care to get into any more of a row with my uncle—and all needlessly.

"Are you giving me your word?" he demanded.

"I'm not promising anything until I can think it over and decide on what's best to be done, Uncle Deck."

"You'll decide now before you leave this office."

He started toward me, but the key was in the door, and I turned it and stood ready to leave.

"You have come back here to fight me, have you? A Sidney fighting his own and nearest blood kin, eh?"

He came close and made threatening gestures. I put my arm across his breast and slowly pushed him back; I gave him good opportunity to note that the arm was a sizable one and mighty hard.

"You plug-hatted dude!" he frothed. "Forgetting the duty you owe to your own because you have had a whirl in the city!"

"I am no dude, Uncle Deck, and calling me names and treating me like a brat, as you used to do, isn't going to get you anything!"

"You are not standing with your own family."

"I can be loyal to my family, but I'm not going to shut my eyes and jump into a row just because you tell me it's your row."

I saw that I had produced an impression and he calmed down a bit.

"There may be a good deal you can do to help me in the thing," he said. "But, blast it! after what you once did to me, I ain't sure I can trust you!" He squinted his eyes and sized me up shrewdly. "You're a Sidney, and the old rat did dirt to you before you left this town. If you ain't willing to rise up now and swoop on him, there's a reason. You ain't stuck on that girl of his, are you?"

The blood surged into my face. I couldn't help it. I was thinking hard about her all through that talk. That was the last thing I would have looked for from my uncle. He had jumped me in fine shape, and he saw it.

"Yah-h-h!" he snarled. "You fool! You devilish fool! It had to be a girl to keep you from doing your plain duty—and I knew it. Nothing but a girl would be putting a twist-bit into your mouth right now!"

"You're wrong! You're all wrong!" I protested, but I didn't sound real convincing.

Nor did he, either, when he started to give me hints about her. His eyes shifted and he stammered. I took him by the arm with a good, hearty clutch and he shut up.

There did not seem to be anything more to say just then, on the part of either of us; plainly, we had squared off at each other!

So I walked out.

I was glad because my first session with my uncle was over. But while I felt relief I knew I had pretty well done for myself where he was concerned. Of course, I had not intended to confess to him my financial condition, but deep down I had felt until then that if worse came to the worst he would see me out of a hole. He would have done something, at least, for my father's sake. But I had been the one to deal family loyalty the first kick. Now my uncle would see me starve and enjoy my sufferings; his grudges followed just such grooves.

Whatever else was ahead, it was pretty much up to me!

I went back to the tavern, for it was some comfort just to look on Dodovah Vose's kindly face.

"Let's see! You've been dropping a word or two about doing business here," he prodded in friendly fashion. "Hope so. It's quiet in town. We're all climbing 'March Hill,' you know—dull time in the country."

"I'm here to start something, sir." I was telling him the truth then. I had just started something over in the town office. I sat down and picked up a newspaper from the table and began to show great interest in reading so that I would not be obliged to talk. I was afraid he would get me cornered. I hung onto that paper as if it were a life-buoy—I read it from title to last line, advertisements and all. It was the *Mechanicsville Herald*, printed in a manufacturing city about thirty miles from Levant, and because I did not miss anything which was printed in it I noted that two concerns wanted cord-wood—and I had just mentioned the matter of cord-wood to my uncle. At all events, I was traveling on a single-track lie in old Levant!

I laid down that paper and did some mighty lively thinking. Then, to reassure myself, I gave my silk hat the least bit of a cock and marched to Judge Kingsley's mansion.

Celene herself opened the door so promptly after my ring that I had a cozy little suspicion that she had seen me coming and had hurried to meet me. She was very pretty in her morning gown.

"Oh, your ankle is so much better, isn't it?" she cried. "I watched you coming across the square."

She stepped back, inviting me to enter by her manner, and I walked in.

"I knew just what to do for it. It's pretty nigh all right."

She led me to the sitting-room, and her mother rose and met me; Mrs. Kingsley was distantly polite, that was all. I was glad even for that much in the case of a Sidney, for I knew that Judge Kingsley's obedient wife was as careful in matching her opinions to his as she was in matching colors at the store.

"I ask to be excused for calling so early in the day," I said, with my hat in the hook of my arm, and putting on my best manners. "But this is a business call and I'm in somewhat of a hurry. You heard me speak to your father, Miss Kingsley, about the wood-lot. Now—"

"I never presume to interfere in my husband's business matters," said Mrs. Kingsley, looking half scared. "I know nothing whatever about his business."

"Oh, I am not asking you to do so—certainly not," I hurried to tell her. "I shall do all my business directly with him. But to do so I need his address in the city. I have come to ask you for it. I suppose he left it."

"Oh yes—so that I may send his mail." She looked relieved and gave me the name of a hotel.

I had not presumed to sit down, though I was sure that Celene's eyes had asked me. I bowed and backed toward the door.

"I thank you. That's all I wanted. I am sorry I was obliged to intrude." I felt that I was certainly doing that little thing well. "I may be obliged to call again, if you will allow me."

Mrs. Kingsley hesitated.

"Of course you may call," blurted Celene.

"I may have to consult with you in a matter similar to this errand to-day," I explained. "I'm sorry the judge is not here; in that case I would not be bothering you."

"I tried to prevail on my husband to stay at home—he is not at all well—there are so many matters which need his attention here," complained Mrs. Kingsley. "If we can help you with any information we'll be glad to do it."

I went away on that, and I guess I left a good impression that I was strictly business!

Feeling sure that the two of them were watching me, I put a lot of business snap into my gait when I returned to the tavern.

"Mr. Vose," I asked, briskly, "how many hitches have you in your livery-stable?"

"Eight," he said, "if I include two road-carts."

"The road-carts are all right, too. I want to use all of 'em, if you can furnish drivers."

"It's easy enough to find men in these slack times."

"And probably farmers and day's-work men in the back districts of the town would like a job."

"You can bet on it!"

"Start eight men going, then, as soon as you can get the horses hitched in. Have the messengers pass the word that I can use two hundred husky men. Each man to report here in the tavern yard to-morrow morning at six-thirty with a sharp ax on his shoulder."

"And what else—tell 'em what else?"

"Nothing."

"But about wages—and what they're to do?"

"Tell 'em nothing. They'll come running in here to find out what it's all about, Mr. Vose. Don't even tell 'em who wants 'em. You and I both know how curiosity itches in this town till it has been properly scratched."

"Guess you're right," agreed the landlord. "If you set out to hire 'em regular style they'd want to hem and haw and haggle about so long and so much!"

"If you want a deposit for—" I suggested, reaching toward a breast pocket which was empty.

"Godfrey domino, no!" he protested, flapping his hands. "If you have had to handle business in those suspicious ways down in the city I'm sorry for you. Now forget money talk between us till it's time to talk."

I was glad to do that, and I hoped that his ideas of time were liberal.

I borrowed some blank paper and went up to my room and figured for many hours, stopping only to eat a good dinner—a boiled dinner in Vose's best style. My plate was piled high twice with corned beef fringed with golden fat, succulent disks of yellow carrots, wine-red beets, snowy white spuds, and odorous turnips. No man could possibly be a pessimist with that dinner under his belt! I had every reason to be the most apprehensive man in Avon County, but I had set my face to the front and I had just naturally made up my mind that I was going to pay for that dinner and for the other things which I had been recklessly ordering. I proposed to put myself into a position where I would be compelled to use every bit of my capital of cheek. The sweat stood out on my forehead, but it wasn't the kind of moisture which could soften my grit.

In the afternoon, every time a steaming horse came homing back to Vose's stable, I felt a funny quiver inside me.

"I reckon you have got a good line on human nature, young Sidney," stated the landlord, when I went down to the foreroom before supper. "From what the men say this rushing around back districts with teams has got the boys all heifered up. Even if they don't come in to go to work, they'll be here to see what in tunket the hoorah's about."

"I have heard my father say that this town was always ready to turn out to a bee," I told him. When I said it another thought came to cheer me—I had noticed that when a lot of men were set at work together on one job the natural spirit of rivalry put pep into the bunch.

When Dodovah Vose went to his kitchen to give an eye to supper, I plucked a telegraph blank from his office desk. I nerved myself to try on my most audacious trick of all. I wrote this:

To Ross Sidney, Levant.—Offer accepted. Go ahead with work. Will settle with you on my return.

Z. KINGSLEY.

I set my jaws and told myself that the message wasn't all falsehood; the last sentence was strictly true, even if Zebulon Kingsley did not pen it.

I folded the paper, stuck it in my pocket, and went again to the Kingsley house. It was brazen business—a dangerous hazard. But I was depending on woman's inadequacy. I felt that I had the two of them sized pretty well. They had never presumed to meddle in the affairs of their master. They would not dare to question his will. I figured that sending him a wire asking corroboration of the message to me would seem to them like bold interference which would bring reproof from him.

I waited, respectfully standing, while they read the message, Celene looking over her mother's shoulder.

"It's more about the wood-lot matter," I explained. "I think you heard your father make me a price on it. Miss Kingsley."

"I remember distinctly, mother. Father said he would sell for two thousand dollars."

"I know it must seem rather irregular," I said, "but in my wire I explained that my people are in a great hurry—and I'm glad that he has been willing to meet me half-way. It means that I am to put on a crew at once and cut the wood—and, of course, it's a safe proposition for the judge," I went on, forcing the best smile I could. "Neither the land nor the wood can be carried away in a shawl-strap before he returns—I think he said in a week or ten days!"

They returned my smile, and for the first time Mrs. Kingsley seemed rather cordial.

"I'm glad you are taking it off his hands," she declared. "It will be one less thing for him to worry about. He has been so troubled by his business. I'm sure that he'll be glad to get rid of a lot more property in the same way."

My soul whispered its doubts!

"I hope that the matter is all clear now and that you have a good understanding, Mrs. Kingsley. You will explain, will you, if anybody comes to you in regard to the matter or questions my authority?"

"I will, Mr. Sidney."

She exchanged glances with her daughter and they seemed to understand each other quickly. While we had been talking I heard the subdued clatter of supper preparations in another room.

"I feel sure that if my husband were here," said Mrs. Kingsley, "he would extend the hospitality of our house to a gentleman who was obliging him in a business matter. Won't you stay and take supper with us, Mr. Sidney?"

Without replying, I gave my hat into the ready hands of Celene and sat down weakly.

I was tickled nigh foolish—I'll admit that. But I was not wholly taken in by that hospitality play. Mrs. Zebulon Kingsley had known too much about me and my breed to feel any great hankering to have me as a guest. But I was willing to bet a big plum that she was thinking a lot about my uncle's hostility and about the judge's fear of that rambunctious town official. And I was also sure that certain matters had been talked over between her and Celene since my arrival in town with such outward emblems of importance and prosperity. Furthermore, had I not fairly promised the daughter that I would do my best in the line of uncle-busting?

So I held on to my emotions as best I could and waited for the subject to come up. It did, of course. I had not been in the house ten minutes before Mrs. Kingsley burst out. She was full of that topic. She saw in my uncle's attitude nothing but a wanton desire to make trouble for a good and great man.

I had been thinking over the matter of that hostility since my morning's talk with Uncle Deck. I had been developing a sharp-ended suspicion that my uncle had something up his sleeve with which to arm that hostility. Judge Kingsley would never have pulled his wife into a row he was having with Decker Sidney unless desperation had moved him. I was bitterly ashamed and grieved when I listened to her description of that unutterable interview.

As for her, she had no suspicions as to her husband's integrity—I could see that! The picture she made of the affair was of a mad dog chasing a saint!

"But what does the man think he can do to my husband? He can do nothing. He must realize it. What has he said to you, Mr. Sidney? I ask you, for I am sure you do not approve his actions."

I looked at Celene, and answered that I certainly did not approve, nor had I ever approved many things my uncle did.

"I will say further that I did what I could to-day to turn him from his grudge."

"But what does he think he can do to my husband?" she insisted. "I suppose he told you."

"No, he did not, madam. He said he did not trust me. He twitted me with having betrayed him once before to the judge—about the doctored horse," I added, with a sickly grin.

"But, of course, you—his own nephew—you produced some effect on him?"

"Yes, I made him so mad he would have struck me if he had dared. That's all the effect I seemed to produce."

Tears came into her eyes. "How will it end?" she quavered.

I did not feel like bragging just then about any powers of mine in the matter; I had plenty on my mind and conscience as it was. I was distinctly aware of being glad I had had that boiled dinner, and plenty of it, and I say that much with all due respect for the blessed presence of Celene at the supper-board. For between my ever-swelling love for her, my self-consciousness at table, my shame on account of my uncle, and my general emotions, anyway, I could scarcely choke down a mouthful. And at the end I was wholly and fairly rattled—that expression seems to fit my state of mind better than anything I can think of right now.

She accompanied me to the door that evening when I departed—Mrs. Kingsley allowed her to go alone, evidently having elevated me to the plane of, at least, a buttonhole friend of the family after hearing of my quarrel with my uncle.

And being rattled, and seeing the grieved anxiety in her eyes, and knowing how much distress must be tearing at her poor heart, I gulped out that I would put my uncle where he belonged. I was saying to myself that I would see him in tophet before I'd allow his persecution to harm those innocent women, and I came nigh saying that to her in my excitement.

She put out to me both of her hands, and I took them. I tossed all prudence over the rail then.

"If there's got to be a fight in the Sidney family, then there'll be one! You tell your mother to sleep easy. I'll take this thing in hand from now on and I won't have your father abused by anybody."

I was talking as big as old Lord Argyle, and I knew I was babbling like a fool—but what can't a girl's wet eyes do to a fellow's common sense?

"We trust you," she said. "You have made me so happy!"

I bent down and kissed her dear hands, first one and then the other. When I straightened up and saw the flush on her cheeks and the shy pleasure in her eyes I went the limit without stopping to take thought. I put my arms around her and kissed her on the lips—and no honest man can look me squarely in the eye and tell me there's any memory like the remembrance of the first kiss from one's own true love! For the first true love is not merely maiden—she has elements of the goddess in her!

Therefore, having presumed so much with a goddess, I was immediately frightened and found myself ready to struggle with apology—and apology did not fit that occasion. So I ran away before I made more of a fool of myself.

"Good night!" I whispered from the gate. "I love you!"

She closed the big door very softly and I gathered good omen from that.

How bright the stars were when I looked at them through my tears! A half-century ago a Yankee poet wrote these verses when he was in love:

When twilight's sable curtain falls,
    Then stars stand thick at even
To act as outside sentinels
    Around the gate of heaven.
That night along the shimmering slant,
    (I tell you true, my brother)
The password was "Almira Grant"
    They whispered to each other.

I knew mighty well what was their password that March night when I walked away from Celene.

I was not fit for any tavern society just then. Impulse seized upon me and I went down into the orchard. True love does not forget his trails and his caches! I found the tree with the hollow trunk and dipped my hand into the hole; I pulled forth the little packet of three rings. I reckoned that when I got my courage and my voice I would have a story to tell her—some evidence of love long-standing to offer—and that I'd find those rings pretty valuable as exhibits A, B, and C.

There were quite a number of gossiping loafers in the tavern foreroom when I marched in at last and took my room key from its hook.

If there had been any doubt among them as to my importance in the world, that doubt must have vanished when they looked on me that night; for if I did not feel at that moment that the world was mine, nobody ever did!

XII

STARTING SOMETHING IN LEVANT

The men were there in the morning—a mob of them. They came riding and they footed it into the village. The tavern office was crowded and the yard was full.

The growing buzz of them woke me before sunup, and I wasted no time in dressing and getting down.

It was just as I had expected—the spirit of a lark was in them. They were not like men who had come dragging themselves to work. The men I knew—and I knew a lot of them on account of my early goings and comings about the countryside on my uncle's affairs—were on my back in a moment, their mouths full of questions.

But I was not ready to talk turkey till I had settled on one point, and I told them to be easy for a few minutes.

I needed one man for a special purpose. I had left the selection of that man for morning, feeling instinctively that I would do better to pick from the crowd than to give away my plans overnight.

I saw him inside of ten seconds. It was as clear a case of the right man for the job as if I had specified and had received the goods.

The man was Henshaw Hook, the best-known man in that section, the town auctioneer. He had the gift of gab, the science of talking all men into good humor, and was as alert in all his doings as a cricket on a hot spider.

I took him by the arm and rushed him up to my room. Mr. Hook had brought no ax to the levee; he told me, by way of explanation, that he had come around out of curiosity. So had a lot of others, I knew well enough.

Dodovah Vose followed us, for I had summoned him by a jerk of my head.

"Now, Mr. Hook, here's the story short and snappy," I told him. "I represent a big syndicate which is buying all kinds of property. I have bought Judge Kingsley's wood-lot for the sake of what is on it—and it must be cleaned off in a hurry. Of course, I can't hang around town to attend to that part of the business. I need an able man who can attend to it." I pulled out my papers and inspected my figures. "Mostly we are after hardwood—cord-wood! Do you suppose you can pull a hundred or so good workers out of that crowd downstairs?"

"Yep!" snapped Hook. "Mebbe more."

He was just as brisk as I was.

The newspaper had given me quotations in its market column, and I had chopped cord-wood in my own young life. Furthermore, in my everlasting scurryings after squirrels and birds I had made many explorations on Judge Kingsley's domains. I was fully prepared to talk business, therefore.

"Mr. Hook, green cord-wood is selling for five dollars a cord. It's a poor man with an ax who can't chop, trim, and pile his cord a day—four-foot length. If you can put two hundred men on that job and will abide by the rules of my syndicate, you can turn a profit of around fifty dollars a day to your own pocket—for I offer you five per cent. on five dollars a cord."

Mr. Hook promptly showed much interest. "You said rules?"

"I said rules!"

"Spill," invited Mr. Hook.

"Get out your pencil and make notes—and I'll ask you to do the same, Mr. Vose, so that there'll be no come-back!"

They obeyed promptly.

"I am to do all my business with you—you are to do all the business with the choppers. You are the responsible party in all the details. You are to keep the books, measuring each man's daily cut and giving him due credit. He is to be paid two dollars and fifty cents a cord—a weekly bonus of twenty-five dollars to the man who comes across with the most cords! No payment to be made for two weeks and then one week's pay will be held back so that the men will not quit on me."

"Don't know about their agreeing!"

"Then the syndicate doesn't want them. There's no chance for argument. We'll see how many volunteer when you put the matter up to 'em. I'm going to leave the speechmaking to you!"

"I'm fairly handy with my tongue," he said, with a grin.

"So I know. And I must be sure that you will not quit. That would disorganize the whole thing. All money to the men must go through your hands. Therefore, Mr. Hook, you must deposit with me, so as to cinch your responsibility, the sum of five hundred dollars in cash before axes start this morning."

That idea did not please Mr. Henshaw Hook—not for a minute! He looked pretty blank.

"I haven't any option in the matter," I stated, coldly. "The syndicate makes its rules—but you can see that's a common-sense one. I couldn't be jumping around the country, leaving behind a lot of operations running by guess and by gosh, nobody financially responsible for the details."

"Corporations have to have their rules, Hen," said helpful Land-lord Vose. "We all know how young Sidney, here, has come along in the world!"

"The Sortwells have advertised that all right," agreed Mr. Hook.

"He isn't working for dubs, Hen!"

"Probably not! But with the judge out of town I can't dig up more than three hundred and fifty this morning, not even if I went and robbed my old woman's work-basket!"

"Needn't worry about that," said Dodovah Vose. "I've got public spirit and I want to see business get a hump on in this town. I'll lend you enough to make up the five hundred."

Mr. Hook devoted thirty seconds to meditation. "Let's see—what did I understand you to say your concern is?" he queried with as-sumed innocence.

"I did not say—we are not advertising; we are pussy-footing so that they won't be boosting land values on us," I said, serenely.

"But among friends—"

"News travels faster among friends than anywhere else. Mr. Hook, I'm not going to risk my job by shooting off my mouth. You don't think I've come back to my home town to work a flimflam trick, do you?"

"I'll grab in on this myself rather than see the plan dumped," stat-ed the landlord.

"I'll go down and put the thing up to the boys," offered Hook, hastily. Fifty dollars and over a day had properly baited this Hook.

Our auctioneer was a good talker! When—as he put it to them amidst laughter—he asked the sheep to separate from the goats, more than a hundred and fifty men stepped to one side and waved their axes as signal that they were ready to go to work.

Fifteen minute later, closeted with Vose and Hook in my room, I was counting the deposit money—a fat bundle of bills; I had made ready for that part of the ceremony and I had an equally fat packet of blank paper in the drawer of my little table. I had not sat at the feet of my crook acquaintances without hearing much about the "substi-tution trick." I worked it then and there on those guileless old coun-trymen.

I merely yanked out a table drawer with the casual remark about an envelope, turned my back for an instant, and then slipped into an envelope in full view of them a financial sandwich; I had made that sandwich by flicking two bills off the money-packet and framing the blank paper. I licked the mucilage, spanked down the flap, and handed the packet to Landlord Vose. I left the rest of the money in the drawer and slammed it shut.

"I suppose you have wax and a seal down-stairs, Mr. Vose. Please daub on a little and lock this up in your safe. Then Mr. Hook and you and I will feel all right about our affairs."

I led the gang to the wood-lot, and that plug-hat of mine must have flashed in the March sunlight about as brightly as the helmet of Henry of Navarre—providing I remember my *Fourth Reader* selection. That wad of bills which I had frisked out of the table drawer was bulked against my ribs in most comforting manner.

I never saw men pitch into a job more cheerfully than those chaps did after I led them over the fence and gave the word. It was a real frolic. Men bantered one another and made side bets on ability and everybody was laughing. Axes sounded in a chick-chock chorus, and trees began to crash down.

I spent the most of the day on the job, for I saw opportunities for extra profits; there was quite a stand of hackmatack, for instance, and there was a lot of cedar which fringed a small swamp. I made special bargains with men to fell this stuff for railroad ties. There was also considerable pine suitable for box stuff; before the day was over a portable-sawmill man, hearing of the onslaught on the Kingsley lot, came hurrying to the village, made a trade for the pine, and paid down a sizable deposit; advertising was certainly paying!

One of the most interested onlookers was my uncle Deck, who drove close to the wood-lot fence and scowled and sliced the air with his whip. He made several trips during the day and was handy by when I started to walk back to the village in the late afternoon. He offered a seat in his wagon and I accepted, for I was all done being scared of him and I was footsore.

"Recorded your deed yet?" he asked.

"No, not yet," I said, airily.

"Probably not, seeing that you haven't got any."

I let it go at that, having no sensible explanation to give a business man like my uncle.

"So, as it stands," he went on, "it's a case of neck-and-neck whether *he'll* jew you or *you'll* jew *him*. As bad as I hate *him* I'm getting to hate *you* worse! I hope he'll stick you. But I doubt it. A young pirate who can step in here and steal a whole wood-lot right under the noses of men who ought to know better is qualified to give old Judas I-scarrot lessons in deviltry."

"I don't blame you for feeling pleased and for praising me, Uncle Deck. I certainly am doing credit to your training."

"But as first selectman of this town I've got a reputation to look after, and where will I get off with one of my blood and name serving time in State prison to grand larceny?"

"Oh, I'm not going to State prison."

"You will, with that old devil after you, surer 'n hell's downhill!"

"We're sort of partners, the judge and I." I decided that I might as well give him a jolt or two, even if his common sense did tell him that I was lying.

"Oh, bah-h-h!" he yelped.

"And as his partner I want to warn you against trying to trig his business affairs."

He almost yanked the jaw off his horse, pulling the animal to a standstill.

"Condemn your young tripe! You are about as much a partner of his as a pullet is partner of a polecat! Don't you talk up to me! If you are trying to cheat him I'll help you do it. But if you are trying to help him, down goes your house!"

"I propose to help him—help his family," I said.

To my surprise he held himself in. "Help him how?" he asked.

"Why, by making you quit hounding him, for one thing. It's time this foolish old row was stopped. I am taking a special interest in Judge Kingsley's family in these days."

"Down to brass tacks, now! You mean just what you say, do you?"

"I most certainly do, Uncle Deck!"

"Don't you dare to call me uncle, you wall-eyed pup! You have gone to leaning up against that girl like a tom-cat cuddling a warm brick, have you? You're letting her fool you along—"

"Shut that dirty mouth of yours!" I shouted.

"Get out of this wagon—out with you!"

I obeyed promptly, for I had had plenty of his society. He waggled his whip-lash close to my nose when I stood in the road. "When you get into State prison, where you belong," he snarled, "you'll have a chum there. For that's where I'm going to send old Kingsley, so help me the living God!"

And he curled the lash with all his might under the belly of his horse, taking it out on the poor brute, and tore away, with the animal on the dead run.

I trudged along in the dust he left flying. A fine chance I stood of handling my uncle Deck!

A precious lot of fool babbling that talk had been at the front door of the Kingsley house the night before!

Nevertheless, I went to the house again that evening, for I had a business excuse. I told mother and daughter that certain urgent matters called me out of town and that I would be leaving early in the morning. I had a word or two to say about my arrangements for clearing the lot so that their minds might be at ease if any gossip came to them; in country communities there are busybodies who are always guessing at mischief and are trying to make trouble.

I remained with them only a short time, for I was afraid they would try to get consolation out of me regarding my uncle and I was not in the mood to do any more lying. I was in a generally uncomfortable state of mind, anyway, and I knew that Celene was troubled by my manner. There seemed to be sense of impending evil hovering over the three of us. Frankly, my uncle's threat regarding the judge had thrown a good-sized scare into me; Uncle Deck had truly acted as if he knew what he was talking about. My own conscience was creaking considerably inside me. When I rose to go Celene did not see me to the door. She gazed at me tenderly when I stated that I would be back in a few days, but some sort of reserve kept her at her mother's side.

The stars were certainly not so bright that night when I walked back to the tavern. In my gloom a memory popped into my mind, queerly enough. I remembered that Dodovah Vose had loaned me ten dollars the night he helped me to escape.

I plucked a bill out of my breast pocket and handed it to him when I walked into the tavern.

"I hope you'll excuse the delay," I pleaded.

"I sure will," he replied, heartily. "You're an honest chap, young Sidney!"

But I was far from feeling honest that night.

XIII

THE MAN WHO TALKED
IN THE DARK

Next morning Dodovah Vose drove me to the railroad station at the Lower Corners. He looked at the trip as a sort of a triumphal parade, and said so to me.

"Some different from that night ride we took, young Sidney," he chuckled. "I'm playing hackman this time so as to take the taste of that other ride out of my mouth!"

Yet, as I rode that morning by his side, I was wondering whether I would have courage to come back to Levant. Panic was in me—it truly was!

"Mighty scared little bug was you that night! But I always knew you had sprawl and gumption in you. Now you're showing the old town a thing or two and I'm proud of you."

His praise made me cringe more than ever.

When we passed the wood-lot a merry rick-tack of axes sounded in our ears.

"Yes, sir! You have shown them all that you can come back here and start something," stated Landlord Vose. He did not realize how infernally right he was. What I had started was setting the willy-wallies to dancing in my soul.

"Things have come along with such a rush that I haven't thought to ask you how you happened to hit it off so smooth with the judge," he proceeded, and my alarm increased.

"I met him on the road, and we turned a quick trade on the spot. He was starting for the city and we had to trade sudden or not at all."

"That hasn't been the judge's usual way in business," he commented, sagely. "I have had some dealings with him myself, and so I know his style pretty well." He gave me a sly, sideways glance. "Yes, I know him so well that I've noticed how he's losing his grip on business."

"And do you think he has been losing money, too?" I plumped at him.

"Well," drawled Vose, "I don't know how much money he's got nor what sort of investments he's carrying or how much money he has been handling for other folks, for he has always been cussed secret in his operations. And the folks who have turned money over to him have been secret, too, for I reckon he has helped them hide their money away from the tax-assessors. But I'll tell you, young Sidney, his money, however much he's got, must be pretty well tied up these days."

I questioned him with a side-glance which met his own.

"Because when old Rollins died a few months ago the heirs lit on the judge for the money he had in his hands—for the heirs are spenders and wanted the money to toss away. The judge's home place is in his wife's name and she mortgaged it to raise the money—and when a man mortgages the roof over his family's head he does need money, there's no doubt about that."

"But there are times when a man doesn't like to sacrifice securities," I said. Somehow I felt as if I had been specially delegated to stand up for the Kingsley family.

"Maybe so! Maybe so!" agreed Vose. "Finance is a strange critter—and the judge is a regular financier. But, I swan, if I like the looks of the strangers he has been doing business with for a long time back. I ain't any kind of a hand to pry into the dealings of men who put up at my tavern. Those fellows always paid their bills and showed plenty of money, but it don't seem to me as if straight business needs to be so blamed secret."

"However, the big fellows in money affairs keep their cards pretty close to their vests," I suggested.

"Maybe so! But he's selling property off slapdash—"

"Mrs. Kingsley says he wants to get rid of some of his cares." Perhaps she had not said just that—but I had taken the rôle of the family champion.

"Maybe so—and if that's the case, it's too bad your uncle Deck is rampaging so. Generally, we all trust the judge and look up to him, and we don't want to see him bothered at this time in his life. But here's your uncle trying to stir up enough sentiment to call a special town meeting."

"What for?" I was more alarmed than ever.

"His excuse is that the town is now so prosperous that we can afford to pay off the whole town debt by a little extra splurge in taxation. Says that with the debt all paid off new industries can be induced to locate here."

"But does that mean anything against Judge Kingsley? It looks to me like enterprise on Uncle Deck's part."

Again Mr. Vose chanted his everlasting and sing-song, "Maybe so!" Then he added: "But I reckon your uncle Deck has more visible property spread around this town than any other taxpayer in it.

110

Maybe he has had a change of heart about money. Maybe he intends to loosen up in his old age. Maybe he wants to hand something back to a town he has gouged all his life. But from what I know of your uncle Deck, I don't think he has grown so cussed patriotic all of a sudden. Young Sidney, I reckon there's a hotter and livelier reason. Your uncle has been nursing a grudge till it's well-grown and all haired out. That grudge is prancing, and he's willing to pay high for a chance to show its paces in public. And there's more in the plan of that special town meeting than shows on the surface at present writing!"

Therefore, when I climbed on board the train I had plenty to think about outside the immediate business I had in hand, though that was enough for one poor mind, Lord knows!

Take everything, by and large, I was in the prime mess of my young life up to date.

The principal reason why I stayed in it, I suppose, was because I didn't know any better! That reason has accounted for a lot of my experiences.

Some of the best fights on the records have been won by men who were worst scared.

I alighted in Mechanicsville in a state of mind I'll not attempt to describe. But I looked at myself in a store window and made up a business face to go with my appearance. I hired the best hack in sight. I started on a round of factories, wood merchants, brickyards, and lumber-dealers. I rode up to the doors of offices in style; I walked in on 'em in style.

It was certainly a new wrinkle in wood-peddling—this plug-hat performance! It opened all doors to me. I don't know what they thought I was, before I opened my mouth, but I was not kept twiddling my thumbs in anterooms; the main squeeze in every office shunted all else in order to greet me. I wonder what would have been my lot if I had come as a stammering farmer, a crude countryman, or a chopper in wool boots!

I sold wood! By gracious, I did!

I found out something all of a sudden. I discovered that I had the art of salesmanship. It's an art, a qualification hard to describe. Every man who has ever bought anything knows what it is and how it has operated in his case.

I sold wood and lumber and sleepers—and the more I sold, the higher rose my confidence in my personality, and I had hard work to control and conceal my hysterics of success.

I worked off onto brick-yards even the crooked limbs, the second-grade stuff which I had seen piling up on my operation.

With every buyer I made written contracts, designating prompt delivery on certain dates, first deliveries to be made within a week and calling for cash payments of two-thirds of value of wood delivered, the whole amount to be paid when final delivery was made.

I went on down the line to another city and then to a third. I sold wood! I sold for three days. Then I woke up and stopped selling. It occurred to me that I might be overguessing on the resources of the Kingsley wood-lot.

I had not a mite of trouble in arranging with the division superintendent of the railroad line for a supply of gondola cars; I was offering something worth his attention.

I left that gentleman in mighty abrupt fashion; he must have thought that I was a very precipitate business man. But while I was winding up my arrangements with him, I looked out of his office window in the railroad station into the windows of a train which was pulling slowly out, on its way up-country. I caught a glimpse of a stern profile with a roll of chin-beard under it. If that face did not belong to Zebulon Kingsley— But I did not stop to do any more thinking on the matter. I galloped out of that office. I had to chase that train a hundred yards down the platform—but I made the last car!

Zebulon Kingsley home ahead of schedule!

I stood on the car steps, getting my breath, giving dizzy thought to the peril I had so narrowly missed. Zebulon Kingsley back in Levant ahead of me, viewing his desolated wood-lot and voicing his fury! Where would my character and importance land after that blow-up?

Did I say that my dizzy thoughts dealt with a peril I had missed? In about ten seconds I decided that I was traveling right along with the peril. I was doomed to drop into Levant in its company.

I might have been mistaken, I reflected. I hoped I had been deceived by a too-hasty glance. I walked down through the train. I was pretty sure of my man when I passed him, though I got a view of the back of his head only. Therefore I went to the front of the car, making an excuse of the water-cooler. I looked back at him while I drank. He seemed to be asleep, for his head was bent down into the folds of the cape he had pulled about his ears. I was so sure he was asleep that when I went back up the car I gave him a bold look to convince myself I had not been mistaken.

I got one of the starts of my life!

Zebulon Kingsley was distinctly not asleep. His eyes were like fire-balls, and he stared straight at me without one flicker of the lids or crinkle of the countenance to show that he recognized me. His face was gray and haggard. He was like a stone man. If he had given one hint by his expression that he knew me I would have pushed myself in beside him, I reckon, and would have come across with my little story. But that frozen face was too much for me. I was doing a lot of guessing about his state of mind, and my guesses warned me to stay away from him just then.

I hurried past and sat down in the first vacant seat.

The feeling I had was that he had found out by letter from home or somehow what kind of a trick I had cut up. Those glaring eyes hinted at unutterable things. He must be in such a fury, I thought, that words had failed him. He was waiting until he stepped foot in Levant to go at me in proper style. Naturally, he would not start anything on a railroad train. I sat there while those thoughts flamed up in me like fire in a brush-heap, and for a long time I found no handy extinguisher to those thoughts.

However, there was a rather comforting packet in the breast pocket of my frock-coat; I got out those contracts and went over them carefully.

I did have some visible emblems of success to stick up in front of his sour face when it came to a showdown. But if Zebulon Kingsley was not willing to start anything in public on a train, neither was I. I studied my contracts, added figures, and tried to keep my mind off the big trouble ahead. But who has ever sat near a bomb with a sputtering fuse and felt in a mood for philosophy? I couldn't even add figures!

The train bumped on and on. It was a long ride.

When we arrived at Levant Corners, I followed Kingsley so closely that we almost walked in a lock-step. I had a sort of crazy notion that if he started to bawl me out on the platform and expose me to the populace I'd choke him and drag him off somewhere for an explanation, for I truly did have a face to save in Levant.

I trod behind him on the station platform. Far up the platform was waiting a man who wore a constable's badge. I itched all over as we approached that man; I fully expected that the judge would whirl and point me out and call for my arrest. But the constable touched his hat respectfully and the judge marched on. I almost bumped into him when he stopped at hail of a citizen. I was forced to go on, then. The citizen had buttonholed the judge on some matter of business, but by the few words I heard I knew it was no affair of mine. I ran my eye over the array of hitches waiting in the station yard, expecting to see Celene Kingsley. But she was not there. Her absence hinted to me that her father was not expected. Then he would ride on the stage! I resolved to walk on and to hail it when it overtook me. I proposed to be on the scene when Judge Kingsley got first peep at what had been his wood-lot. I kept looking behind and noted that he walked past the stage-coach and had started to foot it on my trail. Therefore he was not expected at home, and for reasons of his own had decided to walk.

When I saw that the stage had come on without him and had observed that he shook protesting hand at persons who stopped and offered a lift, I walked on more briskly. He wanted to be left alone, then! His expression had already hinted to me that he had no use for companionship at that time.

At last I could hear my ax-men. Their blades were biting wood in lively chorus, though the dusk was gathering. I realized that the spirit of rivalry was in them and that they were not watching the clock on that job. When I came in sight of the wood-lot I saw that a big expanse had been cleared, down to the bushes; the bared land was thickly dotted with wood which was tiered in cord lots. I hardly recognized the place.

The notion struck me that this was the proper strategic point to await the battle. In the first place, I would not be obliged to waste any breath in telling Zebulon Kingsley that his wood-lot was being cleared; his eyes would inform him on that point. I could devote all my language and energy to the job of enlightening him regarding my activities in the matter, my hopes and his prospects of getting some money. Secondly, considering strategy, my appearance before my men, accompanied by Judge Kingsley, after I got him under control, would put the stamp of authority on the whole affair; I believed I could control him. He certainly would have to take the situation as he found it; he couldn't stick those trees back into the ground again.

Therefore I settled my plug-hat well on my head, pulled out my bunch of contracts, and waited to him to come around the bend in the road.

I reflected that he had looked to me like a man who had a great deal of trouble on his mind. In my young days, when old dog Bonny was dreadfully afflicted with fleas I tied a tin can to his tail to take his mind off his troubles. I believe fully that changing the current of his thoughts for a time proved really restful to him.

It was certain that Judge Kingsley would have the current of his thoughts changed in a very few minutes. He would have something entirely fresh to think about, and I hoped it would do him good, even though I received no thanks.

He seemed pretty much cast down when he shambled into sight, his shoulders bowed, staring at the road ahead of him. But all at once he straightened, threw back his head, and seemed to sniff the air.

"Charge!" I said to myself. And he set his elbows akimbo under his cape and came at a trot.

He tried to rush past me on his way to the fence, but I stepped in front of him and threw up my hands.

"Just a moment, Judge Kingsley! This is my business—"

"Your business be damned!" he stuttered.

Strong talk for a Sunday-school teacher, but it made him seem more human and my courage rose a bit. I had not known how to tackle that frozen figure he looked to be in the railroad train.

"But I'll explain!"

"I'm going to find out what this set of infernal thieves—"

He wouldn't wait any longer, though I was trying to head him off with my arms outstretched. He drove past me and wrenched a post out of the fence and started to climb into the wood-lot. There was only one thing to do—I must get the upper hand of the infuriated old man before we attracted the attention of my busy workers; the dusk was helping me in that respect.

I pulled the stake from him, held him by his arms, and set my face close to his; he was a scrawny old chap and he hadn't any muscle left.

"Judge Kingsley, forgive me—but you must listen. It's best for all concerned. I have bought this lot from you and I am operating on it."

I thought he would choke to death before he got the words wrenched out of him.

"You haven't bought it. You couldn't buy it! There is no money passed. There's no deed. You're a thief!"

I had dropped the bunch of contracts when I grabbed him. I released my clutch in one arm and picked up the packet.

"Here's something to show I am not a thief, sir. You've got to look at 'em. And the middle of the road is no place for our business."

Furthermore, I noticed all at once that the choppers were giving up work and starting for the highway.

Probably the most sensible way was for me to go along to his house, exhorting him to keep his mouth shut till he understood the matter. But a row with him in his own house would be exposing myself to Celene. I held his arm and hurried him across the road and into the woods opposite. He protested angrily, but I kept him on the move until we were in a little clearing which the red western skies still lighted enough for my purpose.

I flapped the contracts under his nose. "You advertised the land—you gave me a price, Judge Kingsley. I know I have been irregular. I cannot stop now to explain why, but I have sold all the wood. Here are the contracts. Hunt up the men and make sure, if you don't believe writing and signatures. I'll let you go and collect your two thousand dollars before a dollar comes to me."

I shoved the papers into his hands and he pawed them over without seeming to understand very well.

"Contracts?"

"Yes, sir! Contracts with responsible concerns."

"I'll have you arrested," he insisted, but his anger was dying out and he sort of whined, "It's my land; you haven't any right to make contracts."

All at once his legs bent under him and he sat down on the ground. There was plainly something special the matter with Zebulon Kingsley!

"Oh, my God!" he mourned. "Are all the blatherskites, thieves, and swindlers in this world on my track?"

"Don't tie any of those kind of tags on to *me*, Judge Kingsley. It isn't fair!"

"You have robbed me!"

"Confound it! Look at the contracts!" He did not seem to be taking any interest in the papers; he merely waggled the packet about like a child waving a rattle.

"First one, and then the other! They have robbed me. I am ruined!"

I squatted down in front of him and made him look at me. I was in the mood for any kind of self-sacrifice. I wanted to beat it into his old head that there was one man who was trying to help him.

"Judge Kingsley, listen to me! You are sure of getting your two thousand dollars for your wood-lot. I say again, go yourself and collect the money. If my estimates are in any way near right—and I reckon I am inside the truth—there's around a thousand dollars profit in this deal, profit I was intending to take for myself. But, seeing that you feel as you do about my actions, I'll hand the whole thing over to you. Take it all! Come to me in the morning when you're feeling better and I'll explain my trade with Henshaw Hook and the choppers."

He looked at me and never said a word.

"I don't even ask any pay for the time I have put in," I said, trying to make myself as much of an angel as I could, now that I was started on the savior trail. "You understand, don't you? All you've got to do is keep my promises to the men and pull down around three thousand in cash!"

In a story-book that would have been his cue to get up and clasp me to his breast. He simply blinked at me. I began to get a little warm in the region of my neckband.

"If that's the way you feel about it, Judge Kingsley," I said, straightening up, "I'll bid you good evening. After you have tucked your three thousand in your jeans, send me a bill for damages and I'll settle."

He called me back before I had taken many steps.

"My head isn't right," he mumbled. "I have been having much trouble. What have you been telling me?"

I went over the thing again, very patiently, for I saw I was dealing with a case which was more serious than I thought. The night was on us by that time. I tore strips of birch bark from a tree, lighted them one by one, and made a torch so that he could examine one of the contracts. Again I insisted that he must take the whole thing over, profits and all.

"I had no right to start in on your property as I did, Judge Kingsley. So I'll fine myself a thousand!"

"I think I ought to call you honest, young man," he said, after a time. "I have hard work to believe that any man is honest in this world just now, but what you say sounds honest. I'll meet you half-way in your honesty."

He asked me to hold more torches. He found a sheet of letter-paper in his wallet, bearing his name printed at the top. He wrote a receipt for two thousand dollars, using the long wallet for his desk.

"I have dated it four days back. Now that I have met you half-way in one matter, young man, I ask you to meet me half-way in another. When you get that money in hand, pay it to my wife. Do not tell anybody that you did not pay it to me." He hesitated a moment. "As to the land—the deed—"

"I have no use for the land, Judge Kingsley. So there's no call for a deed."

"I think you are honest, young man. I believe I can trust you to give the money to my wife—and say nothing about it outside!"

"But I can give it to *you*, sir, in a few days!"

"I expect to be away on business for some time," he said, curtly. "Now understand! Whatever questions are asked by anybody you must insist that you paid that money to me. Your own interest requires it! Show the receipt."

117

"Forgive me to keeping you here so long in the dark and the cold, sir," I pleaded, realizing the situation all at once. "If you'll let me call on you to-morrow I'll have something further to say about the matter of the profits—but I won't bother you any more to-night."

"That's right! Don't bother me to-night."

I waited for him to come along with me.

"Good night, young man," he said. "Step along ahead if you will! I prefer to walk home alone—I have some business matters to run over in my head."

I realized fully that Judge Zebulon Kingsley did not care to have a Sidney chumming with him before the eyes of Levant, and I did not take this dismissal in bad part. I marched off.

But the memory of that face of his went with me. Fifty feet up in the road I stood stock-still. What did it mean—his command to hand over the money to his wife, making a secret of it? What made his eyes burn so redly? What was the matter with Judge Kingsley, any-way? I listened for his footsteps on the road behind me. I heard no sound.

It came to me that Celene Kingsley would have reason to blame me if I left her old father floundering around the woods in the dark-ness.

I went tiptoeing back, my ears perked.

I heard him talking rapidly and clearly, not as one talks aloud in soliloquy, but as if he were addressing somebody. I stepped carefully in through the fringe of trees and I found out that Zebulon Kingsley *was* talking to somebody; he was talking to God!

I listened five seconds and I realized what he was talking about. Then I leaped on him and struck his wrist with the edge of my hand.

He dropped a fat, ugly revolver which had glinted in the starlight. I pounced on it and flung it into the woods as far as muscle, fright, and anger could prevail. When I turned on the judge he had just tugged another revolver out of his pocket, twin of the other weapon. I had a tussle with him to get it, and he fairly squealed in his fury. But I wrenched the thing out of his clutch and threw it; then I pulled him to his feet and patted him all over, as a policeman frisks a prisoner, to make sure that he was not serving as arsenal for more artillery.

"Judge Kingsley," I kept saying over and over, "your wife! Your daughter! Think of them!"

I was obliged to drag him out of the woods by main strength. I propelled him along the highway and he walked as stiffly as some kind of a wooden figure, moved by springs. His eyes stared straight ahead and his face was white in the starlight.

So we came into the village without a word between us, and I led him by dark lanes to his house.

Then he held back and replied to what I had said in the woods as if I had just spoken.

"I *am* thinking of them! That's why I can't face them!"

Oh, the tone in which he said that! Questions were crowding in my throat, but I did not dare to pry into troubles as deep as Judge Kingsley's most certainly were. But I had to have some assurance from him.

"Judge Kingsley," I said, with respect in my voice, "I am meddling, but God knows there was a call for somebody to meddle just now."

"I want to be out of my troubles!" He was trembling like a leaf.

"But you're not so much of a coward, Judge, that you'll shift off all of your troubles on to your family, along with the awful one you were just about to shove on them! I know you're not. I have always looked up to you, sir."

"But nobody can look up to me from now on, young man!"

"I always shall, sir. We all get rattled some time in our lives." I knew I was making pretty poor talk to a man like Judge Kingsley, but I was trembling as badly as he was and I did not know what to say to him.

"I'm only poor Ross Sidney, sir. You know I don't amount to much, but won't you consider that I have done a little something for you this night? I stopped you when you didn't know what you were doing."

"I did know what I was doing," he groaned. "I was doing it because I couldn't go home. I walked up the road to the woods—to my woods on purpose to do it!"

It came to me that fate, or whatever rules human actions, had set me to play quite a part in Judge Kingsley's life, for his private woods were not there—and *I* was.

"Will you consider me enough of a man, sir, so that I can ask a man-to-man promise that you'll sleep on this thing and have a talk with me to-morrow? I have helped you on one matter. I'll do my best to help you in other ways!"

"There's no help for me."

"But let me have a talk to-morrow with you! I beg you, Judge Kingsley. Give me your promise till to-morrow!"

He stiffened up and scowled at me. He resented what I said, I could see. I guess he thought I was trying to be too familiar with him. The old chap's pride was still on tap. I suppose it seemed like lowering his dignity to make any sort of a man's compact with young Ross Sidney. However, I was glad to see pride bristle up a bit in him.

"I never heard of a Kingsley being a coward, Judge," I told him. "Or being a liar, either! You owe me something, sir, and I'll insist on being paid with your promise. So I reckon I have it." I did not give him opportunity to do any talking. I rang the bell at the doer, though he grabbed at my hand to stop me.

"I can't go in now! My face—my conscience!" So his conscience was still working!

"Leave it all to me, sir. I'll fix it."

The maid opened the door, and I led him into the sitting-room. Celene and her mother were there and they came to their feet, gasping with fright, for I was half carrying the judge.

"It's nothing—it's all right!" I told them. "We have been inspecting the work in the wood-lot on the way from the train. It's nothing, I say—just a little touch of the heart. The judge insisted on walking too much." I helped him to a couch. "I'll call in the morning on that business, sir!" I told him. Then I turned to Celene, who was giving me warm welcome with her eyes, now that her fears were subsiding. "Keep your eye on your father during the night," I advised her. "Of course, it's nothing serious in his case—only a little overtasking of the heart—but a bit of home nursing will do him good."

I reckoned I had planted a loyal sentinel over the man who was indebted to me for giving him more days of his life, even though they might be bitter days.

I went to Dodovah Vose's tavern, feeling still more like an overloaded mule—saddled with plenty of my own troubles, to say nothing of other folks'.

XIV

THE KICK-BACKS IN THIS
SAMARITAN BUSINESS

I was too much upset to go to sleep very early that night, even though Dodovah Vose had given me another of those slumber-coaxing suppers of fried chicken.

So Zebulon Kingsley was ruined, according to his own tell!

But what else besides ruin was fronting him? I knew him and the stuff that was in him. When a man like the judge came humping back to his home town, packing a gun on each hip and headed for his woods, there to do himself destruction, it meant something more than that he was flat broke. The fact that he had two guns suggested that he did not propose to take any chances on failure.

His troubles might have skeow-wowed his mind temporarily, I pondered. The fact that he had given me, one of the despised Sidneys, a half-dozen decent words hinted at aberration, as I thought upon the matter. I hoped that he would stay crazy long enough so that he would allow me to poke myself still further into his affairs and his family, and show me a little appreciation. Up to that time I certainly had been using ax and crowbar on the intimacy proposition!

It was my conviction that he would be obliged to be pretty nice to me from that time on. I knew something very private and personal in regard to Judge Kingsley, Levant magnate! All at once I found myself feeling rather like sticking my thumbs in my vest armholes and showing condescension to that man who had loomed so largely before my admiration. At any rate, no Sidney had ever committed suicide or had tried to, unless it might be hinted that it mightily resembled suicide when my father ran the ridge-pole of the Butler barn after wetting down the occasion with a quart or so of hard cider.

I felt decidedly cocky when I started over to his house the next morning. I had his secret—I had manhandled him to save his life. A man might make up his mind to commit suicide, thought I, and then be particularly and almighty grateful, after a night's sleep, because some chap happened along at the right time and stopped him before he had made a fool of himself.

I headed for the front door like a friend of the family.

Judge Kingsley opened his office door in the ell and called to me.

"I do not transact business in my home," he informed me, stiffly.

He tapped the sign beside his door. "Z. Kingsley" was its sole inscription, curtly hinting that no further information was needed regarding that gentleman. "I do all business in my office, sir."

I don't know in just what condition I had been expecting to find the judge, and I had not planned how I would act when I met him, but I know mighty well I had not calculated on the sort of meeting we did have.

I found him just as I had found him in times past when we had had a word or so together—and that was my surprise that day!

I would not have been much astonished if he had fallen on my neck and sobbed out his gratitude; I rather looked for some demonstration. To find him the same old, cold, stiff ramrod was outside all my anticipations. I went in meekly and sat down.

"In the matter of the wood-lot," he said, perfectly at ease and putting that jew's-harp twang in his nose. "I have looked the contracts over. Young man, I don't know whether to compliment you as one of the smartest business men I have ever met, or to have you arrested for an attempt at grand larceny!"

I did not know what to say to that, and sat and fiddled my finger across the brim of my plug-hat.

He put out his hand. "Please allow me to look at that receipt I gave you."

I handed it over—obedient as a pup. He read it and tore it up.

"It is as irregular a document as your operations have been irregular. I will give you a deed, taking back your note and a mortgage—"

"But I want no deed, sir. I said so to you last evening. I don't want the land. You keep it."

He gave me a chilly stare. "My price of two thousand dollars was on the lot—not merely the wood on the lot. The land will be yours when we have passed our papers. I don't know why I should place myself under obligations to you by any such foolish child's play as you suggest."

Say, I felt myself slipping out of the Kingsley family circle as if I were going down a cellar slide in a puddle of soft soap. I made a desperate clutch.

"Judge Kingsley," I said, "I made you another offer last night. I offered to turn the whole proposition over to you—profits and all! I had no business starting in on the operation. If you are in some sort of trouble—"

"Who said I was in trouble?"

"You said so last evening," I faltered.

"Have you told anybody I said so, sir?" he demanded, sharply.

"No, sir! Certainly not."

"If you permit yourself to hint that to anybody I shall promptly brand you as a falsifier and have you before the court on the charge of slander. You must realize that I could secure large damages because a financial man's reputation forms his stock in trade. I could have you sent to prison on a criminal charge."

"I don't see any need of your sitting there and threatening me in that fashion," I protested, with some heat. "I have tried to help you—"

"I have not asked for any of your help—I do not need it, sir."

"I don't suppose you do," I admitted, sourly.

"Certainly not!"

I couldn't figure what his game was—it was his own business, anyway—but I did not propose to have him sneering at me. His manner when he said, "Certainly not!" was mighty nasty. I rose and kicked my chair away from me.

"You needn't show any gratitude if you don't feel like it, Judge Kingsley. You'll never hear a word from me about anything that has happened, but I'm not keeping still because you have threatened me. I'm keeping my mouth shut because I'm man enough to do so! And, by gad! I hope you're man enough, on your side, to show me a little decency and to remember that you have a wife and daughter to protect from scandal and shame. Good day!" I put on my hat and marched out.

I'm making due allowance for the judge's state of mind, but truly that old hyampus did have the natural ability to stir a man's temper. A Kingsley and a Sidney got along together about as well as the two parts of a Seidlitz powder do when they meet in a glass of water!

I slammed the door after me, but I had gone only a few feet when I remembered that I had left behind my contracts. Furthermore, I had not finished my business in regard to the deed and the payments. So I whirled and went back in without stopping to knock.

It was as if he had been playing a part with me with a mask to hide his face! He had laid down the mask.

I looked on a fairly hideous scroll of awful, utter woe. That was his face. He was crumpled down in his chair. He did not look at me. I picked up the packet.

"Are you ready to attend to the matter of the deed, sir?"

He wagged his head weakly from side to side. "Later!" he muttered. "Come later. Come this evening, perhaps."

I went down into the woods and hunted for hours until I found those two revolvers. That face of his was before me all the time.

I expected to look up and find him hunting, too. There were other ways of committing suicide than by shooting, but I did not propose to leave those revolvers around loose, seeing that he had made up his mind to use that means of shuffling off. That face which he had exposed to me showed that Judge Kingsley's soul was near the limit of endurance.

I went about that day sick with fear. My helplessness in the matter was maddening. He was holding me off with his disdain like a man holding an enemy at bay with a pitchfork. And I knew that even if he gave me his confidence there was little a poor devil of my caliber could do in affairs such as his must be.

I wondered if the knowledge that he was ruined was behind his desperate resolve to die. Of course he had a lot of pride, but other proud men had failed in business and lived through it.

I was obliged to confess to myself that the judge must have a deeper motive. I remembered my uncle's threats and wondered what that disturber had up his sleeve.

I almost whipped my courage up to the point of tackling him on the subject, but when I met him on the street in the afternoon and fronted his savage scowl I walked right on past, minding my own little business. His face had an extra touch of flame in it that day. That he had something special on the docket was plain to be seen. I went down to the wood-lot and checked up with Henshaw Hook so as to be out of my uncle's way. His looks rather scared me. Just as I was walking away from the wood-lot at dusk he hopped out of his wagon ahead of me and tacked a printed paper to a wayside tree, glowering at me while I waited at a little distance. It was evident that he meant that paper especially for my attention.

So I walked up and had a look at it when he was out of the way.

It called a special town meeting thirty days from that date. As was necessary in a call of that sort, the purpose of the meeting was stated: "To see what action the town will take to pay off its indebtedness in full. Notice is hereby given that all creditors of the town must present notes or other evidences of claims at that meeting on the 15th day of April."

What did that call signify in the case of Zebulon Kingsley, town treasurer? I had seen behind his mask and I guessed! If I guessed rightly he would feel, when his eyes fell on that paper, like a man who had been notified of the date of his execution.

I started on toward the village, and when I passed Brickett's duck-pond I threw the revolvers into the water.

I hurried to Judge Kingsley's house, for I had the excuse of business, and he himself had made the appointment. There was a light in his office, but it went out suddenly when I was some distance away. I started to run, and then I checked myself. I decided that caution rather than haste was needed. I was right. Standing behind a tree, I saw him come out of the office door in a sneaking fashion, the early evening hiding him. He went around the house, and I followed. Young eyes can see in the dark better than old ones, and he did not spy me where I stood in the dusk, watching him hack off with a jack-knife a section of the family clothes-line.

Stooping and almost staggering he went down into the orchard, and I trod close behind him undetected, for the trees plastered shadows into which I dodged. I waited until he had settled a noose around his neck and had thrown an end of the cord over a limb. I was taking no chances on having any misunderstanding between Judge Kingsley and myself that trip. In my own way I was just about as desperate as he was. I marched up to him, took him by both arms and pushed him against the tree-trunk.

He was in such a state, physically and mentally, that he did not protest or resist; it did not seem to frighten him specially to be overhauled in that fashion. Honestly, I felt like spanking his face as I would have whipped a child. This game of "tag the suicide" was getting on my nerves.

"Judge Kingsley, you need a guardian and I have appointed myself one," I told him, and I was mighty resolute, for I had determined to brace up to him with all the power in me. "You have no right to kill yourself, and you're not going to kill yourself, by gad! not if I have to camp with you day and night till you get back your nerve. I'm going to take you straight to your folks and tell 'em you're out of your head temporarily and will have to be taken to a hospital!"

That brought him out of his numbness, and I knew it would. I believe he would have struck me if his arms had been free. But I needed to have him in another mood than the fighting one. I hit him hard.

"You're an embezzler!" I cracked out. "How much?"

He crumpled, and I let him slide down and sit on the ground, his back against the tree. It was the first time he had ever had that word put to him from man's mouth, even though he may have confessed to himself in his heart.

"Judge Kingsley," I said, bravely, knowing that I had an advantage from then on, "I'm only a young man and I know you don't think much of me. But I'm going to grab in on this thing, whether you want me to or not. I have special reasons of my own. I'll do everything I can to balk my uncle."

125

"You're a spy he has set on me!"

"You're a liar!" I wasn't going to take any of his sneers or his abuse. I hated to talk to him as I did, but only by being coarse and rough and bossy could I hope to pound anything helpful into him.

He stared up at me with his jaw hanging down and I did not let up on my punches.

"I have tried to head off my uncle Deck. I have told him straight out that I am for you and against him. He and I don't speak to each other. I have promised your wife and your daughter that I'll do everything I can to beat my uncle out in this thing. They don't understand it! I don't understand it all. But, before God, my promise to them is holy, even if you do not believe in me! I'm in this affair and I'm in to stay."

He began to wag his head as he had done before that day.

"Brace up, Judge Kingsley! You're not licked yet!"

"Those three selectmen have signed my death-warrant. That notice which has been posted!"

I saw that I had him going and I kept him going. "But when an embezzler stays alive and does his best to straighten matters—"

"Don't call me that name!" he groaned.

"If you will take me into your confidence, Judge Kingsley, so that I can turn to and help you, I swear before Almighty Jehovah that I will set to work for you with body and soul. I *can* help you—I know I can help. No man can feel as I feel and be useless! But let me tell you this much on the other side!" I bent down and snapped my finger under his nose. That was no time for half-way and mealy-mouthed stuff. "If you throw me down after this honest offer, it means that you think I'm too cheap to be of use and too low to associate with. And that's an insult I'll never swallow! So help me, I'll drag you up into the village with that rope around your neck and blow the whole business and hand you over to those who will take care of you. I will! My mind is made up. Take your choice!"

I am sure that with no less bitter alternative could I have jounced any of his secrets out of Zebulon Kingsley.

"I'm just enough of a hellion to do that very thing if you don't treat me right," I warned him, angrily.

"You leave me no choice in the matter," he mourned. "You are—"

"Look out, sir! I'm doing what I'm doing out of pure and honest desire to help you. I want fair treatment."

"Nothing can make my situation worse than it is, I suppose," he stated, after meditating for a time. "On the fifteenth day of April it

126

will become known in town meeting that more than ten thousand dollars of town notes are out, drawing interest and bearing my name as town treasurer. I have issued those notes without warrant."

"But the people who hold them know they are out!"

He was coldly, numbly patient with me, the untamed animal who had promised to pounce on him and drag him to his shame in the village.

"I have borrowed the money in various small lots and in each case the note-holder is keeping absolutely still in order to escape taxation."

"But great Scott! Judge Kingsley, ten thousand dollars for a rich man like you—"

"I am no longer rich. I am ruined. I cannot take up those town notes prior to the meeting. So I shall be arrested as a criminal! I have lost money intrusted to me for investment, but though I have lost it I cannot be prosecuted criminally—it was breach of trust. I hoped to get money to stave off exposure in the criminal matter so that I could set myself to earning more money and restoring what I owe to the investors. But I have not been able to raise that money. That's why I decided to kill myself. I knew I couldn't face it!"

"Did you just find out that you couldn't raise the money, sir?"

He looked up at me, shame and agony in his face showing even in the dark. It began to swell in him—I could see it in his eyes—that longing which comes to every man in deep trouble—the wild hankering to confide in somebody—to rush into confession, to unload the heart, to speak the words which have been pressing to the lips. I was only Ross Sidney, to be sure, but I was a man and Judge Kingsley had been bottling his grief for a long time.

"What I did last was worst of all! Nobody could have convinced me that I would ever do such a piece of folly. Think of me doing such a thing—a man used to the ways of money! A financier! Oh, I have been dreading the scorn, the sneers, the ridicule more than I have dreaded the exposure of my town notes! I want to die!"

"What have you done, sir?"

"My investments were good in years past! I knew how to handle money—but what I did a few days ago!"

"What was it, Judge?" He had been hesitating between his declarations, and therefore I kept prodding him. But confession of his last affair seemed to stick in his throat.

"Oh, I am not guilty—I am not ashamed because I lost money in my investments! The pirates who have manipulated this country's industrials and wrecked the railroads are the guilty ones—they should be ashamed of what they did to the honest investors! But that I should run the scale of speculation as I have—to the depths! Down, down, as I got more desperate! And that I should do what I have just done when I was most desperate—when your uncle was rushing me toward a cell door!"

He twisted his fingers together and cracked his knuckles. I felt like a man waiting for a woodchuck to come out of his hole—getting an occasional glimpse of a nose and seeing it everlastingly dodging back.

"But I had to have money quick. I had lost my grip. I could not raise more money in a regular way."

"When I was in the city I heard swindlers talk about such men, sir. There are blacklegs who go about the country hunting for such men. Have you been swindled?"

"Foully—vilely!"

"How?"

He hooked his fingers inside his collar as if speech had stuck in his throat.

"Laugh!" he advised me. He was as hoarse as a crow and looked as crazy as a coot. "Go ahead and laugh! I may as well get used to the ridicule."

"I don't feel much like laughing at anything these days, Judge Kingsley. I wish that you could understand me better and know how sorry—"

"Yes, and you and everybody else will pity me as a fool to be classed in with the other fools who are gulled by the shell-and-pea game."

"For the sake of Mike, what have you done?" I demanded with a bit of temper, for I was in no frame of mind to guess riddles.

"I—Zebulon Kingsley—a financier, a man supposed to be in his right mind," he squealed, beating his breast as he struggled to his feet, "I bought a gold brick!"

XV

A TIP FROM MR. DAWLIN

While I blinked at Zebulon Kingsley through the gloom I remembered what "Cricket" Welch had once said to me, in one of those sessions where I lapped up information as greedily as a kitten laps milk. He had a flow of language, "Cricket" had, and I wish I could remember his words more accurately. But it was something like this:

"Why should any crook bring on brain-fag by thinking up new ones when the old ones, with gears smoothed by twenty-five centuries of steady operation, work so much better? As long ago as old Solomon was figuring on Temple estimates with the architects, and had quite a reputation in the country round about, a little chap dropped into a village outside of Babylon and gave out that he was The Old Boy's son by Wife 411, and was interested in King Solomon's mines along with his dad. Then he unloaded a gold brick on to a village sucker, first making the sucker believe that the latter was a buttonhole relation of the Solomon family."

I was running that speech over in my mind while I looked at the judge, a little uncertain what to say to him under the circumstances.

"And yet, the fraud did not seem to be barefaced while they were at work on me," lamented the old gentleman. "One of them, the one who came to town first, was the son of one of my old schoolmates who went West when he was young and has been settled there ever since. Young Blake was East on business and dropped into Levant to look the old town over; his father told him to make himself known to me, so that he could carry back news of the folks his father used to know here."

And in my book of notes I had set down the detail of just such a scheme as that!

"They always have a skirmisher ahead of the main push," I blurted. "He finds out about somebody who settled West—and then along comes the son."

"What's that?" demanded Kingsley. "What do you know about it?"

"Then, after the son is well settled, along comes one of father's partners, East, to sell stock, and he has a sample of the clean-up—a big hunk of gold—and it's always a real ingot, too."

"It *was* real," insisted the judge, passionately. "I went to the city and had it tested by a jeweler who is a friend of mine. They offered me a chance to make money on account of my old friendship. It did not seem like a gold-brick game. I could not believe it was. I did not dare to believe it was. I needed money so badly!"

"But it was, sir."

"I mortgaged, I borrowed, I pawned! They offered me a chance to make money because I was a prominent man and could help them sell their stock. They wanted me to be sure that the proposition was a good one—that the gold was honest. They took my last five thousand dollars! My God! I bought a gold brick! I bought it like other fools have bought."

"They always put new trimmings on the old game, Judge Kingsley, and make it look attractive."

He looked at me strangely and did not answer.

"I suppose they worked it as usual," I went on, feeling just a bit proud of my knowledge. I reflected that he might be more thankful for his volunteer if I showed him that I was no greenhorn. His mouth had been running away with him in his wild eagerness to unload the sorrows from his soul. All at once he was showing symptoms of stiffening a bit, as if he wondered why he had opened his heart to such a one as Ross Sidney.

I needed all his confidence—the flow was lessening—and so I "shot the well," as the oil fellows say.

"After they had given you all kinds of nice entertainment in the city, you started for home and opened your package on the train and found a lead junk and a letter advising you to go home and keep still and never believe strangers again."

"That letter—that insult!" he gasped.

"They told you they were starting straight for Europe, and they—"

"So that is what you were in the city for, eh? A blackleg—one of them! Your brazen cheek—your flashy clothes—"

"No, Judge Kingsley, I never tried to sell gold bricks. But it came my way to find out a lot about those fellows who do sell them."

"Yes, you flashy cheat!" he snarled. "You are like that other one! Waistcoats like chromos! Tricked out with gewgaws—airs of a peacock!"

That last word sent a thrill through me, put an idea into my head.

"Was he a big man, Judge Kingsley? Was his name Pratt?"

"No."

"But he brought the gold! He claimed to be the partner. He had a smear like grease across his cheek—a scar. He—"

"You seem to know your confederates very well, sir."

"Judge Kingsley, you listen to me! I have never seen those men face to face, but I have heard of them. I have heard of their tricks. I know how they operate. I know a good many of their lurking-places. I have made it my business to know!" I noted that he was still suspicious, and I put my face close to his and lied with all the fervor that was in me. I needed his confidence, I say. "I did work as a detective until the dirty mess of crooks made me sick of the job. I can help you in this thing! Depend on me! I'm going to help!"

"I have about given up belief in everything!"

"Give me your hand, sir, and promise me you'll offer a good front to the world. Nobody must guess that you're in difficulties. As for the noises my uncle is making, he has never said anything definite; he is merely making threats. Everybody knows about his grudge and folks don't take much stock in him. If you keep a stiff upper lip nobody will guess."

"But they all will *know* on the fifteenth of April."

"If we can grab in ten thousand dollars before then—"

"Do you stand there, young man, and tell me you have the crazy idea that you can pull any of my money back from those scoundrels?"

"Yes, and more with it," I returned, much more bold in my tone than I was in my heart. But when I knew that I had the "Peacock" Pratt gang identified—and probably had located Jeff Dawlin's brother as the man who planted the fraud, posing as the son, his usual rôle, certain wild hopes and dizzy schemes went to whirling in my head.

"We ought to have three thousand in cash in a short time to—"

"A client—a widow is pressing me for money. It amounts to about that sum," he said, dolefully.

"Does she suspect—"

"No, no!" he snapped, irritably. "She is going to be married again, the fool, and wants to hand it to her new husband." He showed a flicker of pride in the midst of his troubles. "There is nobody calling Zebulon Kingsley a thief as yet, except himself and your uncle. I know that I am and *he* suspects," he added, bitterly.

"Then the woman must have her money, sir. We must keep everybody from even suspecting for a time."

I took both his hands in mine. He did need comfort and sympathy, even such as I could offer him.

"I'm square with you, Judge Kingsley. I know how to find those men. I'll go after them. And I know you'll do your part to help me, I only ask you to buck up! Let nobody suspect!"

"I ought to doubt every man in the world after what I have been through! I ought to doubt *you*! Why are you doing all this for me, sir?" he demanded, and then I was glad it was dark there under the tree. I must have revealed confusion aplenty. "I have never shown you any favors, young man. It has been the other way. I never liked your breed."

"I know that, Judge Kingsley, but—" I could not go any further at the moment.

"Well?"

"You see," I gulped, "when I was a little shaver you gave me a quarter and I bought a catechism and studied it and—I guess—I'm quite sure—it made a better boy, and—"

It wasn't convincing, that talk wasn't! He caught me up sharply:

"The truth isn't in you, young Sidney!"

"You told me that once before. And it has been my ambition to show you that you were wrong."

"Bah! I know human nature too well to believe any such rot."

"But you always stood up in Sunday-school, sir, and told us about Christian charity and meekness and forgiveness. You believe in all that, don't you?"

"I have no confidence in you—not now!"

"Not when I'm trying to prove to you that I'm one of those practical Christians?"

"Do not insult me with any more of that balderdash, sir!"

I had just as much of nasty temper as he had, and mine began to flare up in me. I knew that my motives were all right, though I did not dare to reveal them to him—and my innocence made me the more angry.

"You would have made a big hit with the good Samaritan when he came along and offered his help after you had fallen among thieves," I snapped. "I reckon you have never practised any of the charity you have preached. I have never preached, but I am practising! You don't seem to recognize your own religion when you see it acted out instead of being merely printed in a book!"

"You're a renegade, convicting yourself out of your own mouth!"

Oh, what was the use! I walked off a little way. Then I turned on him.

"I have my own reasons for wanting to help you, Judge Kingsley, no matter what you believe about me. But if you feel as you talk, you can go to blazes just as soon as you like. I'm not going to try to round up all the revolvers, ropes, and razors in this town. That rope you have there seems to be a good strong one. Go as far as you like! And I'll keep on in *my* way and will turn the money over to your estate—to your wife and your daughter. You are not the first coward who has knocked out the last prop and sluiced all the mess on to his women folks! Go on! I'll be furnishing your wife bread and butter while you're having insomnia in hell!"

Then I went back to the tavern.

I knew well enough that Zebulon Kingsley would not kill himself that night. In the first place, he was too mad. He came behind me, chattering his teeth like an angry squirrel. Then, again, I had stirred his curiosity, even if I had not given him any special hope. And my threat about handling his money after he had gone was enough to keep Zebulon Kingsley hanging around on top of the earth for a time. I knew his nature mighty well. I would have taken those means with him at first, but I had been hoping that he would accept me on a friendlier basis where I might coddle my hopes; and here was I handling him by the scruff of the neck!

I caught a glimpse of Celene through the sitting-room window when I passed the house. The light was behind her and her hair was like an angel's halo. Ah! there was the inspiration which was keeping me on the lunatic's job I had picked out for myself! As for that old hornbeam father, I was in a state of fury which prompted me to go back, use his ears for handles, and kick him around his premises until he promised to behave himself—and give me his daughter when my task was finished. Well, at least I had reached one interesting stage in my development—I was acting as guardian of the high and mighty Zebulon Kingsley and was rather despising my ward!

That evening I sat till late and went through my note-book and studied the affiliations, the methods, the lurking-places and all other information I had recorded in regard to one "Peacock" Pratt and his associates.

It seemed to me that I had a pretty good start on the thing, even though the future was, as Jodrey Vose used to say of dock water, in a "nebulous and gummy condition."

But I went to bed, nevertheless, in a considerably exalted state of mind. With every day that passed I was getting farther into the affairs of the Kingsley family—and getting into those affairs—

I dreamed of Celene that night, but that was not a matter for special record; I dreamed of her every night.

In the morning I put on a business suit I had bought "off the pile" in Mechanicsville. I had wanted to show Levant that I had more than one suit of clothes. I reckoned that I would feel more sane and solid in that suit. And I did feel that way when I went down to breakfast. If ever a man had business ahead of him I was that one!

But that sane and normal feeling did not sit well on my conscience. I found myself brooding and getting depressed. I wondered why I had felt so exalted and optimistic the night before. How could I have made such confident promises to Kingsley?

While I sawed at that prosaic hunk o' ham the notion of chasing up those knaves and getting my clutch on that stolen money—or any other money—seemed just a hopeless dream. It was surely a crazy idea; I sat there and looked down into my plate and so decided. For all of a quarter-hour I mulled and gloomed there, wondering what had happened to make me so dull and disheartened and doped. I woke up to what the matter was—woke all of a sudden. It was that blamed ready-made suit of clothes!

I was simply plain Ross Sidney! I was right down on the plane of all the men around me. I looked like a tank-town commercial drummer and felt like one. I had no more imagination or horizon than a grocery clerk. All the fantastic spirit of adventure had gone out of me. Perhaps it may be thought that mere clothes cannot do all that to a man! Well, wear overalls to the next grand ball! I'm no psychologist and I have never read Carlyle's essay on clothes, though I am told he describes about what I have felt. I'm merely saying this: when I realized what was the matter with me and felt certain that I needed to be comfortably crazy in order to keep up my clip—why, do you suppose I would ever have tried to bark in front of that show if I had been dressed in a sack-suit?

Yes, comfortably crazy!

I rushed up-stairs and shifted to my knight-errant regalia. Then I went to my job on the run. I reckoned that I was going to be in a devil of a hurry for a while!

I galloped down to the wood-lot, my plug-hat riding tilted back like the funnel of a racing steamer. Those choppers were hearty and happy and were hustling for that bonus; if a few laggards needed pep I injected it. I made estimates, got every hitch in Levant which would cart wood and drag timber and started the cut for the railroad.

The freight-trains picked up the gondola cars as they were ready.

I rushed to the cities and arranged for deliveries, pulled down first payments in good season to settle wages for a week, as agreed with Henshaw Hook, and shuttled back and forth until all the cut was cleaned up on the lot. Gad! how I was counting days! I did not waste any time on Judge Kingsley. I realized that the more I kept away from him, the more I kept him guessing!

I grabbed my first opportunity to take a day off the job and run down to the big city; I made that jump from one of the towns where

I was handling the last deliveries—for I could not make final collections until the railroad completed its haul, and so I had a little time to spare.

There was another barker at the door of Dawlin's place, and I noted with gratification that he was a rather seedy chap. The blonde looked acutely surprised and showed apprehension when I walked right in past her. Plainly, her man had been making some promises as to what he would do to me if I ever showed up again.

And the first glance Dawlin gave me when he looked up from his gazara envelopes showed that he was quite ready to keep his promises.

I beckoned him to his office and walked in there and waited for him. He came on the jump. He was at me almost before I had time to place my plug-hat out of the way of possible damage.

When Mr. Dawlin would close a gazara game right at a moment when suckers were shoving money at him, it was proof that he was specially interested in something else which was almighty important. His language when he burst in on me made it plain that his interest in me was not flattering, though it was intense.

"Oh, if it's that little, foolish, petty matter of the few dollars you handed back to those yaps," I broke in, after I had pushed him back with a swoop of my arm—and, as I have stated, it was a hard arm—"here's your small change."

In my wood business I had promptly changed checks into cash. I pulled out before the lustful eyes of Mr. Dawlin a roll of bills big enough to make a pillow for his Mormon Giant, and I carelessly flipped the edges to show him they were yellowbacks.

"What did the little matter amount to?" I asked, airily.

"Six and twenty-two fifty—and I tossed 'em a five," he said, trying to make a quick shift from passion to pacification.

"And I guess the drinks are on me this time, Jeff," I said, adding a ten-dollar bill to the amount. "Go buy the kind you like."

"But what in—"

"This tells all the story," I said, tapping the roll and stuffing it back.

"But your partners—leaving me in the lurch—not inviting me in for a drag—"

"It had to be a lone play, Jeff—just had to be! But don't think I have all the money in the world cornered in my pocket, even if it looks like it. And I'm not back here simply to give you a treat by letting you look at it. I have located a bigger bundle—but it can't be coopered by a lone play."

"Job for the gang, hey?" he asked, almost drooling.

"Well, for the right operators if they're the real goods. But no amateurs, you know!"

"Condemn it! I have told you about my brother. He's one of the best in the country! Has just pulled off a killing—not very big, but easy and profitable."

"Where?"

"Nothing doing on the where!" replied Mr. Dawlin, warily. "That's all done and the money counted. We always forget *where* as soon as the money is counted." He fingered his nose. "Where is—" he started.

"Same tag," I said, smartly. "You forget and I don't remember. All is, it's there waiting. Can we all get together?"

"When?"

"To-day."

"Blast it all! you ought to know that we can't all get together to-day—nor a week from to-day!" He showed some suspicion.

"Why should I know that?" I looked him in the eye.

"When a job is done East, why, you know yourself they all shoot West—clear to the—"

"You didn't tell me the last job was done East," I said, coolly.

"Well, it was. I can say that much. And they're on their way West—they're going over the Rockies."

"Then I guess I'll declare them out on the job, Jeff. I'm in with some of the other—"

"But that's no way to use a friend like I've been to you! This thing ought to be put up to Ike and 'Peacock.' You must remember that I offered you a lay with them! I tried to use you right. You ought to show some gratitude."

He was fairly whining in his anxiety, but I was mighty careful about showing any eagerness of my own. I scratched my ear and looked rather doubtful and displayed indifference.

"Of course I can't write to 'em—we never write, especially soon after a job. But I have their bearings, Ross. I can put you right on to their trail. They have a job on below the Potlatch country in Idaho. First East and then West—get the idea? It's something about land—this operation. You're bound to bump into 'em; there are not so many men out there as there are here."

"Still, it looks to me like a wild-goose chase," I demurred, hoping to be assured that it was no such thing.

"'Peacock' isn't going to change his style! He's too far away to be obliged to bother—and he sure does like his togs! You can't hide 'Peacock' Pratt if you surround him with a whole county. You'll find him easy, and my brother will be right on the wheel. Wait! If you don't know that country I'll jot down directions and names for you—names of men to ask. I'll give you a word or two for a passport!" He grabbed paper and pen and began to scribble. "What extra the trip costs will be added to your lay. You'll find them square if you get in with them," he assured me while he wrote. "You don't have to discuss any lay for me. My brother always sees to it that I get my pickings from any job I help him to."

He fairly thrust the paper into my hands when he had finished. Really, I was more grateful inside than I allowed to appear in my thanks. I could hardly ask Mr. Dawlin to do more in setting me on the trail of the men I was after. The humor of the thing certainly did appeal to me—and I needed a little something for cheer just then.

Whether I would try to pick their pockets when I arrived up with them, or knock them down with a club, or what I would do I left to the future. I had enough to think of just then—that wood business to wind up and the matter of the future handling of Zebulon Kingsley to attend to—and a crazy chase across the continent ahead of me!

I tucked the paper deep, slapped Mr. Dawlin on the back, and hustled for up-country.

XVI

GRABBING A HUSBAND
AND FATHER

When I laid rising three thousand dollars in front of Zebulon Kingsley on his office table as my card of reintroduction to that glum gentleman, I really jumped him.

The money was in bills and there was a stack of it. A mere check would not have been half as impressive. A lot of men in this world are extravagant because they pay by check; handling real money makes one more appreciative of values, I think.

"I have wound up the wood-lot proposition to the last cent," I informed him. "All collections made, all the men paid, and I hope you are as well satisfied as the rest. There's the cash!"

"How much is there?" His voice trembled when he asked me.

"Count it."

"I'll take your word, and later—"

"You have told me several times that the truth isn't in me. Count that money! I insist!" A bit nasty of me, I admit, but I had resolved to make my bigness, where Judge Kingsley was concerned. I saw no chance of winning unless I made him understand that I was not to be kicked around any more.

I stood over him while he counted. His bony fingers shook. Even though he was handling money—rather a favorite indoor sport of his—I knew he was finding the job a bitter one, with me at his elbow and acting just as if I belonged there. He jotted down amounts as he counted, and then he added the figures.

"I make it three thousand three hundred and fifty four dollars and twenty-nine cents," he reported.

"You are right, sir." I held my little account-book in front of his nose and tapped my totals. "I did a bit better than I figured."

"The two thousand which belongs to me—"

"There are no divisions in that pile, sir. We are not going to have any such argument as we had once before about price and land and deed. You need that money for immediate use and you're going to take it. And don't tell me again that you don't need my help. You do!" Big talk, but he needed it! "But don't you be afraid that I shall ever twit you about this help. Now is there any way of staving off this widow who wants her three thousand?"

"No! I have promised her. After what you told me—I reckoned on—"

"Ah! Then you have been admitting to yourself the last few days that I'm not so much of a renegade and crook, after all!"

His eyes shifted. "You must make allowances in my case, Mr. Sidney!" That looked promising. He was giving me a handle for my name.

"Then we'll pay the widow so that she will not be wagging her jaw while we're away."

"While we're away?" he repeated.

"Yes, sir! You and I are going to start on the trail of that last batch of money you invested."

"But we'll never get money that way."

"How else are you going to raise ten thousand dollars before the fifteenth of April?"

"I have no way of raising it!" he lamented.

"That's it! No sensible, business way! Therefore, we must do the next best—grab from the men who have grabbed from you. It's either that or go steal money!"

I pulled up to the table and before his eyes counted back to myself the money over and above three thousand dollars. I put it in my pocket.

"It's our common purse—for traveling expenses," I explained.

"But it's—" he gasped.

"Yes, it's a long journey, sir. However, I must go and you must go along with me."

"I am not in condition to travel."

"I know that, sir, and I'm sorry. I wish I did not need you on the job, but you must be with me in order to identify those men who robbed you. Your complaint will put them in the jug if we can't scare them and twist the money out of them in another way. I can't do a thing without your presence, unless I catch up with them and knock them down. I may just as well stay East here and commit highway robbery for you!"

I had another reason for insisting on his making the trip with me, but I kept it to myself. If I left him behind there in Levant with my rambunctious uncle barking at his heels and creditors waking up to suspicions, I could not have one moment's peace of mind. I felt pretty sure that he would betray himself by face, his actions, or by suicide or confession. He was in no shape to endure inquisition if he were left where folks could get at him.

"You must go," I insisted.

"Where?"

"It's more or less of a blind run."

"But I must know."

"We're only wasting time by talking it over ahead, Judge Kingsley, because I don't know much about the trip myself."

He began to show temper, and I could not blame him much. My comfortable craziness which I had put on along with my "dream suit" was helping a lot; the judge was frostily sane.

"The project is crazy," he stormed.

"So is the fix you're in!"

"I can tell my wife and daughter nothing sensible!"

"As near as I can find out, sir, you have never told them anything special about your business. Why begin now?"

"Because they are worried. My actions—those strangers—"

"I know, sir. They told me. But when you go away this time you'll be going in my company and that may help with them."

He gave me a look which hinted that he was not at all sure about that.

"We have been in one business deal; it's easy to say we're in another," I suggested, choosing to overlook his manner.

But my feelings got away from me when he began to protest and argue and ask questions about why and where and when. The balky old mule! And I was giving him my soul and service free!

I pounded my knuckles on the heaped money. "We are going to leave this town on the night train, Judge Kingsley. That gives you time enough to settle with the widow and tell your folks something and get them calmed down."

"Don't you dare to browbeat me, young man!"

"Yes, and you'll have time to think the thing over for yourself, sir, before I call for you with a hitch just before train-time! There will be no arguments then. I shall expect you to be all ready with your bag in hand. Go light on luggage. We shall go a long way and we shall go in a hurry."

I left him and went about a few final affairs of my own, and when I finished I was squared with everybody in Levant. Before handing that money to the judge I had paid my personal debts—I felt that I was entitled to that much!

That evening Dodovah Vose loaned me a hitch and a driver and clapped me on the shoulder with great zest and pride.

"When the judge picked you for a partner he picked the right one," he declared. "You make a team which will bring this old town up on its feet. The judge needs you, son. He has been going behind."

And then once more he tried to pump me regarding this latest venture, for I had purposely dropped a word to him that the judge and I were off on a big deal. I knew that a seed planted in Dodovah Vose would bring forth fruit of the sort the judge and I needed.

"You can just hint to folks, if you feel like it, Mr. Vose, that Judge Kingsley and I have seen a way to help this town very much." That was true. "Incidentally, the judge will make a great deal of money out of certain things where his capital has been tied up."

"I've always said he knew his business as a financier. Some of the old tom-cats in this town have been prowling and meraouwing because he has been tied up lately by mortgages; but you've got to bait with money to catch money! Don't fret, son. I'll hand 'em out something now to warm their ear-wax."

"Oh, he knows how to make money for himself and for other folks!"

"Am I too late to slip in a few hundred on this deal?" asked Mr. Vose, anxiously.

It was promptly on my tongue, of course, to put him aside as gently as possible. But I knew that he had been wondering why I had not let him in on the thing before, for truly he had been my best friend in that town. I had no good excuse to give him. I needed his friendship and his loyal good word even more then than in the past, for suspicion was darkly brooding in Levant. I hated to leave behind with him the impression that I would do everything for Zebulon Kingsley, who had been my foe, and would not turn even a little leak of prosperity into an old friend's porringer.

While I was struggling with my thoughts—feeling like a scoundrel reaching for his brother's wallet—a strange notion came to me. It fitted in with that comfortable craziness of mine. If I accepted his money, would I not be pledging my very soul to do and to dare? My devotion to Celene Kingsley I had set at one side as my true and sacred motive. I was mighty sure that I was not at all enthusiastic in regard to her father. However, if I took Dodovah Vose's hard-earned money from his hands—and taking it meant a pledge that he was to benefit from a sure thing—had I not another sacred and even more compelling motive? Truly I had, for my man's honor was concerned as well as my love for a girl!

"What have you handy?" I asked.

"Five hundred," he said. "I ask no questions. I want no promises. I know you'll do your best for me, son. I hate to bother you—but profits come slow in a country tavern, and I'd like to do a little extra repairing this spring."

He was on his way to his rusty old safe while he talked.

So I took his money and went away from him with the warmth of his palm on mine.

The grinding of the wagon-wheels on the grit in front of Judge Kingsley's house brought Celene to the door, and when I did not climb down from the wagon she called to me.

"Will you not come into the house?" she pleaded. I had not intended to do so. In spite of my longing to see her and to have her parting smile go along with me on that amazing journey I was undertaking, I had made up my mind to duck judiciously a meeting-up with the women folks of my traveling partner. But I had no will to disobey when she called to me. I found the judge with his overcoat on and his bag in his hand. Evidently he had thought the matter over! But he did not look like a bridegroom starting on a honeymoon trip, and he scowled at me with as much ferocity as if we were two tom-cats tied by the tails over a clothes-line.

His wife was hanging to his arm and she was white, even to her lips.

"Mr. Sidney, I must know what this mysterious business is."

"I'm sure the judge will tell you what is necessary."

"He will tell me nothing. I have endured much in the past, Zebulon! I have not asked to know much about your affairs," she went on, trying to get a square look into his eyes. "This time I *must* know!"

"I have told you!" From his tone it was hard to tell what his emotions were. The words sounded as if somebody were talking into a tin spout a long way off.

"You have told me nothing except that you are going! You do not say where. You have not told me when you are coming back."

"We don't exactly know, Mrs. Kingsley. But I assure you that the trip is very necessary," I put in.

"I must tell you that mother is not well," said Celene, wistfully. "I'm sure everything is all right, but we must know where you are going so that we may be in touch with you."

"We can keep you posted—when we know where we are," I said; but I did not sound very convincing, I fear. God knows, I wanted to put my arms around her and comfort her and tell her that I was madly trying to save her, her home, her mother, and her father from disgrace and ruin. I guess no man has ever figured out beyond doubt whether it's better to tell the woman everything or to hide trouble as long as possible. When women are proud they never forget the disgrace, whether it is revealed outside or if it's merely kept secret in the household. And in Zebulon Kingsley's case I was proposing to keep the effect of the disgrace as well as all knowledge of it away from those women.

I knew how he felt in the matter! He had chosen revolvers and ropes rather than face them. I was determined to be just as resolute as he—until a showdown was inevitable.

It would be a sorry triumph, a half job, if they were obliged to live out their lives knowing that the master of the household had lived for years in the shadow of prison; it meant the wrecking of all their pride and ideals—no more joy in home or life itself in the case of such women as they. I understood!

The big clock was ticking off minutes rapidly. Our time was short. I shuffled my feet, impatiently wishing that Judge Kingsley would hurry up. His woe-begone, frozen face was making the thing worse every minute he stayed there.

"There is mystery here," insisted his wife. "There should be no mystery about business that's honest!"

"You surely can tell us something to comfort us before you go," urged Celene, coming close to me, pleading with her eyes.

But I knew I must stay away from the edges of explanation in her presence; once I got started, I'd be sure to tumble into a mess. I looked over her head.

"We must hurry, Judge!" I warned.

"I know that my husband would never go into any business that isn't honest," declared Mrs. Kingsley, beginning to show temper. She faced me and her eyes glittered. "But he is growing old, and his judgment may not be what it was. There are always men trying to lead others into trouble."

"That's so," I admitted.

"Forgive mother if she says anything harsh! But we are in such a state of mind!"

Well, so was I!

"I have mortgaged the home over my head," cried Mrs. Kingsley. "I have given the money to my husband willingly—but I will not allow thieves to waste it!"

It was about time for me to assert myself a little. The judge was merely working his mouth like a dying fish, and it was plain that he could be no help.

"I don't blame your mother," I told the girl. I took her hands in mine, glad I could carry away the memory of her touch. "Some of those men who have been hanging around the judge are not good men, but I was born in this town and you know me! I'm helping your father in an important matter. I swear I'm telling the truth. And I'll bring him back safe and sound."

I left her before I should be tempted to kiss her right before their eyes, and I took the judge's bag in one hand and boosted him along with a clutch on his arm.

"We simply must catch that train!" I urged.

It was a sad scene for a few moments. I was obliged fairly to tussle with that woman for the possession of the old man. But I ran him out and left the mother sobbing in the daughter's arms, and they were in the doorway when I helped the judge into the wagon.

"Brace up!" I whispered. "Give 'em just a word or two."

"I'm all right," he quavered. "It's only business! It must be attended to. There's nothing to fret about!"

Wasn't, eh?

"Lick up!" I told the driver. "Lay on the braid!"

We went rattling out of Levant behind a galloping horse and I liked the sensation of that haste. We were chasing ten thousand dollars and had less than twenty days for the job.

XVII

MONEY HAS LEGS

We swapped not a word on the way to the railroad. The judge seemed to be settled down into a sort of numb condition, and I was glad of it, for I did not feel like talking. He stood indifferently at one side when I bought tickets, and I was glad of that also. If I was to be purser and general manager of that expedition I did not want to have a joint debate every time I made a move.

My first tickets took us to a junction point. Then I bought to Chicago.

The judge went along silently, showing about as much interest as a mummy in me, or in the scenery or people. I suppose the old fellow was having a terrible struggle with his fears, his thoughts, and his recollection of the manner in which he had parted from his family. I sympathized with him and left him alone. Once in a while I got a side-glance from him which suggested that he had not abandoned his distrust of me. Perhaps he pondered that he was simply submitting to another form of self-destruction and was willing to let it go at that!

I'll confess this: I was taking so much interest in the world about me that I was finding it hard to concentrate my thoughts on the business we had in hand. I had done no railroad-riding to speak of till then. It seemed as unreal as if I were headed for the moon instead of into the far vastness of my native land. When we went rolling through the smoky fringes of Chicago and I saw that there really was a Chicago, my emotion, as I remember it, was astonishment. But I had already found out that a greenhorn could get along pretty well by watching other folks and by asking questions.

So we crowded into the transfer-wagon on Polk Street and were quickly across the city to another railroad station, where I bought tickets for St. Paul. Before the train pulled out I raided a folder-stand and grabbed a sample of everything in the rack.

I went into those folders like a girl diving into the love scenes in a mush novel; I studied as diligently as if I were a prize pupil getting ready for a contest. I had my nose in those papers for hours, till I could close my eyes and see maps and repeat time-tables and names of cities backward.

So I wasn't at a loss when we reached St. Paul. I trotted the judge right along to a window and bought tickets for Spokane. He was mumbling a monotone of growls in my ear while I counted out the money.

"Look here, young man," he said, when we had left the window, "I am not going to be teamed any farther until you tell me exactly where you are going and what you are intending to do."

It rather surprised me to hear him speak; I had sort of forgotten that he could talk.

"Do you pretend that you expect to get money, racing around like this?"

"I'm on the trail of it, Judge Kingsley—your money, you remember. I'm not doing this for my own amusement."

"You seem to be; I've been watching you, sir. You are plainly relishing this junketing about. I go no farther."

"How much money have you in your pocket?" I asked, mildly.

He looked alarmed. "I did not bring money! You took the money for expenses, you said. I depended on that. I have only a few dollars."

"That's good," I told him. "So there's no chance for argument here on this platform." I waved the tickets under his nose. "I reckon you'll have to stick right along with me, sir, wherever I go."

That settled that rebellion!

When I started toward the train he followed. His face was white, his jaws were ridged, and he was furious—but his anger locked his lips. He did not bother me with questions. That night I hid my money inside my berth-pillow; by the way the judge looked at me I knew he would pick my pocket if he got a chance.

On we went across the prairies of the Dakotas—and the journey was not interesting. It was all dun and dull and brown and monotonous in that late March. When the sun shone it only showed up more of the raw country. Every little while we went plunging through a snow-squall which plastered the car windows and speckled the brown of the prairie.

Then the doldrums got me! All at once I found myself bluer than the old judge had been, even in his deepest despondency. This was a reckless escapade, not a sensible man's project! I had bragged and blustered and made promises there in that little tin dipper of a Levant where the horizon was pinched in by Mitchell's Mountain and Tumbledick Hill. I had got by with my bluff in the wood-lot game and had felt as if I were a big man!

But out there!

No longer was it a string of mere names and a smudge of color on paper to make a map! I was looking out, hour by hour, on the reality of the vastness of the great West. As to the men I was hunting for in that wide expanse—those fly-by-nighters, those human skip-bugs—would they not be dodging where impulse took them? Jeff Dawlin was a mere gambler—willing to take a chance on anything. Had he not taken a mere gambler's chance on my finding those men? If I succeeded he would get his pay. If I did not succeed it was only *my* failure—he had invested nothing—he had no interest in my affairs, except a gambler's.

And what could I do to those men if I did find them? They were at home out there—as much at home as they were in the East. The farther out on those prairies I rolled, the farther away from all confidence in myself I seemed to be. Old Ariock Blake used to say that sometimes he felt as if he were "forty miles from water and a hundred miles from land." I felt just as helplessly up in the air as that! I fairly wallowed in sloppy gloom.

To sit there in front of Zebulon Kingsley in my state of mind and courage and look on his gad-awful sourness of visage was too much for my nerves.

I went to get a drink of water and heard men laughing in the smoking-room. If there were men in the world who could laugh I wanted to be with them. So I went in. They were playing poker, and after a time one man had to leave the train and they asked me into the game.

I was desperate enough to grab at anything that would take my mind off my troubles, so I began to play poker. And when a man sits in to play poker with strangers it's a mighty small slice of mind he has left to butter worry with.

I was away from the judge a long time, and he came hunting me up and caught me at the pastime. Perhaps he feared that his two-legged bank had fallen off the train and he had been worrying; but when he saw me with cards in my hand and money spread out he had a lot more to worry about and his face showed it. He let out of him a sort of moan and went away.

"Your father?" asked one of the men, casually. "Sick?"

"Yes," I said. "I mean he's sick, but he's not my father. He is a big Eastern capitalist I'm escorting West on business."

"Put me next—I can offer him some great chances," said another man.

"I'm afraid he is feeling too bad to talk business—and he is very notional in the matter of strangers. Don't say anything to him; leave it to me." I was obliged to say something about the judge and to block them from bothering him, if I could, for I knew he would not be contented with one inspection of me at my devilish and dangerous occupation. "Don't pay any attention to his actions," I advised.

"He's feeling mighty sick—a long ride makes him sort of seasick."

I was glad I had planted something with the men, for the judge kept coming and sticking his head between the curtains and making strange noises. He went at me in good earnest when he had me at table in the dining-car.

"How dare you throw away my money on gamblers?"

"I haven't done so, Judge Kingsley."

"I saw you doing it in that dirty den of smoke and vice."

"You saw me playing cards, I'll admit. I had to do something to keep from going crazy."

"Tossing away my money! Gambling my dollars—"

"Just a moment, sir! That money is a part of my profits and I consider it a common pot for both of us. I know how to play poker. I have added forty-five dollars to it."

"Do you boast that you have been cheating at cards to help *me*?"

Confound him! he could sting a man with that tongue of his!

"A man can play poker without cheating. Just as a man can do business without cheating!"

I looked him in the eye and he shut up. I had found out that I could get along with him better when he didn't talk. After the meal I went back to the game. I felt that every little helped, provided I could hold my own.

I couldn't resist a quiet chuckle inside when I reflected that I was industriously playing cards for the benefit of Judge Zebulon Kingsley, Sunday-school superintendent of Levant.

I had learned long before how to watch out in a card game, and when I felt little scratches on the backs of the cards and observed that one of the players was doing the gouge act with a specially manicured finger-nail, I turned a few tricks of my own. I felt the full humor of the thing when I calmed my conscience with the thought that it was all for the sake of the judge. When he came to the curtains and glared at me I grinned at him.

I cleaned up one hundred and fifteen dollars, at any rate, before we rolled into Spokane—and I had at least five hundred dollars' worth of respite from my bitter misgivings. When I showed that tainted money to the judge with some little pride and impelled by a spirit of devilishness I couldn't control, I thought for a moment that he would bite me.

"I'm not going to associate any longer with a scalawag. I'm not going to be bullyragged by a scoundrel!"

"However, when we're roaming we've got to do as the roamers do," I told him. Deep in me I was ashamed of the disrespect I was showing him by plaguing him in that fashion, but I felt an almost ir-resistible hankering to do it; he had so long lorded it in Levant. Fur-thermore, he did not seem to recognize in any manner my spirit of self-sacrifice; he had not shown to me one flash of whole-hearted gratitude. I may have had a cloudy notion that he needed to have his spirit of Kingsley pride humbled before he would ever consider me as a likely son-in-law. My ideas then and the memories of my ideas now are not very clear, for I was not in any very calm and philosoph-ic mood those days.

After a carriage had snatched us across Spokane and we were landed on the platform of a station from which trains for the Idaho country departed, he did buck in good earnest.

He was a man of plan and method; he had passed his life in rou-tine. That rattle-brained gallop must have offended every instinct in him.

"I'll not get on that train. I'll go no farther. I'll appeal to the po-lice," he raved. "Give me my share of that money and I'll go home."

"I have mixed it all together—gambling money and all! I would not have you traveling on gambling money, Judge." My pertness added to his anger.

"I'll have you arrested, so help me—"

"Hold on before you put the binding word to that oath, Judge Kingsley. If you dare to put me in the jug away out here away from home, I'll yank you in as an embezzler of town money—and I've got an uncle who is first selectman of the town! A little telegraphing will do the trick. Now let's both of us throw away our bombs. The fuses are sizzling! Climb aboard."

He ground his teeth and climbed!

A fine sort of a brindled, cross-eyed hen was I setting to hatch my son-in-law hopes! But a mood of recklessness was sweeping me then.

I did not buy tickets; I paid cash fares to the conductor, naming a station I culled from the folder. I was not sure what the limits of the Potlatch country were; I proposed to drop in with somebody on the train, if I could manage it discreetly, and post myself by asking questions.

I saw no likely subjects in the car where we were riding—the passengers were mostly women—so I slicked up my silk hat, fixed it at a confident and compelling angle, and went out into the smoking-car.

As I have just said, the spirit of recklessness was flaming in me. I did not dare to let it die down. I lashed my courage and my craziness both together. I was bitterly afraid I might drop back into that paralyzing despondency I had felt back there on the Dakota prairies. That meant that I would became a useless quitter. Only by dint of holding myself in that desperate mood where I proposed to let chance have its way with me, and to grab in on anything that offered, would I have gone through so brazenly with the affair on which I soon found myself entering. It was merely another gamble, it seemed to me after I was in it. It was taking my mind off my more private affairs, even as the poker game had distracted my attention.

I marched through to the front of the smoking-car where the train-boy was arranging his little stock, bought a paper, and walked slowly back up the aisle with a glance to right and left at the faces of the men, hoping to get a rise from that "likely subject" I was hunting for.

One man returned my glance with interest.

After I sat down, well up in the car, I looked over the top of the newspaper and saw that the stranger's interest in me continued. The chap had a broad face, liquor-mottled. After a while he unscrewed the top of a flask and sucked in a long drink. Then he worked his shoulders, jerked at the bottom of his waistcoat, wriggled his arms, and displayed other symptoms of a man who is trying to brace up and to pull himself together. At last he derricked himself out of his seat and swayed up the car aisle. He divided glances between my plug-hat and the frock-coat.

"Excuse me, but it's the clothes," said the stranger.

I nodded amiably.

"I wouldn't butt in and speak to you if it wasn't for the clothes."

Once more I was having it impressed on me that a plug-hat and a frock-coat seemed to be good reliable openers in the jack-pot of chance. I reckoned I'd play the hand.

"You're not a parson."

"I'm far from it, sir."

"The farthest from it I know is to be a lawyer. I spotted you for a lawyer. If you are one I want to talk with you."

"I'm a lawyer. Sit down," was my cheerful lie.

The stranger hauled out his flask. "Do you ever indulge?"

"No."

"So much the better. Lawyers ought to keep their brains cool. Seeing that you've got the brains and propose to keep 'em cool, I've got to keep up my nerve—and so I'll take a drink." He sucked at the flask again. "Where do you live?"

"In the East."

"Then you don't know this country and the laws out in this section," said the stranger, showing his disappointment.

"Oh yes, I do; I used to live out here. That's why I happen to be here now. I'm investigating investments for Eastern capital."

My new acquaintance leaned close, so close that his whisky-saturated breath left vapor on my cheeks.

"I have found out something that's big. I thought I could handle it myself. I have started out to handle it myself. But when I saw you I said to myself, 'There's a squire, and he knows law and probably his brains are cooler than mine.' I've got the secret and I've got the grit, but I need law, too—and I ain't sure of all the fine points. I want you to come along with me and stand at my back and hand me the fine points as I need 'em. What do you charge per day for peddling law?"

"I'll have to know what the deal is first."

"Can't tell you."

I was getting a little shaky on the proposition and raised the paper in front of my face and appeared to lose interest in matters of law. After a time the red-faced individual tapped on the paper with his knuckle, as one would tap on a door. I pulled my shield to one side.

"A chap hates to let go of a big thing to a stranger, even if that stranger is a lawyer. I have walked past a dozen law-offices without daring to go in. Perhaps you don't realize what a big thing I've got. Now listen here! Suppose you were a fellow like I am—a prospector—and was digging around the record-books, looking up land titles, mineral grants, and so forth, and got on to a trail that you followed up and found that a new city had been laid out and lots sold off and buildings going up, and all that—all on a location that wasn't legal? Mind you, I ain't naming any place. But it's on a section that land-grabbers got hold of a long time ago. And they were such hungry land-grabbers that they stretched lines to take in everything that was loose around those parts. There was no one to make any holler about it. It was just so much extra land and it didn't look like real money."

"I have so much business of my own that I'm not interested in making guesses at the business of somebody else," I remarked. I was in that thing about as deep as I wanted to be.

"But how do I know anything about you?"

"Honors are even!"

The stranger knuckled his forehead, trying to think.

"I don't want to trig the best thing I ever got hold of in my life because I didn't buy a little law for to grease the runway," he said at last. "I may as well tell you—without giving out names and places—that those land-grabbers hooked in a section that belonged to a soldiers' grant—and that's why no one ever made a holler. There don't seem to be any particular heirs to side-tracked soldiers' grants that have never been thought worth much. No timber, you see; only plain land. But plain land is mighty good property when a railroad takes a notion to build on to it and comes to an end there and a city starts." The client began to show excitement. "They have laid out lots and built and they haven't got straight title. I have found it out."

"That doesn't seem reasonable," I said. "Railroads and men who are building cities do not make such mistakes."

"But they have this time. The same money that grabbed the land has built the railroad. They think they have got it all buttoned up. They didn't want to expose themselves by starting a movement to make their title straight. They reckon they'll be able to bluff it out with money and pull and influence down to Boisé. That will be easier than to chase around and establish title to a soldiers' grant. But, by thunder! they can't stretch or shrink the hide of old earth! There are set points that have got to be measured from and the measurements will tell the story. And re-locations will have to stand—for the law of the United States can't be built over when the holler is made."

I guess I didn't show much interest—I was afraid to show any. I hoped the man would shut up and go away.

"Don't you believe what I am telling you?" he demanded.

"I am merely wondering how it comes about that you know so much more than everybody else about a section of land that has been surveyed for a railroad and a new city."

"My father was a pioneer in this country. One day, after they began to build the railroad, I was in the record-office and happened to remember some of the things he told me about the days when they were grabbing land in these parts. I looked up records, I did measuring, I did some reckoning, and within the last two days I have made sure that I've got the bind on the city of Breed."

In his excitement he spat out the name. Then he promptly began to damn himself. "I never ought to take a drink of liquor," he declared. "But when it came to me that I could run in there and re-locate the best hunk of that land, I reckoned I needed to have my nerve with me, and so I've been bracing my nerve. But the trouble with me is, when my nerve is braced my tongue is loose. Now I suppose I've got to take you in! But I'm dangerous. However, I'll take you in."

I didn't say anything.

"What do you get a day for your best law work?"

"I don't work by the day." I wondered just how lawyers did work.

"Well, then, name your price for standing by me against the sharks they'll bring to try to beat me out. I don't know anything about hiring lawyers."

"I'll take half." I thought that remark would send him hipering away.

My client's face promptly showed the color of a ripe damson. He tried to say something and merely clucked. After a struggle he managed to control his temper and his voice. He leaned forward and clutched my knees. He spoke low, for there were other passengers near, but the rasp in his tones made up for any lack of emphasis.

"My name is Peter Dragg. If you have never heard of me, ask somebody about me. Ask any one between Buffalo Hump and Cœur d'Alene. I've had a lot of practice in doing things to men who have got in my way. What I'll do to you if you don't back up will put red rings around the moon."

"Well, then, consider I'm discharged!"

"From what?"

"From my position as your lawyer."

"I haven't hired you."

"Then suppose you cast off those grappling-hooks," I suggested, for his clutch on my knees hurt my flesh and my feelings. When he did not let go, I reached down slowly, grabbed his hands and began to pry.

Not a man about us noticed what was going on—the newspaper that I had dropped covered our hands. It was tense and silent testing out which was the better man in that clinch. He had a handsome little grip of his own, I'll admit, but I had diver's hooks at the ends of my arms and I bested him.

"I quit!" he growled, after a time. "Leave go!"

"Listen," said I. "I'm not a lawyer."

"You lie!"

"I *did* lie, but not now. You pass on about your business."

"It isn't my own business any longer—I have put you wise to it."

"But I'm forgetting it. I have plenty else on my mind."

"You don't get past with that kind of bluff," he sneered. "You intend to beat me to it, but you can't."

"Look here, I'm coming across square with you," I protested. "You came and jammed a lot of information on to me. I didn't ask for it."

"I say you coaxed it out of me. Now you've got to come in and give me law on a decent lay. If you don't I'll do you!"

"I'm not a *lawyer*."

"I know better! You're tied up with me—you've got to stick to me."

"But I have important matters which will take all my time."

"I'll take your time from now on."

"Look here! I propose to go on and mind my own business!"

"Then you're spoken for! I'll tend to you before you get a chance to butt in on *my* business."

He leaned back in his seat and pushed his coat aside, inviting my attention by a downward glance.

He was packing a gun on each hip.

"I'll give you about ten minutes' recess to think the thing over," he stated. "If you try to leave this train I'll be after you!"

He went down the car, turned over a seat, and faced me.

I was in a fine way to attend to the business of Judge Kingsley and myself! Whether I went into that fellow's scheme or did not go in, it seemed all the same. In these days, according to what I had read, they were very careless about handling firearms in some parts of the West, and it looked to me as if I had dropped into one of those sections. He took another pull from his flask. The uncertainty of what that intoxicated gentleman might feel impelled to do to me next, in the confusion of his fuddlement, made the shivers run up and down my back. In the ten anxious minutes that passed he pulled that flask four times, and every time he reached for it I made a motion to dodge under the seat. The damnable part of it was that nobody in the car was paying the least attention to us.

Then he came tottering up the aisle and lurched into the seat in front of me. Between two hiccups he sandwiched a threatening, "Well?" Plainly, he was well "pickled" and accordingly dangerous. And, on the other hand, there was a hope for me in his condition. I concluded I might as well be shot as scared to death. I couldn't draw a deep breath as long as those guns were on him.

"Well, what say?" he repeated.

"It's all right!" I mumbled. "But let's make it private. Listen! I'll whisper!" I leaned forward, sliding both hands along his legs, getting close to his ear. I laid hands on both weapons and jerked myself back, holding them low at my hips.

"Make one move and I'll bore you," I growled. "Go back to your seat. Go quick!"

He went. I tucked the guns into my own pockets.

We passed the station to which I had paid fares, and I handed more money to the conductor. I decided to stay on the train, hoping that my client would arrive at his home town, whatever it was, and get off. But he kept right on.

After a time he held up a handkerchief by one corner and waggled it, giving me a drunken and moist wink. Evidently he wanted further conference under a flag of truce, and I nodded agreement after I had made sure that the guns could be come at easily. I agreed because I hoped I could make some sensible arrangement to get rid of this particular bottle imp who had landed himself on to my affairs.

"You think you're a slick one, eh?" My hopes fell, for his tone did not suggest compromise. "You'd better turn around and go back. You're heading into the wrong country. Will you go back?"

"What is the country?"

"Thought you said you used to live out this way!"

"I say, what is the country you're speaking of?"

"The Potlatch section," he growled. "You'd better not get as far as that. You know Shan Benson, don't you?"

"Maybe!"

"You know Ive Hacker, Binn Mingo, Cole Wass—all friends of mine!"

"What about it?"

"Pals, I say! All work together. Pull off our plays together."

"Go ahead!"

"Go ahead!" he repeated, grinding his teeth. "We'll go ahead and make a pot roast of you in that plug-hat! Do you think I'm a lone-hander, without friends? Haven't you ever heard of Steer Bingham?"

My heart jumped. That was one of the names Jeff Dawlin had written down for me.

"And I suppose you're holding out Ike Dawlin for a—" I started, giving him a sharp look.

He smacked his hand on his knee. "Yes, Ike Dawlin. That's the kind of friends I've got who will—"

"A fine bunch to be afraid of if they all are as handy by as Ike Dawlin!"

He stared at me.

"Ike Dawlin is East on a gold-brick game, and you know it," I said.

"East—East—you plug-hat stiff! I'll show you whether he's East or not!"

"He is East along with 'Peacock' Pratt."

My cocksureness made him furious.

"By the jumped-up jeesicks, don't you suppose I know when Ike Dawlin lands back in the Potlatch country?"

"I'll have to see him to believe it. Yes, or 'Peacock' Pratt!"

155

"You follow along on my heels and you'll see both of 'em all right! Next you'll claim to be a friend of theirs, eh?"

"Oh no! If I really thought Ike Dawlin was in the Potlatch instead of back East I wouldn't be headed this way. *There's* one special man I wouldn't want to meet up with."

Mr. Dragg bounced up and down on the seat in his rage. I had prodded him as hard as I could in order to make sure that he knew what he was talking about.

"Damn you!" he snorted. "Then you'll get your dose of Ike Dawlin. I won't eat nor sleep till I find him. And he'll burn up the road getting to you. Ike Dawlin, eh? You don't dare to come on!"

"Keep your eye on me. But if you can dig up Ike Dawlin in these parts come around and I'll hand you a present—maybe I'll hand back your guns!"

Mr. Dragg by that time was not a pleasant companion and I got up and went back through the train. He started after me, and then thought better of it. Probably he reflected that he had me either way. If I got frightened and went back he would be well rid of me as a rival in his scheme; if I came on he had Dawlin and the rest—and I surely believed his word about Dawlin's whereabouts. I did not know whether I was mighty glad that my chase was being guided in such handsome manner or was so dreadfully scared by the prospects just ahead of me that I was half minded to jump off the train; my feelings were very much mixed up.

However, when I met the gloomy stare of Zebulon Kingsley I grinned—I couldn't help it. There was a lot of grim humor in the situation.

"Been raking in more dirty money, I suppose," he snarled, mistaking the nature of my smile.

"No, I have turned a better trick, sir. I have just met up with the most obliging chap I have found in a long time. He knows the man who fooled you into buying that gold brick. He is going to find him for us!"

"Bah!" sneered the judge. "This is only a wild, crazy, helter-skelter chase for—"

"I'm telling you the truth, sir! I never saw a man so enthusiastic about a kindness for strangers! He just told me that he wouldn't eat or sleep till he had found that fellow. Why, he is so headlong about the thing that I'm afraid he'll find the chap before we're ready to meet him in proper style!"

"Hump!" sneered the judge, not taking a mite of stock in me.

I walked away and sat down by myself. There was sad truth in

156

what I just told Kingsley. I was not ready to meet Ike Dawlin and "Peacock" Pratt.

XVIII

THE ECCENTRICITIES
OF ROYAL CITY

I'll confess that it took me a little while to screw up my resolution to the point where I could tell myself that I was entirely ready and willing to meet Ike Dawlin in the circle of his associates.

We had left behind us brown fields where wheat grew, and had passed through the Idaho prune-orchards—a brakeman told me they were prune-orchards. We had come into the hill country and the railroad wriggled its way along the foot of the cañon.

I took it for granted that Mr. Dragg proposed to stay with me. Every little while he came and set his nose against the glass of the car's forward door and glared at me. When we stopped at a station I stuck my head out of the window and made sure that he did not leave the train. The two of us were playing a sort of "even Stephen" game—silent peek-a-boo. I kept carefully away from Judge Kingsley, for I did not care to have Dragg report that I was in the company of an elderly man with a roll of chin-whiskers; Mr. Dawlin might recognize the description and take alarm.

The judge sat close to the window, wrapped in his cloak, and scowled up at the cañon's walls closing in behind as the railroad wound along. He looked as if he felt like a man headed for the innermost chambers of tophet, with the doors slamming behind him. As the hills shut in to the north, my feelings were of that sort, anyway!

And so night came!

I had been asking a lot of questions of that obliging brakeman. My folder named a terminus of the road and I had paid to that point, but I learned that the railroad had been stretched along six or eight miles farther down the cañon so as to serve a mushroom town which was the depot for a freshly discovered mining section.

When the train stopped at the old terminus, both Mr. Dragg and I found ourselves very curious in regard to each other; had it not been for the glass in the car door we would have bumped noses when we hurried to make mutual inspection. But he stayed on the train—and so did I.

It was a young, a very young railroad, that last bit. The train crawled like a caterpillar—and that's a good description, for the cars went bumping up slowly over the bulges in the track. Every now and then we got a side-slat which made me think we were going into the creek.

I was too busy worrying about that train to give much thought to what was going to happen to me when I landed in "Royal City" along with Mr. Dragg. Such, I was informed, was the name of the new town. They certainly do pick good names to build up to in the West, just as Seth Dorsey, of Carmel, built a house on to the brass door-knob he found in the road.

Judge Kingsley was not affording me much encouragement; he sat and hung on to the arm of his seat and glared unutterable reproach at me.

I was considerably glad to get off that train.

But as to Royal City! The place tickled me about as much as if it were a cemetery and I were riding in the hearse. It wasn't even as ripe as that railroad.

My first performance was to step into a mud-hole about half-way to my knees, and I wondered how my pearl-gray trousers stood up under that introduction to the town.

I couldn't see Mr. Dragg or anybody else; there in that bowl among the hills the darkness was something a man could eat! We stumbled over upheavals of muddy earth, stepped into more holes, and made our way across the especially treacherous places along single planks which were half submerged in mire. A few lanterns, tied to short posts, were dim beacons to direct new arrivals from the railroad to the heart of the "city." Quite a glare of lights marked the center of business activity. The slope of the hillside was dotted with bits of radiance from uncurtained windows. In that darkness only those points of light hinted at the extent of this new town. The dots were widely scattered, showing that Royal City was ambitiously endeavoring to cover as much ground as possible.

After threading the course marked by the lanterns we came to a stretch of pulpy mud which was bordered by a sidewalk of four planks abreast, evidently the main street of the place. There were buildings of considerable size on both sides of the thoroughfare, but these buildings certainly did put Royal City into the mushroom class. There was not a bit of stone or brick nor a clapboard or shingle in evidence. The buildings were constructed of beams, boards, laths, and tarred paper. They gave me the feeling that I could pop them between my hands like I'd pop a blown-up paper bag.

A lantern, hung on the corner of a building containing a store, lighted up a sign, "Empire Avenue." The sign over the door of the store advertised the place as the "Imperial Emporium." A fairly huge

159

structure with tarred-paper outer walls was indicated by its sign as being the "Imperial Hotel."

There was nothing bashful about the names picked in Royal City!

The windows of the "Imperial Hotel" shed plenty of light upon the sidewalk in front of it, and I caught sight of Dragg hurrying past as if he wished to be swallowed up in the shadows on the other side. The man had reached the street ahead of us, for he had been in the smoking-car at the front of the train.

I took a chance and led Kingsley into the "Imperial Hotel" and registered in a book that a man in shirt-sleeves tossed at me. I wrote "Adam Mann" and "A. Fellow"—the "A" standing for "Another," of course, and that wasn't bad for a quick grab at names. I did not care to advertise the name of Zebulon Kingsley to certain gentlemen in those parts.

From the corner of my eye I saw Dragg peering in at the window when the man in shirt-sleeves led us up-stairs to a room which held two narrow cots and an unpainted washstand with bowl and pitcher. The walls were of tarred paper.

"Is this all you can give us for a room?" asked the judge, as sour as vinegar.

"What do you expect in a new town—marble floors and gold door-knobs? I have taken care of better men than you and they haven't kicked." He turned on me; I had not said anything. "You seem to have a rush of plug-hat to the brain!"

His impudence gave me my chance. Dragg had located me at that hotel and I wondered if I couldn't turn a little trick.

"We'll move on and look for a landlord with better manners," I said.

"Go ahead," advised the man. "A lot of tenderfeet do the same thing and after they've taken a look at the other place they come back here and beg for a room."

On the street I kept in the shadows. After a time we came to another hulk of paper and boards. Its sign read, "Pallace Hotel."

That extravagance in L's might hint at generosity, I pondered, but I had my doubts.

The "Pallace" had a bar-room in the front of the house and there were many customers crowded at it.

"We'd better go back to the other hotel, bad as it is," suggested the judge. "There are drunken men in there and it is a wicked place."

I put up my hand and pushed Kingsley back from the window into the gloom.

"When one has business with wicked men those men must be

followed to a wicked place, sir. I found fault with the other hotel on purpose. I didn't intend to stay there after I knew that a certain man thought he had located me for the night. It's a wise plan to keep wicked men guessing. Stay back here a moment!"

I stepped along and stared in at the window, hiding my face with my forearm.

I saw Dragg at the bar, and Dragg had a man by the arm and was whispering in his ear. Dragg's face expressed huge pleasure. He slapped the man on the back and bought drinks. After they had tossed off the liquor, Dragg resumed his business at the man's ear.

This man stood out in that slouchy group at the bar as a peacock would stand out among pullets in a hen-yard. He was distinctly a loud noise in the matter of wardrobe. He would have made a lurid smear even among the high dressers who top the crests of the Broadway crowds between Forty-second Street and Greeley's statue. He was of that sort of men who are paunchy and seem to be glad of it, because the extra beam affords them opportunity to display variegated waistcoats to better advantage. I realized that I was looking on "Peacock" Pratt.

After a few moments I tiptoed back to Kingsley, and, without speaking, propelled him to a spot where he could get a view of the men at the bar.

"Do you recognize anybody there, sir?"

"There he is—the man who brought the brick—one of the infernal robbers!" stuttered Kingsley. He was fairly beside himself with sudden excitement. His eyes had fallen first on the most conspicuous figure in the room. "He has my money. I want it. I'll—"

But I pushed him back when he started to rush into the hotel. "I guess that man wouldn't hand you his roll if you ran in there and snapped your fingers under his nose, Judge Kingsley. You recognize him, eh? That's enough for now. I'll tell you that your friend, there, is known in this section as 'Peacock' Pratt, and he's a good man for us to stay away from for the present."

"How do you know so much about these men—how do you know where to come to find them—dragging me across the continent?" demanded the old man. His fury at sight of that smug blackleg had to blow off and I was the nearest object.

"I'll have to confess that I didn't know for sure I was to see this man here to-night. I had my line out and a good bait on, but I didn't believe I'd get a bite so soon. You must keep cool, Judge Kingsley—keep cool and out of sight. Simply seeing that man isn't getting your money. We've got considerable of a job ahead of us."

The judge was all of a tremble while we stood there at the edge of the shadow and watched the room and the drinkers. At last, with a flourish of his hand, Pratt gave orders to the bartender to fill all glasses. We heard his hoarse voice above all others. He tossed a bill on the bar and he and Dragg left in company and climbed the stairs leading up from the hotel office.

"Judge Kingsley," I said, "I left the other place and came over here hoping I could sneak close enough to a certain chap to overhear what he proposes to do about a little matter that I suggested to him a few hours ago. I see that he has found somebody to talk to. We've got a handy sort of house for eavesdropping, but I want you to re-member that the other fellow can hear us, too. Come along with me and keep your head. A lot depends!"

The "Pallace" was evidently more of a free and easy tavern than the "Imperial." There was no register on the planks which served for an office desk. The proprietor looked up at us and leisurely lighted his pipe before answering my questions regarding accommodations.

"Four dollars apiece—two in a room. Pay now. Includes break-fast, and there's a cold, stand-up supper out in the dining-room."

"We bought box lunches from the brakeman on the train; we don't want supper," I explained.

"Price just the same. Supper is there, and I ain't to blame if you don't want to eat it," stated the proprietor. "You needn't look for any place to write your names," he added, noting that my eyes seemed to be searching for something that should be on the desk. "We don't keep books. And half the men who come along here can't write, any-way."

I laid the money in his grimy hand and he fished two cards from his vest pocket and scrawled "Brakfust" on each with a lead-pencil.

"Give 'em up to the table-girl in the morning. Now, gents, all the rooms up-stairs are just alike and there ain't no locks on the doors. Go up and help yourselves to any room that ain't being used. I hope you don't snore, either of you. It's apt to start gun-play from them that's trying to get to sleep in other rooms, and the walls we've got up-stairs don't stop bullets. Sleep hearty!"

The judge followed me, muttering his opinions in regard to the hotel methods in Royal City.

"Hush!" I warned. "Tread lightly and keep still. It's a stroke of luck that he lets us pick our own rooms."

Smoky, stinking kerosene-lamps lighted dimly the corridor up-stairs. Unplaned planks formed the floor, and here again were the walls of tarred paper that had enabled Royal City to grow overnight.

Some of the doors that gave upon the corridor were open, and the rooms were dark and apparently untenanted. Light shone from chinks in the walls here and there, in other places, showing that guests were in their rooms.

I tiptoed cautiously along the planks with ear out at each point where light sifted from crannies. Then I grasped the judge by the arm and thrust him into a room. I lighted the tiny lamp and motioned the old man to take a seat in the single chair. I sat on the edge of the bed.

When a drunken man is on a topic that sops up all his interest, he not only iterates, he reiterates. It is hard to pry a wabbly tongue loose from the favorite topic. Intoxication seems to make the subject fresher and more entrancing with each repetition. The fuddled mind gets into a run-around, as men lost in snow or fog keep on traveling and always return to the same place. I had no means of determining how many times Dragg had been over the subject with Mr. Pratt, but that latter gentleman kept snarling out protests that the narrator did not heed. It was a story about how a stranger in a plug-hat—a shark of a lawyer—had hypnotized him, Dragg, on the train and had sucked out of him all his plans, projects, and secrets in regard to the new city of Breed and now proposed to rob said Dragg of all profits and rake-offs, and if a man could do that and get away with it what would be the use in any honest man starting out in the world and turning a trick for himself, as Dragg had proposed to do? So on and on, he gabbled.

"Say, look here, 'Dangerflag' "—and this seemed a good nickname for Dragg's red face—"don't con me any more as the human charlotte russe—the top part of me is hard! There ain't any such thing as hypnotizing a man when he doesn't want to be hypnotized. You were drunk and you slit open your little bundle of playthings for him to look at."

"If I wasn't hypnotized how did he get two guns off me—and I sitting there not able to move hand or foot or wink my eyes?"

"I'd be more inclined to think you begged him to take 'em as a guarantee of friendship, and offered to kiss him in the bargain," sneered Mr. Pratt. "I've seen you drunk, Dragg."

"But I wasn't to the give-my-shirt drunk stage that time," insisted the other. "I was hiring him for a lawyer—driving a sharp trade with him—and then he hypnotized me and cleaned me out. And he's over there in the other hotel—and I'm going to get to him before he puts me out of business. I'll tell you again—"

"For the love of Jehoshaphat *don't* tell me again!" protested Pratt. "I have got it by heart."

"But you haven't told me where Ike Dawlin is. He is the only

163

man that shark is afraid of. He told me so. He reckons that Ike is in the East. That makes him bold to do me dirt. I made believe that I know where Ike is. I tried to scare him, but the bluff didn't go. He is sure that Ike ain't West. You're Ike's regular partner, and you know where he is. I need him. Send for him, and we'll hold that plug-hatted skyootus here till Ike can whirl in and back him off. Blast him! I could have dropped him if this was ten years ago, even if he was from the East and wore a plug-hat—and I could have got away with it—but the law-sharks have been and tied us all up."

"You want to think twice before you try gun-play on a man from the East who comes wearing a plug-hat," advised Pratt. "It's a pretty good sign that he is from the upper shelves back home, and somebody will be slammed hard if he gets hurt. Keep your hands off a plug-hatter, 'Dangerflag.' I don't believe Ike would dip in, even if he were here. He's too comfortable just now to play scarecrow for your private interests. He might, if I asked him to, of course. But I don't see any reason for asking him."

"I'll give you a half share in the Breed job," promised Dragg. "I've told you I would if you can gaff that law shark."

"The Breed job looks like digging into a national bank vault with your thumb-nail," remarked Mr. Pratt, listlessly. "A lot of law and complications! This re-locating business runs against snags always. I don't mind telling you that Ike and I find the old game a lot easier when we want to clean up an easy make. I'll be blamed if we could sell mining stock the last time we went East. What do you know about that? And then we nudged each other and turned around and speared three easy propositions on the good old gold-brick game. You wouldn't believe they'd still fall—but they do it. It's simply a case of go hunt in the odd corners for the right man. They're there, waiting. We peeled five thousand off the back of an old town treasurer—as soft money as we ever pulled. A town treasurer, mind you! We didn't have to go farther into the bush than that! You can't expect us to be very enthusiastic about a claim-jumping proposition just now—with plenty in our pockets. Gimme a match! When you go to fighting a boom city and a railroad crowd, you've got your work cut out for you—and just now I'm feeling a lot like loafing."

Mr. Pratt was very wordy—but he was almighty interesting. Who was hugging the most money—he or Dawlin?

It was plain to me that the town treasurer of Levant was holding in with difficulty. He twisted on his chair and his face was gray with anger and his lips moved. I scowled a warning.

"Well, you can loaf on *my* job all right if you'll grab in," snapped

Dragg, temper in his voice. "I'm not asking you to break your neck. You have got the thing sized up all wrong. I don't expect to own Breed. I'm going to operate on bluff. The Breed boomers and the railroad will come across rather than have the city set back by a hold-up of everything while land titles are being settled. If they'll hand me cash, I'll keep still, surrender my claim, and the new lines can be run and locations filed before anybody wakes up. They'll see the point all right."

"And I reckon that the lawyer you hired on the train sees it all right, too," commented Pratt.

"I don't know what made me blow myself to him after I had dodged lawyers so long," mourned Dragg. "But the way he was dressed made him look so mighty solid and reliable and honest—and his eyes were nice and brown! He got me! I tell you I was hypno-tized. It wasn't just because I had budge in me. But he'll never get to Breed ahead of *me*. That'll be his game, of course."

"Better make your getaway to-night and beat him to it," suggest-ed Pratt.

Dragg was profane in his rejection of this counsel. He stated that Pratt ought to have more sense than to think a project of that order could be settled by a sprinting-match.

"You know what Callas prairie is in March as well as I do," he sputtered. "It would be a gamble which one of us would get across first if it comes to a race through that ' 'dobe' mud. It's all luck whether a stage-coach or a wagon or a cayuse gets through. I'd have gone around and come into Breed from the south, but I thought I'd rather tackle sixteen miles of Callas mud in March than ride six hun-dred miles in jerk-water trains. See here, Pratt, I've got to have time to operate this thing without that shark hanging to me. He's afraid of Ike. I don't know what made him tell me so—but he was so mighty sure that Ike was East that he wanted to shoot his mouth off a little so as to aggravate me, I reckon. He has got to be held here in Royal City till I can pull off my job in Breed. I'm not going to have him racing me around over the country, with a chance of his queering the whole proposition. Now come into this thing and help me out, will you?"

Mr. Pratt yawned audibly and allowed that he would not.

"Then get word to Ike Dawlin for me," pleaded Dragg.

"I don't think he wants to be bothered," drawled Pratt, indiffer-ently. "I won't send for him. That's final!"

I think it would have been hard telling at that moment who was more disappointed, Mr. Dragg or myself!

I had reckoned specially on Mr. Dawlin. He was boss of the gang, according to his brother's telling. In all likelihood he was better thatched with greenbacks than anybody else in the band.

"Furthermore," stated Mr. Pratt, "I can't be bothered with your business. I have some of my own to attend to. I'm going to jump the train to-morrow and get back to some place where it's safe to wear real clothes instead of a diving-suit or overalls."

And so I was going to lose Mr. Pratt!

To be sure, I had not exactly made up my mind what to do with him if he remained in Royal City; but if he were to start on some kind of a hike and we were obliged to chase him we would betray ourselves and our case, sure as fate. Mr. Pratt was certainly no fool, and would know how to cover a trail the moment he suspected that somebody was chasing him. But I could see no reasonable way of keeping an independent gentleman of his nature in that dump of a Royal City.

"I tell you, you are turning down a good lay when you duck out on this Breed—"

"Oh, hell!" snapped Pratt with all kinds of coarse scorn in his tone. "About all this re-locating business amounts to is that you'll either be bored in the back or boarded in jail! I've been studying the game, Dragg." He grew confidential. "That's why I ran down here to this hog-wallow. Ike and I came. These lines here are run by guess and by gad! There's no clear title back of the land. We figured we would jump in."

"You'd have the law behind you," insisted Dragg.

"Sure! And all the citizens who own guns, too! The trouble is, Dragg, they all know they're skating on thin ice. They are looking for something to drop. And so as to be ready to trouble when it comes they have gone to work and got just as mad as they can stick so that they can put a claim-jumper where he belongs in a hurry. None of it for me, Dragg."

The other muttered.

"I tell you, Dragg," insisted Mr. Pratt, "I'd hate to be the man to put my name on to a re-location stake in this place! Law to back you—yes! But I have been testing out their temper! It's dangerous."

"But mobs don't do up men any longer in this part of the country."

"Perhaps I stated it a little strong, Dragg. But a fellow who tries to put anything over on this town, with the people here in their present temper, will get slammed into the pen—and there's no knowing when they'll let him out!"

166

And if that wasn't a straight tip from Mr. Pratt to a poor young chap in desperate need of good counsel and help in a ticklish matter, then I'm no guesser.

"So it's back up the line for me—where I can buy a cocktail and get the smell of this tarred paper out of my clothes!"

But Mr. Pratt's tip was such a helpful one that, providing Judge Kingsley had had a drop of sporting blood in him, I would have posted a little bet that Mr. Pratt would stay on with us for a while. I could see that the judge had made up his mind already that we had lost our Mr. Pratt.

"Sit here and don't make a sound!" I whispered, and I pussy-footed for the door.

He opened his mouth and I shook my fist at him. I hoped I had on a demoniac expression—I tried to put one on.

"Go to the devil, you and Dawlin, too!" barked Dragg. "If I've got to handle this thing single-handed, the make will be all the bigger for me. I'm all done worrying about an Eastern shyster beating me out of the game on my own stamping-ground. If he tries to take the stage in the morning to cross Callas prairie, I'll smash that plug-hat down over his eyes, yank them guns out from under his coat-tail and blow him into the middle of next week. I'll think up a story that will let me out."

Ah, so Mr. Dragg must be considered along with Mr. Pratt and Mr. Dawlin!

I left the room and hurried down-stairs, hoping the stores had not closed. My mind was mighty busy! I found a store that was still open. It was the "Imperial Emporium" and seemed to be well named, for I was able to purchase there a pair of shears, some spirit gum, a carpenter's lead-pencil, and a huge ball of twine. Then I hustled back to Zebulon Kingsley, who sat livid and rigid, listening to the bragging of the man who had robbed him.

I suppose the stuff I tossed on the bed looked mighty queer to him, and I wasn't just sure about all of it myself. But I did not dare to ask any leading questions in Royal City about claim-jumping and I decided to tumble along alone, doing my little best as an amateur.

Zebulon Kingsley was in a sufficiently volcanic state of mind without any more stirring up.

It's a wonder that I ever got away with what I started on next in my case.

Perhaps his settled idea that I had lost my mind assisted in taming him enough so that he submitted in his fear that I might become violent. I look back now and wonder how I ever presumed so greatly even in the emergency that had arisen. But if "Peacock" Pratt were to remain in Royal City and if Ike Dawlin would join him, as I anticipated, the man with me must not be known as Zebulon Kingsley, of Levant, their victim. So I stood in front of Judge Kingsley and issued an ultimatum.

I'll never forget the look on his face!

XIX

THE JOB OF AN ALTRUIST

The judge sat there with his hat and coat on; the looks of that room did not invite anybody to take any comfort in it.

I leaned close to his ear and told him to stand up. Then I began to peel off his wrappings—overcoat, undercoat, and waistcoat. But when I unbuttoned his collar he pushed me away.

"I'll explain it out to you just as soon as I get a chance, sir," I whispered. "But we mustn't make any noise here." I gathered my courage. "I'm going to cut off your beard!" I had to clap my hand over his mouth to keep him quiet. "I can't argue now! If Pratt lays eyes on you he'll stampede. We mustn't let any of that money get away." I pushed him back upon the chair. "Keep down your hands," I urged. "It's got to be done. Your money is at stake—remember that! What's a few whiskers compared with ten thousand dollars!" I was talking just as if I expected to swap hair for money.

I confess I did not have much of a plan worked out just at that moment—but certain notions were coming to me in sections, as one might say. And the principal notion just then was that I must not let a set of whiskers, even if they grew on Judge Kingsley, flag the whole proposition. That was the first thing to look after, now that we were close to the game—change his looks!

He realized as well as I that we couldn't start any riot there on our side of that paper partition. I don't believe any other consideration would have made him give in to me. If I had been getting his neck ready for the ax his looks would not have been more wild. I clipped his beard as carefully as I could with the shears and laid the tufts, as I removed them, in a little heap on the bed.

Mr. Pratt was thoroughly tired of hearing Mr. Dragg repeat himself; we knew that because Mr. Pratt said so with a lot of vigor and stated that he was going to bed in his own room.

Mr. Dragg advised him to be up early and see what happened to the "plug-hatter," providing said "plug-hatter" tried to get away for Breed on the stage.

"I'll do it," promised Mr. Pratt. "I haven't been having much fun down in this hog-wallow, and I need to have my feelings cheered up."

Then he marched away down the corridor, making the whole building creak and shiver.

Mr. Dragg had considerable to say to himself, in the way of re-hearsing his threats, while he was kicking off his shoes and getting ready for bed. Then his mutterings ended in a rasping snore—and he was off!

I was glad he was asleep because that gave me a chance to talk to the judge, keeping my voice down cautiously.

"I have some other plans, sir! I have had to think pretty quick! But the talk between those scamps has given me a rather good idea, I think."

"You seem to be wasting your time on a lot of silly business," muttered the judge. "This is boy's play out of a detective dime novel, sir. We know where one of the robbers is. We can have him arrested. We can put the screws to him and find out where the other renegade is."

"But that means going to law, Judge!"

"We must let the law handle it from now on."

"We can't afford to do that, sir."

"But the law will—"

"The law will grab the crooks, maybe. But your money will be tied up along with 'em. We are strangers out here, Judge Kingsley. And you don't want the notoriety of the thing. Remember, you bought a gold brick!" He winced, but it wasn't on account of the shears! "Just getting those crooks into jail won't help your case," I insisted. "We haven't much time to turn around in. The fifteenth of April isn't very far away. I reckon it's going to mean getting ten thousand dollars in ten days!" He cringed. "The law is too slow and careful for us just now! They pulled that money off by a trick. We must get it back by— Well, I don't know just yet how we'll get it back—but it won't be by any law business."

"Do you intend to rob them and mix me into more trouble?"

"I'd rob 'em in a minute if I could do it and get away," I told him, calmly. And then, because he was getting excited, I advised him to keep his jaw still so that the shears might not slip and cut him.

When the clipping was done I got my little kit out of my bag and got ready to shave him; there was a tin dish full of water in the cor-ner of the room. Of course he was glad to have the stubble I had left under his chin scraped off, and submitted quietly. However, I knew my real tussle with Judge Zebulon Kingsley was just ahead of me.

On the wall there was a little mirror with glass so wavy that it made a human face seem like the physog of a baboon. I pulled it down and showed the judge his countenance with his whiskers off.

"You see it doesn't change your looks very much, after all, Judge.

Your beard was all under your chin instead of on your face." I didn't want to jump him too suddenly.

"If you have changed my looks as much as that glass represents, you've done a good job," he said, dryly. It was the first time I had ever heard anything like humor from him, and I was cheered and made bolder—so bold that I came right out with it!

"I'll have to change your appearance just a bit more, Judge. I know how to do it, for I did it once in my own case."

I uncorked the bottle of gum. But when I started toward him he did not depend on his hands for defense—he put up his foot and pushed me away. I protested.

"There's no use going half-way in this thing, sir. It only means a mustache for you out of your own beard."

"I won't be cockawhooped up in any such style!"

"Are you going to let those men recognize you as the town treasurer of Levant?"

He glared at me and kept his foot up.

"We're after the money—we're after the money!" I urged. "Just think what a little thing this is you're balking on, sir!"

"But you give me no hint as to how you expect to get the money! I'm at the end of my patience. I won't submit to any more foolishness."

"This isn't foolishness, Judge Kingsley! It's a precaution we must take. I've got a plan to keep those men from jumping out on us in the morning—and they'll be sure to see you." I pushed down his foot and I picked up the hair on the bed and looked resolute. "It's got to be done, sir. I'm going to do it!"

He gave in to me as he had in other cases when I became savage, but I realized that fury boiled in him.

I made a mighty good job of it, if I do say so, but he angrily refused to look at himself in the glass. I used all the hair in his beard and gave him a mustache that fairly cut in half that hatchet face of his; his best friend would not have known Judge Kingsley.

I advised him to go to bed and to be sure to sleep on his back so that the mustache would not be disturbed.

I sharpened the carpenter's pencil and hid the ball of twine under my coat, the judge looking at me as savage as a bear.

"Now what?" he growled.

"Do you know anything about the right way of re-locating a claim?" I asked. "Anything in law about it?"

"It's more likely to be described in the thieves' catechism," he snarled. "I have never owned a copy!"

That's all the help I got from *him*!

Well, if I didn't know much about the regular way, I reckoned I could make considerable trouble in town by blundering along with a little way of my own. So I tiptoed down-stairs.

Apparently Royal City had quit the job and gone to sleep. The hotel office was dark, and when I stepped forth into the night there was no glimmer of light anywhere. Even the lanterns that served as the city's municipal lighting-plant in the streets had burned out or had been blown out. It was a case of grope, but I had looked about carefully when I went shopping and had a pretty good memory for locations.

There was a little pile of laths at the corner of the hotel. I had noticed them when I had lurked in the shadows with Judge Kingsley. I picked up a lath and wrote on its side, well up toward one end, "Relocated. Dragg." Then I pushed the lath down into the mud at the corner of the hotel and tied to it the end of the ball of twine. With several laths under my arm I proceeded a few paces, unwinding the twine, and pushed another lath down and knotted my string about its end. Thus I circumnavigated the hotel, sticking down marked laths, knotting about them the twine. In this fashion I calculated I had declared on one Dragg a re-location of the hotel site—or rather made it seem that Dragg had tried on a clumsy trick to jump a land claim.

With footsteps muffled by the mud of Royal City, moving unseen in the night, I was truly a generous cuss. I located nothing for myself. I took the "Imperial Emporium" for Pratt, and re-located the site of the "Imperial Hotel" for Dawlin. Then I stole back into the tavern, taking off my muddy shoes at the door.

That slatted bed and the snores pealing everywhere kept me awake nearly all night, and next morning I was down before anybody else was stirring. In the gray dawn out slouched from an inner room the landlord, yawning, growling, blinking—beginning his day's duties in a distinctly grouchy frame of mind.

"What time does the stage-coach leave for Breed City?" I asked.

"Nobody but a fool would take a stage for Breed this time of year—but a man who comes out here in March and mud-time, wearing a plug-hat, must be a fool. So you'll leave at ha'f pas' six," was the landlord's genial response.

"And what time is breakfast?"

"Time for you to get the stage. What do you want to ask such a cussed fool question as that for? What do you think I'm getting up to do at this hour in the morning?"

Well, I wasn't in any jolly mood myself. "I didn't know but you might be up to sing a hymn to the morning star."

"Say, you're looking for trouble, ain't you?" bawled the landlord. He came from behind the counter. "I'll cave that plug—"

That made me good and mad! "No, I'm looking for cartridges to fit my guns," I stated, pulling both weapons. "I've got only twelve left—six in each chamber."

My friend checked himself so suddenly that he nearly tumbled on his nose.

"Does the store open early?"

"Yes, sir," said the landlord, quite respectfully.

"Then I'll take a stroll up that way. Make my bacon thick and be very careful not to fry the juice out of it."

There's nothing like establishing a bit of a reputation in a strange town, especially if a fellow has planted seeds of trouble; I could see those laths through the window! I had begun to feel rather devilish.

"Yes, sir," said the landlord. "We aim to please."

I glanced at my work of the evening before as I sauntered along the plank walk. The new laths and the white twine showed up well against the black adobe mud.

Sounds of housekeeping, clatter of dishes and of stove-covers indicated that the proprietor of the "Emporium" dwelt over the store. I rattled the door, and at last the man appeared and unlocked it from within. He was surly and slatted the box of cartridges across the counter.

"Is it because you don't care for early customers that you have built a fence of laths and string about your place?" I inquired.

"There ain't no such thing there." But he hurried to the door. He gazed. He ran to the nearest lath and stooped down and read what was written thereon and cracked his fists together and kicked the lath and stamped it into the mud and swore loudly. "Pratt, hey? 'Peacock' Pratt trying one of his gambling bluffs because titles ain't been settled here yet, is he? If a kettle-bellied catfish like Pratt thinks he can jump a city lot on me he's got trouble coming his way on the down grade with the axle greased."

There was much more that the infuriated merchant had to say regarding the general standing of Pratt, but I did not linger. I strolled into the "Imperial Hotel."

"I knew you'd come back—they all do; but you can't do business with me," the landlord informed me before I had opened my mouth. "Once you turn your nose up at my house, then up it stays, as for as I am concerned! Mosey back to your pig-pen!"

"Very well! But I'll drop back here when the new proprietor

takes hold."

"What new proprietor?"

"I suppose it's a man named Dawlin. I note that his name appears as the man who has re-located this property."

The landlord took a jump and a look and saw the laths and string. He ran out of doors. He was an able-bodied man with a large voice, and he outdid his merchant neighbor in volume of cursing. It was plain that he was well acquainted with the mental and moral qualities of Ike Dawlin.

So I went back to my own tavern. Judge Kingsley was waiting in the office, and the landlord was talking to the old man with considerable affability.

"I was telling your friend here that we aim to please! I reckon the girl can fit you out with breakfast now if you're minded to step into the dining-room."

"Thank you—we'll step in, sir. By the way, there seems to be considerable excitement on the street, Mr. Landlord. Men named Dawlin and Pratt, whoever they may be, have re-located business sites occupied by the big store and the other hotel. I just noticed that the same thing has been done to you; you'd better take a look outside."

By the manner in which the owner of the "Pallace" pounded his way to the street it might have been guessed that the consciences of the pioneers of Royal City were not wholly clear as to their several rights of property. But the manner in which they were taking the re-locations showed that they were entirely ready to fight for what they had squatted on.

"By the bald-headed juductionary of Walla Walla County," howled the "Pallace" landlord, "that tinhorn Dragg has sneaked out of my house in the night so as to do me up, has he?"

"Do you say it's Dragg?" bawled the landlord of the "Imperial" from a distance. "It's Dawlin, up here! He's been boozing here in my house under cover for a week, but he wasn't so drunk, so it seems, but he could dodge out last night and try to steal my property away from me."

Say, I swapped one very large look with Zebulon Kingsley, who stood in the hotel door, staring from furious landlord to furious landlord. The old man had heard enough the night before to appreciate the value of that information in regard to Dawlin.

"It's that skunk of a dressed-up Pratt in my case," shouted the owner of the "Emporium" from farther up the street.

"I reckon I can show any man who tries to steal my property that

I'm mighty wide awake mornings if I do sleep nights when honest men ought to be in bed," announced the proprietor of the "Pallace." He rushed into his hotel, and clattered up-stairs.

"When the wheels of a scheme are running in good shape it's best to stay away and keep your fingers out of the gearing," I said to Kingsley. "We'll go in and eat breakfast."

While we ate, loud voices sounded through the thin walls. Men were crowding into the hotel office. Profanity, denunciation, denial, went on and on. The judge fingered his makeshift mustache uneasily every time the bawling of Pratt was heard.

"Better keep your hands off that and drink your coffee from your spoon," I suggested. "They'll never know you!"

When we were ready to leave the dining-room I warned the judge not to look at Pratt. We could hear him thundering away in the office.

Dragg and Pratt were surrounded by men; the landlord of the "Pallace," the proprietor of the "Emporium," and a grim man with a huge revolver in his hand and a deputy sheriff's badge on his breast were right in the front row.

"You can swear, threaten, and deny till your tongues drop off—it don't go for a minute with us," declared the landlord, "for we all know your style and your nerve. Because you have got away with a lot of hold-ups in other places it doesn't go that you can come here and do us in Royal City."

"Do you think we'd be fools enough to go and put our names on—" began Dragg, but he was promptly interrupted by the landlord.

"Whose names would you put on if you were trying to steal land for yourselves? You thought we'd rather settle than fight, that's what! But we're going to fight."

It was my turn—and my chance.

"Excuse me, gentlemen. I'm a stranger to you all—merely a passing tourist. But I feel it's my duty to state that I heard two men discussing a matter of re-locating land last evening. They were in the next room to mine in this hotel. I recognize their voices. Those are the men." I pointed to Dragg and Pratt.

The deputy poked the muzzle of his gun into Dragg's face to make him stop swearing. "Shut up! Everybody can see that this is a real gent, and if he's got evidence we want to hear it."

"The evidence isn't much," I said, meekly, "but I distinctly heard them say that they could clean up a nice pile of money by a re-location scheme. It was to be bluff to a large extent. If that information is worth anything you're welcome to it. I would hate to see the prosperity of a hustling city like this held up for one moment by men trying to bunco honest citizens."

"You listen to me," roared Dragg. "That hellhound there is lying like a—"

The sheriff slapped him across the mouth. "There's no real gent gets insulted by you in Royal City while I'm boss of law and order here."

Outdoors was a noise of clanking of whiffletrees and the "ruck-ling" of wheels. A stage-coach, mud-daubed from tongue to roof-rail, was pulling out of an opposite stable-yard.

"I've got to take that stage," raved Dragg. "The whole of Royal City can't stop me. I've been monkey-doodled by a shark. He's try-ing to get there ahead of me. It wouldn't work here. I'm no fool. I knew it wouldn't work." He yelled so loudly and talked so rapidly that they listened to him. "My scheme was for Breed—and it was a cinch! He's stealing it from me—that doggone, lying plug-hatter found out that I was going to re-locate claims in—"

"Seem to be convicting yourself out of your own mouth!" broke in a citizen.

"I'm going to Breed by this stage. I've got to go!" gasped Dragg, twisting his throat from the sheriff's clutch.

"You're going into the calaboose right now—and Pratt is going there, too, and Dawlin is going as soon as they get his clothes on him," declared the officer. "Grab a-holt, boys, and help me get on the wristers."

"You men will stay here—and Dawlin, too, till we find out what you mean by this trick," said my landlord. "You don't get out of here to run away and file your location claims!"

"Send a man to the county-seat," raged Pratt. "Look at the records. That will prove that we haven't tried anything on here."

"We don't need any advice from you chaps as to what we shall do—whether it's holding you for a showdown or shooting you out of this place when we have your numbers."

I looked at Mr. Pratt. That remark started my think-works into action. I had my men anchored, to be sure, but that wasn't getting me anything in the money line—and without doubt Royal City would cool down pretty quickly and send the men kiting. When they scoot-ed they would go by rail, of course. That meant difficulties, the thought of which had already discouraged me. I needed to keep those chaps in the open—and the wilder the open the better! In the brush, where it was man to man, instead of in the city where law was safe and sane—and almighty slow! I needed to be quick and crazy!

Mr. Pratt was beginning to get his wits back. He was bellowing so wildly when I accused him and Dragg that he did not seem to sense the situation. He turned to me.

"Damn your lying tongue! What do you mean by putting up this job on me?"

"I have simply stated what I overheard!"

"Heard me say that I was going to jump claims? Why, I told Dragg I wouldn't—"

"You told Dragg that you and your partner came down here on purpose to jump claims!"

He was so mad he was nigh black in the face. "Do I know you? Have I ever done dirt to you?"

I shook my head and looked him over with contempt.

From the time I had left Levant I had been at a loss to decide what front I would put on when I met up with those men who had robbed the judge. I had thought all along that my best plan would be to build on my acquaintance with Jeff Dawlin and use his tips which were to put me next to the parties I was after. Then I might be able to come up on their blind side—if they had one—and—

Well, right there I had stopped. What could I do?

Then I had been hooked by that infernal Dragg! In that mess with him I had allowed chance to swing me and our fortunes. After that squabble with Dragg I could not hope to make much of a hit with his associates, eh? Therefore, I was jumping for the other extreme and I proposed to make Mr. Pratt and his friends just as ugly as insults and injury could serve. I felt like a boy thumbing his nose at angry wildcats. And in my desperation I hoped that the wildcats would come chasing me. Chasing me where? Why not to Breed, wherever that might be?

I certainly was sure of Mr. Dragg, according to his threats and his promises. And if I could stick a few more darts into the broad flanks of Mr. Pratt and leave them stinging it was full likely that Mr. Dragg's appeals to that gentleman would have much more effect than they did the night before.

A couple of citizens came dragging in another prisoner, a red-eyed and ferociously angry person, and I knew by Judge Kingsley's expression that the round-up was complete.

"Who says I did it? Who says I—"

"I say so!" I told him. "You held me up and you asked me to buy twine and pencil for you."

"That's right," stated the merchant. "The gent is right."

"Of course it looked all square to me," I said. "I never heard how claim-jumpers worked!" I told them. "I saw he had been drinking and I thought the string-and-pencil notion was only his bee buzzing!"

It was reckless lying, but that crowd was too much excited to bother with mere details.

"Why, you mutt-jawed smokestack, you, I never laid eyes on you in all my life!" raged Dawlin.

"I reckon my memory is a little better than yours, for I wasn't drunk," I reminded him.

The sheriff was obliged to assign two more men to the controlling of Mr. Dawlin, who was a husky chap. He was far too much occupied to pay any attention to the judge, who stood in a corner and goggled at me with plain and sure conviction that I had gone stark, staring crazy.

"I'll bet you a thousand dollars," roared Pratt, "that—"

"You're a cheap tinhorn. You never saw a thousand dollars."

Mr. Pratt jumped up and down and tried to throw off the clutch of the men who were holding him.

I felt perfectly safe in that crowd; I made up my mind to keep prodding till I was sure that Mr. Pratt and his friends had developed enough interest in me so that they would give up all other business till they had settled their grudges.

I patted my breast pocket. "I always carry ten thousand dollars around with me just to keep the draughts off my chest. I find money better than a folded newspaper," I told him.

I had been keeping my eye on the stage-coach for some few minutes. It had hauled up at the post-office. The driver came out with mail-bags and tossed them into the boot.

"Landlord, will you fetch our valises?" I asked.

"Certainly, sir!"

"I've got a few thousand in my own pocket," yelled Pratt.

"So have I!" howled Dawlin.

"And we'll spend it getting to you," they shouted in chorus.

"It won't cost you much to chase *me*," I said, provokingly. "Cheap skates of your sort wouldn't spend much getting to a man you're afraid of."

That taunt, in the ears of those bystanders, made Pratt and his cronies wild in earnest.

"I'm only going as far as Breed," I said. "I've got to stay there for some time on business. When these good folks let you out of jail suppose you run over and call on me!"

"You don't dare to wait there for us!" said Dawlin.

"I'll bet you five thousand I do dare!"

They didn't take me up on that bet. Perhaps I seemed too certain that I meant what I said. I intended to seem certain. I wanted the company of those gentlemen in Breed, no matter what the risks were. And I was mighty glad when Mr. Pratt and Mr. Dawlin had bragged about the thousands they had in their pockets. I looked into the glittering eyes of Pratt and I knew that even in his fury he was taking much comfort in his belief that I was giving him a straight tip about Breed.

"You don't dare to hang up over there till I come," he snarled, testing me out.

"If I am not there, I'll hand over five hundred dollars to start a city reading-room here," I declared. "I call on these gentlemen to bear witness."

"I hope we won't get the reading-room," stated the landlord, standing with the luggage, "for I want to see a few fresh galoots get theirs."

"It's time to test out whether respectable business men can go about in this country without being insulted and bothered by rascals," I observed. "Come over to Breed after Royal City gets done with you." And just to clinch the thing I snapped my fingers under Pratt's nose when I passed him.

I just naturally knew, that moment, that Mr. Pratt had made a binding appointment with me.

The landlord had hailed the stage, which was surging past through the mud. I was obliged to push the judge to start him toward the door; he seemed to be in a daze.

"But we've got to stay here," he croaked in my ear. "They've got the money on 'em. They brag about it. You'll never lay eyes on them again!"

I hurried him along the plank walk toward the coach.

"Don't fret one mite about that part, sir. If we stay here all we can do is stand outside the calaboose and ask 'em to push our money out through the bars. And I'm afraid they are not feeling generous enough just now."

"But the law will keep them—"

"No, it won't, sir, if I'm any judge of the sporting blood out here. Royal City will be mighty curious to find out what happens when Mr. Pratt and his friends arrive in Breed. And they'll come! Don't worry!"

But the judge was a stubborn old customer! He kept holding back.

"Why not settle it with 'em here?"

"Because I have always read that when a good general has a

179

chance to do it, he picks his own battle-ground and throws up his earthworks before the enemy heaves in sight. I have picked Breed, sir! As to the earthworks, I'll do some meditating on the way."

Already my handy Mr. Dragg had given me the germ of a notion, though, of course, he had not meant to make me any presents.

XX

ACROSS CALLAS

There were four or five passengers inside the coach, and I boosted the judge over the wheel and put him in there. There was no one on the box with the driver, and that was not surprising, for I must say he did not have any coaxing way with him: he had his fists full of muddy reins and looked down on me with his mouth screwed around. I asked meekly if I might ride up there with him.

"If you think a plug-hat is going to help me any getting acrost sixteen miles of 'dobe clay, climb up! But do one thing or t'other damn quick!"

It did not look as if I would be making a specially promising friend, but I climbed just the same.

"Good luck!" said the landlord, "and I hope you'll take it all right from us if we let 'em loose after we have shaken 'em down."

"Send 'em along, sir. One at a time or the lot in a bunch!"

That little speech suited the crowd; I got a lot of friendly hand-waves.

A few rods from the last house in Royal City the muddy street swung to the right and sort of sneaked into the river, as if it were ashamed and wanted to wash the dirt off itself. There was no bridge. The horses plunged into the water and dragged the coach across the stream, floundering in depths that barely allowed them footing.

On the other side of the river the road whiplashed in long curves up the cañon's wall to reach the level of Callas prairie; I should say it was all of a thousand feet above the stream.

I offered to the driver comments on the weather, on the road: I offered him a cigar. I had stocked up with smokes with which to curry favor. The driver paid no attention to the comments and snarled his refusal of the cigar. Even with six horses leaping to their work under the lash, our crawl up the muddy slope was snail-like. The wheelers and swing team got the whip, and the driver heaved curses and little rocks at the leaders. He had nearly a peck of pebbles in a canvas bag at his side. When we were over the rim-rock at last and upon the prairie, I looked for more speed. But no such luck! The straining horses, half-way to their knees in the black mud, could barely move the heavy coach.

After a time the driver left what some flatterers might call a road and took to the open prairie, zigzagging here and there to find solid ground. Then intersecting gullies drove him back into the rutted road again. It was adobe mud—black as zip and as sticky as cold molasses. Every little while the driver was obliged to jump down from his seat and poke the clotted mud out between the spokes of the wheels. Otherwise the coach would have been anchored in spite of the best tussles of the horses.

"I should think they'd have to give up trying to run a stage across this prairie in mud-time," I ventured to suggest to the driver when he came climbing back to his seat after a long assault on the mud-clogged wheels with his piece of joist.

"The mails *have* to go, but the damn fools that I haul don't have to," he retorted, sorting his reins between his muddy fingers. "If you ain't satisfied with the way I'm running this thing, mister, you can tuck yourself into that plug-hat of yours and roll across to Breed City. E-e-eyah! Go 'long, you wall-eyed, splint-legged goats of the Bitter Root, you!"

However, I was thankful I was on the outside; the sun warmed me and the warmth was grateful, for the breeze was chilly on that upland. I could see snow on the far-distant peaks to the south. The passengers inside the coach were plainly far from feeling any thankfulness whatsoever. They groaned and growled and complained. I glanced down over the side during one stop for wheel-clearing, and found myself looking into the face of Judge Kingsley, who had stuck his head out of the window. His false mustache gave him the appearance of an angry cat.

"How much more of this devilishness have we got to endure?" he demanded.

"That's easy figuring, sir! Sixteen miles, sixteen hours! It must be the regular running time on this road."

"I don't want no sarcasm from no one," yelped the driver, straightening up and shaking his joist. "And if any gent reckons he can keep passing out his cheap slurs on this trip he'd better come down here now and get his card entitling him to."

I kept my gaze on the distant mountains, but when the driver climbed back to his seat and kept on cussing me out, I reckoned we'd better have a little understanding for the rest of the trip. I closed my fingers around his arm. It was only a pipe-stem arm—and his eyes were of the sad, pale-blue kind. I said very near to his ear:

"Your breakfast seems to be hurting you, son! The stage company pays you to drive and to be respectful to passengers. Mind your tongue after this."

I was trying on a little something. I have found that when you bluster and shout, the blusterer usually recognizes his own kind and blusters back. But the blowhard hasn't any weapon when a man fights with a look and a quiet word.

"It's the mud. It's getting on to my nerves," whined the man after he had driven a short distance.

"Have a smoke—it's good for the nerves," I invited. The driver's hands were full of reins and whip and pebbles, so I set the end of a cigar to the drooping mouth and the driver bit off the end. Then I held a match while he sucked. And when the cigar was going he turned an appreciative grin on me.

"A fellow can't bluff you much, can he, mister?" he remarked. "I didn't have you sized up right at the start-off, I reckon. Why, *I* couldn't lick a prairie-dog with a hammer. But I bluff out most of the dudes who travel with me. I get a lot of innocent enjoyment that way. It helps pass the time for me on this jodiggered trip."

Out of his cocoon of grouchiness he broke as a real butterfly of chatter. I got a lot of good stuff from him, for I learned the name of the mayor of Breed City and what sort of a man he was—a dry-goods merchant who took his job seriously and hollered about the development of the new place and loved those who said a good word for the municipality.

I also learned that many miners and prospectors from the Buffalo Hump region were mudbound, on their annual spree, in Breed—the nearest town where they could find all the rum and roulette they demanded. The driver stated that one or two of his friends who had a little spare cash for speculation made it a practice to loaf around the gambling-places and buy in from busted players any mining shares that a man wanted to realize on in a hurry. Most of these shares thus offered for sale were shares in undeveloped prospects, the driver explained, but one could never tell when a share bought for a cent would be worth a hundred. That driver certainly liked the sound of his voice when he got started! He offered the confidential tip that the Blacksnake Gully region would develop into the howler of the season. It wasn't being talked of much. Nothing real definite was known outside. He guessed they hadn't opened up anything to prove the hunch some folks had—but mining is like betting on the races. A tip floats in from somewhere—if a hunch goes with it, play it, that was his motto. He had been able to pick up a few loose shares.

The mine in which he was most interested had been located for a long time. Shares had been out for some years, scattered around. He couldn't tell for sure who had started the new stories, but he did know that a friend of his—an humble friend called "Dirty-shirt"

Maddox—was up in this section, nosing around, and he reckoned he'd get some inside information when "Dirty-shirt" returned to Breed.

Of course I wasn't surprised. My idea of the West was a place where every man was trying to unload mining stock on an Eastern sucker.

"The particular claim in the Blacksnake that I'm speaking of is 'Her Two Bright Eyes,'" stated the gossiper. "Mebbe that name is a hunch that it's worth looking into," he added, with a cackle to point his little joke.

I thought of a couple of bright eyes, and felt homesick when the driver drawled the name of the mine.

"Two bright eyes are always worth looking into," said I.

That was some ride!

The stage wallowed into Breed City about nightfall. It had tipped over twice on the way, its wheels sinking into "honey-pots" of mud, rolling over slowly like a tired cow lying down to rest. We swearing passengers had been compelled to pry it up with poles borrowed from a rancher. During these waits and during the meal at a sort of half-way house, Judge Kingsley, mud-spattered, scared into conniptions when he thought of what would be coming behind us from Royal City, miserable as a wet cat, and seeing nothing ahead for consolation, muttered to me constantly his familiar taunt that he was being teamed about the country by a lunatic.

I didn't know exactly what to say, and made him still angrier by confessing that he was undoubtedly correct.

We left the coach in front of the hotel that the driver had recommended, and we stepped from the board sidewalk like passengers disembarking from a boat; the mud in the street was fairly a river of mire.

"Even if you don't like the 'Prairie Pride' very well," my new friend had said, "you'll have a lot of fun watching the White Ghost operate. There's only one of his kind in these parts, or anywhere else in the world, so fur's I know. Folks come from a long ways off and stand around the windows and doors of the 'Prairie Pride' hotel and see the White Ghost perform. Oh no, I don't mean that the house is haunted. The White Ghost is the waiter. He's the only waiter they have in the dining-room. He won't have anybody else there. He prides himself on doing it all alone. Says he is the only waiter in the world who can handle fifty guests and four Chinese cooks single-handed and keep everybody happy and busy eating. He's a little cracked in the head, but he's sure a wonder on his feet. A streak of white lightning would have to whistle for him to turn around and come back and meet it."

Now this bit of information, when I listened to it, stirred in me merely a half-determination to go to another hotel, where the waiter did not give a show along with his services.

How often does man slight some odd tools that Fate lays in his way, especially when Fate doesn't draw his attention to them!

The "Prairie Pride" hotel deserved its name in some measure. It had smooth floors, real doors, and walls of plaster. Its big office thronged with guests, whose character was plain enough. There were slick drummers and bearded and booted miners fresh from the hills, down for a bit of a spring whirl, and there were mining engineers and such like.

We were given a room and at the same time we were given a hint that we'd better hurry to supper before the hungry mob cleaned up all the best dishes. Again my clothes coaxed this courtesy!

"Cross the big dining-room and go into the alcove," directed the clerk, after a glance at my hat. "The alcove is for gents. We herd the others in the big room."

I crossed this main hall a few steps in advance of Judge Kingsley. Men were crowded at the tables gobbling food. No fancy feeding! Men jabbed knives into their mouths and grabbed stuff off plates and smacked their lips and snuffled and grunted. I stopped in the alley-way between these tables to look about. I heard a yell of warning and dodged just in time to escape.

Double swinging doors with spring hinges were burst open by the impact of a foot that must have been swung waist high for the kick. Out into the dining-room shot the individual who had kicked.

It was an apparition!

He was more than six feet tall and as slim as a bean-pole. He wore a white cap, a white jacket, a white apron shrouded him to his heels, and he wore white shoes. He had a white, peaked face and his hair was tow-colored. On a huge tray that he held well above his head dishes were heaped high. He went past me and down the alley-way on the dead run, and wisps of steam from his load followed after, trailing on the air.

"You want to keep out of the road in this dining-room when the White Ghost is on the rampage," advised a guest at the table in the alcove where we took seats. "He's going to get somebody some day fine and plenty. A few months ago he got old Babb Coan, who was down here on crutches, nursing a broken leg, and couldn't get out of the way in reason. But the White Ghost was loaded with empty dishes—just empties. Some day he's going to connect when he's loaded with about seventeen hot dinners."

The next moment a white streak came into the alcove, took half a dozen orders and darted back into the kitchen with a tray-load of empty dishes.

"It advertises the hotel," explained the talkative guest. "Men come here from far and near to see the White Ghost razoo up and down the stretch, but for me I'd rather have more waiters and less slamming. It keeps me nervous, and when I'm nervous I can't do justice to my vittles. I'm all the time expecting to see that man that's doomed to get *his* get it. It'll be a mighty mushy affair."

By this time the White Ghost was back and was scaling loaded dishes about the table with a deftness that a quick dealer shows in a poker game.

And I, still blind to what Fate was preparing for my side of the case, was merely irritated by this tophet-te-larrup!

When supper was over we seized an opportunity when the White Ghost was on an outward trip and escaped.

I advised the judge that he'd better take the key and go to our room and get into bed, and the old man accepted that advice with a sigh of thankfulness. He looked bent, weary, and broken as he climbed the stairs; homesick hopelessness showed in every line of his face and in every motion of his body. I did pity him then!

"Poor old father of the girl with the two bright eyes," I said, not realizing that I had spoken aloud.

A man sidled up and prodded me with his thumb.

"I heard what you said to the old gent just now! Where did you get your tip, pard?" he whispered.

I had already forgotten just what the driver had said.

"You needn't let it out if you don't want to. But there's a little inside guessing in these parts and when you hear a man let drop anything about the 'Two Bright Eyes,' it's reckoned he has had a hunch of some kind."

"I wasn't thinking about that mine!"

The man grinned.

"That's right—keep it sly! But see here, pard, I'm going to test you out a little on this thing. I've got a few thousand shares of the old stock. Took it over in a poker game a long time ago—we gamble mining stocks out this way when we're busted. I'm busted now—and they won't take mining stock at the roulette wheel. I'll sell you five hundred shares of 'Bright Eyes' at fifty cents a share."

He peered anxiously into my face as he made the offer. He was plainly trying to get a hint from my expression, but he didn't, of course. I knew nothing about mining stock.

"I don't want it."

"Twenty-five cents a share, then. I want to chase the wheel."

"You're on a wrong lead, my friend."

Just then a man bumped against me as if by accident and promptly apologized. It was the stage-driver.

The owner of the stock scowled and backed into the crowd in the office.

"I was trying to jolt a little hoss sense into you," explained the driver. "Why didn't you buy that stock? I passed the hunch to you to-day."

"I haven't any money for wildcatting in gold-mines," I said.

The man came close to me and spoke low.

"Don't you remember what I said?"

"Yes, but grabbing gold-mine stock from the first comer—say, my friend, do I look as green as that?"

"Hish! Don't rear up, sir! Please don't! But I know that fellow who just tried to sell. He's fresh in from the hills. He doesn't know what's going on—and only a few do know. But I carry men on my stage who talk and don't know I'm overhearing. I say no more! But I hope you'll take the hint. If I could rake and scrape another dollar I'd buy that stock myself. That fellow has some kind of a hunch—but he has been too far away in the hills to know anything special. I guess he just smells it in the air. There isn't much stock in 'Bright Eyes' left loose these days. I have smelt around; I know! That tells a long story, sir. If that fellow hadn't been off in the hills they'd have got his away from him!"

He was urgent and appealing. I couldn't understand this special interest in me and I told him so plainly.

"I don't exactly know, either," he said, unabashed. "I'm thinking it over and I'll tell you when I get it thought out. Maybe it's your style. I have always hoped to be able to wear a suit of clothes like that."

He surveyed me with candid admiration.

My tartness didn't bother him a bit. He beamed on me—and plainly had taken a few drinks. I asked the driver to tell me how I could reach the mayor's store. My friend offered to conduct me. I had resolved to throw up my Breed City earthworks!

"When I take a liking to a gent I don't do nothing by halves," declared my guide when we were on our way. "You come unwrapped enough to-day so that I could see that you've got real whalebone in your stock and silk in your snapper—and that's the kind of a whip for my hand! You come along with me and I'll introduce you to the mayor. Him and me are chums. He ain't none of your stuck-up dudes. I'll tell him you're a special friend of mine. There's nothing like getting in right."

He left me in the back office of a dry-goods store, sitting knees to knees in the tiny room with a fat and placid man who smiled amiably and seemed to be impressed by my dress and demeanor.

He launched out at me in a way that was surely astonishing.

"You are the kind we like to see coming into our new and growing city. We are anxious for a touch of the dignity and refinement of the East here in our midst. We hope we can offer you inducements which will wean you from that East which, though its traditions are glorious and its civilization is sublime, is nevertheless a bit—I may say, without offense, I trust—effete." By the way in which Mayor David Ware smacked his lips over that sentence I was pretty sure that he was quoting from his inaugural address.

"I'm very glad to have you feel that way toward me, coming here a stranger, Mr. Mayor."

"But strangers are certified to a man of insight by the masonry of breeding."

I thanked him again and proceeded to a matter of business connected with my earthworks.

I told him of the plans of one Dragg, as I had gleaned them from accidental association with that individual. I said that Dragg had now attached to himself two blacklegs and undoubtedly would soon arrive in Breed City for the purpose of taking advantage of technicalities in the land law, jumping claims, holding up enterprises, giving Breed City a black eye outside as a municipality where titles were not assured.

"I am not a spy, a tattletale, or a meddler," I said. "But this matter was forced on my attention when I was on my way here, and I did not want to see a hustling mayor and city set back by the schemes of blacklegs. I had heard of your city and of you, and I said to myself, 'If warning will enable such a city to head off a plot and put the plotters where they belong I'll hurry to headquarters with my information.' Those men are now in Royal City and are on their way here."

The mayor's mild eyes bulged and his face showed his dismay.

"It's plain you are a friend who wouldn't take advantage of our situation, sir. That's shown because you are not trying to operate on the tip this crook gave you. So I'm going to be frank with you, as a friend. We were so anxious to get things moving here that we took a lot for granted in the matter of land titles. Those men can make trouble—or at least they could have made trouble if we had not been warned in season by you. You will find that this city can be grateful, Mr. Mann."

I was sticking to my assumed name.

"Will you allow me to make a suggestion?"

"I certainly will. I'll be glad to have your advice."

"Don't undertake to jump on them, officially, the moment they strike town. In order to have your proof you must wait until they try to operate. Have them watched sharply. If you'll give me permission to take a hand in the matter, on the side, I may be able to bluff them out entirely. I reckon it's for the interests of your city to close the thing up without the public knowing there's any doubt about land titles. Of course I don't need to suggest to you that you make a flying start now and straighten out your law and titles so that no other shysters can come along making trouble after we get rid of these gentlemen."

"Watch me in that line," declared the mayor, thumping his breast. "You're right about handling them with gloves, Mr. Mann. I tell you if you can do anything to help us you will stand mighty high with me and with Breed City."

"In handling them I may be able to make it seem like a personal quarrel between them and myself," I suggested. My horizon was growing wider all the time. "They are dangerous men, but I'm not afraid of them."

"But I don't want you to be a martyr."

"I'm not afraid of them, I say. If trouble does happen here and it seems like a personal quarrel, you will understand it all, Mr. Mayor!"

"Certainly, sir!"

"It may seem strange to have a stranger come along like this and offer to meddle in matters where he has no personal interest. Those men are nothing to me, one way or the other. But I'm for fair play always!"

His Honor warmed to this modest candor.

"The city is behind you in whatever you may do in this thing, sir. As mayor I say it. You'll be backed to the limit. And if you get hurt while you are trying to do a bit of a trick for us I'll be scissored if I don't toss law and order up for a little while and organize a lynching party and head it in person."

"If I thought it would come to that I wouldn't meddle in the affair! The only reason I am offering my services is because I hope to be able to keep Breed City from suffering a setback."

"Hand 'em any jolt that's coming to 'em in the name of Breed City and its mayor." His Honor clapped his hand on my shoulder.

I trudged back to the hotel in a fairly comfortable frame of mind. It's a lucky general who can choose his own battle-field, get to it well ahead of the enemy, throw up earthworks and set a big gun or two in position. So, I said to myself, "Let 'em come!"

XXI

THE SKIRMISH-LINE

I was a bit embarrassed next morning and wondered if I hadn't overdone the thing.

I was waited on by a delegation in the crowded office of the Pride of the Prairie. Mayor David Ware headed the delegation and he introduced the half-dozen amiable gentlemen as leading members of the Breed City Chamber of Commerce. Then the mayor pulled me aside.

"You understand that I haven't whispered a word of what you and I talked about last night. That's to be buried between you and me, but there's nothing like getting in sneck with the big boys of this town. It'll be easier for me when I have to back you up—if it comes to that. I've explained that you're a friend of mine who is West looking for prospects."

"I'm glad to be called a friend of yours—and you told the truth about my business here, Mr. Mayor. We start on a square basis."

With the mayor, followed by the delegation, I was escorted through the main street of Breed City. It seemed to afford the gentlemen honest gratification to follow along behind that plug-hat which I had freshly slicked that morning to the best of my ability. I was lunched at the Chamber of Commerce—a half-finished board structure; I was dined by the mayor at his own home; and I returned to the hotel in the evening to find the judge marooned in the office.

"Please don't scowl at me that way," I pleaded, humbly. "I was afraid you might drop something that would queer the whole proposition. You are looking over your shoulder as if you expected damnation to jump on to your back!"

"Damnation *is* getting ready to jump on to our backs," growled the old man. "One of 'em has got here. He came in on the stage to-night."

"Which one?"

"The scalawag with the flashy clothes."

I had looked for pretty quick action, but "Peacock" Pratt had got away sooner than I expected he would. He had been free with his money, I concluded.

I got down-stairs early the next morning, the judge tagging at my heels. But we were not ahead of Mr. Pratt. I didn't have to hunt for him. He stood out like Jeff Dawlin's "Peruvian cockatoo" would have shown up in a flock of crows. He followed us into the dining-room, and sat down at the same table and scowled at me with ugly fire in his little eyes above their pouches of flesh. Then he leaned across the table. We three were alone when the White Ghost had frisked away after our breakfasts.

"I'm here," said he.

"Glad to see you," said I.

"You're a dog-eyed liar! You didn't expect to see me. You thought you had the three of us canned till you could put something across here. It cost me a hundred dollars to grease the lock of that calaboose—and at that I couldn't bring out the other two. But they're coming! You needn't worry any about that part, you punk-faced Piute!"

He dove a pudgy hand down into the breast pocket of his vest. He got his wallet out and banged it down on the table. It was a big wallet and it was well stuffed. Judge Kingsley gulped when he saw it and his hands worked like claws.

"That's how I'm heeled, and I'll spend it getting you, if it comes to that."

He packed the big wallet back into his waistcoat, galloped down his eggs and bacon, and then banged away from the table. He called back over his shoulder, "I wish I hadn't promised that I'd anchor you and wait for 'em, else I'd take you now and settle my breakfast with you."

"Did you see that money?" gasped the old man. "It's my money. There's a lot of it. My God! I could hardly keep my hands off it."

"It was a nice, fat wallet, Judge Kingsley. I was glad to see it. It all looks very encouraging."

"Encouraging! Where do you see any encouragement? Two more men coming full of blood and thunder to join him—and you waiting here for them to get along! Anybody with sense would have that man grabbed by the police on my charges. I thought you told me you were bringing me out here to make the complaint? Now you're only dilly-dallying. A man with sense, I say—"

"Oh, I suppose a man with sense would never have come out here, at all."

When I went out and stood on the hotel porch, my friend, the stage-driver, lounged up.

"I've knocked off for a few days' vacation," he explained, sociably. "Sent another man for my trip to Royal City yesterday. Mud was getting on to my nerves. You noticed how it was the day you rode out with me. I came nigh queering myself with you and spoiling one of the pleasantest friendships I ever made. I was mighty glad to see the mayor and the boys taking you around town yesterday."

I told him I appreciated his regard.

"There's another reason why I'm taking a few days off," he confided. "I've got a hunch that 'Dirty-shirt' Maddox is about due here. And in the case of 'Dirty-shirt' Maddox it's needful to be Johnny-on-the-spot when he hits town if I'm going to cash in on that grubstake I advanced to him."

I handed him a cigar and he explained further.

"If I ain't here to clap a hand over his mouth to keep the rum out and the news in, he'll get four slugs of language-loosener into him inside of four minutes after striking the first board-walk here and then it's brakes off, all into a gallop and hell-bent up the rise for that 'Bright Eyes' stock."

At a little distance the stylish Mr. Pratt paced his way to and fro on the porch, scowling.

"Please take a good look at that fellow," said I.

"I'll do the best I can without smoked glasses," promised the stage-driver. "I've seen him before—and I never liked his style."

"His name is Pratt," I said loud enough to be heard by that gentleman. "He seems to hold some kind of a grudge against me and is following me."

Mr. Pratt let loose a torrent of cuss words that were fully as highly colored as his rig-out. He wound up by saying, "And, by the gods! I'll get you, and get you fine and plenty!"

"Will you remember that?" I asked the stage-driver.

I realized that I had pretty good control of the movements of Mr. Pratt. For where I did go there went Pratt also. Mr. Pratt was decidedly on his job. Personal hatred moved him and he felt responsible, I suppose, for the interests of the two who were frothing behind the bars of the calaboose in Royal City. He seemed to be guarding me as a morsel for a feast of revenge at which three proposed to sit down. He stuck to me so closely that my big idea became firm enough to handle. The ability to move Pratt, and to be near Pratt at all times by Pratt's own wish, suggested my scheme to me.

When the noon hour was at hand I led the way back to the hotel, and, while I tidied myself for dinner, taking my turn at the mirror in the wash-room, I had an eye for the manœuvers of Pratt, who, was preening and pluming himself, whisking all the stains of outdoors from his clothing, settling his gorgeous tie, smoothing his waistcoat across his expansive front.

I couldn't help it—I grinned in his face when I thought of my plan.

I buttoned my frock-coat carefully and started for the dining-room—and Pratt followed close. On the threshold I cast a look within. The White Ghost was not there—he was in eclipse in the kitchen for the moment. I started through the big hall, toward the alcove, crossing near the swing doors. Pratt came on behind me and I halted and turned suddenly on him.

"I'm going to shoot you now and here in your tracks, where every one can look on," I told him in a whisper—and I kept smiling. "Don't you dare to pull a gun. I've got you covered. I've got a revolver in that hand that's wrapped in the tail of this coat and it's aimed at you. I'm going to shoot you while I'm smiling. There are men looking at me. I'll say that the gun went off by accident. It'll be believed, because we look so sociable. Hold on! Don't you open that mouth to yell. You've got one chance for your life. I'll tell you now—because I'll never have a better chance to get you proper if you don't take that chance I offer."

I was stalling then, for I had not intended to talk so long. Mr. Pratt stood there as stiff as a wooden man.

He took a peep at my hand that was muffled in the skirt of my frock-coat. The unseen terrifies most. His face grew pale. He continued to stare at the hidden thing that threatened his life. My smile broadened—it was no assumed smile—for my wrapped hand was empty.

"You may think that this is a queer place for me to hold you up."

If Pratt could have known what was passing in my mind at that moment he would have agreed. It would also have astonished Mr. Pratt to know that I was just then raking my soul in order to think of something to say next.

There seemed to be an infernally long time between the shuttlings of the White Ghost. I felt like an anarchist who has timed a bomb and finds his fuse faulty. Where in the devil's name was the fool? I knew I couldn't stand there and tell a serial story to Pratt. A dangerous light was coming into the man's eyes. Astonishment had held him for the first few moments, then fear had chained him, but finally panic was plainly breaking out in him, and in such cases a victim will run amuck regardless of consequences. I felt that Pratt was getting ready to howl and leap upon me.

Where was the White Ghost?

The thought came to me that this prolonged absence hinted at one consolation—the White Ghost must be filling many orders—his tray would be heaped to the ceiling.

"Your one chance is—" said I—and then it happened!

Without warning, the swing doors burst open under the kick of the White Ghost's foot and forth from the cavern of the kitchen came the thunderbolt. I had been waiting and listening, and was ready to dodge. The petrified Pratt never stirred a stump. There was a howl from warning diners—a collision, a terrific crash, and Pratt went down under the avalanche. The White Ghost was lugging one of the biggest loads of his career. There were deep plates in which hot and greasy soup swam, there were gravied meats, nappies of vegetables, tea, coffee, macaroni, pies, and puddings. Mr. Pratt was buried under dishes, hot soup blinded his eyes, macaroni was twined around his neck, pies plastered his shirt bosom, and his clothes sopped up liquids. He might have been labeled, "A dinner in eruption!" The White Ghost dove across him and skated along the floor on his nose.

I hurried to Pratt and began to paw the dishes from off him. And having planned just what I was going to do and knowing just where to seek for what I wanted, I dove a hand into Pratt's inside vest pocket and yanked out the big wallet. Other men ran to help me, there was excitement, and in that mess of provisions which I was cuffing to right and left my handling of the wallet was noticed by no one. I was kneeling close beside Pratt and I shoved the wallet between my knees, and when I arose, slid it up under my coat.

There were plenty of volunteers whose hands were out to boost Mr. Pratt to his feet. His eyes were tightly shut and he was bellowing about the pain the soup was giving him. I took the rôle of close friend and ordered the rescuers to carry Mr. Pratt to the wash-room and give him first aid with towels and water. I followed close upon their heels and elbowed Kingsley along with the push. The judge had stood at some distance during our drama. I pulled his hand up under my coat and set it on the wallet.

"Grab it!" I whispered. "Slip it under your coat; get out of this hotel and around the corner. Jam the money into your stocking and stamp the wallet down into the mud. Be careful no one sees you."

It was on me that Pratt's eyes first opened—for I was swabbing the soup out of those eyes with the end of a wet towel.

But when he opened his mouth I swabbed the towel across his lips. Other volunteers were working away at the clothing of the victim with wet towels.

All at once Pratt began to slap himself on the breast and howl. His laments in regard to the hot soup in his eyes had been loud, but in contrast to his latest outburst they were as the voice of the chickadee compared with the roar of the lion. After he had beat upon his breast, he dove a greasy hand into his vest pocket. It was empty. His eyes goggled, his face grew purple, he shouted, he swore, and he raved.

He had been done, trimmed, robbed, frisked, touched—so were his bellowings! He searched his soul for synonyms with which to announce to the world that his wallet had been stolen. And then he accused me—accused me with violence and profanity.

"Just one moment, sir," I suggested, taking advantage of a moment when Mr. Pratt was choking. "You are sure those dishes didn't crack your skull a bit and injure your brain?"

After spitting many oaths, Mr. Pratt declared that he was all right and knew what he was talking about.

"You'll have to back that up," I told him. "Fifty men were looking at you when that thing happened. I have not been out of the sight of those men since. You say it was a large wallet." I unbuttoned my coat and slung it open. "Will any gentleman present kindly search me?"

"He is going too far when he shoots off his mouth about a gent like you," declared somebody in the crowd. "We all saw you. All you did was try to help the son of a gun out of his mess—and that's all the thanks you get!"

"Mistakes are bound to occur. I demand that some gentleman make sure that I have no wallet on my person. My own money is in a roll in my trousers pocket."

A solid-looking citizen searched me, uttering apologies.

"There ain't any wallet on this gent, and you'd better ask his pardon for remarks offered," suggested the citizen.

But Pratt only raved the louder.

"I'd like to say a word just here," called a voice. The stage-driver pushed to the front. "You all know me and you know I ain't any liar. This gent, here, is a friend of mine and he wouldn't do dirt to anybody. He's a friend of our mayor, too." He put his hand affectionately on my shoulder. "But as for that other cuss, there, in the piebald clothes, I heard him make threats not longer ago than this morning that he would get my friend, and get him good and plenty."

"Maybe you think I arranged to have those seventeen dinners dumped over me so as to make the plot a good one, you pie-eyed horse-walloper, you," squealed Pratt, beginning to "weave" in his fury like a caged bear.

"I wouldn't wonder a mite," replied the driver, coolly. "When I heard you threatening to get my friend you was mad enough to try on 'most anything."

"He got my money, I tell you. I felt him at my pocket while I was trying to get my senses back. Blast you all for infernal fools, I've been robbed right before your eyes and you're backing up the thief."

There was a stir at the door and the crowd glanced that way and parted respectfully. It was His Honor the Mayor of Breed City. He stood for a few moments and listened to the language Pratt addressed to me. Then he broke in with authority:

"Just a moment, citizens! There's a lot about this affair, here, that I know and cannot tell. As for that knave who accuses Mr. Mann, I declare on my honor that he is a dangerous foe to this city. He has come here to try to ruin it if his scheme works."

Mr. Pratt at this point managed to control the amazement that was provoked by the appearance of this new champion.

"I tell you, Mayor," he shouted, "you've got the wrong dope about me. Dragg tried to get me into the scheme, but I—"

"You are convicting yourself right now out of your own mouth," broke in the mayor. He marched up to Pratt, finger upraised: "You are as dangerous here as a dynamite bomb. I'll allow you thirty minutes to get out of town. Get to those other two knaves and warn them that they'll be lynched if they show up here—and I'll lead the lynching-bee."

There was immediate change in Mr. Pratt's demeanor and the mayor and the bystanders listened to him. The fat face was lined with grief, and tears ran down his cheeks and mingled with the grub stains.

"I'm not lying about that wallet, gents. I've lost my bundle. It has been stolen. That's a nice word to go out about Breed City—that a visitor to town loses his wad and the mayor backs up the man who stole it!"

"Silence!" said the mayor.

"Then I'll simply say that I've lost my money—and how about law and order in a city that will let a man be trimmed in that style? Hold on one minute, Mr. Mayor! It isn't merely a case of my own money! If it was, I'd shut up now and pass on. But I had along with mine the money of a good friend who trusted me with his roll. I left him in the calaboose back on the trail and I brought out his money to take care of it for him, for he was afraid they'd get to him for it. That's God's truth, Mayor."

In a crowd there may be found champions for the under dog—even when a mayor has turned down his thumb. I heard murmurs. One voice suggested that the matter better be looked into—the good name of Breed City demanded it.

"I haven't much to say in this business, even though this man has accused me," I said in the silence that followed. "Now that you are on the subject of your money, Mr. Pratt, and are making such a squeal in regard to the loss of it, will you allow me to ask you how much of it was money you stole in the East—especially from Zebulon Kingsley of Levant?"

If I had struck "Peacock" Pratt between the eyes the effect could not have been more noticeable. Most of those men who were present had been trained to gauge the human expression in that region of plain and mountain where life itself sometimes depends on the ability to judge between bluff and resolve. His fat cheeks flushed and then they grew pale. That a stranger in the Far West should be able to cast in his teeth one of his latest exploits staggered him. He tried to speak and couldn't.

"Pratt, you have twenty-two more minutes left of that half hour," stated the mayor, after silence had continued for some moments.

"I suppose that has to go for to-day," said Pratt. "But it doesn't go for to-morrow—nor for next day if my friends and I can get back here, Mr. Mayor! Lynch or no lynch!"

He buttoned his waistcoat, took a mournful look at himself in the wash-room mirror, and headed for a livery-stable which a sarcastic bystander recommended. I knew that threat to come back wasn't mere talk. Mr. Pratt had good reason to take the risks!

I took my first chance and escaped from the populace of Breed City to hunt up Kingsley in the little room in the hotel.

"How much?" I was all a-tremble.

"A little over six thousand dollars. Mostly five-hundred-dollar bills. Part of it is tied up in a separate package and marked with Dawlin's name." The judge was not very enthusiastic.

I sat down on the edge of the bed.

"In order to be on the right side and make allowance for delays here and there, we ought to leave here to-morrow, Judge Kingsley. And even then we'd be having hours for a margin—not days. I felt pretty good when I heard Pratt say that he had Dawlin's money along. I figured there would be more between the two of 'em."

"Then it's all over, is it? We're beaten, eh?"

"What do *you* think?"

"I think we are."

"Well, sir," I said, "you and I have always seemed to make more progress when I take the opposite side in an argument. I predict that we shall win out. Please hand over that money."

"The money is mine—it was stolen from me. You're too reckless to handle money. We're beaten, I tell you. I'll send that money home to my wife and daughter. It's something for them to live on. I'll kill myself out here."

Judge Kingsley put both hands over his breast pocket. He was hysterical. There was no reasoning with him and so I rose from the bed, walked across the room, and snapped a finger under his nose. Zebulon Kingsley must not have money in his pocket—in that case I could not handle him or trust him to stay with me!

"Give—me—that—money!"

He stared and groaned and obeyed.

I divided the bills into packets, tucked them into my various pockets, and walked out of the room.

"This money needs an airing," I informed the judge. "I'll take it outdoors and give it one. It has been in some mighty bad company."

XXII

MONEY ON THE GALLOP

In most circumstances, being padded with bills to the amount of six thousand dollars would be comfortably warming. But in my case the possession of that sum only provoked irritation.

I had set out to save Zebulon Kingsley's name and the peace of mind of his family. The sum I had replevined by my scheme of justice fell far short of what we needed—and there was the promise I had given Dodovah Vose, as well.

From the hotel porch I saw my friend, the stage-driver, humping it toward me.

"I have tripped, tied, and gagged him. That was the only thing to do! He got here and he got two drinks into himself before I could slip the bridle on him. In another two minutes he would have been jumping clear off'n the ground, head and tail up, snorting out everything he knows. But I got to him—and I've laid him away, tied and gagged. Go to it, Mr. Mann, go to it, I tell you!"

He certainly was some excited!

"Are you talking about a man or a cayuse?" I asked.

"I'm talking about 'Dirty-shirt'—he's just in from Blacksnake Gully ahead of the news. Say, they've struck a brown crumble in 'Bright Eyes' with gold set into the mush like raisins in a drunken cook's pudding. You're a sport and a friend of mine. I'm letting you in. Come along!"

He ran away a little distance and whirled and halted with the eager air of a dog who is inviting his master to follow. I'll bet if he had had long ears he would have perked them; if he had had a tail he would have wagged it.

"You're a sport—and I know it. Come along," he called.

Along the street came loafing the individual who had tried to sell me "Bright Eyes" stock, and he heard that call.

"You're barking up the wrong tree, pard," he advised the driver. "He's no sport. I have tried him out. He won't take a chance. I gave him a chance on some mining shares."

"What shares?" asked the stage-driver.

"'Bright Eyes' in the Blacksnake."

My friend was truly a good actor. He showed no interest.

"Shift the name to 'blacked eyes.' Yes, and both of 'em closed at that. No good!"

"I tell you there's something in the air," insisted the other. "It's a fair gamble at twenty-five cents a share." He pulled out some papers and walked up to me.

"You look like ready money, my friend. I'd rather play the wheel just now than be rich. I'm tied in here by the mud and it's getting on to my nerves. Take ten thousand at twenty-five cents. I'll close out to you."

"Hold on!" sang out the driver, and he managed to smuggle a wink to me while he was tugging papers out of his pocket on his way back to join us. "If you're in the market for 'Bright Eyes,' Eastern fellow, here's ten thousand shares for fifteen cents a share."

"Don't you come butting in on my market," protested the prospector, elbowing the driver away. "I got to this gent first."

"Those shares have been used all over this section for counters in poker games when beans got too expensive," sneered the driver.

The prospector pulled out more papers.

"If you'll take twenty thousand at ten cents a share I'll pass 'em over. I was intending to hold on to ten thousand shares for a gamble. I tell you there's something, somehow, somewhere, that says the hunch is out for 'Bright Eyes.' But I'll let go for ten cents if you'll take the bunch."

"That's no better offer than you made the other night," I stated.

"I was pretty drunk, then, and I didn't mean to make it. I'm daffy now, I reckon, or I wouldn't be doing it over again."

I stood there and looked them over and for the first time I gave a little real thought to that gold-mine proposition. Up to then the matter had been mere sound, shooting into one ear and out the other. I had been having plenty to think about in other lines.

It struck me that I was being played for a sucker by a couple of mighty awkward amateurs. Talk about Zebulon Kingsley buying a gold brick! That affair had been well buttered by some slick operators. What those two chaps were trying on me was truly raw work. That stage-driver—I didn't even know his name—must have a healthy hate for me hidden deep down in him! I have cuffed a dog in my life and had him show more affection afterward, but I couldn't believe that such treatment helped to mellow love in a human being. I knew it wouldn't improve my own disposition any. In my thoughts I had some excuse for the two. They had probably been brought up to believe that the ordinary Easterner who had not already bought some punk gold-mine stock was thriftily saving up to buy some.

"There's one of 'em born every minute," I remarked to the stage-driver, "but I didn't know I looked so much like one. Run away, the two of you, and fan yourselves with that stock; that's the only way you'll ever raise any wind with it."

"You ain't talking to me, are you—to me—Wash Flye?" inquired the driver.

"I am, if that's your name—and it seems to fit you! But you are not fly enough!"

He opened eyes and mouth on me, stepped back a few feet, and visibly swelled.

"Well, my-y-y Ga-a-awd!" he wailed. "If that ain't using the butt end of the whip on a willing friend, may I never sort webbin's again!"

There was truly something sincere in his distress. But that sudden warming-up to me on the prairie after I had manhandled him, his unaccountable friendliness, his jacking his job for a few days in order to dog me about Breed City—the whole thing was too openly a plant.

"You're a good actor. No wonder you're in the stage business, Flye," was my poor joke.

He looked at me for a full minute. Then he turned on the other man.

"It's you, you horn-gilled wump, with your sashay prices and your drunken man's gab—it's you that has put me in wrong with a friend," he squealed. "He thinks I'm like you are! He thinks I'm in mush with you on a brace! I'll show him and you!" He leaped forward and began to kick the prospector with fury. The latter was a big and rather torpid person and he seemed to be in a sort of daze at first, and stood still while Mr. Flye kicked him. Then he turned and knocked Mr. Flye down; he picked him up and knocked him down again.

It struck me that if this were acting between friends it was getting too realistic. The driver's face was bloody and he lay where he fell, his eyes closed.

I jumped between and pushed the prospector away. He struck at me and I was obliged to hit him a clip or two before he would hold off. We had a fairly good audience, but fisticuffs in Breed, when the muddy season made tempers short, seemed to stir only mild interest.

I found Mr. Flye on his knees and "weaving" weakly when I turned to him.

"I ain't no fighter—I don't pretend to be a fighter," he mumbled. "I knew he was going to lick me if I kicked him. But that's all right! There's three teeth loose an my eyes are bunging! I can feel 'em! But it's all right. If anybody thinks it was a scuffle between friends, he'd better take another think. I've took a licking to show some folks that there's such a thing as being mistook in a man."

I hadn't straightened out my opinions, exactly, but I felt sudden pity and new respect for Mr. Flye, and some emotion even deeper. I helped him to his feet and took him into the wash-room of the hotel and fixed him up as best I could.

"I don't blame you so very much," he kept assuring me, whimpering through his bruised and bleeding lips. "It probably hasn't seemed natural to you—it hasn't seemed natural to me. This world is full of crooks and I s'pose you've been up against a lot of 'em. I done one crooked thing myself once when I kept water away from a drove of hogs for two days and then let 'em drink all they could hold just before I sold 'em live weight to a Snake River drover. But that drover had stolen two cayuses off'n my uncle! I didn't know what I could do to show you, sir! Probably what I have done don't show you. But I've done my best. It was all I could think of on short notice. I'll let a dozen men beat me up if you will only understand that I ain't going to do you or try to do you!"

That spirit of humble martyrdom was certainly getting to me!

"Look here, Mr. Flye," I blurted, "I don't understand at all. Why in blazes are you taking all this interest in me?"

He gazed at me out of those pathetic, pale-blue eyes around which blue-black circles were settling. It was a lingering and wistful gaze.

"I don't know, sir. It came over me all of a sudden. It ain't often I take to anybody. It just came over me. You're a real gent—you knowed just how to handle me. You know how to handle me now! Ain't you doing the friendly act, hey?"

We were alone in the wash-room; the guests of the hotel flocked there only at meal-time.

"You can see how it looked to me—a stranger here—you two fellows chasing me up!"

"I don't blame you, sir," he agreed, meekly. "This world is full of crooks."

"I have some money with me. It isn't mine. I need more in a hurry—it's to save a man's name—save him from death, perhaps!" I couldn't hold in. "It's to save his daughter, too. I'm in love with her. I have been for years! It's all I can think about. When you spoke of 'Bright Eyes' I felt—I felt—" I stopped and gulped.

"I reckon I know how you feel," stated Mr. Flye, wagging that mussed-up head of his. "I know a girl. There's hardly a minute when I ain't thinking about her. She hasn't paid no attention to me, but I'm going to her after I make my clean-up on 'Bright Eyes'! It makes 'em think twice when there's money. I ain't much—"

"I'm desperate—I'm half crazy, Flye! This mine! Are you fooling me?"

He straightened and put his hand up like a man taking the oath.

"I wanted you to get in because I liked you, sir. That's why I was after you. But now that you say that you need money I'm begging and imploring you! If money will do what you say it will in your case, I say 'fore God you'll commit a sin if you don't grab in! I know it! It has come. 'Dirty-shirt' don't know how to lie about it. The strike has been made. Take my word," he pleaded.

"I'll do it," I told him. "I believe you're trying to do an honest turn for me." I put out my hand and he took it.

"Thank the Lord!" he said, and there was a lot of manliness about Mr. Wash Flye at that moment. "That licking was a good investment." He said it devoutly.

"But will that fellow sell now?"

"Can you handle his twenty thousand shares at ten cents—two thousand dollars?"

"Yes."

"When I offered at fifteen I was trying to beat him down to ten. Don't give a cent more. Go show him the money and say you're willing to be buncoed once in your life. And hurry—for the love of Sancho, hurry!"

I found the prospector watching a roulette game with the sour gaze of a busted gambler. He went into the corner with me when I jerked invitation with my chin.

"I've changed my mind," he growled, when I mentioned the stock. "And I wouldn't do business with you anyway, you—"

I unfolded four five-hundred-dollar bills. He stopped his declaration as suddenly as if I had pinched his throat.

"Money is money, I suppose," said he, "though your shin-plasters from the East are poor things alongside the good hard coin."

"There's the bank across the street, and they'll give you the good hard coin, mister."

He pulled out his packet and I verified the amount of the certificates.

I went to the bank in his company, for he seemed to be bothered with the notion that those five-hundred-dollar bills needed me as introducer and sponsor. Then he hot-footed out, weighted with the coin. In spite of myself and of my fresh faith in Mr. Flye, my heart sank considerably when I saw that money take legs. The cashier was one of the amiable citizens I had met in the delegation from the

Chamber of Commerce.

"Making a little investment?" he inquired, sociably.

"A foolish one, I am afraid. But an Easterner who hasn't had a flier in a gold-mine at least once in his life gets to feeling lonesome after a time. That chap has been chasing me around with stock and a story and I have tossed a little spare change to him."

The cashier peered through the wicket and beamed with new respect on a man who could speak of two thousand dollars as spare change.

"There are mines—and then there are mines," he suggested.

I thought I might as well try my new tune over on this piano.

"It's a proposition called 'Two Bright Eyes.'" I tried to seem indifferent, but my heart was only about an inch below my larynx and I could hardly get the words out.

I thought he would never speak. He scratched his nose and fiddled with his ear. I wanted to reach in and shake him so that he would say something, even if he would only say that I had been nicely fooled.

"The property had rather a promising outlook at one time, sir. It was located by good prospectors and afterward two or three other claims were taken in. The section is first-rate!"

Not wildly encouraging.

"But the stock hasn't been much thought of in these parts—it has been footballed around a lot. Still"—he twisted his mustache and waited a few moments—"well, I'll tell you this confidentially, if I wasn't a bank man—and you know we have to move in grooves of caution—if I could afford to do a little gambling I think I would have picked up a small bunch of this loose stock. I got a flicker of a hint from a mining engineer who banks here. Nothing definite—they can't talk much. But I know they have been running new leads. The first development wasn't very scientific, I understand."

"Does a— When they make a real strike—do prices run up pretty sudden?" I managed to ask.

He smiled. "I see you have never been in a mining town when a bonanza toots. Everybody goes crazy. They'll climb over one another to buy stock. Those who can't buy stock go racing off to see what they can grab in the way of adjacent claims. Very exciting, sir! Wish we might show you a circus of that kind while you're in town."

When I went out on the street I found Mr. Flye waiting around the corner.

"You traded?" he gasped. "He's over there tossing away twenty-dollar gold pieces!"

"I've got twenty thousand shares," I said, dolefully.

"Then I'm going to let 'Dirty-shirt' loose. He'll swell up and bust if I don't get that gag out of his mouth."

"But will anybody believe what he says?"

Honestly, a gold-mine was unreal to me! I had Eastern prejudices.

"You go over there and stand on the hotel porch, sir! You'll see almighty sudden how news hits a mining town. 'Dirty-shirt' Maddox don't have to bring a gold-mine down into Breed City. He's the bulletin, that's all. There'll be proof enough pretty close on his heels."

So I went over on the tavern porch. Five minutes later I realized that the bulletin was loose. "It" came whooping around a corner of the street.

Mr. Maddox's nickname fitted him perfectly; in fact, he was well caked with mud from head to feet. Plainly he had not stopped to pick dry spots in his rush down to Breed City. He was shaking a canvas bag over his head with one hand and in the other flourished a handful of stock certificates.

"Who's got 'Bright Eyes'? They've hit it! High grade from Buffalo Hump clear through the earth to Chiny! Whoosh! Who wants 'Bright Eyes'? Here's some that's loose. And there ain't much loose, gents! They have been picking it up! High grade and pockets full of crumble!"

He shook the canvas bag and opened it when men went crowding about him.

"There he is," announced Mr. Flye at my side.

"Looks the part," said I.

"After I had rubbed his jaws where the gag had hurt," confided my friend, "he told me that he ain't more 'n four jumps ahead of the boss engineer expert who is bringing out the samples for the report. All you've got to do now, sir, is to sit tight and look wise!"

My unlucky friend could not do much looking for his part; his eyes were swelled so badly that he could hardly open them.

"Look here, Mr. Flye," I said, with a lot of repentance, "I must seem to you like pretty much of a crab. I don't know how—"

"It was only a gold-mine guess, according to your notion, sir. And I know how an Easterner must feel on that point. But when I have a friend and make up my mind to let him in on a good thing I propose to do it, even if I have to apologize to him afterward for being almighty fresh. So I—"

"Don't make me feel worse than I am feeling!"

There was a crowd in the street of Breed City by that time and

Mr. Maddox, in the center of it, had worked himself into a frenzy of excitement and was offering "Bright Eyes" stock at a million dollars a share.

"Don't mind that kind of talk," advised Mr. Flye. "He's half tight, and his coco ain't just right when he gets to talking in a crowd, but you needn't worry but what his news is all right. And you can see for yourself!"

Several men were larruping cayuses up the street, bags dangling from saddle-bows.

"It's the first of the rush for the 'Bright Eyes' section. Some of the critters out this way can beat firemen for quick action," stated Mr. Flye. Perhaps to emphasize the fact that now at last he felt himself on a footing of intimate friendship with me, he plucked a cigar from my vest pocket and lighted up.

"I see you don't smoke—you probably chaw," he suggested, and he handed his plug to me.

When I state here that I promptly took the plug, whittled off a chunk, palmed it, and put some gum into my mouth, the depth of my esteem for Mr. Flye may be understood. I would rather have chewed that tobacco than hurt his feelings by refusing a friendly offer.

While we stood there a bearded man rode down the street, mud-covered.

"And there's the man who will back me up!" squealed Maddox. "There comes the boss engineer! He knows what's under cover in 'Bright Eyes'!"

But the bearded man rode right through the crowd without answering questions. He alighted in front of the bank and went in, tugging something in his hand.

As a new, and somewhat heavy, stockholder in "Bright Eyes" gold-mine, I reckoned I'd try to get a little information from that engineer—I was quite sure that an Eastern capitalist who wore a silk hat and had a friend in the bank cashier might expect a little more attention than a street bystander. Therefore, with a word to my friend Flye I went over to find out the best or the worst.

XXIII

THE CLEAN-UP

After I had been properly indorsed by the cashier, the mining engineer gave me some mighty comforting information, though I did not understand the technical lingo very well. He was conservative; he was not at all excited. We could hear "Dirty-shirt" still orating.

"Of course that old lunatic doesn't know what he is talking about," said the engineer. "There are always some of that sort to run and rant and stir up excitement and start poor fools off on a wild-goose chase."

He opened a sack and showed me ore and hunks of crumbly rock which looked like nothing special. I had rather expected to see nuggets. He explained that the crumbly stuff was high grade, very much so, but there were only scattered pockets of it in the "Bright Eyes" claim.

"The parties who first located the property," said he, "simply skun in for what pockets they were able to open. They had to pack all their ore out on cayuses and ship it to Tacoma, and there was no profit to speak of unless the ore yielded over a couple hundred dollars a ton. So when they quit the job the mine seemed to be played out." Then he went on with his technical talk, and about all I could do was to blink and try to look wise.

"You can be sure that Newell knows what he is talking about," put in the cashier.

I wished *I* knew. I wanted to butt in with some excited questions. But I did understand that the men who had gathered up most of the stock of the mine were going to build a smelter and tackle the thing right end to. There was plenty of ore and the mine would pay after development was the comforting information handed to me at last.

"I beg your pardon, but how many shares went to you in that trade you just made?" asked the cashier. "That is, if you're willing to tell me."

"Twenty thousand—I bought for ten cents a share."

The engineer showed some surprise.

"I didn't think so much of the loose stuff was corralled in one bunch; we thought what we hadn't picked up was scattered so wide that we wouldn't bother to chase it," said he. "How did you happen to grab in on it?"

I didn't propose to betray Mr. Flye.

"Oh, it was just a gamble! A fellow kept following around after me and I bought to get rid of him."

"Some of you Eastern Yankees certainly can use your noses for something else than to talk through," said the engineer.

"If I smelled a bargain when I bought that stock I reckon it must have been hunch instead of knowledge."

"Well, stick by and stand your assessment for the smelter and you won't be sorry."

Mayor Ware and several other citizens came hurrying to have the news about "Bright Eyes" confirmed. I stood at one side for a time, listening and meditating. When the cashier told them of my lucky strike they were immensely tickled.

"But you know we Easterners never can make a gold-mine seem real," I said.

"In most cases where they're selling stock East the mines are not real. But you're West, now, and you happened in on the ground floor," said the mayor. "I am sorry I'm not there, too."

"You can be," I promptly informed him. "I'm called back home. I'm in a hurry. I don't know anything about gold-mines. I can't come back here to watch my interests. You folks out here know all about mines and values. My stock is for sale if anybody wants it."

"What price?" inquired the mayor. "We might make up a little syndicate. How much do you want for the stock?"

"I don't know," I confessed, frankly. "It's all new to me. I paid ten cents a share. When a gold-mine gets to paying I don't know how much it pays."

"It depends on the mine," stated the engineer. "We can do a pretty good job of guessing in our line, but we can't see all that's underground."

I pulled out my packet of stock.

"I tell you honestly, gentlemen, this seems more or less like a joke to me—and that being the case I'll sell cheap."

"It's really worth par—or it will be in time, I'm sure," stated the mayor, in honest fashion. "We are under great obligations to you, sir, and we don't want to take advantage of you in any way."

"And I feel just that same way toward you, gentlemen," I assured them. "There's always the element of a gamble in mining, I'm sure, though I don't know much about it. Your mine may flush out. I'll tell you what I'll do—I'll meet you on a half-way basis. I'll sell for half price—fifty cents on a dollar. Give me ten thousand dollars and you own the stock."

They stepped aside and conferred.

"I suppose you'll be in town a few days longer!" suggested the mayor.

"If I can get out of here to-night I want to go. I must go."

"I say again, we don't want to take any advantage of you because you are obliged to leave in such a hurry. This may seem like queer talk for business men to make—to offer more than the price asked. But we want you to remember that Breed City is grateful."

"I really am not asking for any presents," I said. That was jackass talk for me to make, and I knew it. Lord! we needed all the money we could scrape. But a funny sort of pride swelled up in me. I did not propose to be outdone in politeness. Never had I had municipal attentions shown to my humble self before I came to Breed City. They did not realize all the good it had done me.

"This is no proposition of that sort," declared the mayor. "But we are so sure of Newell's judgment that we know we shall make big profits on this stock. There are six of us. We propose to give you twelve thousand dollars, so that the amount you have paid for the stock will be handed back to you also. We'd like you to remember that Breed City was good to you to the extent of ten thousand dollars' clear profit."

That asinine pride was prompting me to split the difference with them. But across the street just then I saw the old judge peering about, evidently in a panic of anxiety about me because I had been gone so long with all that money. Another memory jogged me at that moment. I was morally bound to hand Dodovah Vose some profit on his five hundred dollars. Haggling with those enthusiastic citizens of Breed would be feeding my fool pride at the expense of two old men.

"It's a trade, gentlemen, with all thanks to you!"

The mayor was president of the bank and I guess the rest were directors; at any rate, the cashier, in about two minutes, was asking me how I would have it!

I asked for currency—big bills. I had a boyish, eager hankering to lug the money to the judge, to show it to him, to have him count it and feel it and know that he could face the taxpayers of Levant, even if he couldn't satisfy all his creditors. But even bankruptcy, thought I, was not State prison; my uncle would be cheated out of that part of his revenge. My fingers itched and my eyes shone while the cashier nipped at the corners of the bills with moistened fingers. He wrapped them in oiled paper and I sunk them carefully in my clothes!

I made as quick a getaway as politeness would allow.

As I remember it, I left a promise to come back to Breed City and settle down!

210

I caught Judge Kingsley by the arm and hurried him down-street and into the hotel.

The moment we were in our room I began jamming packages of money into his hands.

"Look at it! Feel of it! Smell of it!" I urged. "Judge, I took that money out for an airing and the junket did it lots of good."

He did not understand. I guess he thought I'd merely brought back the Pratt money and had gone crazy while I was out with it.

"There's sixteen thousand dollars net and clear for us, Judge Kingsley! And I reckon we won't hunt up Pratt and hand back the thousand that's over and above his graft from you. He's a liberal gentleman and he ought to be willing to pay our expenses and for wear and tear. Now pack up, sir!" I clapped him on the shoulder. "I can't stop to tell you the story just yet. We'll have it on the way."

I began to pack the money into my pockets.

He was deathly white when he stood up, and he staggered against the wall.

"On the way! Where?" he gasped.

"Home!" I yelled, frolicking like a kid. "Home! And we've got to make a race of it if we propose to head Uncle Deck Sidney under the wire!"

Ten minutes later I was humping around Breed City, trying to find out how I could escape.

The stage would not leave till morning. And that stage would take us to Royal City, and blamed if I wanted to go through Royal City.

I knew well enough, of course, that Pratt had gone back there to join his forces and I could hardly hope that the forces were still in jail.

On the new railroad which they were building into Breed only a part of the rails were down; they were not operating trains. There was no stage line through the broken country in that direction.

The Buffalo Hump Mountains were to the south, and to the east the Bitter Root range raised obstructions.

I had the judge on my back, as it were! I couldn't wake him up to what had happened. He appeared to be mentally and physically prostrated. I myself could have straddled a cayuse and ducked out over the broken country. But the judge must have wheels under him when he was moved.

There seemed to be nothing to do but smash through Royal City, taking our chances. I felt that the citizens there wouldn't see us murdered on the street, but they could not be expected to go along and guard us all the way home. We would have three buzzards on our trail!

I was mighty blue and some scared. I was wishing that I had not indulged that boyish impulse to carry my fortune in cash. I would be fine picking for those devils! Take that money and the judge, and I had two pretty heavy parcels to tug back to the East. The dusk came down on Breed before I had braced myself to make the jump.

No, there was nothing else to it!

In order to catch trains and get to Levant ahead of calamity we must go back across Callas prairie and run the gantlet of those three renegades.

I reckoned, according to my reading of time-tables, that the delay of even one day would bump our plans fatally.

I had tried several times to find my friend, Mr. Wash Flye. I could not get on to his track to save me. I wanted to talk transportation with him, for I was having a mighty discouraging time of it with other parties.

There were four public stables in the city, so I found by asking questions. I tackled the biggest one first. The man in the office was pulling off hip rubber boots with the air of one who has decided to call it a day. He laughed at me when I asked for a horse.

"My friend, every cayuse in my stable that can walk, trot, run, or limp, or even can cover ground by rolling over is hired and has either started for the Blacksnake country where that new strike has been reported or else is going to start with a crazy prospector astraddle."

I offered to buy a horse. He said that he didn't do business that way—he had made promises and would keep them. I asked for names of men who had hired. I found a few and was turned down; they all expected to get rich if they could get to Blacksnake.

I had no better luck at the other stables.

"Bright Eyes" had made me—it looked as if it would also unmake me.

"You can't get it out of their heads in these parts that first-comers on a strike ain't due to be millionaires," one man told me. "If you want a hoss you'll have to carpenter together a new one. The only plugs in the city that haven't been nailed by prospectors are the spare hosses of the stage company—and old Uncle Sam's mail keeps his thumb down hard on those critters."

Then I set my teeth and began to hunt all the harder for my friend. I got word of him here and there, but an eel in a dock quicksand could not have been more of a dodger. It was evident that success had put springs into the legs and restlessness into the heart of this new Rockebilt of Breed City. The trail grew hot—the trail grew cold. It was late in the evening when I finally caught up with him. He was clinking glasses with "Dirty-shirt" Maddox, in a bar down an alley where Breed City's virtuous ten-o'clock-closing ordinance could be more safely violated.

"I've done a lot for you, Mr. Mann, but I can't monkey-doodle with the company hosses at this time o' year when the mud makes double work."

I drew him outdoors and down the alley.

"I'm meddling with another man's secret, my friend, but I'm going to tell you enough so that you'll understand what this means to a poor old man and—and—a girl back East."

At the end of my little speech the driver put out his wiry hand.

"If I didn't do my part to help you in this job I'd have to own up to having a spavined soul and a heart with wind-puffs on it. Go out on the road a half-mile and I'll overtake you with two hosses and a mud-cart."

Before midnight our little expedition was well started across the prairie. The cart was light, the crisp air of the March night had stiffened the mud, and we naturally made better time than with the heavy outfit on which we had ridden to Breed. But it was coming dawn when we got to the rim-rock at the edge of Callas prairie. Far below we could see the chimneys of Royal City, smoking signals of early breakfasts.

During the crawl across the adobe ruts, under the stars, I had canvassed with the driver the dangers that the presence of Pratt and his associate rogues in Royal City held for two gentlemen who desired to mind their own business and travel East by that first train.

"Friends," stated the driver, after he had meditated on the matter, "I'm going to drop you right here at the rim-rock. Just over there is the mouth of a path that leads down the side of the cañon by a short cut—it's all of two miles further by the stage-road where you came up. The path doesn't hit the stage-road anywhere. Now if those chaps are out and free they'll be likely to ram across to Breed by this morning's stage. They want to see you mighty quick and what the mayor said to Pratt won't keep 'em away, I reckon! They must be reckless by now! If you walk down the path you'll dodge 'em—for the stage is just about leaving. There's an old feller named Mike at the foot of the path who'll ferry you. You'll have a full hour to make the train. Take your time down the path so that you'll be sure to miss the stage. If your men are still in Royal City—well, if I was in your place I'd take that train, anyway, even if I had to leave orders behind for the funerals and the flowers."

We climbed down and I started to shove my hand into my pocket. Mr. Flye threw his own hand to his hip.

"Hands up!" he called, sharply. "Don't you pull that wallet! When a chap gets rich overnight like I've done he's pretty touchy when a friend tries to put favor on a cash basis. I didn't think you'd do it, Mr. Mann."

Tears came into my eyes.

"Hands up? Yes, hands up to you, good friend, both hands up to you." I grabbed the driver's fists in mine. "But I don't understand just why you have done for me all that you've done."

"I reckon I smelled out by sort of instinct that you was giving up your time, doing good for somebody else," he said, with a nod at the old man. "At any rate, I took to you, and when I take to a man it's all of a sudden and, doggone it, I just can't help giving him my shirt—if it's clean enough and he'll take it."

He did not trust himself to stay any longer. He lashed his horses, they spun around, dragging the cart on two wheels, and away the outfit went across the prairie. And I never saw Wash Flye any more!

I hurried along and the old man found the path too steep for conversation. In places we were obliged to cling to sloping trees and ease our way down.

We were startled, after a time, by the sudden appearance of a man in the path ahead. He was climbing with haste.

"Well, gents," he called, cheerily, "you're lucky to be coming down instead of going up! But I figured that I'd rather climb up to the prairie and get a little sunshine than stay down there and wait for that stage to get fixed up."

He stopped and wiped his forehead.

"What about the stage?" I asked. I had a vision of Dragg, Dawlin, and Pratt waiting at the river below or lounging in the streets of Royal City, blocking our path of retreat.

"Oh, a tire came off, this side of the river, and the rim caved in. They've propped up the old caboose and sent the wheel back to the blacksmith shop. You ought to have heard those other three passengers swear! I've had a chance to hear it scientific and fancy in my time—but those gents certainly could hang on the trimmings. Especially the fat one!"

"Fat one!"

"Yep! Fat man with a suit of clothes that would put the eyesight of a Potlatch coyote on the blink. They seem to be in a hurry. They're walking up this hill, too. Other two men are derricking fat man up the trail. Are making some talk about getting a rancher to set 'em across Callas."

He clapped on his hat and climbed along.

When he had disappeared, I led the way into the pine growth at the side of the trail, and we found a boulder which would shield the two of us.

Dragg came first—carrying out the suggestion of his name by pulling at Mr. Pratt with all his strength, and Dawlin pushed behind. They halted often and one of their stops was just below our boulder. They were telling each other what they proposed to do to a certain person who wore a plug-hat.

I drew the two guns from my hip pockets, and I could feel the arm of the judge trembling against my ribs.

But after the three went puffing on and were out of sight, I dropped the weapons into a crevice between the ledges.

"No, I did not intend to shoot them," I said, when Judge Kingsley asked questions.

We hurried on down the trail.

"But why did you throw away those two good revolvers?" asked the thrifty old chap.

"I only borrowed them. It might seem like stealing if I should carry them back East. I don't like to have stolen property on my person," I said.

I did not feel like talking. That remark stopped further conversation.

We caught the train!

XXIV

HOW SWEET IS
THE HOME-COMING, EH?

My thoughts, fears, and hopes went galloping ahead of me during that ride back to the East. It's all a blur of memory—wheat-fields, prune-orchards, tunnels, peaks, and prairies—and the old judge sitting beside me, twisting his withered hands and cracking his bony knuckles. It was lucky for both of us that the slow part of the journey was at the start and that we had the clang of mile-a-minute rails under us for the last two days of that race.

Well, I thought the thing over. It was just as much of a nightmare then as it seems now when I am setting it down.

How I ever undertook such a crack-brained, daredevil trip and hoped for anything tangible to fall to me by such a hundred-to-one shot I do not understand even now in clear fashion, in spite of the explanation I have given. We talk about hunches in this world! If I had not obeyed some sort of suggestion I certainly would not have chased those renegades. Only by meeting with them did I stand a chance of recovering any money. That thought and my hankering to use my knowledge about the Pratt-Dawlin gang influenced me a great deal, I suppose. And the conviction that I couldn't spin a thread by seeking money in any other way pried me out of Levant, of course.

I have had something to say about the force of circumstances!

I was not in a comfortable frame of mind at all, though the money in my pockets should have given me considerable cheer. I did not feel that it was my money—any of it. I could not make it seem like anything which belonged to me or convince myself that I had earned it. I had picked a man's pocket for part of it and the rest of that cash had been jammed into my pockets, so to speak. I was not wasting a moment's time on questioning the morality of any of my acts. I reckoned if Pratt's wallet had been stuffed with twice as much I would have kept the plunder.

I pondered on another point.

Judge Kingsley, provided we got under the wire in season, could be saved from the charge of criminality, but he still had his salvation, financially, to work out. He needed all that money and more—and I had volunteered—had forced myself on him as combination courier

216

and savior. It was all settled in my mind, according to my private code, that I must hand over the cash.

I will state right here that the decision I had come to about the money did not rasp my feelings in the slightest. I had read quite a few story-books in my time. If there was ever a case in the whole realm of fact and fiction where the final scene would show loving daughter clasped in adoring lover's arms, and a benignant father raising his hands over them with "Bless-you-my-children" sentiment, my affair seemed to be triumphantly of that sort. Time, effort, and money—it all belonged in the family!

My heart glowed and my eyes grew moist and it was a wonder that I did not blurt out the whole thing to the judge—I felt so sure of him!

However, he had his own troubles to take up his mind pretty completely, I realized. There was no telling what might be happening back home, with my uncle Deck stirring things. If I had timed trains right, and nothing tipped upside down, we didn't have much more than twenty-four hours' leeway in Levant ahead of that town meeting. I asked the judge if the town notes were very widely scattered, and he told me they were not. He had picked special parties whom he could depend on to keep their mouths shut about their investment, and he felt pretty sure that they would hand back the notes in exchange for cash and would ask no questions and would keep still in the future.

"But I can't eat and I can't sleep," he mourned, "not till I have those papers in my two hands!" He put up his crooked claws and worked them. "In my hands—all torn into ribbons—and then into the fire! Just think of it!" He croaked the words and shivered. "Papers—only a few papers! Scattered around town. Papers with ink-marks! Yet they can send me to State prison!"

No, that wasn't the time to talk with the judge about being his partner or his son-in-law. But I did talk more with him in regard to plans for gathering in the notes quietly and quickly the moment we struck town. I had him give me the names so that I could help plan the campaign.

I knew them, of course. They were old tight-wads of farmers in the back districts who would endure lighted candles at their feet for a long time before they would leak any information about their money matters; there were some widows and old maids who didn't know anything about money matters, anyway. The judge had picked well, I had to admit to myself. But there was a lot to do, a mighty short time to do it in, and it had got to be done with the delicate touch a bashful chap would use in picking a rose-leaf off a sleeping schoolmarm's cheek.

Therefore, this was my suggestion to the judge: we'd slip off the train a station below Levant Corners, hire a hitch, and make our rounds of the town's creditors in the back-lots before we showed up in Levant village.

That's what we did.

The lengthened days of April gave us a full hour and a half of sunlight for our ride on our quest. Out of cupboards and long wallets and rosewood boxes the farmers and the old maids dutifully produced their town notes—"for the judge had called on." They seemed to believe that his wish to call in the notes settled the matter beyond all question.

He became once more his dignified, calm, self-contained self, though I could see that it was only by exercise of all his will power.

I had placed packets of money in his hands and he figured interest and made payments.

The first man with whom he did business gave the judge his cue and made me thank the good Lord that I had planted that seed in Dodovah Vose!

"You're looking better than I have ever seen you, Judge! Younger, too! What have you been doing to yourself? Oh, your whiskers are cut off! Improves you!"

The moment we had struck Spokane I bought alcohol and stripped that grotesque mustache from the judge's face. In spite of his haggard countenance, he did look younger.

"It's said around town," proceeded Farmer Bailey—and I held my breath and did not dare to look at Judge Kingsley—"that you've just cleaned up a lot of money in a big deal. Dod Vose has given out first news! We're all glad of it because we have always looked up to you as a financier."

The judge nodded stiffly in acknowledgment of the compliment.

"And I suppose he has made you rich, too, young Sidney, taking you under his wing like he has," suggested the farmer, with a wink. "Your uncle is giving you a black eye for deserting the family—like he done the first time you left town—but I guess you haven't made any mistake by grabbing in with Judge Kingsley."

"I'm quite sure of that," I told Farmer Bailey.

"I hate to take this money, Judge," said the farmer. "It's been safe with you. I ain't a financier like you be. It hasn't been taxed. You bet I have kept my mouth shut!"

"It's only to clear up town business on account of the special meeting which has been called for to-morrow," stated the judge. "I am glad to hear you have kept the matter private. I merely tried to help a few of my friends. And I suggest that you say nothing about having received this money or that you have surrendered a town note. There are disturbers in town who threaten a high tax-rate."

"It's Deck Sidney, thrashing around to make a big show of his authority, now that he is selectman," the farmer grumbled. "He ain't being backed up by the people, I can tell you that! It's all right to be enterprising, but he is too cussed much so. He was around here the other day, trying to nose out whether I held a town note or not!" I felt a thrill of fear and the judge grew visibly paler. "Yes, he hung on and coaxed and threatened and argued. But I knew what he was up to!"

He winked at the shrinking judge.

"He said if I didn't bring my town note into the meeting I'd never be able to collect."

"How did he know you held a town note?" croaked the judge.

"He didn't know! He was round town guessing. I never let on. I knew he wasn't any financier. I knew that you'd protect me, no matter what Deck Sidney might say. I smelled him out, all right! He thinks he is running this town and he tried to bamboozle me so that he could find some more property to tax. I reckon we'll show him where he belongs when it comes to next annual meeting. He's getting altogether too big for his britches!"

We learned much more about my uncle's recent activities before we finished our ride. Evidently, when he had held his nose in the air he had sniffed town notes; but when he had set his nose to the ground and had tried to run those notes to their lairs he had failed. At any rate, the holders protested to the judge that they had not dropped one word—all of them suspecting that my uncle was merely digging out property to tax. The resentful farmers had replied to his anathema with some of their own and the frightened old maids had been too scared to say anything to him. We heard enough to know that he had traveled more or less by guesswork, and had made his quest general, hoping to corner somebody by chance. If we could believe the protestations of the parties concerned, Judge Kingsley's defenses still presented a fair front to the world.

At last, before the evening was old, the judge had taken into his hands the last note.

Then we ordered our driver to hurry us to the village.

"Mr. Sidney," said the judge, when he had paid the driver and stood in the shadows at the edge of the square, "this is not the time to talk over our affairs, but I do want you to step into my office for a few moments."

He led the way.

The big house was dark and a queer kind of a shiver ran through me when I looked at it.

"The devil must have had me in his clutch all these days," muttered the judge. "I have been worse than a lunatic. Not a word from me to my poor folks at home!"

To tell the truth, I had not been giving much thought to our remissness in that duty. I have never been much of a letter-writer in my life—I had been so long without folks who cared to hear from me that the matter of keeping anybody posted on my whereabouts never came into my mind. To be sure, I had Celene Kingsley in my mind all the time, even in the stress of our adventures, but I had not presumed to write to her. During our travels it had not occurred to me that it was any part of my business to prompt Judge Kingsley in any of his family affairs. But now that we were back, in front of that gloomy house, I realized just how brutal the whole thing was.

The judge went to his office door and his hand trembled so violently that the key clattered all around the hole; what with the darkness and his agitation, he could not unlock the door, and I did it for him, gently taking the key from his hand.

I lighted his lamp when we were within. We stood there for a few moments and looked at each other.

"It's so still!" he mumbled. "It seems early for them to be in bed."

"But your folks must be all right," I ventured. "If there was anything wrong we would have heard about it while we have been riding about town."

"Probably! Probably!" His voice quavered and he was all a-tremble. "But it seems so still!"

He sat down at his table and pulled out the notes he had been gathering.

"You are entitled to look on, Mr. Sidney! I wanted you to see me do it. I don't just understand all the reasons yet why you have helped me as you have. We will talk about that some day when my head is clearer. It's all a dream—a dream—a dream—so it seems now." He sort of maundered along in his talk. He did not seem to be at all sure of himself. If the thought did come to me with any force that then was a good time to tell him why I had volunteered as I had done, I put the idea away when I looked at him.

He dumped papers out of a tin tray which stood on the table. He piled the notes in the tray.

"Touch a match to them, sir," he told me. "You are entitled to do it. We will watch them burn. I signed them as town treasurer. One of them would put me into prison. Hurry! Set the match to them!" And I obeyed.

Then, almost before the red embers were dark, he dove his hands into the ashes of the papers and scruffed them about and out of him came the most dreadful cackle of laughter I ever heard.

I was anxious to end that scene as quickly as I could. I pulled a packet from my coat and laid it on the table; I tapped my finger on it to get his attention.

"Here is something I have held out, Judge Kingsley," I informed him. "There's a thousand dollars tied up in this paper. Five hundred of it I accepted from Dodovah Vose, agreeing to put him in right in our speculation. I took it when I started West."

In spite of his emotion the old judge's business sense flared just as the fire had flared in the tray a moment before.

"But there was no speculation—there was no business deal! Why did you take money in that way?"

"I had special reasons of my own, sir."

"But you had no right—it was a private affair—it—"

"And I also had reasons of your own to consider, sir," I broke in. "Mr. Vose asked me to invest for him. I wanted your name to stand well after we were gone. I was under obligations to Mr. Vose and when I told him we had a big deal on I could give him no good reason why I would not turn a little profit his way. That's why the man Bailey is so sure that your credit is now good. You'll find that the news has gone all about the section—"

"They'll be jumping on me for the money I owe!" snarled the judge. "Vose has ruined me if he has bragged. You have—"

"Just a moment, sir, before you say something you'll be sorry for. It's just the other way, I'll warrant! Men will bring more money to you. You can be shrewd and work out of your troubles. Your credit is established. I made a good play when I did it."

"You say there's a thousand dollars in that envelope?"

"Yes, sir! I have handed the other packets to you. I propose to give Mr. Vose five hundred dollars profit—and after I have done that you'll get the best advertising you ever had. They'll rate you mighty high in these parts. Five hundred is a cheap price for what you'll get."

"But I need every cent just now to tide me over," he whined. "You are throwing money away recklessly. Vose can be taken care of some time. Give him his own five hundred—or—or—say it has been invested for him. I will attend to his case later."

221

And do you know what that old rhinoceros did? He reached out his paw to take that packet. I had to pound my fist on his fingers to make him let go.

He stood up and called me names—said that I was taking money he needed. I suppose I ought to have made allowances for the state of mind he was in—his fears—his weakness of old age—his dreadful anxiety which still goaded him.

But I was in a bad way, myself, and I could not pardon that selfishness.

"Confound you," I yelled, "I have a mind to back you against the wall and strip every dollar out of your pockets!"

And then we heard a noise and we turned around, and there stood Celene Kingsley looking at us—looking at me especially with hatred and horror.

"Father!" she cried. "Shall I run and call help? He is robbing you!"

I certainly could not say a word just then, and the judge sat down and gasped and gaped at her.

She came into the room. She was white and pale and thin, but she was no shrinking and anguished maiden. She was showing the female's ferocity in guarding her own.

"I heard you! Confessing that you're a robber out of your own mouth! Where have you been with my poor father? What devilish spell have you put on him—you and the rest of your gang?"

She turned away from me.

"Father, don't you realize that you have come home when it is too late? Oh, God in heaven, why did you not break away from those rogues and come home—or write so that we could ransom you? I know. They have kept you a prisoner!"

"Too late?" he looked at his office safe. I knew what he was afraid of. "Too late?"

She began to sob. "It has killed mother!"

He got up and staggered to her and took her in his arms.

"Your mother dead?"

"It's worse than that! It's her mind—it has gone, and her body is following. She hasn't known me for days. She lies there dying."

I was shocked, but I must confess I did not feel like a murderer. Mrs. Kingsley had been ill when we went away—she had so declared in my hearing.

"Miss Kingsley," I put in, "I'm sorry, but your father and I—"

Her tears ceased and she turned on me in a fury. I knew something about the Kingsley disposition, but I did not know before that she had so much of it in her.

"Sorry! You sorry? I know about you, you miserable low-lived wretch! I have been hunting for my father. Do you think I would look down on my dying mother and not spend every cent I had in trying to find where you had taken him? My detectives have been on that trail you left in the city!"

Able detectives! On the cold and easy trail instead of nosing on the warm one!

"But please listen to me—"

"To more of your lies? No! I know you for what you are—hiding from the police in the city—coming back here to finish the ruin of my innocent father after your friends had been sent here by you to rob him. You don't dare to deny what you have been in the city! Your face convicts you!"

I was perfectly conscious that I was not presenting any lamb-like picture of innocence. She certainly had me on the run when she burst out with that exposure of my city record. But I did not propose to lie down and stick up my feet like a calf ticketed for the butcher.

"Miss Kingsley," I said, slapping the packet of money across my palm—and that was a poor tool to use for emphasis after she had heard my talk to her father, "you must listen—"

"I have been listening just now! I heard you threaten to strip my poor father of every cent he has in the world! Do you deny you said it?"

"No, but—"

"Do you deny that you have been the sort of a man I have said you were?"

She rushed at me, her hands like claws, I was reminded of a sight I had witnessed in boyhood—a shrieking meadow-thrush defending her nest against a sneaking snake.

I looked past her toward the judge. I did hope he would say something, even though I did not expect that he would come out with the whole truth. Honestly, I would have stopped him short if he had started to confess to her anything about the real reason why I was mixed into his affairs. Had not the whole expedition been planned so that the women folks would not know?

Nevertheless, a decent man in his right senses could have made some sort of talk to help me out. But it was plain enough that Judge Kingsley was not in his right senses—he did not seem to have much of any sense left in him; he was doddering around the room, twisting his hands and accusing himself of having killed his wife.

"Please listen," I implored. "You have heard only one side—"

"I will not listen! You, your uncle, the renegades you associate with, you have tried to ruin my father. You weren't even decent enough to be an open enemy—you came sneaking into our home to lie to us and deceive us."

"By the gods," I shouted, "you will listen to me! I don't propose to be kicked around from pillar to post all my life. I am the best friend the Kingsley family ever had. If your father doesn't tell you so, I will. Judge Kingsley, why don't you be a man?"

But he gave me a fishy look and went on lamenting.

She started for the door. "There are honest men in this village—I'm going to call them!"

But I got to the door ahead of her.

"There's another time coming—a better time for an explanation—and you'll be the sorriest girl in the world."

"I can never be as sorry as I am now—sorry and ashamed! To think that I ever put confidence in a creature by the name of Sidney!"

What a glorious home-coming for the paragon of self-sacrifice!

I walked around the square half a dozen times before I dared to go into the tavern. I don't know how I ever got through that interview with Dodovah Vose without betraying my state of mind, but I managed it and excused my peculiarity by saying that I was all worn out by my trip. And he had too much on his own mind in a few minutes to pay special attention to me, for I handed him one thousand dollars and went up to my room without bothering to contradict his excited guessings that the judge and I had cleaned up a fortune. Kingsley, I reflected, might as well have the benefit of the guessing. And, it must be known, hope was not dead in me in spite of my agony.

Something else was very much alive in me. Blackleg, eh? Flashy rogue! Barker for gamblers!

I took off that plug-hat, held it in both hands, and put my foot through the crown; then I kicked it all around the room. I stripped off that frock-coat, grabbed the tails and ripped it into two parts.

Then I went to the closet and surveyed that ready-made suit and the billycock hat with content.

In the morning I would be Ross Sidney, professional diver, ready to go back on the job if there was any such thing as a job for me in all the world. I hoped I would be sane once more when I opened my eyes on a new day. I yanked that fancy waistcoat into ribbons, threw the pearl-gray trousers under the bed, and hurried to go to sleep so that I would not become completely crazy before I could forget my troubles.

XXV

GRATITUDE!

There surely is a lot in this conscious-virtue notion! I had plenty of the quality next morning.

Things seemed brighter. I felt like myself once more. It was inconceivable that the horrible misunderstanding between Celene Kingsley and myself could continue very long; I was ready to make confession as to my temporary lunacy in the city, and my new optimism encouraged me to believe that she would find excuse for me. At any rate, I was soon assured that whatever she had learned from that detective, whoever he was, she had kept it to herself. From that reticence I drew excellent augury that she was not out to ruin me. If she had opened her mouth about my past I would have known it the moment I stepped out on the street in Levant. But every person I met ducked polite salute, and I met many persons because the village was full on account of the town meeting.

At ten o'clock the town hall was crowded and in a short time the cut-and-dried preliminaries were over.

My uncle was with his associates on the platform, and the stare he gave me when he caught my eyes was so demoniac that I was careful not to look his way again for some time.

There was evidence of strained anticipation everywhere in the gathering. I heard voters whispering that Deck Sidney proposed to spring something. But nobody, according to what I could hear, presumed to put in words what they guessed.

My uncle was masking his personal batteries, I saw. An unemotional lawyer explained the purpose of the meeting, and then the moderator called on Judge Kingsley, as town treasurer, to give the financial standing of the town.

Uncle Deck fairly bored the judge with his gaze when the old man walked to the platform and I was as intent with my scrutiny, for I was wondering how Kingsley would get through with it. He was white and somewhat shaky, but he was the same old cold proposition when he faced the voters.

"I hope you will pardon a word on a personal matter," he said, as he unfolded his papers; "but I have returned from a business trip and find serious illness in my family. I have been keeping watch at the bedside of my dear wife and my thoughts are not clear enough to enable me to make the little address I had contemplated for to-day. I will only say that the movement to clear the town of its debt is very praiseworthy and my report will show that the thing may be done with a little extra effort. Our only considerable indebtedness consists of town bonds amounting to eight thousand dollars and current items as follows." Then he went on to give the list of unpaid town orders, of which only a few were extant. "I see here representatives of the bondholders," he added, "who will check my figures if such assurance is required by any voter—and probably most of the parties who hold town orders are in the meeting. I hope the town orders will be presented for payment at once so that there may be no floating indebtedness." He folded up his papers.

My uncle got up and stamped down his trousers legs.

"Now, you voters," he called, "ask your questions!"

But not a voice was raised.

"I'm no lawyer and I'm making no threats," my uncle went on. "But after the way this meeting has been advertised, and after the call that has been made, I reckon that the men who have been holding out claims against this town and who haven't presented them will be left to whistle for their money. I propose to have action taken that will outlaw those claims."

Judge Kingsley turned slowly on my uncle and stood as stiff as a stake.

"To what claims do you refer, Selectman Sidney? Do you question the accuracy of my report?"

"Come out of your holes, you old woodchucks!" shouted Uncle Deck, looking past the judge at the voters. Men scowled at him and grumbled.

The judge walked toward the First Selectman and shook his papers.

"You must talk to me, sir! I am the treasurer of this town and have been for a good many years. Here before the voters I demand that you specify claims."

"I'll specify, then! How about the town notes that are out with your name on them?"

A murmur ran through the assemblage.

"Just one moment, sir! Weigh your words," warned the judge. "You are attacking my financial reputation; there is a law for slanderers and I have many witnesses here. Do you say there is one single town note extant with my name on it?"

"I say there are a lot of 'em!"

This time many voters raised voices of protest and there were hisses.

"That's the thanks a straight man gets for trying to protect his town against a thief, eh?" raged my uncle, his ready temper bursting loose.

"If the judge don't collect fifty thousand dollars damages for this, then I'm no guesser," declared Dodovah Vose, who sat beside me.

Uncle Deck tramped to the edge of the platform and with wagging finger selected a man in the throng; the man was Farmer Bailey.

"Bailey, you hold a town note with Kingsley's name on it! You know you do! Are you going to sit there and see it canceled as no good by the vote of this town?"

Bailey rose slowly and everybody listened in deep silence.

"I hold no note of any kind with Judge Kingsley's name on it."

"Yah-h-h! You have told me that before. But you don't dare to stand here in town meeting and say it under oath."

"Send down that Bible on the stand and I'll take oath and kiss the Book," offered Bailey. There was applause and the judge quieted it by raising his hand.

"I will pay double for any note with my name on it as treasurer, and I will turn the money over to the town as a gift," he said.

I despised him when he made that bluff, though of course he had to do it. Really, in spite of his devilish temper and his spirit of revenge my uncle was twice the man Judge Kingsley was in that moment. I wasn't trying to figure out the righteousness of the thing on either side; the judge was fighting for his very life, as well as his standing, and my uncle, though he was working for the good of the town according to his lights, was satisfying his old grudge—the real passion of his life.

A voter rose and bellowed until he secured silence; they were giving the judge an ovation.

"I want to put in a word here, fellow-townsmen! Money has been borrowed on town notes. A certain eminent man you all know tried to borrow from me and said I could escape taxation. And now he is backed by the liars—"

"And barked at by the liars, too," yelled another man.

"I stand up here for Selectman Sidney, who has given his time and effort to help this town out of the clutches—"

They howled him down. But by this time the defenders of my uncle were howling, too.

"This meeting is going to break up in a free fight if a stop isn't put to this jawing," said Dodovah Vose. He jumped up on the settee and made himself heard. "I move we adjourn!"

The apprehensive moderator put the motion, the judge's friends carried it, and the meeting was dissolved.

My uncle leaped off the platform and came raging at me through the crowd.

"It's you—you damnation imp of Gehenna! Racing and chasing over this town yesterday! I had a line on you. Saving that old whelp from what was coming to him!" He put his hands over his head and wriggled his fingers. "God! I don't know what you have done—you got that money by robbing a bank, probably. But you have done it—you have jumped up and down on your family! You have got to answer to me!"

Men pushed away in panic and left us in a ring. But I had no notion of entertaining the old goggle-eyes of Levant by fisticuffs with my uncle. I folded my arms.

"According to your reckoning, Uncle Deck, I have owed you something for a long time. I want to stand square with you! Go ahead and collect!"

He did not seem to understand at once.

"Go ahead and beat me up! I won't raise a finger." Yes, I would have taken the beating—I knew inside of me that I did owe my uncle something of the sort.

"Not by a dam-site, he sha'n't beat you up," declared Dodovah Vose. "I saved you from him once," he said, careless of revelations, "and I'll save you again."

So, after waiting a minute and enduring my uncle's tongue instead of his fists, I went away with Landlord Vose.

I was not in the mood for any farther paltering or palavering in regard to my personal and private standing with the Kingsley family. I had a collection to make and I proposed to go and make it. I ought to have known better than to force the issue at that time. But youth is headstrong, the sense of my injuries was hot, and I felt that if ever the judge might be willing to show his gratitude that would be the time.

He was crossing the square on his way home and I left Mr. Vose and hurried after. I caught up with him at the front door.

"I want to come in and have a word with you and with your daughter," I told him.

"Impossible," he said, curtly. "I'm afraid my wife is at death's door. And my daughter—she is very bitter!"

"I propose to have you explain enough so that she will not be bitter, sir. It's my due. You know what kind of a service I have rendered. I have made an enemy of my uncle—ruined all my prospects to help you. There are things you can tell your daughter to—"

"How does my daughter enter into any affairs between you and myself? You must let me alone in my sorrow. Later I will pay you for your services. I am grateful. If I were not in such distress I would explain how grateful I am. I will pray that I may be spared till I can pay back to you what I owe."

"Good Cæsar! I don't want your money, Judge Kingsley. I'll work and earn more to help you out of your difficulties. I only ask you to be a man and make your daughter understand—"

"My daughter again! You don't presume—"

"I do presume, sir. She was kind to me until this horrible misunderstanding came up. I expect you to tell her that I am your best friend. It's my right!"

I'll never forget the look he gave me. I'll wager a good bit that the idea of such enormity on my part never came into his Kingsley consciousness till that moment. Even then he did not seem to be just sure that he understood.

"I don't expect anything definite from you or her, Judge Kingsley, until I have made good in the world. But I do look to you to give me a square deal. That's only what you owe to me, man to man."

"I owe you money and I will pay it. There is no other sort of bargain between us."

He stepped into his house and shut the door in my face.

In that damnable situation I was minded to follow him and have it out, even if I were obliged to expose him. However, if death were hovering over that house it was a sanctuary I could not invade. But bitter thoughts raged in me when I turned away; I only asked to be set right with Celene.

I understand that this part of my confession will elicit little sympathy for me from the casual reader who takes the comfortable view that the world is full of girls and if one does not swing low enough on the bough there's always another within reach. But mine was the exceptional case where the first love had become an obsession and all my spirit of persistency was flaming in me. I have not figured out as yet whether the troubles into which my general persistency in all matters has slammed me overbalance the fruits it has brought to me—but I reckon, after all, I'll have to take my hat off to my persistency. If I had been a quitter I would not have played the biggest game in my life—and I'm coming to that right soon.

Once more circumstances were forcing me, though I needed mighty little forcing, to leave Levant at that juncture in my affairs.

"Damn 'em!" I blared out to Dodovah Vose when I stamped into the tavern, "I've got to show 'em! I'll show 'em I can make good."

He blinked at me.

"But you have shown 'em already," he said. He thought, of course, that I was speaking about the general public in Levant. "And if I was in your place I wouldn't give a darn what your uncle says to you."

Less than two hours later Landlord Vose revised that advice. He rushed up to my room where I was sorting some papers, having resolved to travel light when I did go.

"Get under—get under, young Sidney," he gasped.

"Under what?"

"I reckon I mean get out. It's your uncle Deck! Bailey and some other of them yawp-mouths in this place have been twitting and tormenting him and dropping hints, and he's worse than a sore-eared bulldog after a scruffling. He's coming with a double-barreled shotgun. He is! He's drunk, son, and there's no dealing with him. He lays it all to you!"

"I won't run."

"But he isn't responsible, son. To say nothing of what will happen to you, it means that he'll go to State prison. You're sane and sober and you ought to be willing to save him from himself."

Right then Mr. Vose said something which appealed to me. I had stepped outside my family—I had conspired against my uncle—I had blocked his dearest ambition, iniquitous though it was. By hanging around and allowing him to take pot-shots at me I would be aggravating his troubles and bringing more serious afflictions upon him. A dead nephew, shot-riddled, would be a damning exhibit A in his trial for murder!

I picked up my few belongings and escaped from the back door of the tavern, hid in a cross-road till Dodovah Vose's stableman came with a hitch, and I caught a train at a station down the line; hustling out of my native town on the run, by dint of practice, was getting to be one of the best performances in my list of tricks.

I counted my money when I was on my way to the city. I had not been keeping any strict account between the judge and myself; from the common stock I had been paying expenses and spending as loose as peas in order to hasten our journey back East. I found around two hundred and fifty dollars in my pockets, and I reflected, with a sort of grim zest in the humor of the thing, that I could fairly claim most of this money as my own—the tainted cash from my poker profits.

I went straight to Jodrey Vose when I arrived in the metropolis and he looked neither surprised nor overjoyed.

"Where have you been?" he inquired.

"Oh, sort of loafing around up-country—killing time!"

He squinted at me sourly.

"I can't say that you're doing any great credit to my training, young Sidney!"

"You are right, Captain Vose, but I'm turning over a new leaf and I'm out to make good. I am hoping that I can do something in the case of Anson C. Doughty so that I can get back into the diving business and keep on the job hereafter."

"Then you'll go back to diving and keep out from under plughats, will you?"

"Yes, sir!"

He looked at me for a long time and then he pulled out a letter.

"This here," he said, tapping it, "is something more about that *Golden Gate* treasure. There's a new crowd on the rampage about it. From somebody in the old crowd they have got hold of my name. I came nigh trying it on once, as I have told you. But it's a gamble; I am old and I don't want it. You are young and there's nothing as yet for you on the Atlantic coast, and you might grab in on this. They want an Eastern diver because the divers out there are tied up with the big concerns and can't be depended on to keep their mouths shut—so this letter says."

"Probably it's a pretty uncertain proposition, sir."

"Well, you don't expect to fall into anything very certain, do you, a diver blacklisted from Kittery to the Keys?" he demanded, tartly.

"No, sir."

"I know nothing about these people, their plans, or anything. But I'll do this for you, if you want me to. I'll wire this party and tell him I am sending you on. After you are started you can post him from some place as to when you'll arrive. Better give him a wire from time to time to keep his interest up. How's your wallet?"

"I think it's all right, sir."

"If you're lying to me that's your own lookout. Haven't sold your diving-dress, have you?"

"I have it safe in storage, sir."

"Well, I'm glad you kept remembering that you're a diver—and the best one I ever turned out!" That was the first word of high praise he had given me. He got up and shook my hand. "Now go dive, son, and after you raise that four million from the wreck of the *Golden Gate* come back and tell me all about it."

I did not linger in the city; there were too many possibilities in the way of Dawlins and Doughtys.

Two hours later I was headed across the continent with my diving-dress in its canvas bag and the address of one Captain Rask Holstrom written in my note-book. I was pretty dizzy with the haste of it all and felt like the human shuttle between oceans—but I possessed considerable more serenity than I did when I began that lunatic lope with Judge Kingsley.

I had framed a motto and hung it in my soul—"I'll show 'em!"

XXVI

CAPTAIN HOLSTROM ET AL.

My face was set to the West, to be sure, but my thoughts were traveling back over my shoulder to the East. I wish I could say that a lively sense of injury enabled me to put out of my mind Levant and everybody in Levant—box and dice! But I'm not much of a liar.

I do not propose to dwell on the bitterness which stuck in me day after day, along with softer sentiments. This narrative goes into a gallop at about this point and there is no time to be wasted on self-communings. However, if I do not mention my old home and the folks back there it must not be understood that the problem of my life ceased to go to bed with me, rise with me, and keep pace with me as I hurried through the day's work.

I obeyed Jodrey Vose's counsel about giving bulletins of my progress west. After I had bought my railroad ticket and had counted up, I felt that I could not afford to take any chances on those strangers losing their interest in me. I needed a job almighty sudden after I landed in San Francisco.

On the last leg of the journey I was able to forecast the hour of my arrival and I suggested by wire that somebody meet me—knowing that my diver's kit in its duck bag would be identification enough. This telegraph business was shooting arrows into the air and I would have welcomed a return message; I thought they ought to be able to guess closely enough to intercept me somewhere along the line. But, although no answer came, I had the comfortable feeling that they'd be likely to be on the lookout for me. And at last I got my first peek at Pacific waters.

Our train was hung up outside the yard over in Oakland while they opened our track to the ferry, and a chap I had chatted with more or less in the smoking-room on the trip, and who knew my business, rushed out, climbed down beside the roadbed, and scooped a tumblerful of water. He ran back into the car and dumped the water over me for a joke, and I'm so accustomed to water that the joke did not jar me. I took it as it was meant.

"I baptize thee in the name of the Pacific," he said. "Now I hope the old dame will be good to you in your line."

Well, whether she was or not depends on how one looks at those things.

I walked slowly through the ferry-house, hoping to be hailed, and stepped out on to the foot of Market Street into the old San Francisco of the days before the great calamity. In my right hand I tugged along the duck bag that was bulging with my diving equipment. In my left hand I had the rest of my earthly possessions in a grip which was about the size of a ten-cent loaf of bread. It was early evening, and all the lights were aglare.

There was a turn-table for the cable cars at the foot of Market Street. The cars were coming down in constant procession, and the turn-table was busy. It was a regular merry-go-round kind of an affair. It interested me, but it didn't interest me so much that I had no eye for a girl who stood beside me at the edge of the thing. It seemed to me right then—fresh from a tedious train ride, where I'd been penned in with a frumpy set of women passengers—that I had never seen a prettier girl. She had her finger pointed at some one on the turn-table, and was saying "Father!" over and over, with a new inflection on the word every time she spoke it. Her finger traveled as the table revolved, and I was able to pick out father right away. I was right-down sorry for that girl when I laid eyes on father. Father was grinning like a sculpin in deep water, and he was good and drunk, and he was evidently taking a joy ride on that turn-table.

It struck me right then, as a stranger, that San Francisco had a good trait pretty well developed; it was willing to let a man mind his own business as long as he didn't make too much of a nuisance of himself. The street-car men did not push father off the turn-table, and two policemen took a look at him and went off about their business.

I took a good look at the man, too, when the turn-table brought him near me and stopped to let a car on. He had a face about as square as the front of a safe, and his nose was the shape of a safety-lock knob, and was red. His pot-bellied body was set on legs like crooked wharf pilings. I had father sized up in a second. Double-breasted blue coat, cap of blue, with the peak pulled rakishly down over one eye, gray beard which radiated in spills from his chin like tiller spokes—he was a steamboat man, sure! I don't know what in the devil possessed me to butt in and make certain—perhaps I wanted to start something so as to get a rise out of the girl. I'm not naturally fresh and you may be sure I was in no mood for a flirtation. I was crusted with Yankee reserve even when I was young. But that impish air of San Francisco was in my nostrils—did you ever sniff it? It makes your head buzz and your thoughts froth, and it takes hold of an Easterner as quickly as a stiff cocktail grabs a man who isn't used to a mixed drink. You'll do almost anything in San Francisco when the sparkle from that trade-wind gets into your lungs.

234

So I tipped father the wink.

"Give her the jingle when she starts again," I said.

I was right in my guess. He crooked his forefinger, reached down, and yanked empty air.

"Clang!" he barked. In a few seconds the turn-table began to revolve again. Father gave me as silly a grin as I ever saw on a grown-up man's face. "Yingle—yingle—yingle!" he yelled in falsetto. And away he went!

I never got a more awful look from a pretty girl than I got from that one when I turned and caught her eyes. There was nothing shrinking or bashful about her when she was mad, so I found out then and there.

"You fool! You have started him all over again."

"He seemed to be well started before I came along, miss." It was that confounded air that was making me reckless and saucy.

"Clang!" yelped father, coming around again. "Yingle—yingle—yingle! Pull in them port fenders and mouse that anchor; we're going outside this trip."

"Just see the fool notion you have gone and put into him when he was all ready to come along with me!" she blazed. She knocked her little knuckles together in as fine a state of temper as I ever viewed spouting in a female. She turned suddenly and drove one of her fists against a man whom I had not noticed till then. He was tall—as long as the moral law, as we say East—as thin as a pump-handle, and he had a tangle of gray whisker and beard on top of him that made him look like a window-mop. He fell down when she hit him. She kicked him with the point of a little shoe, and he came up, unfolding in sections like a carpenter's two-foot rule.

"Slap this man's face, Ike, and send him along about his business," she commanded.

But he only teetered and grinned and drooled, and winked at me over her shoulder.

"Oh, you are only another drunken fool!" she raged; and she stretched on tiptoe, and beat his face with the flat of her hand. "You have stood here without putting up a finger to help me get him off that turn-table, where he's disgracing himself. I wonder whether there are any real men left in San Francisco!" She was in such a state of mind that I was mighty ashamed by then, I tell you that!

I dropped my baggage and took off my hat.

"I don't know much about San Francisco and the real men, miss," I told her, "for I've been in town only about five minutes. I reckon it makes an Easterner dizzy to be rushed in and dropped here.

I didn't mean to make trouble for you. Seeing that I've made it, I'll unmake it if I can. Do you want your father—saying it is your father—brought off that turn-table?"

"No!" she snapped, still spiteful and all worked up. "I want you to think up something else for him to do on there as soon as he gets tired of doing what you suggested."

Well, it was up to me to butt into that affair still farther—I could see that. I couldn't sneak off and leave that girl feeling that way about me. I hopped on to the moving turn-table, took father by the arm, and told him his daughter wanted him to come along. He braced himself and shook loose.

"Nossir," said he. "I've paid my money, and I'll stay aboard till I get to where I'm bound."

"Look here, you are not getting anywhere, man. You are only riding around and around, making a show of yourself, and there's your nice daughter waiting for you."

"It's no place for a daughter—going where I'm going. Daughter ought to be in bed." And then he braced himself back still farther, and—well, I suppose I'll have to call it "singing" in order to describe the sound:

"I'm bound for the foot of Telegraph Hill,
    To the Barbary Coast so gay.
I'm starting there for a peach of a tear—fill
    'Em up all round—hooray!"

I took hold of his arm once more, and it was some arm.

"Look here," he snarled, squinting at me, "I don't know who you are, but I'll let you know who I am blamed quick."

I don't know just what he might have done to me if he had been sober—but he wasn't sober. I was, and my line of work had made me lithe and quick. I snapped my man before he had time to open his mouth, and ran him off that turn-table and presented him to his daughter with my compliments. He kicked and thrashed around in a logy style, and I kept him circling so that he could not get foothold, on the same principle that you keep a boa-constrictor from hooking his tail around a tree.

"Where will you have him delivered, miss?" I asked, as politely as I could.

"Father, you come along with me this instant!" she cried. "We don't want strangers interfering in our affairs any longer." She said that to him for my benefit.

"I don't mean to be interfering, miss," I pleaded. "I only want to square myself for being thoughtless and starting trouble for you—more trouble, I mean."

She put her hand against me and pushed me away from her father—no, I can hardly say that I was pushed away. That hand was too little to push a man of my size. But the gesture of pushing was enough for me. I let him loose. She reached for his ear, but he dodged away, cantering like a cart-horse, and whooped that he was bound for the "Barbary Coast." The human belaying-pin with the oakum top-knot followed, plainly relishing the fact that the procession had started. The girl took a few steps in pursuit, and then she stopped and began to cry. She had grit—I had seen that—but after a girl gets about so mad she has to cry on general principles.

"Look here," I told her, "I'm a stranger, all right, but you need a man's help right now. I'll help for every ounce that's in me if you'll say the word. But I'm a Yankee and I need to be asked."

"He has a lot of money in his pockets," she sobbed. "He must pay out that money to-morrow morning. He will be butchered and robbed where he's going. I never saw him so silly and obstinate before. His head has been turned by some good luck which has come to him. He—"

"I haven't got time to listen to details, miss. He's getting out of sight. I've got to work quick. I'm square and decent and honest, and I'm mighty sorry for the scrape you are in. Do you want me to chase that father of yours for you?"

"Yes," she gasped; "yes, I do."

"About all I'm worth in the world is in that bag there. It's my diving-dress. I've got to leave it."

"Your name is Sidney!" she cried, her eyes opening wide on me. "You're the man we came to meet!"

So, after all, I had butted in on my reception committee!

"And that's Captain Holstrom?" I demanded, pointing up the street.

"Yes! Yes! Hurry, sir. I will watch your bag! I will stay here. Hurry, sir! He has gone up Market Street, but he'll turn to the right pretty soon. That's the way to the horrible Barbary Coast."

I patted her shoulder—I couldn't help it. She looked up at me through her tears. And off I hiked, leaving my earthly possessions in charge of a girl whom I had met for the first time less than ten minutes before.

Of course, I knew what every one knows, whether he has been in San Francisco or not, that Market Street cuts straight across the city from bay to ocean. But at just what street on the course Captain Rask Holstrom proceeded to port his helm and swing to starboard blessed if I had the least idea. I didn't know the name of another street in the city. I knew what the Barbary Coast was in San Francisco. I had read descriptions of its dance-halls, its dens, its haunts of iniquity, and its dangers. And here I was, galloping straight toward it before the creases of a railroad journey across the continent were out of my clothes. That is to say, I hoped I was galloping toward it, for I wanted to catch father for that nice girl.

Captain Holstrom was out of sight among the crowds on that long Market Street before I had started the chase. I didn't dare to run too fast.

San Francisco, as I have said, seemed to be inclined to let a man tend to his own business, but I didn't want to provoke some ass to start a "stop thief" yell behind me. I craned and peered ahead as I trotted on. I stopped for a moment at the head of streets which led away to the right—the girl had said he would turn to the right—but I caught no glimpse of a bobbing blue cap nor of a lofty thatch of grizzled beard and whisker.

I took a chance after a while, for Market Street showed ahead an upward slope and I couldn't spot my man there. I turned off to the right, and hurried. I didn't know what street I was on. I came to a square at last where there were a statue and a fountain, and there were large buildings on the right. I ran across the square, and the next moment I realized that I was in Chinatown—and I had read of that part of San Francisco, too. I knew then that I was headed toward the Barbary Coast all right, having a memory of what I had read. But in a few minutes I was lost in a maze of narrow streets which traveled up and down the little hills. I was peering and goggling here and there. I must have looked like a tourist trying to do Chinatown in record time. I came into a street or alley that was roofed—and I came out again, for it seemed to be closed in at the upper end. By that time I realized that not only had I lost Capt. Rask Holstrom, but that I had also succeeded in losing myself—a rather silly predicament for a young man who so boldly offered himself as knight errant to a damsel in distress.

I stood still and wiped sweat out of my eyes, and addressed a few pregnant remarks to myself on the subject of a man's making a fool of himself for a woman. However, I had a mighty good reason of my own for wanting to meet up with Captain Holstrom—and to safeguard that money of his, for I hoped to rake some of it down in wages.

XXVII

MR. BEASON HORNS IN

A white-livered, sneaky-looking chap sidled up to me and stuck out a dirty card.

"That's my name on there," said he; "Jake Beason, and I'm the best Chinatown guide that's on the beat; I'll show you everything from joss-house to hop-holes."

"Do you know the Barbary Coast?"

"Do I know— Oh, come now! Why, say, I live over that way," he snarled through the corner of his mouth; and he looked at me as though I had insulted his intelligence.

I decided that I would be plain and direct with that chap.

"I'm on the trail of a steamboat captain by the name of Holstrom, and he is two-thirds pickled, and has money on him. Do you think you know the places where a man like that would be likely to drop in?"

"What's the lay—a touch and a divvy?"

"Nothing of the kind. I'm his friend, and I want to catch him and take him home out of trouble."

"The same old stall," he sneered. "You've got to let me be a friend, too."

I reached out and got my crowbar clutch on that fellow.

"I don't suppose you ever had a man tell you the truth, son," I said, "so I'm not going to blame you much. I say that I'm after this man to take him home to his daughter. That's truth, and it's on my say-so. If you propose to call me a liar, out with it, and we'll settle the thing."

"She stands as you say—and you needn't pinch so," he whined.

There's nothing like a good grip to press home conviction in a sneak.

"I'll give you ten dollars if you'll locate that man for me before the evening is over," I told him. "I'll make it twenty dollars if you'll turn the trick inside of an hour."

"I know all the joints—I know the steamboat hang-outs."

"It ought to be an easy trick. He is with an old belaying-pin who has enough hair on his head and face to stuff a bolster—and I heard somebody call him Ike."

"Aw, that's 'Ingot Ike.' Everybody between Dupont Street and Telegraph Hill knows that old hornbeam and his everlasting hum about three million dollars' worth of buried gold ingots. Come along! I ought to pull down that twenty easy."

"Let me tell you one thing," I said, chasing along with him. "I'm not worth robbing. I'm going to keep close to you, and if you put me against any frame-up I'll get you first, and I'll get you quick." And I grabbed him by the wrist and let him have that honest old grip once more. I kept hold of him. And led thus like a blind man through this street and that, by short cuts along dark alleys, across courts, and now and then skirting vacant lots, we came at last into purlieus that my ears, eyes, and nose told me must be that "Barbary Coast so gay," as Captain Holstrom had caroled.

Out of open doors came liquor fumes and music blended, if there is any such thing as blending noise and odors; the two seemed to be associated there so regularly and invariably that my senses told me that they were blended.

The women sauntered on the sidewalks; the men loafed there. We two seemed to be about the only ones who were headed for something definite.

"We'll tap the regular joints first," said Beason. "If he's pretty drunk he won't be using his mind much to think up new places to go. He'll fall into the rut like a ball in a crooked pin-game."

I was young enough to be interested in that panorama of iniquity. I would have gaped longer than I did in those places, but Mr. Beason proved to be a very active guide. That matter of twenty dollars proved to be like a bur under a bronco's saddle. He would gallop into a place, leave me to goggle at the antics on the dance floor; he would weasel his way through the crowd, chop out a few staccato questions, and then yank me out with my eyes behind me and my chin hanging over my shoulder like the tailboard of a cart.

Beason rattled me down another length of street—and if the folks we bumped hadn't known him I reckon we would have had a few things on our hands besides that man hunt. They all seemed to know Beason. He snapped questions right and left.

All at once my guide got a clue. He barked a few more questions at this illuminative party, and turned and scooted back along our trail.

"The old cuss has taken to a back room," he gasped. "I ought to have figured that he would be hiding."

He rushed me around corners, across streets, down alleys, and into more streets. We came up against a saloon at last where the front window was lettered in red paint, "Holding Ground Cove." Knowing, as a deep-sea diver, that a good holding-ground means a mud bottom, I could have thought up a highly moral and somewhat humorous apothegm on that name for a saloon if I had had the time; but Mr. Beason was cutting corners on Time that night. He rushed me into the saloon, into a back room at the rear, and when he didn't see what we were looking for up-stairs we went. There were cribs of private rooms, furnished with bare tables and hard chairs—drinking-rooms. From the half-open door of one came the cackle of much laughter, and we peeped in.

A girl, whose face was painted in almost as gaudy hues as her red stockings, was standing on a table in the middle of the little room.

Capt. Rask Holstrom was seated in a chair, straddling the back, and was busily engaged in tickling the girl's nose with the tip of a very long peacock feather—and wherever he secured that feather I never found out. But always leave it to a hilarious drunken man to find something odd to carry around with him. In the room was the human belaying-pin, also seated. But his chair had evidently slipped from under him when he tried to lean against the wall, and he was jack-knifed down in a corner, with his broomstick legs waving in the air, and was surveying the scene between that frame. He was squealing laughter in a key that would have put a guinea-hen out of business.

"There's Ingot Ike," affirmed Beason, "and if t'other one is your pertickler friend then I'll cash in."

He held up his cheap watch, with his dirty forefinger indicating the hour.

"I get the twenty with nine minutes' 'velvet,' if that's your friend."

But Captain Holstrom did not display any very ardent friendship for any one just then. He turned an especially malevolent stare in my direction and poised his peacock feather like lance in rest. I could see that something was going to break loose there mighty soon, and after what I had told Beason I didn't want that young sneak to overhear. It would be like him to come back with a gang and "do" me on the excuse that I was a stranger who was "frisking" Captain Holstrom for his pocketful.

I hauled out two ten-dollar bills mighty quick, and passed them to Beason. He held one in each hand, pinched between thumb and forefinger, and looked at them in turn, wrinkling his nose with as much disgust as though he were holding lizards by the tails.

"Soft money," said he, "and the stink of the East still on it! I'll bet you both of these poultices that you haven't been in San Francisco twenty-four hours—and how do you happen to be such a pertickler friend of a China Basin steamboat cap'n, hey?"

A freshly arrived Easterner is always given away by his paper money.

"Who's a friend?" inquired Captain Holstrom, the one eye I could see as staring and as baleful as the "eye" on the peacock feather.

"Look-a-here," said I, bracing up to him savagely, for I knew that soft soap wouldn't grease the ways, "I want to know what you mean by running away from me after my telegrams to you."

I whirled on Beason, pushed him out of the room, and slammed the door in his face.

"You have been paid," I yelled at him through the crack. "Now, keep your nose out of the rest of the thing, or I'll pinch it off."

"See here," growled Captain Holstrom, vibrating the feather as menacingly as though it were a sled stake, "don't you know a private party when you see one?"

I walked right up to him.

"My name is Sidney. I'm the diver you are expecting."

"You're a liar," he returned, promptly.

"I tell you you were down to the ferry to meet me. I pulled you off that turn-table!"

"Who are you?"

"I am Ross Sidney, I say! You're expecting me. I'm a diver."

But he did not show the least evidence of understanding what I was talking about. It's a familiar phase of drunkenness in many men—that dogged determination to hang on to one notion and admit no others.

He shook his head and waggled the feather under the girl's nose.

"This is a private party," he growled.

"But your daughter is waiting for you—she is very much worried about you and the money."

"Say, who does this money and this daughter and this room here belong to, anyway? Who do I belong to? Who am I? Ain't I Rask Holstrom, fifty-six years old, and fully able to take care of myself anywhere between Point Lobos and India Basin?" He squinted at me along the peacock's plume. "Who are *you*? You say my girl is at the ferry, hey? How do you know she is there?"

He leaned back in his chair, dropped the feather, and yanked a canvas bag from the right-hand pocket of his trousers. It was a plump bag, and a heavy bag, and it plainly contained hard money. He banged it down on the table with such a thump that the girl hopped and squealed, and it barely missed her toes. He pulled another canvas bag from the left-hand pocket, and crashed that down. This time he

242

connected with the girl's toes. She screamed in pain, leaped down from the table, and began to hop around the room, kicking her foot out behind her. She stumbled into a corner, braced herself there, and began to swear volubly, clutching the tip of her faded red-velvet slipper in both hands.

I had not broken in on his monologue. I could not match him in roaring. Then for the first time he seemed to note that the girl was not in an amiable state of mind.

"You've insulted my lady friend. I'll have your life for that!" He plunged out of his chair and drove against the wall in his unsteadiness.

The girl was profanely advising me—no, entreating me—to kill the "drunken fool." I didn't blame her for her ire, and I could excuse her language. To shift from a tickling under the chin to a mally-hackling of toes was a little too strong for a woman's nature even if the toes had been cracked with money.

That was no time for fine figuring as to ways, means, or chances. Before Captain Holstrom recovered his balance I grabbed his sacks and stuffed them into my pockets. I started for the door. I had a sort of muddled memory of a maxim, or proverb, or something of the kind which says that "where a man's treasure is there will his heart be also." It occurred to me that Captain Holstrom's body would go with his heart if I made off with that money, and I preferred to have the body chase me on two legs rather than be lugged on my shoulders. If he would chase me back to the ferry the situation would be simplified. Of course, mine was a crazy expedient, considering the place where I was, but it was a crazy evening, anyway.

"I'm not stealing it," I yelled at him as I opened the door. "I'm going to give it to your girl, and if you run hard enough you'll see me give it to her."

I had plenty of help in opening that door. There were men outside who helped me so promptly and unanimously that it was evident they had been lying in wait.

Two of them grabbed me by the neck as they would have clutched a bat stick in choosing sides in a game of three old cat. They rammed me back into the room. There were three other men who came in, and one of them was that rat of a Beason.

They were all talking at one another, and Beason was spitting words the fastest. But Captain Holstrom drowned out all other sounds by a bellow of delight. He knew these men, all right. He seemed especially tickled to behold the two men who held me. He slapped them on their backs, cuffed their faces with drunken affection, and adjured them to hold me tighter.

"He took my money! He stole it! He insulted a lady friend of mine. He's been chasing me and picking a row with me for three days," he lied, or else the rum he had been drinking had elongated his notions of fame.

"You see, I get your twenty, Mr. Keedy," insisted Beason. "I told you straight. I called the turn on this fly guy. He's what I told you he was. You just heard what the captain said."

I was mighty busy just then with the two men who were holding me, and Captain Holstrom was giving me some slaps which were drunkenly heavy, but not affectionate. However, I heard what Beason said, and I saw the man whom he called Keedy pass over a twenty-dollar gold piece. Beason grinned at me and scuttled out of the room. The Keedy person pushed the scolding girl out after him and slammed the door.

I did not like the looks of the Keedy person—no, not at all. I may have instinct in such matters; I don't know. A diver is obliged to do most of his work in pitch darkness and by the sense of touch, and such work may develop instinct in general. I won't stop to discuss the question.

But that yellow face with a black mustache smacked across it like a smear of paint, and arrows of eyebrows shooting up northeast and northwest from a regular gouge of a wrinkle between the man's eyes wasn't the kind of physog worn by the deacon who takes up the collection in a Sunday-school. He stood with back against the door.

"Go through him, gents," he directed. "And hand me the gun when you come to it."

There wasn't any gun, but they got the two sacks of gold, and my little stock of paper money as well. Then they gave me a shove into a corner, and all of them stood off and looked at me. The excitement had brought old Ingot Ike on to his feet and he joined the ring of spectators.

"You are in bad," stated Mr. Keedy.

Silence gives consent; so I kept still.

"Who is backing you in this job? Where's the rest of your gang? You're in here without a gun. Now, where's the main party?"

"The main party," said I, mad enough now to do a little talking, "is down at the ferry, foot of Market Street. She is that old fool's daughter, and she was crying when I left her. I'm just in from the East, and when I came out on to the street from the ferry this evening, setting foot in San Francisco for the first time—"

"You're a liar!" yelped Captain Holstrom. "You've been on my trail for seven days, and you have just knocked me down when I was entertaining a lady friend and wasn't looking. You robbed me. The money was found on you. But Rask Holstrom has got friends who won't see him done. Here they are. And into the dock you go, blast ye!"

"You're in bad," reiterated the Keedy person, narrowing the crease between his eyes.

"If you're a friend of Captain Holstrom, see if you can't pound it into his head that I'm the diver he is expecting."

"You're the what? Is your name Sidney?"

"That is my name."

"Rask," snapped Keedy at last, "were you down at the ferry turn-table as this man says? You've been pretty drunk. This thing here is taking a new tack. I'd like to believe this chap here if I can."

"Might have been there," owned up the captain.

"*Was* there," stated that old fool of an Ike, who had been standing by without a word in my behalf. Now he was ready and willing to leap with the popular side. "I was there with him."

"Was your daughter there with you? Did you leave her there?"

Captain Holstrom looked a little ashamed, and hesitated.

"She was there," stated Ike. "She was following us and trying to get my noble cap'n to go along with her, but it wasn't right to bother my noble cap'n when he was happy over a lucky trade."

"The two of you must have been good and fine," growled Mr. Keedy. "Look here, Cap, I believe this gent is telling a lot of the truth about you. No matter now about his high jinks with the coin. I want to believe what he says. As your partner, Captain Holstrom, my advice to you is to hustle out, get a cab, and get to that ferry station in quick time. If that diving-suit is there bring it back here."

The captain rolled out of the room, growling, but subdued.

Mr. Keedy gave me what was for him an affable smile, a hitching up nearer to his nose of that paint-streak mustache.

"We may as well start in an acquaintance," he said. He passed my pocket-book back. "My name is Marcena Keedy, partner of Cap'n Holstrom. Step up here, gents," he commanded the two men who had squatted my windpipe. "This is Number-one Jones; this is Number-two Jones." They ducked salute. They had paint-brush chin beards and cock eyes, and were evidently twins. "First and second mates, new hired for the *Zizania*." He did not bother to introduce Ingot Ike.

He pushed a button on the wall.

"We'll take something to gum the edges of sociability, gents. There's nothing like gents starting in sociable when they can, and staying sociable as long as they can, providing any gent proves himself all right, as he says he is."

He gave me a significant and mighty sharp look, sat down, and jigged one leg over the other, trying hard to keep up his affable smile.

We kept on being sociable for half an hour or more.

At last back came Capt. Rask Holstrom. He was tugging my duffle-bag, and on his heels was his daughter. She had my little valise. She did not show any especial symptoms of embarrassment at being in such a joint alone with men. She walked straight to me and gave me the valise. What was better, she gave me a smile.

"I misunderstood you, sir, on short acquaintance," she said. "I hope you will excuse me."

She looked me straight in the eyes without coquetry, a gaze as level and candid as that of man to man.

I gulped some reply—I don't know what. I wasn't half as cool as she was.

Keedy right now put that yellow face between us. The affable smile wasn't there. I got a quick and sharp impression that he didn't relish the way the girl and I were getting chummy. She was putting out her hand to me, for I had made a motion as though to shake on our general understanding. He took her hand and whirled her around and pointed to a chair.

"You'd better sit down, Karna dear. We're going to talk a little business, and you can listen, for you are too much father's girl to be kept out of any deal of ours."

She pulled her hand out of his, but she went and sat down without shaking my hand.

"Father's girl sees more clearly every day that he needs a guardian," she said, with a rather hard laugh. "Thank you, Mr. Keedy, but I do not need your invitation to stay."

Captain Holstrom looked very sheepish. It was plain that he had been listening to some plain and frank opinions on his way back from the ferry station.

He tried to act unconcerned, and spying the drink I had not touched, started to lift it to his lips. His daughter snatched it away and sprayed the liquor on the wall. He sat down, coughing behind his hand. I had seen men like Capt. Rask Holstrom before—a bully and a braggart among men, but half a fool where women were concerned—pliable in the hands of the loose female, and mortally afraid of his own womenkind.

The men in the room were silent for some time. Keedy was looking at Holstrom; then his eyes fell on my canvas sack at Holstrom's

246

feet. He spoke to me in almost the same fawning tone he had used with the girl. It was that almost indescribable air—that cheap assumption of gentility that a professional gambler uses when he is prosecuting his business, and it rather jars on an honest man.

"I'm sure it would be almighty interesting to me and to these other gents and the lady to see an Eastern diving-suit. I reckon you're pretty much up to date back there."

Liar and knave himself, he wasn't exactly sure I had been telling the truth. He wanted to see the goods. But I did not mind much. I knelt on the floor, and opened the sack and dug out the equipment. This yarn of mine goes back before the days of the compressed-air chamber which the modern diver carries on his back just as an automobile carries fuel. But I had a mighty good suit, almost a new one. There wasn't a dent in the helmet or a patch on the rubber or canvas.

"We have had a long talk, this gent and I," said Keedy, after he had squatted like a frog and had peered at all I had to show him. "I'm naturally a man to get to cases quick. I'm open and free with them I take a liking to."

He went to the door and peeked into the corridor.

"Number-two Jones, you stand here and keep an eye and ear out," he directed. "Now, Brother Sidney, you Eastern chaps are apt to be pretty cold-blooded, and you need first-hand evidence. I'm going to open up to you one of the biggest prospects you ever heard of—reckoning that, as a human being, you simply can't resist coming into it. If you don't see fit to come in after it has been opened up to you—well—" He scowled at me like a demon, snapped his fingers above his head, and turned on old Ike.

"Get up and take the floor," he directed.

"First-hand evidence is what counts," went on Mr. Keedy. "Now, here's a man who has told his story over a lot of times on the waterfront. He has told it so many times it has grown to be a joke. They've given him the nickname of 'Ingot Ike.' Lots of big things in this world have been buried under a joke."

He leaned back in his chair and twisted up the ends of his mustache.

"Court is open for first-hand evidence, gents. Ike is the first witness. I'm going to ask him questions and make him answer snappy, for if he ever gets to rambling on this story of his he'll make it longer than a dime novel. Look-a-here, Ike, what was the steamer *Golden Gate*?"

"Passengers, bullion in ingots, and general cargo 'tween here and Panama."

It was rather comical to see that old bean-pole straighten up and try to imitate the snappy style of Mr. Keedy.

"What was your job aboard of her?"

"Quartermaster."

"What happened to her?"

"Caught fire off coast of Mexico when she was bound for Panama, beached well north of Acapulco, rolled over and over in surf, what was left of her, and bones still there. Three ribs show at low tide if you know where to look for 'em."

"What was she carrying for treasure?"

"Over three million dollars' worth of gold in ingots in her strong-room abaft second bulkhead, between pantry and boiler-room."

"Was the treasure ever recovered?"

"Wreck was abandoned to underwriters, and after underwriters had worked for a long time, keeping very mysterious, they reported that they had got the ingots all out of her. Then they came away. Everybody believed that the underwriters had cleaned out the wreck, just as they reported they had. But I was in that wrecking crew. I kept my eye out. It was a bluff about getting that treasure." The old man began to show excitement. "Their divers couldn't get at it. They didn't have nerve, and they didn't have the right outfits in those days. The underwriters didn't want it shown that they hadn't pulled up the stuff. They knew that every Tom, Dick, and Harry would go down there, peeking and poking around that wreck, and that some fellow might think up a way to call the turn.

"So they bribed the divers, and the divers brought up fake boxes of gold, and the report was made that all the treasure had been taken from the *Golden Gate* wreck. But it's all there, gents. The underwriters haven't been able yet to think of a sensible way of getting at it. They don't want to make another splurge and attract attention till they're sure of what they're doing. Them's facts what I'm telling. I know. I haven't done much of anything but keep tabs. I don't care if they do call me Ingot Ike. I know what I'm talking about. The trouble down there has been that the old Pacific has rolled on and rolled in and piled up sand over that treasure, and they didn't know how to handle the proposition in those days."

"The idea is, Brother Sidney," broke in Keedy, "first-hand evidence informs us that three or four millions are cached in a place we know of. Now, because man has failed once, years ago, when man wasn't as bright as he is now, is that any sign that man shall give up? Captain Holstrom and I say, 'No.' We're partners. We have been talking over this proposition for a long time. Now, up to date, are you in any way interested?"

I was, and I said so.

"There they lie," said Keedy, "bars of yellow gold. Boxes and boxes of shiny gold. More than three million dollars' worth of finest gold—and only a little water and sand over 'em. No bars to break through, no vaults to drill. Only sand and water—and we ought to be able to match that sand with grit, and the water with good red blood."

There are some men who can talk about money, and it will not start a thrill in you.

Marcena Keedy could talk about gold in a way to make your soul hungry. He rolled the sound in his mouth—a big, round, juicy sound—as a boy sucks a candy marble. It made the moisture ooze in my own mouth to hear him talk.

Mr. Keedy gave over leaning back in his chair. He sat on the edge of it, and leaned forward.

"It's right at this point that we go into this thing clear to the necks, my friend. I have studied men a lot in my life. I can see about what kind of a fellow you are. If another fellow opens up to you in honest fashion you are *with* him—and if you can't stay with him you are not going off and squeal and hurt him. There's nothing half-way between Holstrom, here, and myself. We're partners. We're in together, whole hog. I'll spread the cards for you just as they are spread for the captain and myself. He and I have been having a run of good luck to date in our partnership. We'll have some more first-hand evidence. Rask, how was it you got the inside clinch in the *Zizania* matter?"

"For the benefit of a man from the East, where they ain't as shrewd as the Yankees think they be," stated Captain Holstrom in his husky voice, "I will say that we've got a devilish good close combine on the water-front—we fellows have been on the job for a long time. When the Government auctions off anything we get together and fix the top price at which any bid shall go, and then we cut the cards to settle who shall pick the plum at that price. It means that the lucky man will pick a bargain, don't forget that. Price can't be budged above that bid—and it's a blamed measly price." He smacked his lips. "So that is how I have got hold of the old *Zizania*, Government lighthouse-tender and buoy steamer, side-wheeler, one hundred and seventy feet long, new derricks, boilers in fair shape, and engine fresh overhauled. I've cut the cards for eleven years, and this has been my first look-in. But it's worth waiting for. I could junk her and make four times what I pay for her."

"What *we* pay for her," corrected Mr. Keedy. "Remember that

I'm your partner. Now I'll take the stand myself. Holstrom here sold his tugboat the minute he struck luck on the *Zizania*. He pulled what money he had in the bank. He lacked half the price, at that. He was going to borrow on a bill of sale. 'No,' says I to him. 'Bring along your cash to the place where I'm dealing faro. I'll go in partner with you and double your pot.' Holstrom knew that when I talked that way with him I was square. Some men would have double-crossed him and pulled the pickings for the bank. I ain't that kind," declared Mr. Keedy, pulling himself up virtuously and giving the girl a side-glance. "I know who my friends are, and who I'd like to help. And I can deal faro! Don't worry about that! Captain Holstrom walked out with his pot doubled. The money goes down on the *Zizania* to-morrow morning, making up the balance after the forfeit money was paid. That's the way Holstrom and I do business after we have come to an agreement." He gave the girl a look which he intended to be melting. "I said I'd do it, and I did it."

"I'm ashamed of my father," she said, crisply.

"I don't much blame you, Karna," stammered Captain Holstrom, missing the point of her rebuke. "For me to go and do what I done after scooping in that money was a fool performance, and I ask the pardon of all concerned. But I reckon my head was turned by having all that good luck come in a bunch. I just went into the air, that's what I done. But I'm back on earth to stay now."

"Let us hope so, partner," chided Mr. Keedy. "That crazy Beason and our new friend here made such a racket chasing you through the Coast that I heard of it, and started out on the chase myself. It has turned out lucky, but that's no credit to you."

The girl stood up. "I have listened, and now I understand. If you want to keep my respect, father, you'll hand back the part of that money which is stolen, and borrow enough to make your payment."

"Hold on, Miss Karna!" cried Keedy. "That money wasn't stolen. A man who tackles a faro-bank isn't stealing if he wins."

"I heard what you said a few minutes ago, Mr. Keedy."

"And I said it to show I can be a friend to those I like. I've known you a long time, and now when I've had a chance to show you that I'm a friend you can't afford to chuck me."

He jumped up and went near to her.

"No more faro for me—no cards any more," he said, dusting his hands before her. "I know you haven't liked to have me do it."

"I have never made any remarks to you about your affairs, Mr. Keedy. It's only when my father gets mixed into them that I protest."

"I reckon that after all the years I've dealt crooked for the sake of the bank I've got the right to deal crooked for once in my life to help my friends," muttered Keedy. "But I'm all done with faro, I tell you, Karna. We're all going to be rich. I want you to remember that I've done my full share in this thing."

Captain Holstrom banged the sacks of coin upon the table.

"You bet you have, Marcena. And you're my partner. I stand by you. I never saw a girl yet who didn't have foolish notions. But they grow out of them." He winked at Keedy. "This money goes down on the old *Zizania* to-morrow morning. She's ours from snout to tail—from keelson to pennant block. And she's going to make our everlasting fortunes. You shall see, Karna, my girl!"

For a moment she stood there, her eyes narrowed, her cheeks flaming up, as fine a picture of protesting and indignant maidenhood as I ever laid eyes on. Then she compressed her lips and choked back an outburst.

"Yes, I *shall* see," she said at last. "For I shall go on board the *Zizania*, and stay there and watch you, father, and try to keep you out of State's prison for the sake of my poor dead mother."

"It has been all right for you to live with me aboard the tug," growled Captain Holstrom, blinking sourly at her. "But this is a different proposition. This is going to be a man's game."

"With one woman along," she insisted.

"You have got to stay here in the city," he declared.

"If you leave me here alone, deserting me for men who are leading you into dangers and trouble, you'll find me dancing in one of the worst holes on this street when you come back. I swear it!" she said.

She did not raise her voice. There was no elocution, and hysterics were absent. But there are women who can say a thing and make you believe it. Captain Holstrom cracked his knuckles and gasped, and said nothing. Keedy ran his thin tongue along the line of his sooty mustache.

"As a partner, I'm in favor of keeping a good girl near her father," said he.

"You are not a partner in my family affairs, Mr. Keedy!" cried the girl, hotly.

Keedy, much embarrassed, and willing to hide his feelings, turned to me.

"We seem to be drifting off the main subject, Brother Sidney." I wanted to yank him up for calling me by that title—resentment surged in me as hotly as it did in the girl. There are some men who seem to make your soul feel sticky when they try to be intimate.

I told him I'd like a night to think the matter over.

"All right," said Keedy, dryly; "I'll take you with me to a place where you can do some steady thinking and won't be bothered. Stuff your things back into your bag."

As I plodded along the narrow street with him, my sack propped on my shoulder, Captain Holstrom and his daughter passed me in a cab.

Mr. Keedy's voice and manner were well padded with velvet that night, but he couldn't fool me. He caged me—that's what he did. I remember that I slept in a closet of a room, and Mr. Keedy was on a cot in the room which opened into the hall. I didn't mind any of his precautions. I had made up my mind to go along. I was dog-tired and slept all night.

XXVIII

SORTING THE
CHECKER-BOARD CREW

Mr. Keedy evidently desired to impress on me that his hankering to make sure of my company during the night was inspired by pure and sudden friendship.

When he came to awaken me his mustache was lifted so high in an amiable smile that the twin sooty wings seemed to stick out of his nostrils. He hoped I was getting to like the West and the folks there. I returned that up to date I had not been homesick—a conservative statement, and true; I had had no time to be homesick.

He paid for my breakfast; further evidence of friendship. Then he called a cab and took me and my belongings down to the berth of the *Zizania*. The old steamer was docked in a place which, so he told me, was the China Basin, and we wormed our way through alleys and junk-piles and got aboard.

We hadn't hurried that morning, and the time was well into the middle of the forenoon.

Captain Holstrom was stubbing to and fro on the main deck. He wore a fine air of proprietorship, and welcomed us with a flourish of his hand. He patted his breast, and the crackle of paper sounded.

"Money paid," he reported. "Them's the dockyments. Come up into the wheel-house. There's the place to talk the rest of our business."

Marcena Keedy did most of the talking that forenoon. He loved to lollop the words "three million dollars' worth of gold ingots" in his mouth. He had wormed out of me at breakfast-time admissions enough so that he knew I was favorably disposed. He proposed to try to take advantage of me and I saw his game and resolved to do some bluffing on my own part. He put a lot of verbal plush around his propositions, but I could feel the hard nub just the same.

After all that conversational fluff he wanted me to sign a contract to take day's wages for the job—double pay for the days when I recovered any gold.

I turned that wages suggestion down, flat and final. You would have thought I had money plastered all over me.

"It has got to be on shares," I said.

"You doggone bean-eater, have you got the nerve to talk shares on an investment of a diving-suit against our steamer and our information about the *Golden Gate*?" stuttered Keedy.

"That isn't the way the thing shakes down, Mr. Keedy. You have made it plain to me that you're gambling in this—it isn't a straight deal."

He swore at me, but I didn't mean the thing the way he took it.

"If you were going down there," I said, "with a big expedition, and proposed to build coffer-dams, and all that, and go at it scientific fashion, I would hire as a regular diver. I couldn't demand anything else. But I'm not merely investing a diving-suit, as it stands. I'm playing a lone hand in the diving part of the scheme; I'm investing all my experience, all my skill; I'm investing life itself, for, as near as I can find out from what you say, it will be up to me to know how to get that gold, and then go get it. I want one-third of the velvet after all bills are paid, and I want a contract drawn before I start."

Perhaps I wouldn't have jabbed the thing so hard at Holstrom, but I did not propose to be the monkey for Keedy. I looked innocent and suggested that they'd better talk with another diver. Keedy flapped like a speared fish for half an hour—and then he came over. Captain Holstrom walked up and down with his hands behind his back during all the talk. I judged from his general air that he was viewing the whole thing as more or less of a dream, and did not want to get too wide awake about it from fear of losing courage and interest.

"There's one thing about it—you'll work harder if you have a lay," said Keedy.

That's usually the way with the grafter or loafer—he's afraid the other fellow won't work hard enough.

Frankly, I did not have any very brilliant hopes in regard to that expedition, for if old Ingot Ike had told the truth about the failure of the underwriters, I figured that the diving proposition must be a tough one. Keedy was hot about it, for he did not know enough about such work to judge chances; as for Captain Holstrom, ever since he had won this *Zizania* elephant he was in a state of mind which made him ready for any project, even to putting wings on her and starting for the moon.

I didn't pay much attention to the outfitting, except to make a list of such equipment in the way of lines, hose, air-pumps, and such matters as I needed for my part of the work. Keedy and Holstrom turned around and borrowed money on the security of the steamer, this debt to stand against our partnership. Keedy seemed so sure of that gold that he did not stop to ask me how I was fixed to stand my share in case of utter failure. Therefore, with plenty of funds to work with, we were ready for sea in short order, and to sea we went, swashing out past Point Lobos, the sea-lions hooting at us as we passed their rocks, and started down the coast.

I leaned over the rail and watched the shore melt in the hazy distance, and did not blame the sea-lions for their derogatory remarks. I did not know much about steamers, but I realized that the *Zizania*, condemned Government tub, wasn't anything to brag about. She was a real old ocean-walloper, a broad-beamed duck of a thing, thrashing her warped paddles, her rusty walking-beam groaning, her patched boilers wheezing—a weather-worn, gray, and grunting ocean tramp.

Like all craft of the buoy-boat model, she had much deck room forward of the bridge, and here were nested, as dories are nested on a Gloucester trawler, four forty-foot lighters. Plenty of anchors accompanied these scows—huge, rusty second-hand anchors which Captain Holstrom had bought from junkmen. The *Zizania* was naturally slow, and this load forward now made a snail of her. Hawsers and chains encumbered her deck space everywhere—age-blackened ropes, and iron from which rust scales were dropping. Captain Holstrom had ransacked the wharfs for hand-me-downs. Even the men whom he had shipped looked as though he had secured them at a rummage sale.

"It's a checker-board crew," the captain had informed me as they straggled on board. "Half black men, and half white. That's the only way to sort men when you're bound on a long cruise. Keep the blacks mad with the whites, and vitchy vici, and you've always got half the crew on your side in case of trouble. There can't any general mutinies start when you've got a checker-board crew. Number-one Jones has the white men's watch; Number-two Jones has the black watch; and as soon as we get this stuff stored and the rest moused on deck I'll have Number-one sick his bunch on to Number-two's, and let 'em fight long enough to get good and mad. Then they'll sort of neutralize each other for the rest of the cruise."

That system of gentle diplomacy was new to me, and I loafed around and kept an eye out, for I have always had a hearty relish for an honest scrap. Furthermore, in explaining to me later, the captain had stated that I was expected to jump in with himself and the mates and break up the fight with clubs when it had progressed far enough.

"You see, we want to leave both sides mad and neither side licked," said Captain Holstrom. "It will be like cooking in a hot oven. The thing mustn't get scorched on. I know how to handle it. Jump in when I say the word."

He had given me these instructions leaning over the sill of the pilot-house window soon after we had got away from the dock.

"Not that the doodah will start for some time yet," he added. "But I'm a great hand to have things all ready and understood. You can be looking up your club between now and to-morrow."

I glanced into the wheel-house as I walked on. Marcena Keedy lounged in solitary state on the transom seat at the rear, puffing away at a cigar.

"You're always welcome in here," he called. But I had no appetite for the companionship of Mr. Keedy.

It occurred to me, with just a bit of relish in the thought, that Miss Karna Holstrom probably was of similar mind in regard to Mr. Keedy. She had taken a seat in the wheel-house when she had come on board that day. Now she was in her state-room, which was the cabin on the upper deck near the bridge, planned as the captain's apartment. Either she had pre-empted it or Captain Holstrom had assigned her to it. I had seen that the Joneses—Number-one and Number-two—were in berths near my quarters below, and it was plain that partners Holstrom and Keedy had quartered themselves in the mates' room on the upper deck.

Miss Holstrom's door was on the hook, and I caught a glimpse of her more by accident than by design. She nodded without speaking, and I raised my cap and went below to the main deck.

I got there in season to see the lighting of a fuse which exploded Captain Holstrom's "checker-board" plans ahead of scheduled time.

The first man I met on the deck was Ingot Ike. He was gnawing at a hunk of gingerbread with his snags of teeth, and was grinning amiably.

"This is going to be a comfortable trip for me," he confided. "I find I know the cook. It's a lucky thing if you stand in well with the cook. Him and me was shipmates together on a Vancouver packet. He's the Snohomish Glutton." He opened his eyes and looked at me as though he expected that I would show astonishment. "I said—he's the Snohomish Glutton," he repeated, more loudly.

But my face remained blank.

"You don't mean to tell me that you never heard of the Snohomish Glutton!"

I shook my head.

"You nev—You don't—You ain't ever—" Ike took another drag at the gingerbread, and swallowed hard. "Why, the Snohomish Glutton is known—the Snohomish Glutton, he has eat at one setting—Oh, shucks, if you ain't ever heard, what's the use!" He started on, but whirled and came back and shook the hunk of gingerbread under my nose. "I suppose if it had been writ and printed in a book you Eastern perfessers would know all about it. Thank God, in the West we know a lot of things that ain't printed in a book!" Then he stumped away.

Well, I concluded I would stroll along to the galley and take a look at the cook, and be able thereafter to say that at least I had seen this notable of the Pacific.

There was a spacious galley on the old *Zizania*. I looked in through an open window which commanded the port alley. A fat man was chopping kindlings. He was a thing of rolls and folds of fat—a gob of a man. There were narrow slits near his nose marking his eyes, but his eyes seemed to be shut by fat. A little, round, pursed-up mouth was in the middle of his face, and from this came wheezy grunts as he chopped.

While I was watching him, an object bounded into the galley door and leapfrogged him, darting past me through the window. Before I could turn my head the thing, whatever it was, had disappeared around the corner of the alley.

The cook straightened up, and by an effort opened his eyes enough to stare at me. I expected a deep, gruff voice. But he had a real tin-whistle pipe.

"What did you throw at me?"

"I didn't throw anything. Something rushed through the galley—I didn't see what."

"Things don't hit a man unless they are thrown," he insisted. "I may look funny, but I ain't funny. I don't relish having things thrown at me."

He gave up trying to hold his eyes open, and went on chopping.

I was getting my breath ready to protest when the thing came through once more. It was a monkey. But it missed the cook's back, for the broad shoulders heaved as the ax came up. The monkey slipped, slid across the chopping-block, and down came the ax. The animal squealed horribly, flung itself past me through the open window, and fled. It went like a shot, but I got the fleeting impression that its tail was gone.

"What did you do then?" asked the cook, squinting at me suspiciously.

"I tell you I haven't done anything at all. That was a monkey. He came from somewhere. He ran through here. I think you have cut off his tail." He peered about. "There ain't no tail here," he whined. "There couldn't have been any monkey here. This ain't any place for a monkey to be. There may be monkey business here—and you're getting it up. You go away from here!"

I'm afraid the Snohomish Glutton and I would have had trouble then and there, but just then a man came rushing into the door of the galley. He had the monkey under his arm, upside down, and he was pointing quivering finger at a bleeding stump of a tail. I couldn't understand what he was bawling. I found out afterward that he was a Russian Finn and could command only a few English words even when he was perfectly calm. He was not calm now. I never heard a man rave so. The monkey joined him with hideous screams.

The cook listened for a time, puckering his fat forehead. When he found that the man was talking a foreign language he upraised his ax and swished it around in circles near the Finn's head. A cook in his galley is lord supreme in his domain, and the sailor probably knew as much. The ax was menacing; it was coming very close, and the Finn already had one exhibit of that cook's ferocity under his arm. He allowed himself to be backed out, and the cook slammed and barred the door.

"What did he say?" he asked me, in his piping tones.

"I don't know what he said."

"I reckoned it was some kind of Dago swearing, and I don't allow a man to swear at me. Most likely it was swearing."

"You cut off that monkey's tail," I insisted. "I thought so when he squealed. Now I'm sure of it."

He went to peering around again, whining to himself like a fat porcupine who is being badgered.

"There ain't no tail here. I didn't cut off his tail. I didn't see him so that I could cut off his tail." He started toward the window with a look as if he proposed to resent my suggestion that he had been cutting off monkeys' tails. I passed on. I figured that I might as well try to argue with a Sussex shote as with that shapeless mass of fat. I would have saved a nasty bit of trouble for myself, perhaps, if I had remained and argued. And my trouble later that day—and that monkey with the missing tail—was the seed from which— But that's getting ahead of the story.

There ware really three messes aboard the *Zizania*. There was the captain's mess aft, with special dishes, which was entirely distinct from the crew's food. On the port side was set out the food for the black half of the checker-board crew, and on the starboard side the white half received their provender.

We were at dinner in the captain's mess. It was our first meal at sea—our first meeting at table.

When Miss Karna came in we were just sitting down. The captain was with us, having left one of the Joneses at the wheel. Keedy lifted his paint-streak mustache against his nose in a smile, and pulled out a chair beside his own.

"Sit here, my dear," he said to the girl.

She walked past the chair, came around to my side of the table, and sat down. She did not toss her chin or sniff, as some girls would have done, to show dislike of Keedy. She was a cool proposition, that girl was.

That left the chair beside Keedy the only vacant one at the table. A plump little man had been standing off at one side, waiting for the last choice of seats. He looked rather bashful, and his round face was shining with soap, and his hair was plastered down at the sides and combed up in front in a fancy cowlick. You could see that he realized that he did not exactly belong at that table. Therefore he had scrubbed himself up for the occasion.

Captain Rask Holstrom did not trouble himself with any of the finer graces of society. He gruffly introduced the little man as Romeo Shank, chief engineer, and told Shank to slide into the chair beside Keedy. "We ain't drawing any fine lines between ship's officers on this trip," stated the captain, bluntly, for the benefit of all concerned. "Get to table while the grub is hot, and get it into you—that's the motto. Business before style is the idea aboard this boat."

He began to shovel food industriously with his knife.

Keedy hitched away from his table-mate a few inches, and looked across at me, and deepened the wrinkle between his eyes. But he could not spoil my appetite. Something else which happened the next moment pretty nigh did it, though.

A black man leaped into the saloon through the forward door by which the waiter came and went. Two other black men were at his back. They stopped just inside the door and dragged off their knitted caps. They had the appearance of being a delegation, and an excited delegation at that. It was plain to be seen that they had come rushing aft without stopping to figure on consequences. The leader carried something in front of him, and it was looped over the blade of a wicked-looking knife. He held the object at arm's length toward Captain Holstrom, pointed at it with the vibrating finger of his left hand, and yelped shrilly like a dog. He was too excited and too furious to put his complaint into words.

"What have ye got there—a snake?" yelped the captain, gulping down a mouthful, and wrinkling his nose like one who had suddenly come upon something disgusting.

"We find him in our kittle—we find him dere. Yassuh! We eat 'most to de bottom, and den we find him," raved the negro.

Captain Holstrom snapped up from the table and strode over and squinted at the object which dangled from the knife blade.

"Dey cook for us in our kittle a monkey tail—dem white men cook dat for us, and laugh," squealed the negro.

"And you think that some of those cheap white jokers put it in, eh?"

"Dey laugh all de time since when we pull him out. Yassuh, it's a lot of fun for dem men."

Captain Holstrom rubbed his nose thoughtfully, and stared down on the thing which had savored the black man's dinner.

A happy thought seemed to strike him. He turned his head and winked at me.

"Take that thing out and whack it across the face of the white man you find laughing the hardest," he commanded. "When he gets up to hit you pitch in." He came lurching back to the table. "I didn't intend to have the row till to-morrow," he informed us, in an undertone. "But this is too good a chance to miss. We'll get that checkerboard crew on a war basis where they'll stay put."

The black men were lingering at the door, trying to get the captain's meaning through their wool.

"Excuse me, Captain Holstrom," I said, "but I think I know how this thing happened—and I feel it's too bad to have innocent men beaten up." I started to tell what I had seen, but he swore and broke in on me.

"Don't butt into something that's none of your business!" he snapped. He roared at the men: "Go do what I told you to do. Go punch the jokes out of that white gang or you'll have no peace the rest of the voyage. Get out of here before I kick you out!"

It sounded like a very pretty row, judging it from where we were sitting in the saloon. It began in a very few minutes.

"Mr. Number-two Jones," directed the captain, "go out there and oversee, and let me know when it's time to break the clinch." He loaded up his plate once more and kept on eating.

In about five minutes the mate returned. "I reckon it's about time to knock 'em apart, Captain Holstrom," he advised, shoving his head in at the door. "No great harm done, but they're chewing each other bad, and that means expense for plaster and salve."

If I hadn't already lost my appetite for dinner, that grisly statement from Mr. Number-two Jones would have fixed me. I pushed back from the table.

"Come along, Sidney," commanded the captain, kicking his chair out from under him. "Come settle your dinner. I'll find a club for you."

"I'll obey the orders you gave me first, sir," I called after him; "I won't butt into something that's none of my business."

"Do you mean to say—" He had stopped and whirled on me.

I was sore because he had snapped me up so short before them all. I thought my explanation should have been considered.

"I mean to say that this fight was needless. You started it; now you can stop it."

Mr. Keedy had been lighting a cigar, and it was plain that he did not intend to venture out into the mêlée.

"Look here—I tell you to come along," yelled the captain. "It's your duty."

"Not on your life. I'm no ship's officer! I'm along as a diver, not as a prize-fighter."

Captain Holstrom looked ugly enough just then to tackle me as a preface to his job forward, but after cursing a moment he followed the mate. The riot was increasing, and it was plain that he was needed in the field.

Keedy leaned back and scowled at me through his cigar smoke.

"I didn't know I had picked a quitter," he sneered. "We're tackling a job that needs sand. You ain't a tin horn, are you?"

I didn't answer and the back of my neck began to itch; I suppose if I had had hair there like a dog's, the hair would have bristled. That itching in the neck when you're mad is a survival of the old days when men had lots of hair on 'em.

I started to walk out of the saloon. Miss Karna was sitting there, looking at us, and her presence rather complicated matters for a man who was getting madder all the time, as I was. The other officers had chased along on the trail of Captain Holstrom.

"A second-hand diving-suit doesn't stack up very high against what we're putting into this thing—Captain Holstrom and myself," he insisted. "There was something going in from your side in addition to the diving-suit, as I understand it. But a coward can't invest grit."

I stopped at the door and walked back toward him.

"A what?" I inquired.

"I said 'a coward.'"

I slapped him—not hard.

"Now come up on deck with me, Mr. Keedy. You've got to come after that. There's a lady here."

261

"I'm going, gentlemen," said the girl. "Don't mind me." She looked at Keedy and set her lips.

But Keedy jumped up and pulled a gun instead of putting up his fists.

"I don't fight that way, Mr. Keedy," I told him. "I have no gun. You'd better put yours up. You can't afford to kill me—not yet!"

"No—and that's the devil of it," he blurted, after waiting a moment. "You have taken advantage of—of—"

"Of your hankering to get money into your paws," I snapped back at him. "If you won't come up and fight man fashion, I can't make you, but if you ever call me a coward again on this trip I'll put in a little evidence to the contrary with these." I showed him my fists.

He rammed his revolver into his hip pocket and stamped out of the saloon.

I found the girl looking at me, wrinkling her forehead.

"I beg your pardon, Miss Holstrom," I apologized. "But an itching to strike that man has been in my fingers for some time."

"You ought to have waited until you had an excuse to strike harder than that, Mr. Sidney. I have known Marcena Keedy for a long time. A man like you with a big job ahead ought to be able to keep his eyes to the front all the time. Now you will have to keep looking behind you. I say—I have known Mr. Keedy for a long time."

She went out.

I followed a few minutes afterward, and I went with my head down, and I was pretty thoughtful. Captain Holstrom and I bumped together in the doorway. He shoved past me and threw a club into a corner.

"I hope you can dive better'n you can fight," he snorted.

Then he bawled to the waiter and demanded his piece of pie.

XXIX

THE TELLTALE RIBS

There was nothing especially interesting about that prolonged grunt of the old *Zizania* down the California coast. She rolled and thrashed, and the brisk trades spattered spray over her bows, and she certainly took her own time in moving along.

We all settled down to endure the trip as best we could, but it was a rather surly party. Forward, the blacks and whites nursed their scars and their grudge; aft, Keedy and I scowled at each other so much that nobody could be happy around where we were. Miss Karna walked the deck alone, or read, or embroidered in her state-room; once in a while I got a glimpse of her through the door while she was at work. She continued to sit beside me at table, but she was very cool and distant. I don't know as I tried to have her anything else. I would have liked to lean over the rail and talk with her, though I never presumed to speak to her on deck. Take a fellow when he is young, penned aboard a slow packet, a pretty girl near him all the time, and you bet he cannot confine all his thought to the scenery and his job.

She truly was a pretty girl! I can see her now as she strode to and fro on the upper deck, her hands shoved deep in the pockets of her white sweater, and drawing it forward so that it set off her plumpness. There was a sort of indescribable tousle to her hair, if I may put it that way. I don't know what the color was—there's no name for those shades of copper and brown and all that. I know I liked mighty well to see the sun shine through that hair.

I loafed below and forward considerably. I found a lot to interest me, particularly a job that the Russian Finn was on in his spare time. He was making a new tail for his monkey. He explained to me half tearfully that the monkey would never be safe or happy otherwise. I had pretty hard work to understand the man's broken lingo, but I gathered that this especial kind of monkey needed to spend a portion of his time hanging head downward from his tail in order to be well and contented. Once or twice since the tail had been amputated the monkey had run up the foremast or the derrick, and had confidently tried to throw an imaginary tail over a rope, and had tumbled to the deck, where he had squatted and moaned and examined the stump with confused and pitiful attempt to understand the phenomenon. I could sympathize with the Finn's fears when he said that "some day he fall over the board or break him damn neck." The cook's random blow had left some inches of the stump, and to this with marline and glue the Finn deftly fastened by an "end-seizing" a wire covered with furred skin. I wondered where he secured this skin. He owned up to me. He had captured and killed one of the cook's pet cats, and the cook had never opened his eyes wide enough to detect the crime, or to behold where the skin of the defunct was performing vicarious atonement.

This catskin-covered wire was hooked at the end. Edison, I reckon, never watched the testing of an invention with greater raptness than the Finn displayed as the monkey, after a thorough inspection of the new appendage, clambered aloft to where a rope swayed invitingly. I confess that I shared in that interest. It proved a surprising success. The monkey swung from the hook, chattered, and grinned, and came down and sat for long minutes scrutinizing the thing, running busy little fingers along the furred wire.

"I may need an inventor with brains when I get at my job down below here," I told the Finn. "I will remember what you have done to your monkey."

But when the time did come, it was the monkey instead of the master who served.

As day followed day, and we finally raised the loom of the southern California mountains in the blue distance on our port, Ingot Ike came out of the lethargy in which limitless supplies of soft gingerbread seemed to involve him. He talked to me with the brown crumbs sticking in the corners of his mouth, and his spirits rose higher each day. He was like a thermometer which was being brought nearer and nearer to heat. His talk became more eager, his demeanor more alert, joy more intense.

"After all I've talked about it, and told 'em about it, and argued, it's coming true at last," he kept repeating to me. He had fastened himself to me with especial insistence during the voyage. "You're the one who is going to get it, who is going off this boat right down to where it is, where you can lay your hands right on it, sir. Won't it be a grand feeling when you lay your hands on the first box?"

"Yes," I admitted, "it will—when I lay my hands on it."

I did not say that with any great enthusiasm. If Ingot Ike had not been so full of gingerbread and glee he would have seen that I was pretty much down. That San Francisco cocktail had got well worked out of me. I'd had plenty of time to think the whole thing over during that wallow down the coast. A man could be hopeful, in on shore, with Mr. Keedy rolling the word "gold" over his tongue like a luscious morsel. I had been hopeful—and desperate. But after days at sea in that rickety old tub, with her rotten equipment, her bargain-sale fittings, her makeshift crew, with her whole grouchy, suspicious, and reckless atmosphere, I decided that I was a fool and would have been better off if I had gone out and hunted for a legitimate job. I had ahead of me the fact, according to old Ike, that other good men had tried and failed. I had behind me just then the sure feeling that Mr. Keedy proposed to do me up as soon as I made good, provided I did so by some lucky chance.

The last stage of the voyage south was made with old Ike posted in the crow's-nest, his beak thrust out, and his mat of hair fluttering in the wind. He was so excited that he forgot to wallop gingerbread between his toothless jaws.

Number-two Jones, who wasn't a bad sort, gave me some information about the coast which was in sight of us since we had crossed the mouth of the Gulf of California. He had sailed those waters before. He had a somewhat misty remembrance of where the steamer *Golden Gate* had gone ashore, but he had never been in the vicinity of the spot, for the sand-bars obliged craft to keep well offshore.

According to his recollection, the wreck had occurred along the Guerrero coast, somewhere between Orilla and Acapulco. The doomed steamer, after she had caught fire, was headed for the harbor of Acapulco, almost the only haven on the coast, but an outlying sand-bar tripped her many miles north of her destination and she went to her grave. Mr. Jones confessed that he did not know just where; he would be obliged to hunt fifty miles of coast for her if it were up to him.

But Ingot Ike had the memory of a monomaniac on the subject of the *Golden Gate*. He peered under his palm at the hazy sky-line; he threw back his head and snuffed into the east like a dog treeing game.

Captain Holstrom started the lead going as soon as Ike had asked to have the *Zizania* hug the coast more closely. He knew the reputation of those hummocks and submarine plateaus of sand, and the howl of the leadsman rather astonished me when he reported, for on the Atlantic coast, to which I had been accustomed, we would be in deep water with a coast-line so far away in the hazy blue of the east. At a distance which I judged to be at least two miles offshore we were getting a report of only fifteen or twenty fathoms.

At last Ike began to swish his thin arm. "Ye'd better down killick, Captain!" he screamed from the crow's-nest. "We're laying off of her. This is the place." He scrambled down and ran to the wheel-house. "If you put her in closer than this she'll roll her blamed old smokestack out."

Captain Holstrom accepted that advice promptly, though the shore-line was at least a mile away.

He yelled shrilly, and splash! went the port anchor. When she had swung wide he sent down the starboard mud-hook, and she headed the rolling Pacific, riding easily to the heave of the giant sweepers.

A little thrill tingled in me as she came to a halt. We were on the ground at last.

It was now up to me!

There were plenty of other men on that boat, but there was only one man who could reach out and put his hand on that treasure, and that was myself. The thought did not help to cheer my despondency.

Captain Holstrom was immediately busy with a huge telescope which he lifted from its rack and leveled across the sill of the wheel-house window. Old Ike was excitedly counseling him, jabbing a digit toward the shore.

"Follow down from that second nick in that hossback mount'in," the guide suggested. "Them is my bearings. You ought to see them ribs fairly plain against the white where that surf is breaking in-shore."

There was silence after that while the captain squinted through the glass, twisting a section now and then to sharpen the focus. His daughter was in the wheel-house at his side, her face tense. She had never intimated to me, of course, what her ideas were in regard to this treasure quest. She may have held the whole project in the same contempt in which she seemed to hold Keedy, its chief instigator, or old Ike, its prophet. But I stole a look at her, and decided that she was interested now.

Well, anything with intellect above that of a steer would have had to be interested at that moment.

We were hoping that yonder under those rollers lay three or four million dollars' worth of gold—gold enough to buy everything that man or woman could desire.

Even the blockheads of the checker-board crew, who could hope for no more than their wages from the quest, were staring over the rail from the main deck forward, their mouths open. Marcena Keedy was eating a cigar instead of smoking it.

"Them ribs ought to be there, Captain," insisted the old man, wistfully. "The rest has been buried, but them ribs have stood all the swash for years. They ought to be there."

There was another long silence.

Then Captain Holstrom straightened up. "They're there!" said he. He beckoned to me. I was at the rail. "Come in here," he directed. "It's your next peek—for yonder is laid out your job."

I had good eyes and I spotted the objects right off. There were three curved ribs of a ship outlined against the white of the breaking rollers beyond. The telescope gave the view relief and perspective, and I saw that the ribs were well outshore. Many yards of tossing water, so I judged, were between them and land.

"Well, what do you think?" he inquired, when I passed the glass back.

"I'll tell you after I've been down, sir. A diver can't afford to waste guesswork on the top side of water."

The girl shook her head when her father offered her the telescope, and Keedy came in and took his look.

"Away in there, is it? Well, what are we waiting for out here?"

Captain Holstrom looked his partner up and down. This sudden exhibition of a lack of a practical knowledge took his breath away for a moment.

"We're waiting out here because we have got to stay here, Marcena. This is as far as it's safe to go."

"We might as well sit on the Cliff House piazza and boss the job as be out here," grumbled the gambler.

"I don't know what sort of an idea you had about getting this treasure," retorted the captain. "But if you had paid attention to Ike when he was telling about the lay of the land you ought to have realized that we wasn't going to tie up to that wreck and have Sidney hook bags of gold on to a fish-line for you to pull up."

"I'm down here to have a general oversight in this business," said Keedy, "and I propose to be near enough to the job to oversee it."

Captain Holstrom looked a bit disgusted. "We might rig a bos'n's chair for you on one of them ribs, and cut a hole in the water for you to look down through. But see here, Marcena, don't get foolish about this thing. All you've been thinking about, so I judge, is of them boxes of gold, and you haven't stopped to figure on the way of getting 'em. I have figured. I've talked a lot with old Ike when you wasn't listening, but was dreaming about them ingots. Now you listen to me. Let's start in without a row and a general misunderstanding." He began to dot off his points with a stubby forefinger.

"We can't anchor the *Zizania* any nearer. There isn't holding-ground on that sand, and we've got to have plenty of water under this steamer in case of a blow. See those lighters forward? I bought 'em after I got a general understanding of the lay of the land here from Ike."

"You bought a lot of things without consulting me," said Keedy, showing his grouch. "What *am* I in this thing—a passenger or a partner? Seeing that my money is in it, I propose to have my brains in, too."

The man acted and talked in a way to indicate that he was starting out hunting for trouble. It began to look to me as if there were worse shoals ahead for our partnership than the shoals of San Apusa Bar. Mr. Jones had given me that as the name of the place where the wreck lay.

Capt. Rask Holstrom did not have the steadiest temper in the world. His eyes narrowed.

"Every man for his own line, Keedy. I'm not presuming to tell you how to deal from the box, nor how to size the buried card in stud poker. Nor I don't need any advice from you when it comes to handling a job of work in tidewater. I've waited till I got here to tell you my plans. When I can talk and you can see the layout at the same time, I'll not be wasting so much breath; even those faro-game brains of yours can take in what I'm getting at. Now, hold right on! This is going to be a square deal, and you can sit close to the jack-pot. Those four lighters are going overboard, and we'll moor them in a chain between here and the shore. We can splice the cables so as to allow a hundred fathoms between each one. That will make each lighter a sort of a bridle anchor for the others, and we ought to get the inshore lighter mighty nigh the wreck. You can stay on that lighter and have your meals brought if you hanker to."

He snapped out that last remark while he was backing down the ladder from the bridge to the main deck. The sneer that went with it did not improve the state of Keedy's feelings.

"I'll show this aggregation whether I can boss a job or not," he growled.

I decided right then that if Keedy tried to boss me from that inshore lighter the partnership of Holstrom, Keedy & Sidney would get a fracture in the second joint much wider than the one which was already widening there. I looked after him when he strolled away, and I reckon if he had turned around and given me one of those nasty looks of his just then I would have run after him and hoisted him a good one under the coat-tail—gladly taking the consequences. I had never hated Anson C. Doughty any worse. Keedy had grafted himself on to the project with stolen money—and now he was insulting the rest of us by placing us in the rogue class with himself and in need of watching.

I suppose I looked very blue and ugly and disgusted as I stood there at the rail, scowling first at Keedy and then at the streaming white of the surf which played beyond the ribs of the wreck.

The girl spoke to me. She leaned from the window of the wheelhouse, and there was a note in her voice I had never heard before. All her brusqueness was gone. She was sort of confidential and wistful.

"You don't think much of this scheme, do you, Mr. Sidney?"

I was in the mood to agree with her. "There must be an almighty good reason why those other fellows did not recover the treasure, Miss Holstrom, providing old Ike is right in what he says and that they didn't get it. I can tell better after I have been down."

"I have never seen a diver at work. It is very dangerous, isn't it?"

"That depends on the job. I have been as deep as one hundred and seventy feet, Miss Holstrom, and I felt perfectly safe, though the pressure made my nose bleed. Another time I was down in only four fathoms in the wash of a lee shore, and they couldn't keep my lines and my air-hose clear, and they pulled me up near dead. That's a lee shore yonder, and I'm afraid I'm going to find some very good reasons why the other divers didn't succeed. Sometimes I am tempted to believe that they did get the gold and that old Ike's talk is simply a dream."

"I think the whole affair is a nightmare—I mean this trip," she declared. "I don't believe the good Lord is going to allow a man like Marcena Keedy to succeed in any decent enterprise."

I rubbed my ear and looked at her for a few minutes. I had been turning over a thought about this expedition in my mind for some days. I did not know whether to say anything to her about it or not. It would be giving Captain Holstrom a pretty hard dig. But I blurted it, for she knew I had something on my mind and bluntly demanded to know what I was thinking about.

"Perhaps this is the kind of a scheme where the devil will help his own, Miss Holstrom—and therefore Keedy belongs in the thick of it as chief manager. He'll win on that basis. I don't know much about admiralty law or maritime justice. But it may be that this treasure has not been officially abandoned. Perhaps taking it is stealing it. I know that the *Zizania* got away from port with papers as a trawl fisher. I know I have no business talking like this about your father's affair. But if it's to be real stealing, perhaps we'll succeed with Keedy in the game," I said—and it was a pretty clumsy joke. It fell flat.

"I hope my father will wake up," she said, curtly, looking down on him where he was giving off orders about clearing the big derrick. "Sometimes I almost believe in evil spirits and in control of a man's mind by another man—in a wicked way, I mean. But I thank God there's one of the Holstrom family who can't be hypnotized by Marcena Keedy. That is why I have come on this voyage—my father needs a guardian."

She came down the steps from the wheel-house, and went into her state-room. I walked aft, for the *Zizania* had swung with the surges, and was tailing toward shore, and I wanted to look at the place where my work had been cut out for me.

Keedy met me amidship. He came out from behind a lashed life-boat, and it struck me at once that he had been in ambush, spying on me. That was before he had opened his mouth. He did not leave me in any doubt when he began to talk.

"Let's get to an understanding about Miss Holstrom, Sidney," he rasped, leveling his finger at me. "You let her alone. No more buzzing her behind my back or her father's."

"Keedy, you have started running after trouble to-day. In my case, you'll catch up with it mighty soon."

"Then let's make believe I have caught up. I'm going to marry that young lady. And no cheap Yankee masher is going to stand around and make sheep's eyes at her. That's business and you keep your hands down. You slap me again, Sidney, and I'll drop you in your tracks—even if the gold stays there till we can get another diver." He had his hand on his hip, and his eyes were fairly green.

I started to tell him what I thought of him and his chances with that girl, proposing to throw in a few remarks about what I should do if I wanted to. But I shut my mouth suddenly. I had no right to stand out there and insult a girl by quarreling about her with a fellow of that stripe.

Vastly different were the circumstances and the relations of the persons concerned—but I felt the same rankling of resentment which hurt my pride and my feelings when Jeff Dawlin growled his warning in my ear. I hated to leave any false impressions with Keedy. I did not propose to have him think I envied him anything he possessed or thought he possessed. Pride and the spirit of brag—that was it—prompted my answer.

"Look here," I shot out at him, "I have a girl East who is worth more than all the gold you expect to find in that wreck over there. What do you think I'm out in this God-forsaken country for? What do you think I'm gambling along with you for? It's so I can grab off enough money to make a showing when I carry it back home and pour it into her lap! Don't you worry, Keedy. I don't want any of your girls. There's one who is waiting for me back East!" How a man will lie when he gets to talking about girls! I snapped my fingers under

Keedy's nose and walked on aft. I felt considerably relieved because I figured I had taken some of the conceit out of him. I had a lot taken out of myself when I returned.

Miss Karna Holstrom met me. She gave me one of those up-and-down glances which seem to sting like the flick of a long lash.

"I have no objection to your discussing your love affairs with Mr. Keedy, my dear sir—though I question your good taste. But I must ask you not to discuss me with him."

"I assure you I did not!"

"I stepped into my state-room only to get my cap. I was walking on the other side of the life-boat when you were talking."

"But I—"

"I'm sure you understand my request, sir." She walked on.

A fine partnership—that of Holstrom, Keedy, and Sidney, treasure-seekers! And there was a silent partner whose silence just then, along with her disgust, sent a crimson flame into my cheeks.

XXX

THE LOCKS OF THE SAND

Right away I found that Captain Holstrom knew how to "team" a crew. He started that checker-board outfit of his to humping in good earnest after he and I had planned out the details of setting the stage for the work ahead of us.

We needed to reach as long an arm as possible toward the wreck.

Inside of four days after we planted our mud-hooks on San Apusa Bar, we had our string of lighters in place.

First we anchored them and then we linked them with one another by cables because the sandy bottom inshore from the steamer afforded poor holding-ground for the anchors. Having a number of lighters hitched together in this manner, the chain made a sort of spring cable for the lighter nearest the wreck where the scuffling surges were piling high over the shoals. The scow nearest the shore thrashed about in rather lively style, but I figured that I could do my work from it in pretty fair fashion. At any rate, by our system of cables, we planted the lighter less than three hundred feet from the upstanding ribs of the *Golden Gate*. It was about the best we could do, considering our limited equipment.

On the fifth day all was ready for me to go down for the first time.

Of course I had been allowed to pick my own helpers, and I had been giving them lessons for some time. I chose Mate Number-two Jones to tend hose and lines, and Chief-Engineer Shank was to manage the air-pump. I had found them to be steady and reliable men. I owned a Heinke diving-dress which had cost me six hundred dollars, and with the right men "up-stairs" I was not worrying about my ability to get down and stay down—even if I had been off my job for a while. As to what I would be able to accomplish when I got down on ocean's floor I was not quite so sure.

While I had been waiting for the lighters to be moored I had pumped Ingot Ike daily.

He did seem to know what he was talking about—and I had to admit that. The matter of the treasure of the *Golden Gate* had crowded everything else out of his mind, and left his memory mighty clear. He drew a plan of her with a stubby pencil, and went into minute details of description. He said the ribs which showed were forward of the room where the treasure had been stored. The fire had been aft and amidship, and when she had struck the sand she had buried her nose, and these ribs were planted so solidly that the surf had not been able to beat them down. As a quartermaster who had known his ship, he was able to tell me how many paces aft from the standing ribs should be the spot where the treasure lay.

They made ready the best life-boat on the *Zizania* for me and my equipment, a big yawl with sponsons. Captain Holstrom did not propose to take any chances with that outfit during the ferrying process. He went as coxswain, and I was not surprised, of course, to see Keedy scramble in even before I had lowered my diving-dress over the side. What did surprise me was to have Miss Karna show up as a passenger. When she stepped past me and went down the ladder my eyes bugged out. I thought 'twas somebody I had never seen before. She wore knickerbockers, and was gaitered to the knees, and she went into the life-boat as nimbly as a midshipman, asking a hand from no one. I could have cracked Keedy across the face with a relish for the way he rolled his eyes at her.

She showed the good sense of an out-of-door girl who understood a thing or two when she picked that costume. Embarking and disembarking with that surf running under a keel was no job for a girl in skirts.

When we came up beside the in-lying lighter we were climbing white-flaked hills of water and coasting dizzily into green valleys. Those waves of the old Pacific which had marched across seas from the lee of the Society Islands were certainly making a great how-de-do in halting on those sand-bars of the Mexican coast; and inshore there in the shallows the surf had a nastier fling to it than off where we had found holding-ground for the old *Zizania*. It was a case of every one for himself in making the transfer from the life-boat to the lighter. I was ready to assist the girl, but she set foot on the gunwale, sprang with the heave of the boat, and landed on deck as lightly as a bird; she could not have done the trick more neatly if she had worn wings on the shoulders of that close-fitting sweater.

There was one cheerful moment for me on that day of anxiety; Keedy was the last passenger out of the life-boat, and he teetered and made motions to jump, and flinched and squirmed and backed water like a swimmer afraid to plunge in. When he did jump at last he stubbed his toe on the deck of the lighter, and raked that hooked beak of his across the planks. I grinned at him when he staggered up, holding to his bleeding nose, and I went to overhauling my diving-dress, whistling a tune.

I found Number-two Jones and round little Romeo Shank to be

helpful handy-Andys after the instructions I had given them. The girl never missed a motion they made in getting me ready. I felt a warm finger trying to worm its way under my rubber wristbands, and I turned to find her looking at me with a great deal of concern. She explained that she wanted to be sure that no water could leak in, and then she seemed to think that she had been just a bit forward, and she blushed.

The next thing I knew she was sturdily fetching one of my twenty-pound shoes, and stood there holding it ready for my helpers. I had gone down a good many times in my life, but I went that day with the happy consciousness of helpful interest in my poor self.

Then they set the helmet on to the breastplate and gave it its one-eighth turn into the screw bayonet joint, and set the thumb-screws. My front eyepiece was hinged like the window of a ship's port-hole, and this was open. The girl bent down and peered at my face.

"It seems a terrible thing for you to be closed in there—for you to go down into that raging water," she said, her face close to mine.

"Wish me good luck, and I'll go humming a tune," said I, smiling at her.

"With all my heart I do," she answered, a catch in her voice.

I shut the frame, and Mr. Shank set the turn-screw. With a man on each side of me, I scuffed my way to the ladder, and went over the rail of the lighter. I waited at the foot of the ladder—about ten feet under—until I felt that little pop in my ears which signals to the diver that his Eustachian tube is open, and that the pressure is equalized. Then I yanked the rope to ask for a taut life-line, and let go my hold.

The sun was bright and the bed of the sea was of sand, and I found good light below. There was a heavy sway to the water even on bottom, but I was strong, and knew how to handle myself. I found my footing, and started along.

My only tool that day was a peaked-nose shovel. I crawled along, using it for a push-pole.

I found the bottom to be a succession of bars, which were parallel with the shore—waves of sand, so to speak, ranging from six to ten feet in height. It was a slow job working one's way across them. However, they assisted me—there was no danger of getting off one's course. I needed only to proceed at right angles to the bars. Through my bull's-eye in that dim green light I could see ahead for some distance. So at last I came to the timbers of the wreck. There was a long tangle of these, a great mass of wreckage hidden by the sea and protruding but a little way above the sand which the eternal surf had packed down. I kept along toward shore until I came to the timbers

which, so my eyes told me, must be the ones that marked the location of the wreck. They went looming up through the water. I clung
to one of them and rested. I was having no trouble with my air, and
now that I had reached the scene of the work that fact comforted me.
The movement of the sea in that shallower water was considerable,
and now and then a heavier roller jostled me about. But I began to
plan out a system of lashings that would anchor me.

Then I got down on my belly, and started to measure paces along
the edge of the timbers, following Ike's instructions as to distance.
There was mighty little that was encouraging about the spot which I
finally located as the probable site of the treasure-chamber. Sand was
billowed and packed there, and the place was quite free from wreckage. It occurred to me that the other divers had dug the timbers away
at this point. As I was feeling fairly fresh, I decided to use my shovel
a bit.

After five minutes' toil at that sand I began to perceive why
the others had failed, providing Ingot Ike was correct and they *had*
failed. In the first place, there was not the footing on that bottom that
a submarine diver needs. I skated about almost helplessly when the
heaving sea clutched at me. When I tried to drive the shovel into the
sand I was pushed back, and the tool made only scratches on the bottom. Without a prop or a brace, a diver cannot pull or push horizontally with much force even under the best conditions, and when I did
succeed in getting the shovel into the sand and scooped a hole, the
particles began to settle back, driven by the swaying seas. The giant
Pacific was jealous of the treasure it had engulfed.

There was nothing more for me to do down there that day. I began to feel that pain above the eyes which warns the diver. I gave
the signal for return, and went back at a lively pace, for the taut line
helped.

I saw none of them on the lighter until my helmet had been removed, for when a diver ascends to the air his bull's-eye becomes
covered with mist in spite of the wash of vinegar which has kept the
glass clear below. Marcena Keedy was in front of me, looking at my
hands, and acting as though he were wondering where I had stowed
the find I had made below.

"Well, it's there, isn't it?" he demanded.

"From what little I have been able to find out, I reckon it is
there," I told him; "and it wouldn't surprise me much if it stayed
there for some time." I was in no mood to encourage that polecat,
who was plainly thinking more about that treasure than he was about
any dangers I might have been through. He drew that streak-o'-paint

mustache up against his nose and looked like a dog about to snap. I turned away from him so as to have something better to look at. There was the girl beside me. She sure was an antidote for the poison of Marcena Keedy's evil eye. Her red lips were apart, and her little hands were clasped, finger interlaced with finger.

"Thank God you are back safe, Mr. Sidney!"

She wasn't looking at me as though she were wondering in which pocket I had hidden an ingot of gold.

"It was not dangerous," I told her. "It was disappointing, that's all."

I ignored Keedy. I looked past him to Captain Holstrom, and related what had happened below. It was a mighty interested crowd that stood around me and listened.

"The idea is," I wound up, "this is no 'reach-down-and-pick-it-up' proposition."

"That's what I call doing damn little in an hour's work," growled Keedy. "You ain't down here to tell us how hard that job is. We have heard all about that from the other divers. You are down here to get that gold. You bragged around what a devil of a diver you have been, and now when we have to depend on you, all we get is some more conversation. Have you got us away down here and let us in on a dead one?"

"If that money was in a faro-bank instead of a sand-bank," I told him, "you would be just the man to get it out—you have had plenty of practice in that line. But this happens to be an honest job, and it needs something besides false cards."

Then I kept on talking to the captain:

"After giving the thing a good looking-over I have begun to figure on a few plans. I'll paw over and size up the stuff on the *Zizania* this afternoon and see what there is in stock to help me." I told Mr. Jones to unstrap my shoes.

When Keedy saw them peeling off my dress he had a few more remarks to offer about the kind of a "hot diver" a man was who called an hour a day's work. If I had brought up an ingot in each hand from that first trip he wouldn't have been grateful; he would have wanted to know why I did not bring up the whole box.

I had a dirty job of it that afternoon pawing over the old junk on board that steamer, but I managed to sort out some material that fitted into my scheme, and it was ferried to the lighter.

I went down again the next morning at sunrise, for the southwest trade-wind had quieted during the night, and the swell wasn't quite as energetic as it had been under the push of the breeze the previous day.

I had the same spectators. Miss Karna, looking like a pretty boy in her knickerbockers, had plainly determined to keep in the front row, and I'll own up that her presence put ginger into my efforts. I reckoned I'd show her the difference between a man who could do and dare and a sneering loafer of the caliber of Keedy. A handsome girl usually has an effect of that sort on a young man.

When I reached bottom under the lighter they lowered an old mushroom anchor to me. I unhooked it, and started to roll it along the "windrows" of sand toward the wreck. It took every ounce of strength in me to boost it up those slopes. I had lashed a crowbar to the anchor stock, and when I finally got the thing to the wreck and had rested I stuck to the job, though I had really done as much as was advisable at one descent.

I loosened up a sizable patch of sand with the crowbar, and settled the anchor in the hole, stock upright. There was no need for me to pack the sand back; the Pacific Ocean would attend to that part of the job. The Pacific was altogether too busy in packing sand, though. It did not discriminate between an anchor which I wanted made solid and treasure which I wanted set free.

I went down a second time that day. I carried small chains and a broad shovel. I lashed myself to the anchor's stock, and with that support as a fulcrum for my body I dug into the sand with the crowbar, and fanned out the loose particles with the broad shovel.

But it was like the reverse of the story of the man who set out to carry water in a sieve. The sand kept running in. If I had been able to stay down there night and day, and have my meals brought to me, and could have worked without rest or sleep, I might have been able to dig a hole in that sand and to keep it dug out until I had come to that treasure. As it was, I toiled until my head seemed splitting, until blood ran from my nose, and I felt the first weakness of that peculiar paralysis of the limbs which divers experience when they pass the limit set for endurance under water. I lashed my tools to the anchor, and was pulled back to the lighter.

Human arms had given up—human strength and grit had failed. But I knew that through the hours of that afternoon, through the watches of the night, that old, miserly ocean would keep toiling on, rolling sand back into that hole, patting it down with unseen fingers, locking a door over the treasure that would serve the purpose better than doors of steel or bars of bronze. I should find all my labor undone when I came back to that anchor.

Therefore I did not lark and play when I was dragged over the rail of the old lighter. I stumbled to my seat, and sat and wiped blood from my face when the helmet had been twisted off the breastplate.

"Four hours since you went down—you're sure a wonder!" muttered Shank, patting my dripping shoulder.

I was embarrassed—a bit shocked—when the girl hurried to me and began to wipe away the blood with her little handkerchief. I tried to push away her hands. It didn't seem right to have her do such a task. But she resisted me. She kept on.

"You poor boy!" she said—or I thought she said it; I was not sure. There was pity in her tones—a caressing kind of pity, such as comes right from a woman's heart. I was astonished. She had been stiff and curt toward me—and was rather short with every one else, for that matter. She had never seemed tender even toward her own father.

But she murmured again in my ear, leaning close to me, "You poor boy!"

I'll admit I was glad to hear her say it—I needed sympathy; but because I mention the girl and her little ways please do not jump at the conclusion that I was falling in love. She had overheard a declaration which established my standing with her and, I suppose, made her feel freer in my company. Oh no! I was not falling in love!

Sitting there as I did with forty pounds of lead on my feet and eighty pounds of it across my shoulders, with air in my dress puffing me out like a giant frog, dripping with brine, and hideous with blood-smeared face, I wasn't much to look at in the way of a lover. And outside of the pity she had never by flicker of eyelid, or tone of voice, or touch of hand intimated that she was interested in me except as a young man who was tugging at a hard job and deserved a little encouragement.

"It's all—all useless—down there—isn't it?" she asked.

"No; it's a glorious job, and I've just begun on it."

"But it's wicked for you to suffer like this."

"I was never so comfortable and happy in all my life—never so full of courage."

Keedy was listening and I felt like tormenting him. He stuck his face down to mine. It was not a pretty face. His nose was swathed in absorbent cotton, which was held on with straps of court-plaster.

"Well, let me in on why you're so happy," he snapped.

"It doesn't happen to be any of your business," I informed him.

"Ain't I a partner in this thing with you?"

"When I get ready to tell you anything about my work, I'll see that you are informed. Or, if you want to make the trip, I'll tuck you under my arm and take you down to-morrow. I'd be delighted to do so." He looked at me a little while and his eyes narrowed.

That evening I had a talk with Capt. Rask Holstrom. Marcena Keedy was not in that conference. I walked the upper deck until Keedy had gone, grunting and growling, off into his state-room. Then I hunted up the captain where he was lying on the transom in the wheel-house, puffing at his pipe and looking rather sullen. I knew what was ailing him. I had refused earlier in the evening to come into the wheel-house while Keedy was there.

"Being a plain and blunt man, I may as well say what's on my mind," stated Captain Holstrom, sourly. He did not arise. He squinted at me from under the vizor of his cap, which was pulled low over his eyes. "You ain't dealing with me and Keedy open and frank as your partners. You ain't giving us full particulars. You was down four hours to-day, and came up looking blue and scared, and then just talked flush-dush with my girl. We ain't down here for anything except straight business and results. Your two eyes are the eyes for all three of us. When you have used 'em down below there we're entitled to have full report. Me and Keedy ain't at all satisfied with the way this thing is running on."

I sat and looked at him, and waited to hear whether he had any more to say.

"No, sir, we ain't satisfied," he repeated.

"I'm glad Mr. Keedy isn't satisfied," I told him. "I wish he would get so dissatisfied that he would quit this expedition. And I don't intend to kowtow to him and make him satisfied."

"Well, I'll be damnationed!" exploded the captain, pushing back his cap.

"You needn't be, Captain Holstrom. What I say doesn't have any reference to you at all. I hope my relations and yours will stay as they are—no, I hope they will improve as you know me better. But that gambler has grafted himself on to this scheme. He isn't a practical man, as you are. He sneers at me and my work—and God knows it's hard and dangerous work. He expects impossible things, and it doesn't do any good to come up out of that hell of water and explain to him. Every time he opens his mouth I feel like jumping down his throat and galloping his gizzard out of him. There! That's rough talk, but I mean it. If Marcena Keedy doesn't handle himself different where I'm concerned there's going to be serious trouble aboard here. Hold on a moment! Hear me through. I respect your good judgment and I know you are willing to work hard. I'm ready to talk to you at any time when that sneak isn't around. What you say to him after that about plans and expectations I don't care—that's your own business. But I'm sorry you don't hate and distrust him as much as I do. Now I'll tell you what I found down there to-day, and how the thing looks to me." I told him.

"Then, if all that is so, we may as well up killick and go home, eh?" I never saw a more disgusted look on a man's face, or heard a more melancholy tone.

"I haven't told you that to discourage you, or to cry-baby myself. I'm giving you the facts, and I hope you're practical man enough to keep from sneering about my efforts the way Keedy does. I'm doing all that a human being can do—but you've got to face facts, Captain Holstrom, and I've been giving you facts, I say. That's the situation—that's all! You know as much as I know. If you have ideas, think 'em over and give 'em to me. I'll keep on trying to think up something myself." I went off to my state-room so as to give him time to do that thinking.

XXXI

A TASTE OF BLOOD

The old Pacific was in her usual welter next morning. The big seas were rolling up from the equator, and we could hear them booming in on the coast-line.

As I look back on that nightmare off the bars of San Apusa I think the day when I went down with the anchor was the calmest day of our stay. With the everlasting thrust of the trades behind them the billows rolled, rolled, rolled, rolled—seethed and surged—giant green soldiers with the white plumes, charging that sandy shore. I got to feel after a time that they were soldiers in real earnest, and that they were after me—poor little midget, who was trying to accomplish the impossible.

At breakfast Mr. Shank ventured to remark politely and somewhat nervously that he was supposing I would not try to go down that day.

And I told Mr. Shank rather brusquely that of course I should go down, and added that if we were to wait for smooth water in soundings on the lee shore of the Pacific Ocean in the season of the trades, we should have brought plenty of knitting-work and novels.

Captain Holstrom, from the head of the table, smiled and winked at me with the most cordial expression I had ever seen on his face. I decided that one of my partners was regarding me in a more amiable frame of mind than he had before I had made that little speech to him. Mr. Keedy scowled at me, and I was glad of that mark of his continued disesteem. It occurred to me that perhaps I was weaning the captain from Keedy, for Holstrom snapped his friend up rather short two or three times during the meal.

I went down that day with more weights. The tug of three rollers inshore was tremendous for a buoyant man, even in the comparative calm of the previous day. I realized what I would meet up with this day, and I was not disappointed in my reckoning.

I was tumbled from hummock to hummock of the submarine sand-bars. I was knocked down, and then was stood up once more. Sometimes I was lifted off my feet, and then I was rolled and pressed down and pinned to the sand till it seemed that I would never get on my feet again. Part of the time I was thrust ahead as if the Pacific were trying to make me walk Spanish—and then I was yanked backward on all-fours like a big crab.

I knew a whole lot about undertows, and I realized that I was having an experience with a particularly crazy one.

Men who have observed and studied think they have a pretty good line on the notions and the moods of the sea—but take it from me as a submarine diver, they haven't. If one is standing on a rock and looking out on it, or sailing across it in a safe boat, the ocean becomes a matter of "beautiful surf," or an expanse more or less hubbly with waves.

But get down into it—get down deep where it can play with you, twirl you, toss you, suck your breath, provided it can throttle your air-hose—where it can work all its schemes and its spite. You will find out that the ocean has a new trick for every day.

There are beaches where persons have bathed in safety for years. Then all at once some day a shrieking man or woman is seized, as though by some hidden monster, and is dragged off to death. That mighty and erratic force is called an undertow. It is now here, now there. It is born out of diverted currents, checked tide rips. It sneaks up bays, seeking prey; it roams along open beaches. I know a lot more about undertows, but that's all for now.

I was in one that day off San Apusa. Wind, tide, a current wandering off its course—one of the currents that is uncharted and which is known only by some diver who meets it on its wanderings below the surface, had combined, and had come to play in the vicinity of the wreck of the old *Golden Gate*.

I struggled on toward that wreck. Say, I met an old friend of mine. It was the mushroom anchor, and it was doing a sort of jig on top of a sand ridge when I first saw it. Evidently it had been lonesome during the night, and it had come to meet me. It was at least one hundred feet on the sea side of the wreck—and I had left it with fluke buried close to the ribs. If that undertow had dug up that anchor it might be doing other things. That thought came to me like a flash of hope. There's no telling what an undertow will do when it gets to prancing, you know!

I unlashed the crowbar from the anchor stock and tumbled on over the ridges. I found myself in an opaque yellow light instead of in the green radiance I had found on my other two trips, and I knew that the sand was in motion inshore. When I came to the wreckage of the steamer I did not know my way about. The undertow had been dragging away the packing of sand here and there. More bulk of the débris was displayed, so far as I could judge by touch and by what I could see in the dim light. I groped my way along to the great ribs which showed above water, in order to get my bearing. It was a fight to get there. I was thrashed about and tossed and slatted. I wasn't exactly sure when I did get there, for other parts of the wreck had been uncovered so much that one could easily be deceived in water in which boiled so much sand that it was like working in soup.

However, I toiled back after I reckoned I had located the marker.

Yes, the old Pacific had truly had a change of heart since the day before. The unseen fingers of that freakish undertow had been at work—they were still at work. They were scooping out sand instead of piling it in. I can best describe the appearance of things by saying that there was a smother of sand in the swirling water. Now and then the water cleared when the undertow let go its tuggings for a moment, and I could see parts of the steamer which formerly had been hidden from me.

When I had counted the paces that should bring me in the neighborhood of the treasure, I set my crowbar into the sand with all the strength I could muster, and twisted it around and around in order to loosen the stuff. It was wonderful how quickly the water dragged away what I set free from that pack.

A bottle came bouncing up out of the hole. I dislodged pieces of broken crockery. Ingot Ike had said that the treasure had been stored in a compartment of the ship near the pantry. The sight of that jetsam encouraged me. I stabbed with all my might, drove the crowbar in again and again, struggled to hold myself on bottom, and muttered appeals to that undertow in my frenzy of toil. I do not know how long I worked. I do know that all my sensations informed me that I was remaining beyond my limit of endurance. But the conviction came to me that this was not a chance to be neglected. I was in a fever of hope. I wanted to show that coward of a Marcena Keedy that a strong man could call the bluff of a loafer's sneers. I wanted to convince Capt. Rask Holstrom that he had not picked out a piker, and perhaps I wanted a girl to give me the smile which success ought to win.

Well—and here's to the point!—all at once, when I was near fainting, my crowbar struck something which was not bottles or crockery. I managed at last to get the point of the bar under the object. I could not see what it was. I only knew, as I worked the bar, edging it around the thing to dislodge the sand, that the object was oblong and had corners.

My buoyancy and the swing of the rolling sea would not allow me to pry with any great force. I could only pick at the sand and coax the box out. In the end I had it where I could get my fingers under the edges—and there's one thing a diver can do: he can lift with the strength of a giant, the air in his dress assisting him.

Yes, it *was* a box, so I found when I had it out. It was a heavy box even when lifted there under the sea. It was a small box, and there could be only one reason for such a small box being so heavy—it was one of the bullion boxes. Of that fact I was convinced.

I carried several small chains at my belt—my lashings in case of need. I circled the box with chains, and secured it to my body as best I could, then clutched my arm about it for greater safety. As I worked I grew more excited—I had drawn first blood in my duel with the old Pacific. Excitedly I pulled the line to send my signal to the lighter, asking for help on the return. They told me afterward that I gave the emergency signal. Perhaps I did. They had been waiting for a signal for so long that they were in a state of panic. They feared that I had been drowned, for I had been down for hours. When they got my double tug, so they told me later, Number-two Jones gave a yell, called every man on the lighter to the rope, and proceeded to give me a run home in emergency time.

The first yank took me off my feet. Overballasted by the box of gold, I tipped head down, and butted the summit of the first hummock of sand with my helmet. My neck was snapped to one side and my head got a tremendous rap against the side of the helmet. I did not strike ground again until I reached the next ridge. I struck that and bounced, and I think I took a recess on breathing right then and there. I have not much recollection of the rest of that three hundred feet of rush back to the lighter. I know I hit a good many hummocks, and I must have passed away into dreamy unconsciousness when the drag upward through the water to the rail of the lighter began.

They told me that when I came over the rail I was bent double, and it was some time before they saw that I had something tucked in my arms.

I heard somebody shout, "Oh, God, this man is dead!" But I was just getting my wits back then. I opened my eyes. Two of the crew were holding me up, and Shank had my helmet off. He yelled like a maniac:

"I'm wrong! He ain't!"

"I'm mighty glad you're wrong, Shank," I told him. My voice was pretty feeble, but the memory of that box came back to me, and my thoughts were dancing even if I couldn't dance with my body just then.

I tried to look around after that box, but I lost interest in it the next instant. It's pretty hard work for me to tell you what happened, and tell it in a matter-of-fact way, as I'm trying to tell the rest of this yarn. When I looked around I saw Karna Holstrom on her knees a little way from me, her face as pale as the white foam on the waves, her eyes wide open. I think her ears had been closed by horror when Shank had let out his first yell.

"You're alive!" she cried. And the next instant I was very much alive, for she leaped up and ran to me, and threw her arms around my neck and kissed me squarely on the mouth. Then her face was no longer white. It flamed.

"I didn't mean to—I am sorry—it was a mistake!" she gasped, and she broke out and cried like a baby. But I caught her hand before she could get out of reach of me, and pulled it to me and kissed it.

"Ah, if I *had* been dead you would have waked me up," I told her.

"I've a blamed good mind to kiss you myself!" roared old Holstrom from somewhere behind me. Then he let out a whoop and came and capered in front of me.

"You've brought up twenty thousand dollars' worth of gold!" he informed me. "Five ingots, with the assay mark on 'em, and each worth four thousand dollars. That's the kind of a diver you are, Sidney! All together, men! Three cheers for the greatest sea diver that ever wore lead shoes!" And the men gave the cheers while he pounded his fists on my back.

I got a view of Marcena Keedy when I turned my head around. Mr. Keedy was not showing any interest in my condition—not he. He was sitting on deck with the open box hugged between his knees, and he was feeling over those bars of gold like a lover fondling his lady's cheek.

"I can't say I'm stuck on the style of that critter," mumbled Shank in my ear. "He yanked that box away from you before we had fairly swung you inboard and before anybody knew you was alive. He pried it open, and has set there making love to it ever since."

Old Ike was squatting in front of Keedy on his haunches, and was drooling like a hound watching a butcher.

"It's there! I've always said it was there. It's there all bright and shining. They all have hooted at me because I have said it was there. Now what do you think?"

"Nobody has been a game sport in this thing except you and me," said Keedy, sticking an ingot up under Ike's nose. "Nobody would back your hand till I came along. I've had to talk everybody over before anybody would do anything. I know how to play a hand with a buried card in it. I've played that hand to the limit, and now see what has happened. When you fellows are passing cheers around you'd better hooray for the man who has turned the trick—for the man who kept at it till he got you down here."

He gave me a nasty side-glance and snuggled the box under his legs just as though he had recovered property which belonged to him.

"Where there's one there's the rest of 'em, eh, Sidney? You have found the nest of the beauties, eh? Well, do we get another nice little box to-day? We may as well open the game with forty thousand while we're about it."

Shank was leaning close to me, unscrewing the wing nuts between the breastplate and my collar-band. He began to swear very soulfully in an undertone, and he kept on swearing when he got a look from me that indorsed all his sentiments in regard to Mr. Keedy.

"There are three millions down there—and twenty thousand is only a flea-bite," declared the callous knave. I don't believe he noticed that I was half dead when I was pulled up—or cared a rap about my condition, anyway. "I'm strong for bulling the game when it's coming your way. What do you say, Sidney, if we make the first day's ante forty thousand?"

"Captain Holstrom," I said, "a man who has been banging the soul out of himself for five hours in a diving-suit is in no condition to talk to a skunk like that over there. Can't you say something?"

I must confess that the captain did rise nobly to the occasion. A tugboat man who has spent most of his life fighting for berths in the maze of shipping along the San Francisco water-front needs considerable hot language in his business, and Captain Holstrom was in good practice.

"So I've got the two partners against me now, have I?" snarled Keedy. "I had to fight to get the two of you into the proposition, and now that you're making good I've got to fight both of you to keep the thing going, have I? Thanks for the hint as to how you propose to hold cards—but I serve notice right now that you can't whipsaw me between you."

He looked as evil as a door-tender in Tophet, but his threats did not trouble me.

That evening something happened that indicated further cleavage of associations on board the *Zizania*, whose checker-board crew had set an example early in the cruise.

Ingot Ike came to the captain and myself in the wheel-house.

"Now that we're beginning to haul in the bright and shining stuff that makes the world go round I'd like to know where I'm going to get off when the divvy comes," said he. And he was more than a little insolent in the way he said it. It was a good guess that he had absorbed more or less of the insolence of his new running-mate, Marce-

286

na Keedy.

Captain Holstrom was pretty short with the man. He informed old Ike that when the work was done and we knew what the profits would be he would be handed a lay which would make him comfortable for life. "That was the understanding between us when we started out on the gamble," said the captain. "You haven't got a dollar ahead now—you never did have. A lot of money wouldn't do you any good, anyway. You don't know how to keep it or how to spend it."

"That ain't any of your business!" declared Ike, with heat. "We have begun to get up that gold. We'll get all of it. It's there, just as I said it was. I want ten per cent. of all that comes over the rail, and I want it without any strings on it."

"And if you got it laid into your hand you'd be around in six months borrowing from me," said the captain. "If this thing comes out as it ought to, I'll put enough in trust for you to pay you a hundred dollars a month as long as you live. Now go off and dream of that, and be happy."

"Happy your Aunt Lizy!" yelped the old man. "See here, me and Keedy is the whole thing in this, and—"

Captain Holstrom arose and grabbed Ike and tossed him out of the wheel-house door.

"Them two fellows," he confided, wrathfully, to me, "will be charging me board on this trip, besides taking all the profits for themselves, if I don't watch out."

I did not confide to the captain any of my doubts that evening in our talk. I was hoping for the best. I had recovered one box with the assistance of my enemy, the old Pacific. I understood the queer and notional quirks of undertows. I realized that history might not repeat itself in this case—but the Pacific coast was new to me, and I was not ready to believe that I had happened on the only case of an undertow scooping sand instead of piling it and packing it. I went to bed, tired as a hound after a chase.

And I went down into the sea again the next day, still hoping. Yes, I was fairly confident—so confident that I carried a pair of ice-tongs. My experience of the day before had shown me that this tool was just the thing with which to grapple one of those boxes and lift it from the sand.

There was plenty of motion in the depths of the sea. But I realized that it was not the motion of the day before. The swaying water thrust me ahead over the hummocks with more force than it pulled me backward. The water was clear and green once more. Where, oh, where had my undertow gone?

I had ground my crowbar into the sand where I worked the day before. I could not find it, and after a survey I saw it had been covered by the drifting sand. Portions of the wreck which had been in sight were hidden again. The hole where I had wrought so valiantly was filled and smoothed. It is wonderful how quickly currents of water can make changes in sand. I had seen instances before in my submarine jobs; now I was beholding a more striking case. After inspecting the scene I judged that the treasure was buried more deeply than ever. The ocean had plenty of loose sand with which to work, and had used it. I tell you honestly I never suffered such an awful feeling of disappointment. The pang was worse because I had been successful once.

It was as though my enemy, the ocean, had decided to give me one bite of the fruit of success in order to whet the appetite of my expectations. It had not relented in order to do that—it had played a devilish trick on me. It had shown me that the millions were there—money enough for all that life or love might require in this world. I had got a peep—had got one taste—and the malicious ocean had tucked it all out of reach once more, and was making faces at me with the wrinkles of that hard-packed sand.

It was useless to remain down and exhaust myself. I signaled, and returned to the lighter.

As soon as my bull's-eye cleared after I came up out of the bubbling water I saw Keedy. He was perched on the rail near the lifeline coils, looking down at me like a fish-hawk eying its prey. For a moment I was glad I did not have another box. I enjoyed his disappointment.

Then, after my helmet was off, I told Captain Holstrom that a change in current had piled up the sand and that nothing could be done that day.

"That's it!" raged Keedy, smacking his fist into his palm. "You wouldn't take my advice yesterday. You wouldn't follow your hand when the cards were running right. I understand about those things. That was the time to double the ante! I know how to play the game for what it's worth. There ain't any brains in this whole outfit except what I've got under my hat. I see it's up to me to go down there and show you how to do this thing."

"I'll be out of this diving-dress in a few minutes," I told him. "You're welcome to use it."

I had a wild hope that he was mad enough to go down—angry enough and gold-hungry enough. It would have settled the case of Keedy if he had gone down—soaked with rum and tobacco as he was. But he swore and walked away and jumped into the life-boat—so much of a coward that he wanted to put as great a distance between that dress and himself as he could.

I can describe the happenings of the next two sad weeks in two words, "Nothing doing!"

Not that I didn't go down. I went every day. I tried all kinds of tools. I sat up nights to think, and worked days under water until they had to pull me back to the lighter, riding on my back over the sand hummocks, so weak that I could not use my feet and drag my lead-weighted shoes. But the old Pacific had given us our one mouthful of bait, and now was mocking us. If I loosened sand the ocean took that sand and piled it higher over the treasure. And all the time Keedy glowered and growled and swore, and said I was not half trying.

One morning Captain Holstrom came banging on my state-room door before I was awake. He tried to tell me something, fairly froth-ing at the mouth, but the words tumbled over each other so rapidly that I couldn't understand. He was jabbing a slip of paper at me, and I took it and read:

To HOLSTROM AND SIDNEY,—With two partners working against me, I claim the partnership is broken. After this I'll work on my own hook, and I'll have a man who is a real diver, not a dub; and I warn you not to bother me in any way.

"Partnership broken!" yelled the captain. "And how do you sup-pose he has broken it? He sneaked away in the night. He took Ike and four of my crew and the best life-boat. But that ain't the worst. He took the gold—all of it! Took the twenty thousand. He had the key to the safe."

"Why did you let him have the key to the safe?"

"Because he howled around that he ought to have some office as a partner, and wanted to be treasurer. He has trimmed us for twenty thousand, and he'll use that money to fit out another expedition. He has done us good and proper, and there ain't anything sensible we can do about it."

I reflected a few moments, and decided that, considering the kind of a project we were working on, we could not afford to chase Keedy and howl. In the opinion of certain persons interested in that wreck, we might appear as thieves, ourselves, if the thing became known in Frisco.

I tried to say something to Captain Holstrom about being well rid of Keedy, but I do not think he heard me. He was too busy stamping about and swearing. That was truly a dark-blue morning on the *Ziza-*

nia.

They were certainly weary and hopeless days which tagged on after that. I kept going down, for I hoped to meet up with another obliging undertow. But San Apusa Bar did not seem to be a popular resort for undertows.

In about ten days we got another hard jolt. A little schooner came swashing up in the lee of the *Zizania*, and a boat was rowed off to us. The two men who leaped over the rail introduced themselves as Mexican customs officers for the district off which we lay, and they wore the uniform to prove their identity. It had been reported to them, they said, that we were seeking treasure from the wreck of the *Golden Gate*, and they told us we must stop such business at once and sail away or we should lay ourselves liable to arrest and imprisonment. They had a lot to tell us about what the law was, but I have forgotten. Maybe they were giving us straight law, and maybe they were not. Neither Holstrom nor I knew.

The captain did know men if he did not know law—and he was a man who had mighty keen sense for a crook's trail, having had a lot of experience with crooks on the water-front. He rubbed his red knob of a nose for some time, and listened. Then he invited the customs men into his sanctuary of the wheel-house, and called me along with them.

"I know all about who has been talking this over with you, gents," he told them. "I reckoned he would make down the coast in that life-boat he stole from me. He stole that boat, he stole my men, he stole what else he could lay his hands on here. He is a yaller-faced faro-dealer. He never told the truth, he never dealt square cards, he has always cut a corner on every man he had business with. I don't want to see you fooled. I'm the captain of this steamer. You can see I'm something of a man. This is my partner, and you can look at him and see that he is no crook. I'm going to get right to the point, gents. Do you want to do business with a square man or a crook? You might as well be open with me. Men have to live down here in Mexico. I know all about this customs business along the coast. You've got to do business to live."

They blinked hard, but they did not protest.

"I don't know how much of a 'hot rock' he dropped into your hat, but I'm prepared to drop in a bigger and a hotter one."

I had never heard that expression about a "hot rock" before, and I was obliged to listen a little while longer in order to understand that Captain Holstrom was talking thus bluntly about a bribe.

"In one case you're doing business with a crook—a thief. He'll turn around and do you when he has used you. In this case you are dealing with a man who has a name along the water-front, who owns this steamer, and who is here to make a dollar for himself and for you. You are men with brains and you can size up chaps pretty well. I'll bet you didn't like the looks of that whelp with his cat's eyes and his mustache cocked up—come, now!"

They blinked harder.

The captain leaned to me and whispered in my ear: "Run and tell Karna to give you every gold piece she has got in her pocket. Dig over your own pockets. Tell the Joneses to dig. Bring it here. I've got to keep 'em on the run with conversation."

I returned with my collection, and the captain added the contents of his own pocket, banging the coins on the transom. Then he swept the money into a little sack and drove the sack down into the trousers pocket of one of the officers.

"That's only posting a little forfeit that we'll do as we agree," cried Captain Holstrom, heartily. "We are here where you can watch us, gents. But you can't watch a fly-by-night like that coyote who has been lying to you about us. Keep your eyes out—stand by us—and you'll get a 'hot rock' in your hat that you'll need both hands to hold up. We'll see the other man's stake and then raise him out of the game—and if we don't, then come and seize the steamer."

He followed the men to the rail, shook hands with them half a dozen times, and they returned most urbane grins when they rowed away.

As soon as they were out of ear-shot the captain cursed them in horrible fashion and shook his clenched fist at them under pretense of waving farewells.

"So that's what Keedy done as quick as he got down coast to a port, hey? Cleaned us out of what he could lug, and then sent them critters here to finish the job. He probably thinks he is going to make a clear field here for himself by strapping us for every cent, and then setting the customs on to us as soon as he can drop another 'hot rock' into their hat so as to raise us out."

"Don't those men feel bound in any way after taking money from us?" I asked him.

"They feel bound till the next fellow gets to 'em, my son. Do you see what we have got cut out for us? By the jumped-up Judy, we've got to get that gold—and we've got to keep ahead of everybody else in getting that gold, because them custom-house blood-suckers are going to stick to the juiciest crowd. I don't know what kind of an outfit Keedy proposes to bring back here, but he has got twenty thousand dollars in his fist, and a man can do a lot of business on charters with twenty thousand dollars. And we haven't got a sou markee."

He stamped into the wheel-house, shaking his fist above his head, and I walked up and down the upper deck, thinking some thoughts which I do not care to call back to mind.

XXXII

PER MISTER MONKEY

As she had done many times in those days of gloom and doubt, the girl came out of her state-room and walked with me. Her companionship was a consolation. She looked up at me from under her tousle of curls and swung along by my side with an easy air of comradeship.

The word "comradeship" best expresses our attitude toward each other. After that explosion of her feelings on board the lighter, when she had kissed me in front of the whole bunch, she had coated herself with just a little ice, and my Yankee reserve and sensitiveness detected it. It was as though she had hinted to me that I would be a cad to presume further because she had taken a woman's interest in my misfortune. In fact, she had dropped a few words in regard to women making fools of themselves when they are too frightened to know what they are doing.

Furthermore, she stuck to that knickerbocker costume of hers, and I found myself forgetting half the time that she was a girl, for she clambered about over the truck aboard the old *Zizania* as no girl in skirts could, and never needed a hand on her trips to and from the lighter. She wore those clothes with such frank assurance that the garb was the only suitable one for the circumstances, with such lack of self-consciousness, that after a few days it really seemed as if the other men had forgotten that we had a girl aboard.

Perhaps that accounts for the fact that when one of the firemen rushed past us a few minute later he was using language such as he would not have used had he been properly mindful that there was a lady in hearing.

The fireman came from the depths below-decks, and was chasing the Russian Finn's monkey. He was so intent on the chase that when the fleeing monkey invaded the sanctity of the upper deck the fireman came along, too. There were several breathless instants in that part of the pursuit which we saw. You will recollect that this monkey had a false end to his mutilated tail—a curved wire, which was covered with cat's fur. As the monkey fled, screaming and swinging the heavy end of the tail from side to side, the hook caught, first on a stanchion, then on a life-boat prop. The monkey had not entirely mastered the science of handling that new tail, or else he was too excited just then to remember its limitations. When he had his own pliant tail it didn't matter if a loop hooked around an obstruction. But now when the wire hooked itself the monkey was obliged to back up and unhook that inflexible loop. Each time he stopped he lost all the lead he had gained on the fireman.

Four times in traversing the upper deck the coal-heaver was near enough to make a crack at the monkey with a grate bar. Each time the monkey unhooked himself just in time to be able to dodge and continue the flight. Finally the fugitive made the ensign mast by a rousing leap, shinned up, and hung over the dingy gilded ball at the top. I don't understand monkey talk, but I'm sure that the yells he sent down were just as pure profanity as that which the fireman was howling up at him.

"Hey, there, my man," I called, "that kind of talk doesn't belong up here."

He shut up, gave the monkey a long and blistering stare, and came back toward the ladder. Sweat was running down through the soot on his face, and that face showed that he was in no pleasant frame of mind.

"I asks to be excused," he said, "but that—" he gulped. "Seeing that I can't talk about it before a lady and be polite, I asks to be excused again and I'll be going."

I followed him to the head of the ladder and stopped him just as he was on the first rounds.

"What happened?"

"We're keeping up a little steam for the derrick windlass and the pumps, and that gimlet-eyed, snub-nosed hellion got into the bunkers when I was on deck, and turned on my wet-down hose, and shifted twenty tons of dust coal out to where it's all got to be shoveled back. I'm going down to write out notices for a funeral and, by Jabez! I'll guarantee to have the corpse ready!"

"Shifted twenty tons of coal!" said I, surprised. "It must have taken him some time."

"I guess you don't know what can be done in fine coal with a stream of water when you bore it in," snapped the fireman. "That wire-tailed gabumpus wasn't in there five minutes. He has laid in wait and watched me sprinkle coal. He turned her on full bent and bored. I'll get him, and I'll get him good!" His smudged face went out of sight down the ladder.

There are some ideas in this life which steal up on a man and whisper to him, and keep whispering for a long time, until at last he overhears—and then he plans and toils, and in the end an invention results.

Then there are other ideas which march up to a man and hit him on the head.

Twenty tons of coal shifted in five minutes by a monkey and a hose! The idea that hit me was like a hammer blow. My head wasn't clear all at once; I was dizzy. The details were hazy—but there was the idea hammering at me. It was such a glorious idea that I walked aft to that ensign mast, looked up, and took off my hat to that monkey. I know he misunderstood my act. I know he cursed me as another enemy. But I did not care. I had got used to being misunderstood and underrated aboard the *Zizania*.

I turned around and found the girl looking at me with wide-open eyes. "This isn't insanity," I told her. "It doesn't run in the Sidney family. But an idea has just come to me out of a monkey's prank, and it's such a wonderful idea that I don't dare to talk about it until I have thought it over. I guess you'll have to excuse me, Miss Karna; I've got to go into my state-room and pound at that idea while it is hot."

I did not sleep much that night. I was wrestling with a notion as the old chap in the Bible wrestled with the angel. And when morning came I was positive that an angel of a notion had come to me. I told Captain Holstrom at breakfast that I was not going down that day. But when he turned a doleful look at me I grinned so amiably that he snapped his eyes, thinking, perhaps, that he was not seeing just straight.

"I'll have something to tell you later, Captain. It'll sound better to you when I have made certain that we have got stuff aboard here to work out an idea."

That became my business after breakfast—to hunt the *Zizania* over for certain material. I invited Captain Holstrom along with me, and took two men for helpers.

My first quest was for hose. The *Zizania* carried canvas hose for fire purposes, stacked here and there on racks. It was not in prime condition, for the old *Zizania* had been condemned along with her equipment as far as Government purposes went.

We got that hose down and measured it, and found rising two hundred feet of stuff that was serviceable. I needed three hundred feet to cover the distance between the lighter and the wreck. I made inquiries about canvas. The steamer had a suit of sails for her two masts, and the sails had been unbent some time before and were stored. Before the day was over Mate Number-two Jones had men at work cutting that canvas and sewing it into hose of a diameter to fit the fire-hose. Of course, it was crude work, but I was obliged to do the best I could with the materials at hand.

That evening I called a conference. Captain Holstrom, his two mates, and Engineer Shank assembled in the wheel-house, and I explained as best I could what my preparations meant.

Remember, please, that at the time of which I am writing hydraulic mining had not been tried, and men in those days had no conception of what a stream of water would accomplish in moving soil.

I told those blinking confrères that I believed I could direct a stream of water on that sand below the sea and bore a hole down to that treasure. The only one in the party who showed one glimmer of enthusiasm was Mr. Shank. And even he did not get up and hurrah. He nodded his head sagely and admitted that "stranger things had happened."

"But you've got to use our steam-donkey for your stream," growled Captain Holstrom, "and you can't get the *Zizania* any nearer shore than this without wrecking her. You're only planning on three hundred feet of hose."

"That's all I need, Captain. Mr. Shank can build us a plunger-pump with brakes, and we'll put the whole crew on to the beams, and have 'em give an imitation of a firemen's muster."

Mr. Shank nodded again, and allowed that "stranger things had been done."

"How did you happen to think of this cussed scheme, anyway?" inquired Captain Holstrom, not trying to hide his disappointment.

I promptly decided that I would not confess that the thing had been suggested to me by a monkey with a wire tail. I looked at the scowling captain, and I could imagine the wealth of his language if I should tell him any such thing. So I took all the credit to myself—and it was not much credit I received from those solemn listeners. The most I got out of Holstrom was the sullen statement that no matter what I did next the situation couldn't be any worse than it was.

The work went on the next day, and the day after, and the day after that. It was slow business making that hose so that it would be anyway water-tight. And the wooden force-pump took a lot of time in the building, rude affair though it was. It had a plunger—two ends of wood on an iron rod, and the brake-beams were long enough so that a dozen men could get a clutch on them.

I don't remember how much time we used up in getting our makeshift apparatus into such shape as would warrant it being used for the trial.

I do remember this—and remember it all too well!—before we were in readiness for the test of the hose and our pump a small schooner came rolling up the coast and anchored well inside of us, even nearer the wreck than our lighter from which we had been operating.

This was no customs boat. Within a few hours we abroad the *Zizania* knew that Marcena Keedy was in command of the new arrival, and that he had brought two divers and was full of hope and curses and brag.

Where Keedy secured his men and his craft we did not know—for social calls were not exchanged between the two vessels. But a lot can be accomplished in a few weeks when a man has greed to prick him, a grudge to settle, and twenty thousand dollars to back him.

Capt. Rask Holstrom had been in the depths of despair before the arrival of Keedy; now he found a hole leading into the subcellar of his despair, and retreated still lower. He had no faith in my new contrivances. He wanted me to abandon work on such folderols and go down and stand over that treasure. He could not seem to see with my eyes. He knew that millions in gold were at the bottom of the sea—I had recovered a sample of it. He felt just as though it lay there unprotected, and that the first-comer would get it. As a submarine diver who had struggled against the difficulties of the situation, I was more serene. I didn't know what sort of prodigies in the diving line Keedy had secured as my rivals, but I was not ready to admit to myself that they would succeed by ordinary means where I had failed after exerting every ounce of effort.

Using Captain Holstrom's long telescope, I saw them going down. They went together. Evidently Keedy had concluded that if one diver had failed, two ought to be twice as good, and succeed.

Captain Holstrom remained at the end of his telescope until he acquired a permanent squint. We had hard work to get him to drop the glass long enough to eat. Day after day, as soon as it was light in the morning, he was in the wheel-house, balancing the glass across the window-sill, watching Keedy's schooner. He evidently feared and expected to see uncounted wooden boxes of ingots come tumbling up over her rail.

My equipment had been almost ready when Keedy arrived, but now another consideration held me back. I did not propose to let the other crowd in on my methods if I could help it. No matter what Captain Holstrom and his associates thought of the feasibility of the scheme, I had a lot of confidence in it, and was not willing that a rival should know enough about it to copy any plans.

Therefore I set my crew at work building a wall of boards about the lighter, leaving only a door for my exit over the side. I wanted to conceal the pumping operations. As to the divers whom I should meet at the scene of the wreck, I trusted to other measures to conceal my system.

I was out on the lighter to superintend the building of the wall, and more especially to oversee the setting of the force-pump and its attachments. I did not like the looks of the sea on that last day of our work. It looked murky and slaty as the big rollers surged under us, and I remembered that it showed that same color on the day when my friendly undertow had helped me. I was tempted to go down and investigate, but I had seen the men from Keedy's schooner go over-board, and I concluded to keep away from contact with them until I was ready for serious operations.

Inclosed in my wall on the lighter, I was busy about my own af-fairs, and did not peep to see what was happening in the neighbor-hood.

Captain Holstrom remained on the *Zizania*, in close companion-ship of his only intimate of those days—his long telescope. But Kar-na Holstrom was at my side while I worked, cheering me by her wise little comments, her bright eyes taking all in, her quick mind grasp-ing all the possibilities of my scheme.

It was a rather cheerful little group there in our pen. Even Num-ber-two Jones was whistling in jig time, for all the apparatus was fit-ting together as slick as a schoolmarm's hand in a fur mitten. And then in through the door burst a human thunderbolt in the form of Capt. Rask Holstrom.

He was bareheaded and his gray hair was scruffed up like the bristling mane of a mad bulldog. He was not able to manage words for about a minute, but he wasn't voiceless by any manner of means. He roared and leaped about and smote his fists together. He picked up our hose and flung it about himself like an insane snake charmer. He kicked at the wooden pump with his stub-toed shoes until I was obliged to push him away. Then he grabbed the hose once more, and reeled it about himself in senseless fury, for all the world like a cater-pillar weaving its cocoon. His square face was a war map of rage, and in the center of that face his red nose gleamed like a danger sig-nal.

We stood and gaped at him. There wasn't much else we could do as long as he remained in that awful state. He paid no attention to his daughter's questions and appeals.

I took a peep through the cracks of the boarding to see whether the old *Zizania* were still afloat; I had a horrified suspicion that she had sunk or burned. She floated serenely, sweeping up and down on the crested waves.

After letting off his surplus of steam in howls, Captain Holstrom was able to manage speech at last.

"They've got it!" he yelled. "They're getting it! I've seen 'em pull two boxes of it over their rail, and they're dancing jubilee around the deck." He flung down the coils of hose, and stamped on it, and spat the most vicious oaths I ever listened to.

"They're getting it—they've got it—and all you're doing here is fooling with a damnation squirt-gun that ain't no sense and no good—and I told you so in the first place. Keedy was right. I ought to have stuck to Keedy. I've known Keedy. He was a friend of mine till you came along and broke us up. I had promised my girl to him. He ain't setting around darning second-hand canvas"—he kicked the hose—"when he ought to be up and about, doing real business." He rushed at me and clacked his fists under my nose. "I'm all done with you! I'm going to Keedy and crawfish and offer him the steamer and my equipment for a lay with him and his men. I'll offer him my girl. You'll marry him if I have to hold you up in front of the minister by the ears!" he informed her, whirling and shaking his fists under her nose, too. "I've had all the silly notions and lallygagging I propose to have, and what I say goes after this. It's business from now on."

He started to plunge back through the door like a clown through a hoop. A couple of his men were holding a yawl beside the fighter.

I had used my submarine grip on Captain Holstrom once before when he was drunk. I used it now when he was sober—and the grip held. I grabbed him and yanked him back, slammed the door, and set myself against it.

"You can't dissolve partnership with me in any such way," I informed him. "Especially not right now, just as I've got the world by the tail."

"I'll show you whether I can dissolve partnership or not," he barked; and he began running about the inclosure, roaring threats and peering here and there. He was plainly hunting for a weapon of some sort in order to beat me away from the door.

"Karna!" I called to her—the first time I had ever addressed her so familiarly, but that was no time for niceties. "Karna, it's no use to plead with your father. He's no better than a lunatic. He's going to throw everything into the hands of that thief of a Keedy. It mustn't be done!"

The captain had found a club and was coming at me. She put herself between us. He knew better than to raise his club against her, and he kept dodging back and forth to get past her. He paid no attention to her protests and appeals.

"Mr. Shank—Mr. Jones," she cried, "take that club away from my father. He is not in his right mind."

"It would be mutiny—mutiny and State prison," stammered the mate.

"I'm his daughter—I'll go into court if it ever comes to that! I order you to do it!"

"Keep the others off, and I'll do it," I said in her ear, and I rushed past her.

Holstrom struck at me viciously, but my rush had taken him by surprise. I caught his arm and the stick, and tore the weapon away from him. But to down him and subdue him was a different proposition—and a very husky job he made of it for me.

He was broad and sturdy; he was sober, and he was beside himself with rage. The spectacle of that gold going into the hands of Keedy and his gang had made a lunatic of him for the time being. I got no help from the others. Men of the sea and ships, they had a wholesome fear of what would happen to mutineers when that matter came into court. I struggled with that old rascal until every muscle in me throbbed with the pain of tension, and I thought the blood would burst through my face. No matter about the details of that long fight. But at last I got him down; I rolled him on his face. I pulled his hands together, kneeling on him, and the girl lashed his wrists together when I appealed to her. She lashed his legs as well, for I decided to take no chances with him while he was in that mood.

When I got my breath I leaned over him and spoke my little piece:

"This is tough business for all of us, Captain Holstrom. I don't know what may come out of it. I'm prepared to take my medicine if I've done wrong. But you have started in to run amuck. You ought to know what Keedy is by this time. He has done you once. He would do you worse the next time. If you weren't crazy at this minute you'd realize it. I don't propose to stand by and see you heave your best chance over the rail in any such fashion. I demand twenty-four hours to make good on my scheme. Twenty-four hours—that's all. I know how those men got that gold. I got mine in the same way. But they won't get any more; I know conditions down there; I've been all through it. You listen to me, I say! I'm going to take twenty-four hours—and if I've got to keep you tied up while I operate, then it's tied up you stay. I'll take all the responsibility of this mutiny, men," I told the crowd on the lighter. "I'm a partner in this expedition with a signed contract. Twenty-four hours from now I'll hold out my hands and let you tie me up if I haven't made good."

That was pretty bold talk, and I'll confess that I did not know just where I was going to get off. But to let Captain Holstrom run away to that rogue of a Keedy just when I was on the eve of my experiment—to allow Holstrom to hand over everything to that he-devil—was too intolerable.

"We'll take the captain back to the steamer," I told the men. "I'm assuming all responsibility."

"I'll share it with you," said the girl, stoutly.

Captain Holstrom seemed to have lost his voice. He stared at us and gasped like a fish newly heaved on deck. He was silent while we carried him to his state-room on the steamer. We left him tied up well and his daughter was his caretaker and jailer by her own choice. She was showing the grit of a young catamount in that emergency.

All of it was about as bad as it could be. But it was going to be worse.

XXXIII

THE HEART OF THE MILLIONS

I was about at daybreak next morning. The man who predicted the first eclipse of the sun and was waiting for it had nothing on me in the way of a case of nerves. I kept away from the captain's state-room. I had plenty on my mind without loading up with any more trouble.

The first thing I saw when I came on deck was a little schooner which was lying-to a few cable-lengths from us. She looked familiar. A boat was slid over her rail. Through the telescope I saw two men in uniform take seats in the stern-sheets. They were those customs chaps who had visited us before and they rowed past us toward Keedy's schooner. I turned the telescope and saw that somebody in Keedy's crowd was wigwagging a flag furiously.

I saw something else through the glass. Keedy's divers were going down and I could imagine with what kind of tongue-lashing he had been urging them to "follow their hand."

For an instant I had a wild notion of calling for my boat crew and beating them to it. Then I looked out over that quieter sea, and felt sure that the freakish undertow had gone off to play elsewhere.

"Let 'em go down and learn a thing or two," I said to Romeo Shank, "and then come up and tell Keedy that the Pacific Ocean is something of a gambler itself when it comes to 'following your hand.'"

I knew well enough that I'd better stick around pretty close aboard the old *Zizania*, for I was sure we would be receiving a call from the customs men. They would find our treasury bare, and they would find the captain of the expedition trussed up in his state-room. They would probably come with another "hot rock" which had been dropped in their hat by the prospering Keedy.

Yes, there was only one station for me that morning!

The visitors arrived in less than an hour. They tried to smile when they came over the rail, but it was a mighty sick smile.

I led them into my state-room, and did not pay any attention to their questions about the captain. They talked broken English, and little of it, and so there were no words wasted. In a few minutes I knew what was wanted. We must up killick and get out. We were there without authority; we were breaking laws; we were stealing other men's property.

I tried to talk about Keedy and his gang. How about them? The officers shrugged their shoulders and scowled at me. Ah, that was the Government's business, not mine, they told me. They were attending to that case. Had I not seen them going over there also? Yes, all should be used alike—but we must go or else they would report, and a gunboat would be sent to drive us away—yes, to confiscate our ship. So!

Captain Holstrom had been right in regard to them—I found that they were blood-suckers, looking for the juiciest proposition, and Keedy had got next by some plan—perhaps by being a better liar.

I stared at those knaves for a few moments, and did some tall thinking quickly. I was really getting used to quick thinking by that time.

When I jumped up and asked to be excused for a moment they smiled and settled back on the transom. Perhaps they thought that I proposed to raise Keedy out of the game.

I found Mate Number-two Jones on the main deck forward.

"They have called the turn on us—say that we must get off the coast," I told him. "Keedy has bribed them over our heads. I tell you, Jones, I'm going to get that treasure! I've got to get it. This isn't mere brag talk. You are posted on my plans, and you believe in them."

"The scheme does look good to me," admitted the mate.

"If these men leave here tied up to Keedy they'll send a gunboat and shoo us off—and they've told Keedy, of course, how to dodge her. Jones, those men have got to stay aboard the *Zizania* until I make my try to-day. And, by the gods! I'll bring up enough to show 'em that we are the people. You come with me!"

"What for?"

"We've got to lasso those chaps and hitch 'em to the stanchion in my state-room. They've got to stay here till I test out that hose."

"Look here," objected Mr. Jones, fumbling at his nose, "seems to me there's altogether too much tripping and tying aboard here. It beats a round-up of steers. We're going to get into a lot of trouble—we're in it now. You wait till the captain gets loose, and see if we ain't!"

"Tying two more won't make it any worse than it is. I can't make you do what you don't want to do, Jones, but I believe you're too much of a man to let me play this thing single-handed. We're fighting Keedy now. If I fail in getting at that gold to-day, all we've got to do is to up mud-hook and steam north—we'll have to do the same thing if we let those grafters go over the rail now."

Jones was a cautious man, but he was a loyal one. I kept on urging, and at last the battle-light flickered in his pale-blue eyes.

"Blast their thievish souls!" he said. "They've taken all the money I had in my pockets—and now they're thumbing their noses at decent men. I'm with you!"

We grabbed ropes, rushed up to my state-room, and fell on the men before they could scramble to their feet. They were wizened little chaps and we tied them without any trouble.

Then I went below and leaned over the rail where their boat was tossing.

"The gentlemen are staying here for some business," I told the two rowers. "They tell you to go back to the schooner and wait till they signal for you with our ensign." They didn't look entirely satisfied, but they rowed away after I had ordered them to fend off.

I stationed two men at my state-room door and I hunted up weapons and armed some of the crew. I ordered them to keep off everybody until I returned from the lighter.

I spoke to Captain Holstrom through his state-room window. I told him that I would bring him a present before sundown. He did not reply—and when Captain Holstrom was mad enough to keep his tongue between his teeth I felt that only murder could express his feelings.

The door was on the hook, and a little brown hand was thrust out to meet mine.

"Good luck, brave boy!" she whispered. "I know you'll do it."

"I can't fail after that word from you," I told her.

Then I ran down the ladder and jumped into the boat where my men were waiting for me.

I found a heavy surge running under our lighter, but the swirl of sand was no longer darkening the water. I had reckoned right in regard to that undertow. Keedy's men were still down and I could imagine them wasting their strength on the sand which had been packed back overnight.

Our water-hose had already been coupled in makeshift fashion, and the last work that morning was to wrap the joints as best we could. Then I set the men at the brakes and told them to "give her tar," as the old-fashioned hand-tub foreman would say. The hose was strung about the deck of the lighter.

After they pumped for five minutes I found that the hose was not so tight as I had hoped. Wheezing little streams punctured it here and there, and the joints leaked. From the end of our home-made nozzle of sheet iron the stream barely trickled. I was disgusted—but I was not wholly discouraged. When I state this you may see how desperate I had become. I was resolved to fight that thing through to the last ditch. I was determined to take that hose down and try it out. I had the misty and hopeful notion that the pressure of the sea on it might make some difference, that the wet hose might retain the water better, that after the plunger had swelled a bit we might get more force.

All those straws and others did I grab at by way of bracing my courage.

The captain of the expedition trussed up in his cabin like a steer calf—only waiting his opportunity to deal with me!

Two customs men also trussed up—also waiting to deal with me!

It can be readily understood that there were some decidedly red-hot goads at my back that day to drive me down under the sea.

I had not been able to convince Captain Holstrom that all my work and struggles and investigation and failures up to then were a good investment. But as a submarine diver I knew that they had been. I had been spending my nights on a sleepless pillow, docketing those experiences and drawing lessons from them—plotting, pondering, and planning.

When I went down I was ready for my job in so far as a man, by pounding his brain, can be ready for all emergencies.

I had piled the lead on to myself. Around my body from hips to armpits I had a canvas belt with five pockets, each pocket holding twenty-five pounds of shot, part of the junk of the old *Zizania*. Around each leg above the ankle I fastened another bag of shot holding fifteen pounds. My helmet had weights weighing thirty pounds. In addition I wore my regular breast and back weights. That is to say, when I was rolled over the side of that lighter I, a one-hundred-and-eighty-pound man, was weighted with about two hundred and fifty pounds of metal.

I went with bare feet and bare hands. I knew that if I ever did succeed in boring that sand, holding that hose in my hands, my feet would have to serve as hands for the purpose of feeling out objects.

Keedy's men had come up before I gave the word to lower me. Number-two Jones had peered through the cracks of the boarding, and had reported that they had come over the rail without bringing treasure, and that Keedy was stamping up and down the deck, wagging his fists over his head. I could imagine from my own experience what kind of language the cowardly slave-driver was spewing out.

I found myself on the bottom under the lighter, and started to make my way toward the wreck. I was loaded like a pack-donkey, outside of the tremendous extra weight of lead I carried. But I was taking everything which my judgment counseled as needful for success.

I was obliged to drag with me my life-line, my air-hose, and the heavy canvas hose for the water. In addition to those, I towed a double line which was hitched to a pair of ice-tongs, and the points of those tongs were filed to a sharp point. I carried the tongs at my belt. If I found treasure I had this method of sending it to the lighter and of dragging back the tongs to myself. I had had one experience in serving as a carrier and I did not want to repeat the job.

I tell you, I felt like a mighty poor and puny little ant when I started away on the bottom of the sea, climbing those sand ridges. The sea clutched and tore at those wriggling lines, at my air-hose, and was especially ferocious in tackling that heavy water-hose. It seemed as if the Pacific resented that scheme of fighting it.

It was a mighty struggle I had. I was tossed and tumbled. I was banged and buffeted.

But in the end I arrived at the wreck. Under ordinary circumstances that stunt alone would have finished a diver's work for a day—but I had left matters above the surface in such condition that I could not face them just then.

I dropped my water-hose, and went back fifty feet along the line. Past experience with the weight of the surges had suggested another trick with which to fight the giant Pacific. I had brought a small anchor, and, with this set into the sand as best I could do it, I anchored my air-hose and water-hose about fifty feet from the wreck. I proposed to let the ocean wreak the most of its spite on the two hundred and fifty feet between that anchor and the lighter. I figured that I might be able to handle the other fifty feet, no matter how ugly the surges were.

I crawled back to the wreck and found my bearings. There were the "cat scratching" on the sand where the other divers had spent their energy that morning. I grinned—I couldn't help it. They had just had their own experience with the tricks of a Pacific undertow.

Well, the great and awful moment had come for me!

In the years that have passed since then the vivid memory of that moment has never left me. I wake up in the night even now, and the thrill of it shakes me.

If my scheme did not work, what would become of me when I went back to the surface of the sea?

If my scheme did work, what was I facing down there? I was proposing to bore into that sand—to sink into it. No such plan had ever been tried by a human being up to that time. Was I not digging my own grave?

I sat down on the sand, Turk fashion, like a tailor on his table, pointed the nozzle down, holding it against the sand, and gave the agreed-upon signal for water. It took a long time in coming, and it was an agony of waiting. Then at last I felt the hose swell under my arm. I pressed the nozzle harder against the sand. I cannot describe my delight. I felt that my dreams were coming true, for when I jammed the nozzle down I found that the sand was moving. That stream had merely trickled above the surface, but now a pressure was created when I held the nozzle hard against the bottom of the sea. Yes, the sand moved under me. It began to boil up around me. It swept and swirled in yellow clouds. I realized that I was boring a hole about as big as a barrel, and into that hole I was gradually sinking. I was on my way! I did not know where I was going—but, bless the good Lord, I was on my way! The sand in that boiling water made all dark. Down and down I went slowly, my bare feet searching eagerly.

But though I descended more rapidly as the swirling motion increased, I felt no boxes. Had I, then, happened upon a straggler among the boxes of gold on my earlier trip? Had my rivals also found two more stragglers from the main treasure—loosened boxes which had been forced out of the chamber by the impact of the wreck on the bar or had worked near the surface of the sand by the action of a sucking undertow? If that were true, it meant that Keedy's men were dumped if they stuck to shovels. Provided I could reach the treasure, and could keep my own system a secret, I was headed toward a glorious victory, and could depend upon the ocean to keep off others—but was I headed toward victory? My feet touched nothing that had square corners. And yet, to the best of my judgment, I had already gone down at least ten feet in that hole in the sand.

Down and down—five feet more, so I reckoned. Then my heart gave a jump. My feet had touched something. It was smooth and hard and flat, and spread under me horizontally. But I soon discovered that it had too large a surface to be a box of ingots. I could not bend over to feel it with my hands, for the rush of the whirlpool of sand and water about me, sweeping upward, would not allow me to force my helmet and the upper part of my body down. I must depend on my bare feet to tell me what I had struck.

After a time I knew. It was boiler plate. I could feel the round heads of bolts. Whether this plate formed a part of the treasure-chamber or not I did not know. But it was an obstacle which must be passed. I turned my nozzle in front of me to clear the way. I wanted to reach the end of that iron plate.

In two ticks of an eight-day clock I was in a mess that has been my nightmare ever since. I began to get a thorough education in what sand will do under water when it is submitted to the force of a stream from a hose. The instant I turned that nozzle in front of me the sand rushed in from behind. I was grabbed as tightly as though the eight feelers of a devil-fish had encircled me.

It must be remembered that this whole proposition was an experiment so far as I was concerned. I did not know then how quickly a stream of water can affect great quantities of sand under the sea, let that sand get in motion. Tons can be moved almost while one takes a breath.

This shift was so sudden that I was not prepared for it. My legs were pinioned, and my arms seemed to be clutched at the elbows. The sand was packing in around me from behind. I was so scared that my hands loosened on the nozzle. A roller snatched the hose from my grasp.

The nozzle was up-ended and began to sizzle away over my head. It kept the sand moving there, and the murky water still swirled about my helmet, and the pack was not allowed to settle on my head. But as to the rest of my body, it was as if I had been immersed in molten metal and it had cooled around me. In a few seconds I was immovable. I was buried completely in sand, except for my wrists and hands. In clutching for the hose, as it had been yanked away, I had raised my hands above my head, and they were now waving in the swirl of the whirlpool. I groped and stretched and strove, and at last I felt the tips of my fingers on the nozzle. I managed, after a while, to tilt it down a bit so that the stream played along my arms to the elbows. The temporary release of my forearms did not help me. I couldn't get hold of that hose so as to turn the nozzle full upon myself. The sand kept packing more closely about my legs and body.

After a time my aching hands and arms were obliged to give up the fight. I had became so weakened by my struggles and strainings that I was faint—I was as feeble as a baby.

I have read about men in awful peril who have resigned themselves to die. Mentally I was not resigned when I first gave up struggling—not for some time. I came out of that first faintness, wide awake to my danger, filled with frightful fear, mad with the longing to live. But my case seemed hopeless. The stream was keeping the sand in motion still about my helmet and over my head, but my hands informed me that the pack was gradually settling, that the sand was piling up around my neck slowly but surely. In the boil of that water the particles were drifting over me.

I might live minutes, I reflected—I might linger there for an hour or more—feeling that sand-pack around my head until it choked the valve of the helmet or pinched off the current in the air-hose.

Never was I so hungry for life as when I stood there pinioned hand and foot in the Pacific's bed, feeling the sand piling up against the glass of my helmet, sifting around me to chink the little cranny where the air bubbled from the valve. And all because a stream of water would not swerve ten inches and pour itself in my direction.

Then something surprising happened to my soul in its agony. I'm telling the truth.

When I had made up my mind that effort was useless, that I had done all that I could do, and that death was certain, a strange feeling came to me and took away my fear of death. I fell into a quiet and really exalted frame of mind. I floated in dreams. Cares of earth and worries of the world, lust for gold, and even the love of woman seemed very small matters. What did it all matter? I was dying. Peace came to me.

Is it not probable that kind nature or a kinder God thus smooths the way into eternity when the great moment comes? Men who have been nigh the last gasp have swapped stories with me and we all agree.

I had no notion of the length of time I had been down. In my mistiness of mind I did not bother about time. In the case of a submarine diver, the hours are marked off by his sensations, and he knows when he has stayed down long enough. If my men had told me that I had been on the bed of the ocean for a day and a night I should not have disputed them. I must have been near death, for it is said that when one is dying all of life that has been lived comes before the mind and passes in review, as though the mortal soul were preparing its brief for the use of the recording angel. I remember that this last was a strange idea which came to me there in the sand-pack which was slowly heaping itself over my head.

Then something happened. It was something which should have amazed me, but I reckon that my brain was too numbed to feel amazement.

The nozzle above my head gave a sudden yank and rapped my knuckles. It righted itself. That is to say, it aimed downward and began to pour water directly at and over me. I felt the stream rather than saw it. I could not see in that smother of sand. But my arms came out of the mold in which they had been pinned. I grabbed and groped for that hose with all the desperation that was in me. I held to it with all my strength. It was lucky that I seized it as I did, for I felt the rollers tugging at it once more as though some devil of the sea had given me one more chance in order to tantalize me, and was now resolved to finish me finally.

I did not know what had happened above to cause the sudden deflection of the stream. It was enough for me to know that some freak of the waters had turned the hose. I found out later what had occurred, and I may as well explain at this point, lest you think I have told merely of a case of story-book Providence.

I have related how I anchored my lines fifty feet from the wreck. That anchor, so I found later, had been pulled out of the sand, and the surges had bellied the water-hose in toward shore, over my head, and the aim of the nozzle had been changed in the snap of a finger. It surely had been touch and go with me, for once the surge had taken up the slack the next wave must have jerked the hose out of my hole. I had grabbed just in time; I had melted my sand mold and was free.

Common sense advised me to quit the job forever. The uncertainties of trying to move sand with a stream of water had been impressed upon me in horrible fashion. But common sense is not allowed to rule a man when he is after gold in this world. I had found out what that stream would accomplish if it was used properly. I had learned one lesson which I could not forget, and I was sure I would not make the mistake of letting the sand catch me from behind again. I knew, on the other hand, what would happen to me when I appeared above the surface without my ransom fee of yellow gold. I preferred to stay and fight sand instead of men. There, in the boil of the roiled water, I resolved to stay down.

I tried another experiment with the hose, and was vastly encouraged. I had been wearying and wondering how I would get back out of the hole, for I feared that the life-line, playing over the edge of the sand, would not allow the men on the lighter enough direct pull to help me much. Now I needed to rise from the hole for a little way in order to attack the sand at another angle so as to pass that plate of boiler iron.

I slackened the force of the stream from the nozzle with my palm, and the sand began to pack in below me. The uprush of the swirling water helped me, and I was able to work myself slowly upward. Then I began to bore again.

I realized now that something must have happened to my anchor, because the rollers were giving me battle for the possession of that water-hose in fierce style. But I hung on, and found myself sinking into the sand. I went down more rapidly, for I had already softened the surrounding pack. After the awful experience I had just had, I was more of a lunatic than sane while I made that second attempt. My brain swirled as dizzily as the water which swept up from the hole. As nearly as I could estimate, I went down at least five yards before I struck anything that was solid. And when my feet, already sore from the grinding of that sand, felt what was below them, the whole of my being gave three cheers—not cheers with the mouth, but those silent cheers with which a man's soul yells its joy. I had touched a box. There were its corners—there was its unmistakable shape.

After wild struggles and contortions, I was able to set the points of the ice-tongs into its sides. I gave the signal on the drag-rope, and I could feel the surge of the men on the line. But the angle of the rope over the edge of the hole would not allow them to lift very hard. The box was too far away from the lighter for their efforts to amount to much. But as they swayed away I kept the hose playing upon the box and under it. It did seem damnably slow work. But it came up, inch by inch, slowly and surely, until I was out of the hole, and standing about knee-deep in the sand. I had a tug of war of it then!

The box was not out of the hole. The rollers tugged at my lines and wrenched at me. Once or twice I was fairly floored. I would fall with my legs pinioned fast, and would lie exhausted until I could get strength to stand up and wash myself free with the hose. In order to get back out of that hole at all, I was obliged to slacken the stream and let the sand pack in under myself and the box—and when the stream slackened I was obliged to drag my legs out of the packing sand.

But I was free at last, bless the good Lord! And I had a box of gold. It was not a mere stray box, salvaged with the help of a freakish undertow. It was a box which I had torn from the heart of the hoard below. Yes, I was sure that I had been to the heart of the treasure. And where I had been the Pacific was already stuffing back the sand, locking the door once more on the gold it had taken for its own. Let Keedy's men come down! Let them waste their strength. I had the key to that situation—and I alone.

I tugged a signal to shut off the water. And as promptly I gave them pull-up signals on my life-line and on the drag-cord of the tongs. I wanted to get above the sea and breathe the fresh air of the good God, and look into the eye of the blessed sun, and give praises. And, oh, the awful weariness in every bone and muscle of me! I lay down and let 'em pull me back. I had no strength with which to manage that weight of metal which loaded me down.

When they got me upon the deck of the lighter, and had twisted off my helmet, I lay for a long time without words. I motioned to Number-two Jones to remove the cover from the box I had brought. The sight of those ingots gave me the goad once more—ah, it takes gold to make the human soul gallop!

"Gold, gold, yellow gold,
Hard to get and harder to hold."

This quotation burst from Mr. Shank. His round face was radiant, and he came and leaned over me and patted me on the head. He did not seem to have any better way of showing his joy. It was a wildly excited crew which crowded around me; they were still more excited when I sat up on deck at last and told them I was going down again. The fever was in me. I wanted to go back to the *Zizania* with gold enough to convince Captain Holstrom and those knaves of customs men that there was no fluke about our proposition. I wanted to raise that infernal Keedy out of this game for good and all.

It was mighty tempestuous water in the vicinity of the wreck, and putting the lighter nearer was not to be thought of. But I discussed with Mate Jones the possibility of dropping our yawl back toward the wreck at the end of a cable, so that the men could lift the treasure-boxes more directly. We had brought extra men that morning for the pump, and a crew for the surf-boat volunteered. The gold lust was seizing the whole of us. I went down again, feeling sure that the wicked labor of getting the box up through the sand would be lightened for me.

I took another anchor, and on my way to the wreck I refastened my hose lines to the bottom, rigging the second anchor as a bridle, so that the strain would be eased on the one which I had set into the sand.

Down I bored again, my tongs at my belt, my hose in my clutch. And I stayed down until I had sent three more boxes up to the surf-boat. While I was toiling down there I knew that I was setting a dangerous record for myself—I could not hope to equal it on the days which were to follow. It was plain that I had penetrated to the heart of the treasure, but I had penetrated to other things as well. I found all the sculch and broken crockery of the wrecked pantry and the bar of the *Golden Gate*. Yes, I sent three more boxes to the lighter; but when I crawled over the rail later my hands and feet were bleeding, and the sand had ground into the wounds. Already my skin showed where the grinding of the boiling sand was wearing the epidermis. Even the rubber of my suit was showing wear.

I was a sorry-looking object when I staggered into Capt. Rask Holstrom's state-room. He fairly slavered in his rage and tried to leap at me. I reckon I did look like a beaten man. But the next instant my men came tramping in with the boxes of gold. There were four of these glorious boxes, and each one was open and showed the ingots.

"Your friend Keedy got his two boxes by the fluke of an undertow," I told him. "I have got mine by science and a system which will give us the rest of it. Now, Captain Holstrom, I'll accept your apologies." And I cut him loose.

I did not mention any apologies due from me to him. I wanted to rub it into the old squarehead so thoroughly that he would never get the smart of it out of his skin. I wanted to let him know that I had set a ring into his nose, and that if he ever tried to run amuck again I was the man who could catch him and trip him.

He gave me one look, gasped one gasp, and I knew that Capt. Rask Holstrom had abdicated his throne. I was boss. But I had no time to listen to his slobbering thanks just then. I took one of those bars of gold in my bloody hand and started for my state-room. I shook the ingot under the noses of those customs men. And they, too, knew that I was boss when I got through with them. I had not come back that day from hell and the bottom of the sea to mince words with any loafers—Captain Holstrom included.

"Here's gold worth four thousand dollars in good Yankee money, you low-down renegades. You take it and get off this steamer. If you are good, and come around here like gentlemen about a month from now, perhaps I'll drop another rock into your hat. I don't promise—it all depends on how you act. But if you come back too quick—if you try to squeeze us for more rake-off—I'll go down to headquarters and buy your blessed Government, and have you put into prison or shot—for before this thing is ended here I'll have more than three million dollars behind me. Now you can either make a dollar quietly or you can make trouble. Suit yourselves."

I cut their ropes and pushed them out of the room and ordered our ensign set to signal their boat.

I didn't have to offer them any apologies, either, and I was not in an apologizing mood that day. They did the apologizing while they were waiting for their boat, and I scowled while they were begging me to forgive the mistake they had made.

Yes, I felt pretty much like the boss of the outfit. But when Karna Holstrom came with hot water and a basin and bandages and ordered me into my state-room, I went as meekly as a slave who trembles when the finger of his master is pointed.

XXXIV

AMONG THIEVES

I did not go down next day, and I watched the descent of Keedy's divers with indifference that was pretty nigh serene. Captain Holstrom stamped around restlessly, for he couldn't seem to get it into his mind that the Pacific Ocean was on guard. But he did not venture to make any suggestions to me, and I decided that I had trained him in pretty fair shape.

I had good reason for delaying my next descent. It would not do to take chances with my diving-dress, which was showing signs of being frayed by the swirling sand, and I put in a busy day with the two Joneses, stitching an extra canvas suit to wear over the rubber dress. I improved on the ice-tongs by having a set of steel spring hooks made so that by means of long handles I could push them over a box without stooping and fumbling. Also I had a long rod of steel turned out for me, and with this I could probe the sand for boxes.

I had no way of knowing whether Keedy or his divers suspected that I had secured any treasure. I knew that after a night of action of the sea there would be few traces left where I had disturbed the sand. But I also knew that Keedy would certainly be wondering why we had built the wall around the lighter, and therefore we doubled the guards who had spent the night there since we had installed the pump, and gave the men orders to shoot any man who tried to climb on board.

We started work on a bigger and more elaborate pump, having tested out the principle of the thing by means of the first one. I needed more stream. While Shank was building this I went to work again, using the old equipment.

I waited each day until the other divers had been down and had climbed back into the sunlight, empty-handed. Then I slid overboard from our lighter as secretly as possible, and did my day's work. I averaged three boxes a trip by working myself to the limit of my endurance. It was reported to me that Keedy climbed into the rigging of the schooner whenever the surf-boat was eased back toward the wreck, and that he remained there on watch. How much he saw we did not know, but the men in the boat crowded together whenever a box was raised. From what I learned afterward, I found that Keedy thought we were operating some kind of a dredge, and that his divers reported to him that we were not making any impression on the sand.

So he sat calmly in the rigging, spying on what he could see, and reckoning that we were wasting our time the same as his crew.

Before the end of a week the new pump was finished and I had almost five hundred gallons a minute at my command.

I do not mean to be profane, but I must state that when I got that new stream to operating it was hell for me down below—and no other phrase seems to express the case.

I have already mentioned the refuse of that wrecked pantry and bar; from out of the holes I bored rushed up bits of broken bottles and crockery, slashing at my bare feet and hands. I could not protect them.

The stream from the nozzle—a three-inch stream—stirred such a mush of sand that I worked in pitch darkness. I had to have bare feet and hands in order to feel my way.

After a time, my feet were swollen to twice their natural size. Finger-nails and toe-nails had been worn off by the grinding of the sand, and the skin had been eaten off. The sand even penetrated my dress, and my knees and shoulders were chafed raw. My back, under the dragging weights I was forced to wear, was about like a piece of pounded steak. I was suffering the limit of human agony, but I was mad for success—I was crazed by the gold lust. I was bringing out a small fortune every day; one day I recovered six boxes—one hundred and twenty thousand dollars! But I was still just as hungry for the gold that remained at the bottom. I set my teeth, gasped back my groans, and kept at work.

All the tender ministrations of Karna Holstrom could not mend my hurts, and I would not listen to her appeals to me. She begged me to give up the fight. She urged that we had enough. But I was as crazy as the wildest man who ever hunted gold, and the pain I was in made me more of a lunatic. On several occasions I was pulled back to the lighter in a dead faint, and fought with Number-two Jones because he would not send me down again that day.

I cannot go into the details of these days of nightmare. I can only say that I kept on.

We soon had plain hints that Keedy was getting suspicious and uneasy. One night a crew from the schooner made a desperate attempt to board the lighter. On other nights they made other tries, and shots were exchanged before they were driven off.

One day when I was at the bottom of the hole I had bored and had just succeeded in fastening my hooks to a box, I got a shock that made me believe the end of the world had come. Something hit me on the top of the helmet with a thud that knocked me senseless for a moment. I reached out quickly with one hand, reserving the other for my hose, and felt the breastplate of a diver. I realized what had happened then. One of Keedy's men, sent to spy, had stumbled through the sand swirling from my pit, and had fallen in on me, not dreaming that I had been able to dig a fifteen-foot hole.

In the tangle that followed, it was a wonder that either of us escaped.

By the way the man struggled I knew that he was terrified out of his senses. He clung to me desperately, as a drowning man might cling to a rescuer. Then he gave his emergency pull, and yanked me with him when he went up.

I had a raw temper which went with my raw surface in those terrible days. I left hose and box and went up with the caller, dragging my knife from my belt. I kept clashing the knife against the front bull's-eye of his helmet, and after we had been dragged together for some distance from the edge of the hole, and the sea became clearer, he perceived what I was doing. He let go his clutch, and it was well he did, for I was in a state of maniacal fury. I would have ripped his dress from crotch to neckband with my knife if he had not escaped from me just as he did. I went back and recovered my hose, and after a time got the box. Then I returned to the lighter, for I was too unnerved to work any longer that day.

As I lay on deck that afternoon, a shapeless, hideous thing of bruised and macerated flesh, I wondered whether I would be able to work any more.

When I was under the sea I was fairly beside myself with the excitement of the hunt. I could grind my teeth together and groan and fight my way through the sand, for there was gold at the bottom of the hole I was digging. And every time I went down through that fifteen feet of smother I knew that death raced me to the box of treasure and back. Under those circumstances, a man is desperate enough to forget his bloody cuts and raw skin. But I felt like a pretty weak and useless tool as I lay there on deck.

Karna Holstrom was with me. She had insisted on becoming my nurse. I craved her companionship, I'll admit, but I wanted to hide myself from her eyes. Her father was in his state-room, busy at his job of adding more sheets of iron, more bands of steel, to the treasure-chest he had taken it upon himself to build. We could hear the bang of his hammer. Captain Holstrom worked days at that huge chest, slept on it nights with the key lashed into the palm of his right hand, and betweenwhiles cuddled those ingots rapturously. In his way, he had become as insane over the matter as I was myself.

The girl and I were in the lee of the deck-house, to get out of the trades, and we did not see the boat when it came off Keedy's schooner. Had I seen it coming, Keedy would never have been allowed to board us. But all at once he appeared before the girl and myself. I felt a fierce impulse to get up and beat his face off him, even though my hands were as sore as the exposed nerve of an aching tooth. He got that flash from my eyes, and looked meek for a moment, but then he saw the condition I was in and became insolent.

"Better listen to me," he said. "I'm on. I know your system. But I should say you're all in, Sidney. You need help. There's enough there for all of us. I've got two good divers. I'm over here to propose that we call the row off, and I'll send my men down to work with your contrivance and give you a rest."

That proposition from Marcena Keedy, after what he had done to us in the matter of that twenty thousand dollars, and after what he had tried to do to us in the affair of the customs men! I felt the language begin to roil in me as the sand roiled under the force of my stream from the nozzle.

"Miss Karna," I pleaded, "won't you please run away? I want to talk to this dirty dog. And send your father here with a club."

She did not leave me. She came closer, and gave Keedy a look which would have wilted any other sort of man.

"You can't afford to be foolish over what's past and gone," insisted my ex-partner. "I left because you wasn't making good—wasn't holding up your end of the partnership. You fell down. Now if you can deliver goods we'll call off all trouble and start it over again."

"Captain Holstrom," I yelled, "come here quick! Bring your hammer! Hurry! Knock that devil overboard!" I shouted when the captain tore around the corner on the gallop. His eyes were bulged out, and he had his hammer over his head, for I guess he thought from the tone of my voice that pirate had boarded us. His expression did not soften any when he laid eyes on Keedy.

The gambler put up a lean forefinger. "You'd better hark to what I say, friend Rask." He went over the same talk he had had with me.

"Not by a continental tin dam-site!" howled the captain. "And how you have got the gall even to look the way of the *Zizania*, much more come aboard of her, is what gives me a callous over the collar-button. Get off'm here!"

"You don't dare to drive me, Holstrom, after I've come to you with a fair and open proposition—ready to take the first step and let bygones rest. You can't afford any big talk! Why, you're only stealing this gold, whatever of it you are getting! This is pirate business—the whole of it. Now you be careful how you try to raise me out of the game."

That taunt about our rights there at San Apusa came from a rascal and a gambler, but the taunt made me think—and it stung, too. To tell the truth, I had done a little thinking about our rights in the matter of that treasure.

"You're infernal thieves, and you can't make yourselves out anything else!" Keedy insisted. "And you can't afford to throw down another thief who is willing to come in and help."

Captain Holstrom shot out a swift kick and missed Keedy. He made a crack at him with the hammer, and missed again.

The Keedy person had had experience with the captain, probably, in past times. He ran for the ladder and escaped into his boat.

"You are fools, besides being thieves," he informed us, standing up when he was a safe distance away, and shaking his fists. "Don't you understand what I can do to you?"

Captain Holstrom returned the fist-shaking with too much alacrity to be misunderstood.

"All right," bellowed Keedy; "have it your own way, you fools! I'll do you so good that you'll never know you were ever in the game." He was so mad that he let out a little more than he intended to, so I reckoned. "There are men who will pay me more for what I can tell 'em than any rake-off you can give me, anyway." He was rowed away to his schooner.

"That means?" I suggested, swapping looks with the captain.

"I suppose it means that he is going to blow this thing to the underwriters."

"Then we are stealing this gold, are we?"

Captain Holstrom fingered his red knob of a nose, and looked away from me.

"I don't know much about law," I went on. "I supposed you knew something about our rights in this thing—if we have any. I tell you, it's going to be pretty tough, Captain, if I've been through all this hell only to have all our great hopes grabbed away from us."

"Men have to take a chance in this world, Sidney. Damn the law in a case like this! The gold was there, and nobody was trying to get it. We had a right to try for it."

"But wasn't there any legal way?"

"Oh, a drunken lawyer in San Francisco told me something about power by attorney, but it meant chasing around and getting hold of claims by shippers, or something of the kind—and that meant blowing our plans and letting a lot of grafters in on us. I simply cleared from the custom-house as a trawler and came away, minding my own business."

"And now somebody else will take the job of minding it," I complained. I did not have much philosophy or courage about me just then. My hands and feet and shoulders were aching too miserably; and had all my suffering and daring been thrown away?

"Let's go home, father," pleaded the girl.

"Go home!" he yelped. "Sail in past the Golden Gate with this gold? Lug it back where coyote lawyers can get their whack at it until they've trimmed us for every ounce? Well, I guess—not!"

I wondered if he proposed to sail around in the middle of the Pacific Ocean, cuddling those ingots for amusement, the rest of his life; but I had neither strength nor taste for any more complaint or argument at that time. It was a mighty dismal outlook, according to my way of thinking. I saw that I was tied up with a man whose sole notion was to get the gold without bothering his head about how he was going to keep it. Later, Keedy's schooner frothed out past us, standing to sea, and headed north.

I did not go down again for almost a week. Courage is always a man's best asset, but courage in the job I had undertaken was pretty near my whole capital. And courage had left me—I had to admit it. I had been doing honest work with all a man's grit and strength and will. I had wrecked my body and wrenched my soul in effort. Yes, the work part of it was honest, but how about the honesty of our undertaking? I had got some plain words from Keedy—and I got no consolation from Captain Holstrom. I was daredevil enough and plenty in those days, but I was not the sort of a daredevil who would make a successful pirate.

I sat on deck day after day, and bore with my agonies of body and wrestled with my soul. An idea had come to me as I had struggled with that problem of our rights. It was a rather vague idea. Of only one point of it was I sure—its success depended on getting as much of that gold as I could tear out of the sand.

Thinking upon it, hoping that good would come from it, brought my courage back to me. I was again ready to undergo tortures and to face death.

XXXV

SUBMARINE PICKPOCKETS

A new arrival off San Apusa Bar had interested us for a couple of days. It was a husky sloop with a leg-of-mutton mainsail—a broad-bellied craft on which a dozen men showed themselves when it sailed past us to take up a position near the site of the wreck. This sloop seemed to be of a build to ride the surges easily, and ventured much closer inshore than we had dared to anchor our lighter. The men did not visit us, and displayed no desire to meddle with the secrets of the equipment on the walled-up scow. We wondered who they were, why they were there, and left them alone.

I went down and crawfished my way over the sand windrows, but I could make only slow work of it, for I was stiffened by my days of inaction. But that new idea of mine went along with me for my encouragement.

I had hardly put myself in position, ready to call for my stream of water, when I got a rousing surprise. Down through the sea came rushing a naked man. The depths were fairly clear, for I had not begun to stir the roil with my nozzle. His eyes were wide open and staring, and I reckon that I peered at him through my bull's-eye with eyes just as wide open. When he arrived close to me he dropped a rock from each hand, his diving weights, and grabbed me, hanging to my belt. I sat right there on the sand and gaped at him. His mouth was shut tight—he was holding his breath.

In a short time another naked man came down like the stick of a sky-rocket. He dropped his rocks and grabbed me, and the first man let go and went swimming up to the surface. Then came a third man and replaced the second.

I began to feel like a candidate for office in the receiving line. I wanted to ask some questions about what this function meant. But for good and obvious reasons I could not carry on a conversation, and I did not know the deaf-and-dumb alphabet.

Along came the fourth man. I noticed that each man wore a narrow belt with a huge knife fastened in it. And that's all the man did wear. The sight of the knife made me rather nervous. A man under water, straining to hold his breath, his eyes bulging with his efforts, is a savage-looking object at best. These men were plainly Mexicans, and they looked particularly savage. I felt pretty sure that they were not diving down there to cheer me in my loneliness or to ask me to run for mayor.

Then it came to me all at once who these men were. As a submarine worker, I was interested, of course, in all sorts of jobs under the sea, and I had read various accounts of the Mexican pearl divers. I knew that they could descend long distances and could remain under water, many of them, for ninety seconds. One man succeeded another, diving in rotation. I remained there without moving, staring at them until I began to recognize faces. They were making me return visits. I realized that they did not propose to carve me—the first man could have done that on his first call. Therefore I got my nerve back and decided to go to work. I signaled for water.

It occurred to me that my new friends might find that the "fogo" I stirred with that hose would be a little too much for them. I resisted an impulse to bat them away from me with that nozzle, a considerable effort in self-control, for my temper was pretty short in those dreadful days.

They stuck to me bravely at first when the sand began to swirl. There was an itching under my ribs when the sand made a pall and darkness settled on me. I was afraid that one of my callers might become peevish and ram his knife into me as a hint not to muddy that water.

It was not easy to hold my position and work with a man anchored to me. But I was not bothered for long.

The tug at my belt ceased suddenly, and I knew that they had given up. They could not find me in that smother.

They resumed operations again when I got up my first box. In working my way out of the hole I decreased the flow from the hose, and when I reached the top of the sand the swirling particles were settling and were being washed farther inshore by the surges. In a clearer sea down came those devils once more, and fastened to me, one by one, like leeches. They tried to clutch the box, but it was too heavy for them. It was hoisted past them up to the surf-boat, and once more I drove the nozzle into the sand and forced them off me with a whirlpool of mush.

They were more bothersome the next time I allowed the sea to clear. Two dove at a time, and grabbed me, and almost lifted me up with them. I was furious, but I did not try to beat them off. I kept on about my own affairs as best I could, and allowed them to hang on to me. There were a dozen of them above, with knives, and I had no hankering to tackle the pack. I was not sure as to their motives, anyway. One rip of a knife would have put me out of business. But they did not offer to use knives.

I did a short day's work and went back to the lighter. Captain Holstrom had watched their diving operations and was full of eager questions.

That night we doubled the guards on the *Zizania*. But no boat came near us.

My friends were ready for me next day, and resumed the same tactics. I carried a bigger knife, and kept my eye out as best I could. But before I got the stream started they were coming at me three at a time. They kept lifting me off bottom, and I wasted a lot of valuable time and much of my little stock of strength before I got down on the sand and began to bore. They were ready for me again as soon as I got up with a box and the sea had cleared a bit. One of them brought a rope, and tried to get it around a box I was handling, but I had my tongs well set, and my men hoisted the treasure away from them. Then they began to interfere with me so savagely that I quit in disgust and signaled to be pulled up.

I was half crazy with rage, and frantic because this sort of business was putting me where I could not realize on that idea which I was nursing.

After listening to me, Captain Holstrom set his cap well down over his ears, jutting his chin, set his teeth, and called for his boat. He was rowed over to the side of the little sloop. He came back very soon and he was not looking pleased.

"I couldn't get anything out of that bunch except a few grunts and a lot of jabber," he reported. "They make believe they can't understand the English language. They want graft, I suppose. They'd understand, all right, if I was to carry over a slug of gold and dump it over the rail. But I'm about tired of feeding gold to everybody who comes along here."

"This isn't our gold to give away to all comers," I told him. He blinked at me, and did not seem to understand. I did not go into that side of the question any further, for I was not ready for much argument at that time. "I'll not stand for any more 'hot rocks,'" I told him.

"Nor I, either," he agreed. "Begin to feed gold to those chaps, and they'll think we are scared of 'em and they'll want the whole mess."

To show them that I was not scared, I went down the next day, and I had a wire edge on my temper. I balked at starting a knife duel, however, and after a struggle got my hole started.

I struck something new that day in the ruck at the bottom of the hole. I found ingots loose in the hodge-podge of pantry wreckage. A wooden box had been smashed. I had a slit and a sort of deep pocket in the canvas overalls affair which protected my India-rubber suit. As my toes located loose ingots, I sifted the mush of sand with the fingers of one hand, captured the gold, and stuffed it down into the deep pocket. I came up with a box, and my breeches were bagging with gold.

Then came the climax of my strained relations with those greaser divers. I've heard of pickpockets operating everywhere, almost, but I reckon that I'm the first and only man who ever had his pockets picked at the bottom of the sea. The first devil who got to me as the sand settled, in groping for a handhold on my dress, felt the loose ingots. He got one, but he did not get away with it. Trouble or no trouble, knives or no knives, I had got to the limit of my temper. I gave him a jab with the end of my sheet-iron nozzle, and as near as I could judge I took a hunk of meat out of him as neatly as a woman could operate on dough with a doughnut cutter. The edges of that nozzle had been whetted on sand until they were as sharp as a razor blade. The fellow dropped that ingot and darted upward, blood streaming behind him. Another diver was coming down to take his place, but when I jabbed at him with the nozzle he whirled like a fish and went up, giving me an awful kick when he started.

I reckoned I had thrown down the gage of battle, and I was not minded to stay there and meet the pack, for I was weak after my extra struggle down in the hole. It had been a tedious job gathering that loose gold. I saw the box started on the way to the surf-boat, gave the emergency signal, and was yanked back to the lighter at a lively clip.

Later that day, being in a proper and ugly frame of mind, I tucked a rifle under my arm and had myself rowed to the neighboring sloop. I found the spokesman of the crew ready to talk English that day, all right. But when our conversation was ended I had received a surprise. No demand was made on me to a "hot rock." I found that I was dealing with men who had deeper motives. It took me some time to understand that they were not holding out to a big offer. The man at the rail wrinkled his nose and sneered when I angrily told him that was what they were after.

"It's what I'd expect a gringo to tell me," he said. "But we are not here to do business with thieves. You have no right to be here. You may pick and steal, but it will not amount to *that*!" He snapped his finger above his head. "We shall do our business with those who will have the gold in the end, with those who can pay and will pay. And we have a man who will see that we are paid."

My wits had been sharpened while I had toiled at San Apusa Bar.

323

I was able to see farther into the ways of guile than before I had met a man like Marcena Keedy. I had a flash of suspicion that was almost instinct.

"So you think you have made a better trade with that renegade, Keedy, do you?" I flung at him.

I was sure I had guessed right; the man's face betrayed him.

"Oh, we are honest men—not thieves," he called back. "We do not deal with thieves. We came here to stop you from stealing. But you do not stop. Now we shall see. We have kept our knives in our belts. But you have set us an example. You have tried to kill a man who did not offer to hurt you." He leaped up on the rail, and aimed a long finger at me. "We can fight the way you do. If we catch you there on bottom again you'll be pulled up with six of these sticking in you." He patted the knife in his belt.

There are men who can threaten and who cannot impress others. It is easily docketed as bluster. There is another kind of a man who gives you a look and a word, and you know that he means what he says. I went away from that sloop feeling that if I were desperate enough just then to commit suicide, an easy way had been opened for me.

I went and tumbled into my berth, and viewed the ruins of that idea which I had been building so prayerfully. It looked to me then, in my despondency, as if Keedy was holding mighty good cards. If he had decided to turn informer, he could demand and would undoubtedly receive a noble rake-off. It was probable that he *would* inform—for that would be his natural, lazy method of making his money out of the thing. The posting of the pearl divers in behalf of the underwriters would be an additional feather in his cap; on the other hand, if he proposed to come with a backer and new equipment—having discovered my system—he had good reasons for leaving men behind him who would hold us in check. If Keedy returned with steam-pumps he could rip the bottom out of the Pacific. Our makeshift equipment would not be two-spot high.

And how soon could he return, whether he came piloting the underwriters or came on his own hook as a rival "thief"? I talked with Captain Holstrom on that matter the next day. He rubbed his nose and scruffed his hair, and could not guess.

I asked the captain for his estimate of the amount of treasure in our chest. He told me that we had rising three-quarters of a million.

"Captain, it has become a matter of touch and go—live or die—with us. With less than a third of that gold in our hands, we're in no position to do business when the pinch comes. I'm going after the rest of it!"

"But you said you knew them greaser pickerel would poke their knives into you. God knows I'm hungry for the rest of the treasure, Sidney, but I'm no Marcena Keedy."

"I'm going down at night, Captain Holstrom."

"It can't be done."

"It *can* be done. After I get my stream started I'm in the dark even when the sun is brightest. I know the way from the lighter to that wreck, all right. I've dragged my way there times enough with a trail of blood behind me," I told him, sourly. "It can never be any worse than it has been. We'll take extra chances, moor the lighter nearer the wreck, get rid of the surf-boat and crew, and leave those greasers guessing."

I want to say, to the credit of the captain, that he opposed this undertaking of mine. His daughter— But I will not dwell on that point. It harrows my soul now to remember the manner in which I opposed my obstinate and reckless will to her honest grief and her almost frantic protests.

I went down that night. I gave 'em three boxes before midnight. I ate a lunch, and gave 'em one box more before I quit.

I have no ambition to make this story a rival of Fox's *Book of Martyrs*. I have already given some idea of the physical state I was in. I think I became numb to pain, accustomed to agonies. I cannot explain otherwise how I ever kept on, night after night. I haven't the courage to write down what I suffered.

But out from under those grinning greasers—grinning their sneers at us daytimes—I dragged one and one-half million dollars' worth of gold ingots inside of two weeks—and they never suspected that I was under water.

During the last of that nightmare, I felt as if I were working with my chin over my shoulder. I was looking for trouble. I was expecting disaster. I was scared to the marrow. I am not referring to any feelings I had on account of the pearl divers. Their bug eyes had never detected me in what I was about. I knew that darkness protected me more surely from any attack by them than iron walls would have done.

But I worked nights with the constant feeling that the red and green eyes of a steamer were coming up over the horizon. When I was awake daytimes I peered into the northern sky hour after hour, expecting and dreading to see the trail of smoke which would announce the coming of Marcena Keedy and those whom he had notified.

My conferences with Captain Holstrom had been scant and rather brusque. There were some points in that idea of mine that I had not thought out to my own satisfaction, and I had not found the captain to be especially helpful in attacking problems. He was wholly taken up in helping to pull that gold in over the rail, in storing it, in guarding it.

His daughter knew why I stared at the northern horizon, and why desperate worry added to the other woes I was suffering in that tophet of toil. She had resigned herself to the situation when I had persisted in keeping on. She became, as before, my wistful nurse. She talked to me as she would have soothed a madman whom she hoped to win back to sanity. Well, I was a lunatic in those days—there's not much doubt of it. It was madness made up of fear, desperation, agony of physical pain, lust for gold—all forcing me to do work which no sane man could have accomplished in my condition of body.

She dared to break her usual silence on the matter of the treasure when we were on deck one afternoon after my sleep. She had been gazing at me sorrowfully while I stared into the north.

"Oh, what use is it—this dreadful work and worry? You have told me that you feel like a thief in it all. You sit and stare into the north as though you were a wicked man, instead of being so brave and successful in the most wonderful work a man ever did. You are getting their gold for them. But you feel that they are coming to take it all away—and call you a thief. You cannot deceive me as to your thoughts."

I had to acknowledge to myself that her woman's intuition was in fine working order. I understood what men were, naturally, in affairs where big sums of money were involved. These men, provided Keedy had done as I supposed he had, would have Keedy's lies about us to inflame them still further in addition to their natural greed.

But she was no quitter on one point. She clenched her little fists and kept on:

"I say fight back! It may be their money—somebody's money—but what good did it do them or anybody else until you came here with your strength and your courage and your brains and got it up from the bottom of the ocean? I don't know what the law is about such things—I don't care. I've heard you and father talk, but I only know that often in this life law is one thing and justice is another."

"There are the laws of salvage," I told her. "We could turn this money over and wait for the courts to decide. But I'm afraid of what may happen if we do that. There's that renegade Keedy with his lies;

there are the customs men of Mexico, and all that mess of international law to complicate things. Keedy can claim partnership; the shippers can claim shares, I suppose; this one and that one can dip in their fingers; and lawyers can tie the matter up; and God only knows when it will all be untied so that we can get what we have honestly earned. We may have to fight for our liberty, for men are crazy enough to try to make us out thieves, providing they can get hold of much money by lies and injustice. I have been pounding it all out in my poor head, and I can't seem to believe that the law is going to give us what we ought to have. For, you see, this thing isn't like anything else that has ever happened."

"I say fight!" she insisted, her eyes alight, her cheeks flaming under the tan. "You have fought the ocean for their sakes as well as your own—and you have won. Keep on fighting! Plan something, do something—get into some position where they will have to come to you and beg for what's theirs. You have earned the right to make them beg. And you know you have!"

Yes, I did know it; and on that belief I had based my idea which had served for my encouragement. Her advice and her woman's spirit in the matter heartened me. She had acted like the lady of the castle of whom I had read. She brought to me my helmet and shield, and was sending me out to battle as a brave woman should. I started to tell her more about my idea—but we were interrupted.

There was a queer noise in the direction of the ladder which led to the lower deck. It was such a prodigious puffing and wheezing and grunting that anybody might suppose that we were going to receive a visit from a hippopotamus. The Snohomish Glutton, the cook of the *Zizania*, appeared to us. I had not laid eyes on that individual for weeks. He stuck in his pantry like a hermit in a cell, reveling in the steam of food, stuffing himself even while he was cooking for others. He rolled rather than walked across the deck, and stood before us, propping up the rolls of fat which shuttered his little eyes.

"I don't know how much there is or where you're keeping it," he blurted, without preface, in his tin-whistle voice. "I don't ask questions—I stay in my pantry and mind my business. But I serve the niggers in the port alley and the whites in the starboard alley, and I hear both sides. But there's only one side now. They said that the monkey's tail started the row. But they've forgotten the row. Gold will make men forget 'most anything. They've got together at last. They are going to grab for it. They thought I haven't been hearing because my eyes were shut and I seemed to be asleep."

"What do you mean, my man?" I demanded.

"I mean that you can play checkers on that checker-board crew now, sir. It has settled into a solid board—white and black mixed. The Russian Finn is captain. He killed my cat. I have said I would get even with him. He is captain, and they are going to drop on to that gold and run away."

"They have planned a mutiny?"

"Mutiny and all the side dishes that go with it. I have heard. I wasn't asleep when they thought I was. I've got to go back. I have duff in the pot."

He backed to the ladder and let himself down, rung by rung, grunting more terrifically than before.

The girl leaped to her feet. She held her clenched fists above her head. Her white teeth showed beneath the crimson of her parted lips. She drove her hands down at her sides.

"Oh!" she had gasped, when her hands were above her head. When she drove them down her woman's soul spoke its anger and horror. "Damn the name of gold!" she cried; and I would not have indorsed a milder phrase even from her.

For weeks my head had been full of seething particles of schemes relating to my central idea. I reckon it needed a shock—needed the desperate occasion of instant action—to make those particles cohere into resolve. For a moment I was stunned by the prospect of this new danger; and then a course of action came to me in a flash of inspiration—it was the result of all the thinking I had been doing, without making up my mind to act.

I hobbled to find Captain Holstrom in his state-room. I had to push him back when he had heard a dozen words of what I had reported. He had grabbed his pistols and was rushing to kill off a few prospective mutineers as an example to the others.

"You have got to do what I advise in this matter, Captain. I've been making plans. We've got not only this crew to consider, but Keedy and those he is bringing down here. He is coming. We may as well make up our minds to that. I want you to go down on the main deck as quickly as you can and order the crew to get out planks and start in making strong boxes. Privately, you and I will overhaul the junk for scrap iron, for chains and cable. Get after the men. Hustle them. Make it a hurry-up job. Busy men won't have time to talk mutiny. And say to one of the mates, when you are giving off orders, that you are going to pack the treasure into boxes suitable for handling. Say that loud enough so that all the men will hear."

"I'll be joheifered if I don't believe I've got to handle a lunatic as well as a mutiny," flamed Captain Holstrom. "Are you advising me to pack up that gold so that it will be easy lugging to the crew?"

"As soon as they believe that it is going to be packed so as to be easy lugging there'll be no mutiny until those boxes have been made. You've got to do as I say. You ought to have had your lesson by this time that I know what I'm talking about."

He shuttled his eyes when I looked at him. He was remembering those past matters in which he had made a fool of himself in resisting me. I was willing to explain my plan to him, for I was not trying to humiliate Captain Holstrom. But just then I had a feeling that every moment counted. One instant more and I knew what the pricking of my mental thumbs had meant. Mate Number-two Jones came clattering along the deck from below. He shoved a red and greatly troubled face in at the door.

"Get your guns, Cap'n Holstrom," he panted. "They're grumbling and mumbling. It means mutiny."

"Take your guns with you, if you like," I told the captain. "But go down there as cool as you can. Give off your orders as if you didn't notice anything. And be sure to throw out that hint about why you want the boxes made. This is no time to bull this game of ours."

Captain Holstrom was no fool, and he knew when a man was in dead earnest. I pushed him and he went. I'll have to confess that he qualified as a good actor when he arrived on the main deck.

I was looking down from the bridge, and I saw the men of the crew exchange winks and grins behind the captain's back.

The model crew of the crack ship in all the world could not have shown such willing obedience. They went to their work on the rush. Saws rasped and hammers banged. There was clattering of iron and hum of industry.

Captain Holstrom left the work in charge of his mate, and came back to his state-room to resume his watch over the treasure. I closeted myself with him.

"Now, we'll get down to the bed-rock of the proposition, Captain Holstrom. We have agreed—you and I—that Keedy is about due here. We don't know who will come with him. But we can be mighty sure that they'll be no friends of ours. We'd be playing the parts of idiots to keep that gold on board the *Zizania*. But there isn't a harbor nearer than Acapulco where we can land it; we can't lug it ashore on the open coast through the breakers; we can't dodge all around the Pacific Ocean with it. Right now, there's another complication beside Keedy and his crowd. We have still more desperate thieves right here with us. The mates and Shank are safe. To-night the five of us will get busy, pack that gold in the strong boxes, and drop it overboard."

"Great guns!" groaned the captain. "I said you was crazy, and now I'm sure of it. Dig it all up, and then throw it away again! No, let's not put it in the boxes. Let's hoot and holler and cavort around the deck and heave it overboard, one ingot at a time, so as to see who can make the biggest splash. Come on—let's have fun!" he raved.

"I am far from being crazy, Captain Holstrom," I informed him, giving him the hard eye so steadily that he blinked. "To each box we'll hitch chain long enough to reach to the surface. That chain will have rope cable—say ten feet of it—hitched to the end, and the rope will be buoyed to a small spar. The box and all the chain will lie on bottom. The small spar with its rope cable will swim well under the surface of the water. In case we want to raise the box we can catch the rope and spar with a rake, or else drag for it with a chain between two boats."

"I hate to see that gold go under water again," mourned Captain Holstrom.

"It's that or stand by and see mutineers lug it off or lawyers divide it."

He writhed like a speared fish when he pondered on the alternatives. I went out on deck and left him to think, confident that his slow mind would finally swing to my way of making the best of a bad matter.

The checker-board crew was at work in a real frenzy of effort. I have no doubt that each man secretly told himself that he was building his own box—and he was putting his best work into his treasure-carrier.

The summer evening was long and the crew labored on after their supper. According to my best judgment, when darkness shut down on their labors there were boxes enough for our purpose. The men went to their rest on the berth-deck in the forepeak of the steamer. Captain Holstrom had remarked, casually, in their hearing, that he would wait till next day before packing the ingots. From my post on the bridge, though the dusk had deepened, I caught a cheerful wink or two between man and man, and they went below looking like cats who had been promised a full meal of canaries.

In order to encourage general peace and confidence, the mates allowed the usual deck watch to go below and sleep, and the lazy sailors were only too glad to do so.

When they were snoring in satisfactory chorus, Captain Holstrom slid their hatch over and barred it so as to guard against a surprise by peepers. Before two bells after midnight the last box of our gold had gone gurgling down over the taffrail. The last spar winked out of sight under the surge.

"It's gone!" groaned Captain Holstrom.

"Thank God, it has!" said I, and felt the girl's little hand snuggle comfortingly into my unsightly fist.

XXXVI

THE TERROR FROM THE NORTH

The next morning Captain Holstrom ordered the checker-board crew assembled on the main deck, forward. He appeared on the bridge and leaned over the rail like a candidate ready to make a stump speech. But, unlike a candidate, he had two revolvers strapped to his waist and in plain sight.

"I have a few words to say to you critters down there," he began. "I know all about what you have been planning to do. I have watched you peeking and spying around this morning for them boxes. Well, you won't find them. Them boxes are a good way off." He pointed a stubby finger down at the Russian Finn. "You come up here!" he commanded. The Finn turned pale and shook his head.

"You come up here and I'll promise that you won't be hurt. I want you to take back a report to that gang of yours. If you don't obey a master's orders and come up here," continued the captain, pulling a gun, "it will be mutiny—and I know how to deal with mutiny. I'll shoot you where you stand."

After a little hesitation the Finn climbed the ladder. The captain led him into the wheel-house, into all the state-rooms, and took him on a general tour of inspection of the upper deck.

"Now you can see with your own eyes that there isn't any gold up here to mutiny about. You go back and tell that gang what you have seen—or, rather, what you didn't see." He pushed the Finn to the ladder.

"I give you all liberty to hunt over the lower part of the steamer from forepeak to rudder," declared the captain over the rail. "You can help yourselves to all the gold you find. But I can tell you that there ain't an ounce aboard here. That gold is stored where you can't get it." He swept his hand in a gesture which embraced the horizon. "If you act like men from now on until this cruise is over, you'll be paid like lords. If you hanker for mutiny, start in and mutiny. Them who live through it will never get a cent; them who are killed can't use gold where they will fetch up; it will be too hot to handle!"

The men fell to muttering among themselves, but I could see that they had been cowed. The report of the leader made them still more melancholy. They divided at last—the blacks from the whites—and went about their tasks.

"I want to say, Sidney, that you showed good judgment," said the captain, as he went to his state-room. "But I don't feel like giving three cheers—not while that gold is back on the bottom of the Pacific Ocean."

Well, there was gold to the value of about a million yonder on the bottom in that wreck of the *Golden Gate*, but I had no appetite for more gold just then. I knew that I had reached the limit of my strength and courage. I had won more than two millions from the greed of that miserly ocean, and had given it back again in order to make another fight against the greed of men.

I sat on deck and endured the pains of my tortured body, and waited for the inevitable when it should come down over the horizon from the north. Half a dozen anxious days dragged past—and then it came!

A trail of black smoke signaled it—they were using lots of coal and were in a hurry, as that banner of black indicated. Framed in Captain Holstrom's long telescope, it took form as a big ocean tug. She seemed to leap angrily across the sea as the surges rolled under her, and the bows churned up white yeast.

There was no hesitation in the manner in which she came on. She bore down on us with a speed which seemed to say, "Here we come to take our own!"

We counted at least a score of men aboard, using our glass. And when the tug slowed off our quarter we saw that most of the men held rifles in the hook of their arms.

"It's what I have been expecting," I told the captain. "They have come down here proposing to treat us as pirates. How would you feel right now with gold aboard here?"

Captain Holstrom wagged his head mournfully, and seemed to lack words with which to express his feelings.

"We are going to make fast to you," bawled a man, with a voice like a fog-horn. "Mind how you perform."

That was a reckless performance even for a tug in that sea, but they rigged a row of fenders and put her alongside with much clanging of bell. A dozen men leaped on board the *Zizania*. Some were guards who carried rifles. There were three men who seemed of importance. I spied Marcena Keedy on the upper deck of the tug, holding to the funnel stays. He did not venture to come on board us with the others.

"Let them do the talking," I whispered to Captain Holstrom as the three were climbing the ladder. "Just stand on your dignity as master of this steamer." And the captain did so in a way that highly satisfied me. He chewed a toothpick and displayed much indifference.

"I bid you welcome, gents!" he informed them, stiffly. "And you can see that I ain't looking for trouble—otherwise I might have a few words to say about your way of boarding this steamer. If it's ignorance of rules and etiquette, I'll overlook it."

"It's business, Captain Holstrom," snapped the spokesman, a chap who wore a hard hat and looked as though he had just closed a desk in an office. "We are from San Francisco, and represent the underwriters in the matter of the *Golden Gate*."

"Step into the wheel-house—it's my office," stated the captain. He pointed to the muzzle of the first rifle, rising over the edge of the upper deck. "If those fellows come up here I shall consider it an insult to me as a peaceful man and master of this vessel."

The man hesitated.

"We're no pirates," remarked Captain Holstrom.

The man gave orders to the gunmen to remain below.

"If you are not pirates," he said, when we were assembled in the wheel-house, "you can show it by turning over to us the gold you've dug out of the wreck over yonder."

The spokesman was a rather excitable fellow. He began to tap his finger on the captain's breast. He showed documents with seals and all the other law-shark trimmings.

"You have no right to come here and operate. Have you got attorney's powers? Have you got anything in the way of permits? No, you haven't. That gold belongs to other people. Give it up and save trouble."

Captain Holstrom threw a sort of helpless look at me, stifling some emotion. I realized that he was at the end of his dignity and that in about ten seconds he would begin to use his talents in the line of profanity.

"Excuse me if I say a word here," I broke in. "I am a partner in this enterprise."

"You're using a polite word for this kind of a job," sneered the man.

"You may represent the underwriters," I said, "but to all intents and purposes the underwriters had abandoned the treasure."

"We shall take our gold, my friend!"

"Rights or no rights?"

"You have made it a grab game, and we're in on the grab!" He was mighty overbearing and offensive. Law was behind him, a fortune was concerned, and he was showing the usual spirit of the greedy world.

334

"You have full powers in this matter so far as the underwriters are concerned, have you?" I asked.

"Absolute." He waved his papers under my nose. "Issued due and regular by the court and the United States."

"But don't you realize that you are not in the United State, sir?"

"There's got to be more or less dog eat dog in this game. We happen to have the cards. If you don't hand over that gold, we shall put a crew on board this steamer, guard it with rifles, and set this boat into waters where we have jurisdiction. I'll be frank to say that then we can beat you in court in the lying game, because we start with law behind us, and you're handicapped. I say this to show you that you'd better fork over."

I was holding my temper. For the sake of my own conscience in this affair, I wanted the other side to lay all their cards on the table; in their insolence and confidence, they seemed inclined to do so, for their plain intent was to intimidate us.

"What do we get out of it for ourselves?" I inquired, meekly.

"Remember that you came down here on the sly, thinking you were going to get away with the whole thing. It hasn't been your fault that you haven't. I think that we can premise to keep you out of the penitentiary if you act sensible. I'm not making any rash promises."

There we had it! Contemptuous disregard of all our rights because they thought they had the upper hand on us!

I have hinted before this that men became monsters in the presence of much gold. From my own experience I knew the insanity which gold stirs in a man. I had foreseen some such attitude as this on the part of the men who would come to claim the treasure. A grab game, eh? And success to the best man!

I looked at that fellow—at his white hands and his flabbiness—a man who had never done an honest day's labor with grit and muscles. He had given me his code. I told him as much.

"And I thank you for giving me that code," I went on.

I stripped the bandages off my hands. I tore the wrappings off my feet. I showed them sights which made their faces turn white. I ripped the shirt from my back and exhibited that spectacle of ragged flesh.

"You have given me your code, I say! It's going to be a grab game. All right! Have it your way. Go hunt this steamer from top to bottom. You're welcome! Prove that we have any of your damned gold! Go ahead!"

I hobbled out of the wheel-house and went into my state-room, and they began to hunt the *Zizania* over. And I heard what Captain Holstrom said to them after they had finished.

"Now, gents, you have made sure that there's nothing on my *Zizania* that belongs to you. You're aboard here without any rights. I just want to remark that I'll give you five minutes to get aboard your own boat and cast off, and stay cast off'm here, yourselves. I've got some men who can fight—and I've got a two-pounder in my junk-heap. I'll put a ball through that tug that will disturb her innards seriously."

They went silently and grudgingly—but they went. I enjoyed the expression on Marcena Keedy's face as the tug backed off. I came out on the upper deck and gloated down on him. They anchored their craft a little distance from us, and I could readily imagine the council of war that started among them as soon as their mud-hook bit the holding-ground.

A boat put off from the tug next day, and the three important-looking men were in it. But Captain Holstrom warned them away from us. The spokesman shouted his message. He was angry, and he still dealt in threats. In order to impress upon those gentlemen that we were not at all interested in their threats, the captain and I turned our backs on them, and after a time they bawled themselves out of breath and returned to the tug.

They kept up those tactics for most of a week. They were certainly stubborn and insolent persons, and they were fighting for big money. But the more they raved and threatened, the more at peace with myself and my conscience I felt. We were fighting for our own now, and they had established the code.

Then at last the boat came with a white flag. The spokesman politely stated that they had come to talk some business in private, and begged to be allowed to come on board.

Miss Karna was with me on deck when they climbed up the ladder. She had resumed her woman's garb, and they stared at her in frank astonishment and admiration. She did look particularly sweet, her little cap on her curls, her sweater displaying her winsome curves of beauty.

She seemed to astonish them, I say. The next moment she astonished *me*. She walked into the wheel-house by my side, and was the first to speak.

"Gentlemen," she said to the three, "you have seen with your own eyes how this poor boy has suffered. You can't see how I have suffered as I have watched him do what he has done, but the marks are on my soul, I know. There is law in the world, and all that, and men are too apt to get angry in law when there is much money concerned. Can't you all keep from being angry to-day, and be wise, and decide on what is right?"

They looked at one another and the spokesman stammered something about being over there to have a heart-to-heart talk.

"May I not stay?" she asked, wistfully. "I won't say a word to bother you—I won't move unless you start to quarrel—and then I'll only remind you that there's a lady present." The queer little smile she gave them started the grins on their faces. The ice was broken. Those men were human once more. The girl had given the magic touch to the conference.

We had not been getting anywhere at all, in the past, and we woke up and realized it as we stood there with the girl's presence toning us down. It had been man's bluff and bluster; they had arrived ready mad and I felt that I knew what ailed them outside of the mere money part of the thing.

"Gentlemen," I said, "if it hadn't been for Marcena Keedy's tongue you would have shown a better side to us when you arrived here." Nobody seemed ready to say anything for a moment and I went on. "I reckon he told you that he was our partner and that we have cheated him."

"He had quite a story to tell when he reported the matter to the underwriters," admitted the lawyer.

"After you sized him up, you naturally decided that men who could cheat Keedy must be the champion renegades of the Pacific coast! I can't blame you much for the way you came banging up against us. I don't know what else he has said to our prejudice, and I don't care. Now that you are here with us, face to face, and we're down on a real man-basis, we don't need to paw over what a liar has said. I want you to call that man Keedy on to the *Zizania*, even though he poisons the air. What I have to say I'll say in his hearing."

I'm pretty sure that Keedy did not relish making that call, but the men who went after him brought him. He had a gambler's face and nerve and he put on his best front; he even disregarded Miss Karna's presence and lighted a cigar to appear more at ease, and I plucked it from between his jaws and flung it out of the window.

"I want the floor for only a few moments, gentlemen," I told the group. "I'm going to tell you how this expedition was organized, how this person Keedy fitted in, and what happened." And I did tell them.

It was necessary for the lawyer to appoint Capt. Rask Holstrom as special guard to keep Keedy's mouth shut while I talked, but the rules of a court-room prevailed after that.

"I'll admit, gentlemen," I said when I had finished my little story, "that we have acted like children so far as the legal side of this thing goes. But it seemed only a crazy scheme at best when we started out—I couldn't feel that I was dealing with any reality. After we arrived here we did the best we could, and we have been too busy to study up law. But I want to say that Captain Holstrom and I are not thieves by nature. I'll show you a thief, however. There he stands!" I pointed to Keedy. "He stole from us a box of bullion worth twenty thousand dollars. I know that he recovered two more boxes. Now that you are proposing to handle this matter man-fashion, Captain Holstrom and I stand ready to give to owners what is fairly their own. I advise you to ask Keedy what he proposes to do!" The lawyer asked him in mighty prompt fashion.

"Up to date nobody seems to be making any showdown except in talk," said Mr. Keedy. "I'll cash in conversation just as far as anybody."

"But how does it happen, Keedy, that when you gave us your other information you did not say that you had any of the gold in your hands?" asked the lawyer.

He scowled and did not answer.

"If these men turn their bullion over on a square lay, are you prepared to do the same?"

"I'll talk business after I have seen them turn it over."

"That's a rather queer attitude for you to take, Keedy, after your talk to the underwriters and to me."

But the renegade did not show any inclination to come across with anything definite.

I knew well enough that he could not. His try with those divers had cost high and it was safe to presume that he had realized on every ounce of the bullion his men had recovered and had planted the money. My rancor was deep and I walked up to him and declared my belief.

"You understand, Keedy, that you must produce the bullion or its value in money or our bargain doesn't stand," said the lawyer.

I did not need that declaration to be assured that the villain had sold us without regard to our rights or our safety. And sudden fervor and determination thrilled through and through me. I proposed to show those men from San Francisco the difference between Marcena Keedy and the partners on whom he had pasted his dirty label. Mere talk was not as convincing proof as I desired. I had already made an investment of my best strength and all my courage and I had much

338

to show. But I felt that if those men could see with their own eyes what that investment signified in the way of human endurance, they would meet me in more generous spirit when we came to make our bargain.

Up to then the legal papers had only been waved under my nose in threatening manner. I asked permission to examine them, and the lawyer was very obliging. They were all-embracing, even to granting powers of attorney to the underwriters' agents to handle the matter in all its aspects.

"Gentlemen," I said, "I'm going down after the rest of that gold, and every box will be put into your hands as it comes up."

I got a glimpse at the girl's face, but I did not dare to look into her eyes. Her cheeks were white, and she was gasping protests which nobody heeded, for those men were listening to something which filled their ears just then:

"And after you see how I am bucking hell for your sakes, well, then we shall see what you have to say to me—man to man!"

XXXVII

THE FRUIT OF THE
TREE OF KNOWLEDGE

If what I have just written sounds as if I wanted to pose as a hero of melodrama, I have produced a wrong impression. I was playing a big game and I was using all the hard, cold and calculating wit I possessed. As I have said, I proposed to operate on human nature. After all, I was in no position to demand anything from those men, in spite of the bluff we were making in regard to the treasure we had recovered and concealed. I had a healthy fear of what the courts might do to us in a case where stolen property had been hidden. It was up to me to cultivate a spirit of generosity in them—and that was why I went down again, though every nerve and fiber in my racked body made protest. But I went down under better conditions.

The tug had powerful pumps and a considerable quantity of good hose. She was manageable in shoal water, and by means of her hawsers and well-set kedges we were able to swing her in, for the day's work, fairly close to the wreck.

There is no need of further dwelling on details—and it would be necessary to supply the details by somebody's word of mouth—somebody who watched me, for I don't remember much of what happened. I was a lunatic, I suppose; my human machinery was operated by a single mania. As I look back I am unable to separate the nightmare from the reality with any amount of clarity. Therefore, we'll allow all that to hang in limbo, seeing that this is a plain yarn and not a study of psychology.

However, I can remember flashes through the dark curtain, and of a few of these I will make mention, for they have a bearing on the tale.

There was a period when I was in the mood for babbling. I could feel my dry tongue clacking away inside my jaws like a clapper in a wooden box and wholly beyond my control. That tongue was telling all my story about my love and longing and ambition in my boyhood days—telling the story to somebody who patted my cheek and crooned sympathy—somebody who did not annoy me by dispute when I said that I would never live to see Levant again—somebody who promised to carry there the three rings and tell my story and fulfil my requests. It was a dream full of agony for me—rather it may be called a dreaming reality. I wanted to stop that clacking tongue. I wasn't operating it. It was telling a lot of truth which I did not want published. It was putting me in wrong, I felt, just as if some enemy were tattling about me. It was mine and I hated it furiously for what seemed to be betrayal of me. I wasn't standing for what the tongue said.

Then there was a period when I forgave the tongue many of its past offenses, because, at last, it did good service for me in man-talk to men. It was steady and convincing and I was conscious that it had helped me to win in some big matter. Then, later, there was a time when there were shots and shoutings and dismal trouble of some sort. And, last of all, in the blurred imaginings, mixed with the real, came the long-drawn-out, misty, groping, wondering consciousness that I was out of strife and trouble and agony. But I could not come out of the shadow—I knew that many days and nights came and went while I was trying to grasp something which I could know was reality.

I was dreaming that I was back in my old room in Dodovah Vose's tavern, and that dream seemed to last for days. Then all at once I woke up and I was truly in that room.

By the open window sat Capt. Rask Holstrom and he was junking up a Red Astrachan apple with his jack-knife. He poised a cube of the fruit on the tip of the blade; looked me square in the eyes, and asked, in a matter-of-fact way, if I was feeling more like myself that day.

There was no doubt about my being in Dodovah Vose's tavern! I made sure before I opened my mouth. There was the old quaint smell of the place, and I could always trust my nose. For my ears there was the whining squeak of the windmill pump in the stable-yard. I touched the irregular seams of the silk crazy-quilt, and, to delight my eyes, the brass handles of the ancient high-boy in the corner blinked back the radiance of the afternoon sunlight. All my senses were satisfied, for I could almost taste, as the breeze flicked my lips, the savor of fried chicken which came floating in through the window. And after my senses told me what they did, I felt at ease and dismissed all the shadows and imaginings. Never did a man come back to his right balance of mind in more commonplace fashion.

I decided to be just as matter-of-fact as Captain Rask. I told him I felt pretty fair. Parts of my hands were bandaged and I was aware that my feet were tied up.

"Have another apple?"

So I had been eating apples from Dodovah Vose's orchard! I used to steal from his trees—especially the early-autumn fruit. I must have been giving the impression that I was pretty nigh all right, even though the kink in my brain had kept me on the side-track so far as I was concerned, personally.

The captain junked an apple into quarters, pared them, and gave me the fruit. I think Eve tempted Adam with a Red Astrachan!

The captain sat and rocked and munched. Confound his old pelt, why didn't he start in and tell me what had happened?

He clacked his knife shut after a time and yawned.

"So, as I was telling you before you had your nap, Karna and I may as well move on. There isn't much more that's sensible we can do for you." I wondered just what they *had* done!

"Where is Karna?" I called her "Karna" quite naturally; it seemed to me that my clattering tongue had been that familiar for a long time.

"Oh, I guess she's just resting up a little in her room. She is bound to be nursing you most of the time, though you don't need so much attention, so far as I can see. Do you know, Ross, in spite of what you and I were saying to each other yesterday, that girl o' mine still insists that your mind isn't right, and that you're off the hooks. She says there's something that hasn't come back to you!"

God bless that girl's intuition! I felt the tears coming into my eyes.

"Women folks are always seeing something a man can't see—because it isn't there for him to see!" declared the captain. "I have made her keep her mouth shut best I could! Nice thing it would be to have it go out in business circles that you're a lunatic. That old hippohampus uncle of yours would try to get himself appointed your guardian. He makes believe to be a great friend of yours, I know, when he calls, but I reckon he's only hiding that old grudge that Vose has told me about. *There's* your friend, Ross—Vose! He's the old boy to tie to!" I was getting considerable information from Capt. Rask Holstrom without weakening his confidence in my sanity.

"And then, outside of Vose, it has really been a good thing for you to get back here near your girl," pursued the captain. "Now you take Karna on that point! I say women folks have too much imagination. When you told me you wanted the Kingsley girl to stay away from you till you was fit to look at, why, then you was showing hard, ordinary common sense. In spite of all that Karna or anybody else said about her coming in here, I done just what you asked me to do—for I believe in men standing by each other. But, as I have told you, Karna was bound to have it that a screw was loose because you didn't want your girl first thing! And Karna has been bound and determined to hang on here till she is sure you're all right with your girl. But I can't see that your girl is in any great pucker about you! She hasn't showed up!"

The sweat started out on me. Into what sort of a tangle had my affairs been drawn?

"But I've got a good girl, even if she is flighty in her thoughts—as I suppose girls' nature is about this lovey-dove business. I used to sit and hear you talk to her on the *Zizania* about those three rings and that girl back in Levant—all mush, mush right in the middle of that wind-up job—and, I swear, if I didn't think you were crazy then, though she wouldn't have it that way! Said you were all right. Karna and I never did seem to agree very well on much of anything. After the settlement with the underwriters, when you were right as a trivet and wanted to stay on the Coast, then she insisted that you were out of your head—as I don't mind telling you now when we're going—and she fairly picked you up and lugged you back here. You were too sick to help yourself, you know! Made me help her do it! For you and your girl, said she! I ain't sure but what you *was* a little delirious there at times. But being here with Vose has done you good. However, I like West the best. So, as I say, I reckon Karna and I will pack up and start back. Furthermore, you know, I'm summonsed for that trial."

I merely stared at the old gossiper.

"I don't want to be too hard on those critters," he said, musingly. "There was a big temptation and Marcena Keedy knew how to stir 'em up. When he lolloped that word 'gold' around in his mouth he always made me drool."

Didn't I remember, also? Only too well!

"No, I'm going to use some discretion in my testimony," Captain Rask chatted on. "I have been running over in my mind what happened. Now, if you're a mind to, let me kind of rehearse it over to you so that you can check up my memory. I'll hate to have any lawsharks tangle me on the stand. If I make a slip catch me up on it."

I assured him that I would, and I settled back in bed with great joy in my heart.

He gave me the most wonderful story I ever read or ever listened to—wonderful because it concerned myself, my friends, my hopes, and my fortune; wonderful, because I was in it, acted in it, and now for the first time was hearing what I had done. He droned out the hair-raising narrative without showing special interest in it, confident that I knew the happenings as well as he; at the most interesting point, in order to collect his thoughts in regard to Marcena Keedy, he stopped and pared and munched an apple; I was saving my own face in the matter and I did not dare to prod him.

I am not minded to make much account of the details of that story. In this yarn I have been telling what I do know—not what I have heard from another man's lips. Let this much suffice: I recovered the rest of the *Golden Gate* treasure, so far as human knowledge of it went, the jettisoned gold was dragged for and raised, and then mutiny, which had been secretly organized by Keedy and the Finn, developed into a bloody battle which had been won against numbers by the rifles of the lawful guards. Keedy would not fight—he had prodded the other poor devils to do that—and the San Francisco men took the law into their hands when the *Zizania* was on the high seas and hung Keedy from the derrick boom.

So, there's enough in a nutshell to make quite a book by itself!

And then while Captain Rask meditatively wagged his jaws on another apple I lay and gnawed my nervous lips and wondered how much money I had in the world! I did not dare to ask questions. I felt as bitterly fearful as a straitened merchant who has lost all run of his bank credits and is afraid to ask his bank how he stands; the fear of giving one's self away becomes terror pretty vital!

"However, I'm going to pass the rest of my days without worrying about their troubles," declared the captain, again clacking shut his knife blade. "They brought it on themselves, though I shall swear on the stand that Keedy told them into the scrape. You and I did right by the faithful ones—especially *you,* for you could give out a better line of talk—when we pulled that hundred thousand out of the underwriters and added it to the hundred thousand of our own. They're satisfied, even the Snohomish Glutton in his new restaurant, and Ingot Ike, who has gone to board with him. Clear consciences—that's what we've got, Ross!"

But how much clear profit? The fact that we had handed out one hundred thousand dollars was a consoling bit of information. There naturally must be plenty more where that came from!

"Do all the folks here—do the people in Levant know how well we're fixed?" I faltered.

"Sure! I ain't ashamed of it. Are you? I haven't let the yarn lose anything by the way I have told it. It has been a good way of killing time."

So everybody else in Levant, except myself, knew how rich I was!

And then that infernal old tiddlywhoop yawned, got up, and stamped out of the room, saying that he was going to stretch his legs.

I didn't have spirit enough to stop him and ask the great question.

I don't know just how wild I looked while I sat there, but I know I felt wild. Then Karna Holstrom came into the room.

I was conscious that my features were not obeying my volition. I had not been able to make that clacking tongue of mine behave; now my face was just as disobedient. I wanted with all my heart to beam gratitude and joy on her, but I seemed to be trying to manage a stiff mask. If she had turned and escaped in sheer fright I would not have blamed her.

I entirely mistook the expression on her face when she stood there and stared at me. Her eyes were wide with what appeared to be terror. Her lips parted and her cheeks grew pale. Then she ran to the side of the bed, plumped down on her knees, set both her little hands about one of mine and cried, "Thank the good God! You have come back—you have come back!"

And that's how a woman knows.

The balm of her tears bathed my hand when she put her forehead down and hid her face. It was not white any longer—the warm color flooded it and I ought to have been content for a time with what I could bring in the compass of my gaze. But I wanted to have a blessing from her eyes, and when I struggled to lift her face she suddenly released my hand and hurried to the window and sat down.

"I didn't mean to make a fool of myself that way," she panted. "But when I saw your eyes I knew you had come back—and it has been so long—and the others haven't understood!"

"When I came to myself, just now, Karna, your father was here and I didn't confess to him. What I know now and what you have known all along we must keep to ourselves."

"Yes! Nobody has believed what I was so sure of!"

We sat there in silence for a long time.

"Do you remember?" she asked, almost whispering the question.

"Only flashes. Not much. But your father has just been chatting on, and now I have the story without his realizing what news he was telling me."

I was the first to break another silence:

"I know from what he said how faithful and self-sacrificing—"

"You force me to remind you how much we owe to you, sir. It makes me very uncomfortable. It's twitting me of a debt which father and I can never pay. Please don't!"

So there was conversation closed on that point; I did not feel like making Karna Holstrom uncomfortable.

"It's all coming about just as it should. It will be all right from now on," she said, after a time.

She had recovered all her usual serenity; she was the girl of the *Zizania*, cool and distant. I was irritated by her manner. That aloofness was not a square deal between folks who had been through what we had suffered together. It seemed to me that I was not being treated right—first that matter-of-fact manner of Captain Rask and now this coolness on the daughter's part. Her first greeting had given me an appetite for more of the same sort. Of course, I didn't expect to be welcomed back from the shadows with a brass band and speeches—but some kind of hankering or dissatisfaction was gnawing inside me and I felt ugly and cross and childish.

"I haven't intended to go too far in anything, sir. But I have been so anxious to help all I could—forgive me, but father and I do owe you so much! Don't scowl so! I'll not mention debts again. I hope you won't think I was too eager—and that I meddled. But I went to her! I did not want her to misunderstand! It was due you and due myself—and her. So I have explained everything. I have told her the story. It will come about all right—just as you hope—I am sure! I did not intend to stay here—but I have been worrying about— But now you can speak for yourself!"

She rattled it off so fast I couldn't get in a word. She looked relieved when she had finished—as if she had been carrying around something very disagreeable and had handed it over to somebody for keeps. And I was obliged to wait quite a while before I dared to trust myself to reply to her. What she had handed to me seemed to be about as gratifying as if she had dropped a sea-crab down the back of my neck and then sat back and expected me to give her three cheers.

"Look-a-here!" I yapped. "Where did you get the notion that I wanted you or anybody else to act as my attorney over there?" I jerked my thumb in the direction of the Kingsley house.

"But your head was not right—I knew it," she stammered. "I was afraid there would be a misunderstanding—and after what you made me promise on the *Zizania*—"

"Don't you know that I was as crazy as a coot?"

"But I knew that deep down in your heart you must love her."

"A crazy man doesn't tell the truth."

"Oh, he does when he is revealing his real soul."

"I wasn't revealing any soul. I was babbling away—and I knew I was talking fool talk and I couldn't stop my tongue. I didn't mean that guff. And now you have got this thing all tangled up by talking to Celene Kingsley. I can do my own love-making!" That temper of mine was working in fine shape. And Karna Holstrom was no wilting daisy in temperament!

"From what I know of you myself, and what *others*—I call no names—have said, you are about as well qualified in that direction as a catfish." She jumped up and stamped her foot.

"But I know now what love—"

"Mr. Sidney, you have just insulted me because I tried to be your friend. And your *sweetheart*," she sneered, "has no better manners than you! She has not even thanked me for bringing you to her! I do not understand! I shall go to her at once and tell her that you are in your right senses at last. After this you handle your own love affairs. Don't you mention the word 'love' to me again!"

She marched out and banged the door so violently behind her that all the brass handles on the old high-boy were left jingling shrilly—as if the high-boy had gone into a spasm of giggles over my comeuppance!

In a few minutes the kindly face of Dodovah Vose appeared at the door, his eyes full of solicitude.

"Fall out of bed?" he inquired.

"No, out of heaven," I snapped. He came in and shut the door and showed anxiety.

"See here, son, you seem to have a turn for the worse all of a sudden. You've been gaining fine. But your eyes look crazy to-day. And what you just said—"

Say, I came nigh bawling out Dodovah Vose, right then! Nobody seemed to know anything about my case except Karna Holstrom—and she knew too blamed much!

I rolled myself out of bed and stood on my feet.

"My Lawd!" gasped my old friend, "you mustn't do that. It's against her orders. You're sartain out of your head!"

"Don't you worry one mite about my knob," I shouted, cracking my scarred knuckles against it—and the pain in the knuckles made me all the uglier. "I'm not going to be nursed and fussed over any longer. I have been nursed too much already. They're even nursing my own private business—and making it sicker all the time. From now on I'm going to tend to my own affairs. Mr. Vose, help me get these bandages off my feet!"

He stood back and flapped his hands and protested. I knew he felt that I had become a lunatic, and so I convinced him by walking up and giving him a good, sane stare.

"Do you think I'm going to stay in bed the rest of my life—a man who has so much to live for as I have?"

"That's right—a man who is wuth—"

At last somebody was going to post me on my financial status—satisfy my wild eagerness to find out! And I stopped him.

"Shut up," I fairly barked. "I don't want to be reminded of that every five minutes. Excuse me, Mr. Vose. But get my clothes."

I had made up my mind that only one voice in all the world should tell me what my sacrifice had wrung from the Pacific for my own self! Silly notion, eh? No matter. I felt that a certain pair of lips would bless the information when it passed them.

A half-hour later I was dressed after a fashion. I walked downstairs, or it may be better to say that I scuffed and skated down, for I could not squeeze my feet into shoes and was provided with a pair of Dodovah Vose's slippers—carpet affairs with a hectic rose on each instep.

I found Captain Holstrom on the porch with my uncle Deck; their chairs were tipped back and they were confabbing in most amiable fashion. My uncle grinned at me, and I floundered for words because I wasn't sure what I had said to him prior to my awakening or just what our diplomatic relations were. His grin encouraged me.

"Damn it," he ejaculated, "I've said right along it was best for you to be up and around. But Cap's girl would have it t'other way. Feel all right, sonny?"

"I'll feel better, Uncle Deck, if I'm sure that you and I will never have any more misunderstandings. As we have said—"

I stopped there and waited, figuring that I had left about the right kind of an opening to find out what we *had* said. My uncle arose and clapped my shoulder.

"Sonny, I tell you again, now when you stand man-fashion in front of me, that the night when I took my first trick at sitting up with you we fixed it all! For I found out how you felt, underneath, about *him*! And about the whole proposition!" He nudged me. "I'm taking my comfort these days watching him. No more liberty than old Potter Crabtree's day-grinding hoss—around and around in an everlasting circle. I hope he'll live long enough to pay his debts—that means a considerable stretch of enjoyment for me. I wouldn't trig his wheel for all the world!"

That was how it stood, eh? And I let it stand, for I wasn't just sure what my private sentiments were in regard to Judge Kingsley at that time. Furthermore, I had some very special business of my own on my mind. I turned to Captain Rask.

"Where is Karna?"

"Reckon she's over saying good-by to your girl."

My uncle stared at me—I must have been telling him things

when he sat up with me.

Saying good-by! Then she probably had told her father that she was ready to go away. I started across the village square, sliding along in my huge slippers like a man walking on snow-shoes. I banged the big knocker on the front door of Judge Kingsley's mansion and the maid admitted me. I was not bashful that day—I walked right into the sitting-room.

If I am any judge of expressions I did not interrupt any amiable and confidential tête-à-tête. The two girls rose and, after a few moments of constraint, Celene Kingsley asked me to be seated. I told her that I preferred to stand; I reckon that I wasn't sure that I *could* sit down; the stiffness of the whole situation made me feel as if I did not have any joints.

"I have finished my errand," declared Karna. The red was in her cheeks and there was no encouragement for me in her eyes. "I will say, Mr. Sidney, that I have apologized to Miss Kingsley for meddling in matters between you two. I thought I understood and I have tried to help. I deserve exactly what I have received! I assure you both that I will keep out of the way after this." She started for the door, but I was standing where I could block her. I supplemented my interference by an appeal to the lady of the mansion.

"Will you ask Miss Holstrom to remain for a moment?" I entreated. And Miss Holstrom did remain, biting her lower lip with impatience.

"I haven't had much time for thinking on what to say," I confessed. "I don't know how to talk to ladies very well, anyway."

My face was flaming—I could hardly control my voice—I felt sure that I was committing a dreadful sin in point of etiquette and all that—but once more I was playing a big game in my life—bigger, even, for the sake of my happiness than when I offered to go down after the remainder of the treasure of the *Golden Gate*. I was operating again on human nature—and that nature was in the complex little personality of Karna Holstrom who pressed impatiently at my elbow, frowning at me. I knew with all my heart and soul that unless she stood in the presence of Celene Kingsley and myself—as she then stood—and heard the truth about my boyhood folly, my cause was lost; because the pride of a girl makes the way of a man with a maid a mighty doubtful proposition.

"May I hope that you have found out that I am not the scoundrel you believed me to be?"

"I know the truth now. My father is wiser! I am trying to find words—"

She hesitated, just as if she did not know what she ought to say to me, and I could not blame her for feeling pretty uncertain. She looked at me with a sort of kindly and tolerant expression—but, good heavens, there wasn't any love in her eyes! I had found out what love-light was like when Karna Holstrom kneeled beside my bed that afternoon!

As I have confessed and have shown, I was pretty much of a blunderer in affairs with women. But do me this credit in your estimate: I had not come into the presence of Celene Kingsley that day harboring any more illusions as to how I stood with her. I was awake! Think back with me! Never had she given me a word of affection. Rather, her tolerance of me had been plainly inspired by her zeal in her father's behalf. After that piece of brazen idiocy of mine, when I had taken her in my arms, she had been careful to keep out of my reach. Allow me to say that I had been doing some swift and coherent thinking on my way from the tavern.

In my soul was the shamed consciousness that I had been making a real thing out of a dream—and had been babbling unwarrantably. I was a pitiful object as I stood there between them—I deserved punishment at the hands of both of them. For I had made free with Celene Kingsley's name and had misdirected Karna Holstrom's devoted obedience to a promise.

I say, I knew with all my heart and being that I had never struck a spark of real love from the condescending nature of Judge Kingsley's daughter; I knew that I loved Karna Holstrom with all the tender devotion one pours forth to the true mate.

Yet I dared not say a word lest I should appear as an atrocious cad seeking release from the old love before taking on the new.

Equally did Celene Kingsley's high-bred delicacy restrain her tongue; I understood that she did not want to betray me as a mere cheeky boaster.

So we stood there looking at one another, three as unhappy specimens of humanity as there were in Levant that day.

"I am too much of a fool to know what to say and how to say it," I blurted, and the tears ran down my cheeks.

It was Celene who stepped into the breach; she wasn't in love, and she was cooler than the other two in the party.

She walked up to Karna and took her hands in caressing grasp.

"Don't you understand, dear?"

"No," faltered the poor girl.

"I hoped you could understand without obliging me to speak. I hoped you would guess when I refused to discuss certain matters with you—I made you angry, and I'm sorry."

"I know I meddled—"

"My dear, I understood you all the time! I understood my old school friend, too!" She reached out her hand and drew me close to Karna. "He has been very noble in his help in a great trial in my family, dear! I owe my happiness to him. And I'm speaking out, rather boldly—rather bluntly, because I want to help him in obtaining his great happiness. I know what must happen to make him happy." She put Karna's hand in mine. "Now, my dear, do not force me to disparage one of the best young men I have ever known by telling you that I never dreamed of him as a husband—nor was I anything else to him except a school-day fancy, a—"

"An inspiration to set me on the way to make something of myself," I insisted.

"And now—say it, Ross Sidney, or you're a coward—say it, and let me hear it! She deserves it!"

"I have found out that real love differs from boyhood fancies—and I—I—want to—"

She gently pushed us toward the door while I was stammering.

"You want to tell a dear girl the sweetest story in the world, Ross Sidney! My blessing on you both. Good night!"

We did not speak to each other for some time after we were out of doors together. I took her arm in gentle manner and led her steps away from the tavern. We could see its lights in the early dusk, and I wanted to keep away from lights for a time.

I was glad the autumn dusk had settled—a sliver of new moon was a comforting sight for a lover.

"I guess neither of us knows very well how to talk about love, Karna," I told her, hobbling along beside her as best I could. The judge's orchard was shaded by the evening's gloom, and when I turned down there she did not resist.

"I'm sure I'm mighty awkward about making love," I went on, "but God knows I want to learn how."

"Why do you think I can do any better as a tutor in love than as an attorney?" she asked.

"Because I'll be such a willing pupil, dear."

"I heard you inform Miss Kingsley with a great deal of earnestness just now that you have found out what real love is like." She couldn't keep all the naughty teasing from her tone, though her voice trembled. "Who is the fortunate one?"

Then I caught her to me, and with her warm cheek close to mine and her lips near and never denying caresses, I told her and I convinced her.

"I think," she admitted, after a long time and after many words there in the blessed shadows, "that you are entitled to your diploma, Ross. You are showing me that you know more than your tutor. But is there a woman who is not jealous when she is in love? Here!" She pressed into my hand a little packet; it contained the three rings. I drew her along to the cleft tree. I dropped them into the hollow.

"One for fancy, one for folly, one for the freakish dreams of boyhood!" I told her. "All buried! Come back to the tavern, precious girl! I want you to tell Dodovah Vose how to decorate the parlor for the wedding!"

She reached on tiptoe and plucked two apples from the old tree. She gave one to me.

"An apple of gold from the only woman in the world," I said.

"Don't say 'gold' to me, Ross! Don't! A boy of your age with half a million safe in the bank—"

There was my news at last! I kissed the lips which told me!

Then, eating the sweet fruit of our new knowledge of life and of each other, we went on our way up through the whispering trees toward the welcoming, glowing windows of the old tavern.